ANDRE... ... is the author of *Sleb*, *All Fur Coat*, *64 Clarke* and *Criminal Records*.

# ANDREW HOLMES

## Criminal Records

SCEPTRE

For my brother, Dave

# Acknowledgments

Thank you very much to the following: Jocasta Hamilton, Henry Jeffreys, Antony Topping, all my early readers (you know who you are by now), Phil Slade (who designed Betty) and all my family, especially Claire.

# 1973

She shouldn't have put the little one in the paddling-pool. Not when she was so tired from night after night of 3 a.m. feeds and splintered sleep. Worse than that, she'd been drinking.

Shouldn't even have put water in it. Not with the drought.

She'd had a visitor. He'd told work he was on a viewing but really he'd come to see her, see the baby. She'd put him to good use, getting him to inflate the paddling-pool while she relaxed on a sun-lounger nearby.

They've improved since then, sun-loungers. This one had vicious metal tubing, frayed polyester, unexpected lurches if you sat on the end. She'd let the straps of her dress drift down her arms, and wore large sunglasses, occasionally peering over them to watch him. He'd stopped a moment, looking at her with peevish eyes and a grumpy mouth. But pretend-peevish. Pretend-grumpy. Smiling back, she'd sipped from her tin of lager, into which she'd pushed the ring-pull of the can; it clinked as she drank. Her other hand dangled from the side of the lounger, occasionally reaching to prevent Mark toppling over.

Mark – nowadays he'd be called Nate, or Donte, or Ethan,

or Jacob. Or *Kian*, if he was particularly unfortunate. Mark was a good, proper 1973 name.

Mark was seven months old and he'd only started sitting upright the week before, so occasionally he toppled over. Mostly she caught him, even though he was fine on the blanket; fine as long as you watched him, and she did, mostly – mainly to be sure he stayed in the shade and didn't ram handfuls of grass into his mouth. Everything went in there nowadays. She watched Mark because she loved to see his little exploring hands and the intent expression of discovery on his face. She liked to hear the contented, sated sounds he made as little wooden bricks were grasped successfully and raised to his mouth; tiny little fingers curled around them, gummy gums biting down.

'You're not falling asleep?'

Over the way he held the half-inflated paddling-pool by the valve and screened his eyes to look at her.

The lounger was set to upright but tilted back enough so that when she spoke, she spoke into the sky. 'How can you tell?'

'I can see under your glasses. Your eyes closed.'

'I'm not falling asleep,' she said. 'I'm just resting my eyes.' She left it a beat. 'But keep an eye on Mark just in case, eh?'

Her eyes closed again and she smiled up at the sky. He resumed his inflating.

'Hey.' The next moment (or was it a couple of moments later?) her eyes snapped open, and he was standing over her, gesturing at the pool. She glanced down at Mark, happily upright, gnawing a wooden brick. Her little angel.

'All done.' He had his jacket slung over his shoulder, needing to get back to work.

'Oh,' she said. 'Well, let's put some water in it at least –

before you go.' She pushed her sunglasses up her nose. 'Just a splash.'

'Sooz . . . I really should go.'

'But I'd have to carry the buckets by myself. If we both did it. Or maybe . . .' she stretched on the sun-lounger and felt his eyes on her body '. . . if just you did it, then I could have a couple more minutes in the sun.'

He laughed at her cheek, how *spoilt* she could be, and he felt proud, and handy, and a good man to have about the place. Sighing, he laid his jacket down.

Moments later he emerged from the back door with a bucket, poured the water into the paddling-pool then dragged it towards the sun-lounger on her instructions. Mark looked at this rather colourful piece of rubber that had suddenly appeared on the other side of the lounger, seeming to know it was intended for him. The wooden block went flying in an arm-flapping explosion of excitement that sent him toppling over.

She reached and righted him, cooing, 'Wait a minute, angel, let's get it ready first.' She dipped fingertips into the water and called, 'Put some warm in it!'

'You're quite sure you don't need your lawn doing while I'm at it?' he said sarcastically. But she didn't. All she needed was more water for the pool.

One bucket later and her guest had left, with a final frustrated noise. She lifted Mark into the pool and sat him up in the water, the temperature just right.

After a moment of uncertainty he was grinning and splashing, wetting his face so that his eyes and smile seemed to sparkle. When he was settled, she reached to the other side of the chair and passed his wooden blocks into the pool, one of which he immediately picked up to resume gnawing. She laid herself sideways on the sun-lounger, making her eyeline almost level with Mark's, bringing her arms forward to hold him, gently splashing water on to him.

She thought about the frustrated sound her visitor had made and smiled, but felt warm inside. Things might have been different once, maybe, and she was being unfair to him by hinting there might still be hope. But there wasn't. Mark, still gumming the wooden block, was staring at her, and she stared back. They smiled at one another. No, there was no hope for her visitor because Mark had set her love clocks back to zero. There was only him now. Anything else was just trimming. She smiled, listening to the splash of the water and the contented sound he made with his brick, thinking how it, he, this, was perfect. She closed her eyes.

Which snapped open an instant later, with her thinking: *Christ*. Almost nodded off there . . . Can't bloody fall . . .

Her thinking that in the micro-second before knowing that it wasn't just an instant between her closing her eyes and opening them.

The man from Willow Street was ι
screams.

## Sleepy Tiddlers

Where had it started, all of this?

That was what Charlie wondered later: which was the domino that dropped? What event set the chain in motion?

That crackhead offering to suck him off, maybe.

Or that beardy bloke who ran Guilty Pleasures coming up with a better name and, to add insult to injury, having a radio show to promote it. Bastard.

Or Charlie climbing on top of Bea in Norfolk, a little ashamed of his tummy, truth be told, thinking maybe he was letting himself go in his old age (old being his mid-to-late thirties), and distantly fearful that Bea would leave him as result (because that waiter had been staring at her, he was sure of it); wondering if the two glasses of wine he'd had with the meal would make his little tiddlers sleepy. (Sleepy or not, they'd done the job.)

Or not that moment, not one dominated by Pinot Grigio and penile tissue. Another. Mary being born. The sma[ll] matter of becoming a dad. Boy to bloke to husband to fa[ther.] All without him seeming to participate, as though his [life] climbed into a reliable family car and driven off, l[eaving h]im open-mouthed and waving in the driveway, going, 'Hey, Life, come back . . . Wait for me . . . I just need to find a warmer jacket and *then* we can go . . .'

Or a blister pack of paracetamol, empty. Lots of them, everywhere.

Or his brother, Leo, informing him, 'My flat's burning down, mate. I went for a crap and when I came back my fucking flat was on fire.'

Christ, his flat. He owned it – owned it outright. Leo going on to say it didn't matter if it was burning down, he was coming over to Charlie's house that minute – he slurred it, way too drunk to drive – and for Charlie to hang on, that he had something to tell him, something important.

Leo: 'There's something you should know, mate.' Like that.

Charlie: 'What? What do you mean? Leo . . . *are you pissed*?'

Not long after, Charlie had gone to bed.

## Eight Glasses of Water
## and No Packets of Crisps, Please

The next morning Charlie Watson woke up in his warm bed, in his house in Bentham, which is a town at the top of the Metropolitan line, just outside the M25.

He still had a bit of a tummy, though it had shrunk since Norfolk. There was that to be said for sleep deprivation at least. Still, could definitely do with losing a few pounds – if he had either the time or the inclination for diet and exercise.

Charlie didn't eat red meat, but he did drink wine like it was going out of fashion. The one sort of cancelled out the other. He ate wholemeal bread, and there was usually salad in the day somewhere, plus a bit of fruit. Oh, and he drank water, when he remembered, or was reminded to, which was pretty much always if you ever watched TV or read a magazine or looked at a newspaper. *Yes*, he sometimes felt like screaming, I'm trying to eat five portions of fruit and veg a day and drink eight glasses of water and get half an hour's worth of exercise that leaves me out of breath. But I've also got a living to earn, and now a two-month-old baby to care for, plus a collection of old vinyl that needs constant love and attention, and an Apple Macintosh that sucks life into a kind of Bermuda Triangle of time so it disappears and you're never even sure it was there in the first place; like, first it was 5.30 p.m., and you were trying to configure a printer, next thing you knew it was 11.28 p.m. and you were still trying to configure the same printer.

So naturally the good diet and exercise and eight glasses of water and five portions of fruit and veg are going to slip by the wayside a bit. Sorry, but they do. And I'll end up bolting down a cheese sandwich and two Mini Rolls followed by a bottle of wine. And I'll take the empty bottle of wine out to the green recycling bin of shame, that tottering, clanking pile of bottles precariously waiting for a week next Monday, which, according to the council timetable attached to the fridge with a magnet, is the next time the glass-recycling people will come.

I'll try to be *really* good but, you know, I'm too busy trying to be a bit good. I'm doing my duty.

And doing it, he pulled himself from his bed, which was cosy and comfortable, and contained his wife and baby daughter, both sleeping, their worlds complete.

The radio had said the weather would break last night and it had. Day after day of soul-sucking heat (welcome at first, of course, but we've all got our limits) had finally been interrupted by the monsoon. July rain had attacked their home like angry villagers. It had thumped the windows, smacked the brickwork. The gutters had overflowed. The semi-detached next door had one of those half-hearted conservatories with a plastic corrugated roof, and the noise of it was like endless, cacophonous static. Not that it would have kept them awake. Oh, no, the reason they'd been kept awake was the two-month-old baby girl in the room next to theirs.

She'd only been in her own room a couple of nights. Before,

she'd been in with them. She hardly slept, but even when she did, her snuffling and shuffling was as loud as air-raid sirens to Charlie and Bea. Hollow-eyed and almost beside themselves with exhaustion, they'd finally and, despite their fatigue, reluctantly, given in to the advice from Bea's mother and moved the little Moses-basket-on-a-stand into the adjacent room, the baby monitor up so loud that Charlie could hear the click and bubble of water-pipes – a sound he couldn't even detect when he was *in the room*.

At least her snuffling and shuffling didn't keep them awake when she slept in the room next door.

But she hardly ever slept.

So, status: another exhausting night. Hour upon hour of monitor-distorting screams; of raised hopes in those brief moments between screams, then dashed ones when they began again, the pause only so that she could gather breath to scream louder; of arguments over what best to do – to let her scream like their parents advised or pick her up as the books dictated; to feed her again or wind her, change her, adjust the room temperature, take her for a drive, sing to her, dance with her . . . *throw her at the bloody wall*.

Now (of course, because it was morning) the baby slept the sleep of the innocent. She slept like only an eight-week-old baby can and, looking at her, Charlie felt his heart fill with so much love he thought it might bulge from his mouth like a big corny cartoon Valentine's heart. Blissfully unaware of the emotional weight she carried, she lay with her mouth making reflexive sucking actions, having relaxed into sleep while breastfeeding. Beside her, lying on her side where she'd dropped off mid-feed, was Bea, her sleep a snatched, disturbed but grateful beast, at the mercy of little Mary. Charlie watched his wife and daughter for a moment more, then hunted around for his clothes.

He pulled on a pair of jeans and a faded black T-shirt that had the Casablanca logo on it – standard dress for a man still clinging to his youth, even one facing the sudden debilitating and stupefying pressure of responsibility.

Not that he was jobless or anything. Until two months ago, a trip to the hospital and the injection into his wife's spine, otherwise known as an epidural, he'd considered himself an entertainment entrepreneur. He was, after all, the owner of the Cheesy Vinyl Roadshow, which wasn't so much a road-show, actually, it was more, uh, a *concept*.

Okay, mainly he played records (records, note, *not* CDs) like 'Take My Breath Away', and 'I'm In The Mood For Dancing' and anything by Donna Summer to rooms full of drunken middle-aged people *but* – he did it in an ironic, conceptual way.

There were two flies in his ironic, conceptual ointment. First, financial necessity meant that he had to cast his net wider than the sussed urban tastemakers who were his natural constituency so the ironic bit was mostly lost on his audience. Second, the beardy bloke who ran Guilty Pleasures had come up with the name Guilty Pleasures, which was, any way you looked at it, a better name than Cheesy Vinyl. Plus Beardy Bloke had his own radio show and a thriving website. The Guilty Pleasures parties at Koko in Camden were a popular celebrity hangout, and not long ago the *Guardian* had called Guilty Pleasures 'a putative global phenomenon'.

How could Charlie compete? That was a rhetorical ques-tion, but he answered it anyway. He couldn't. He couldn't compete. He just did a thing that was *a bit like* Guilty Pleasures, and only then when people got it, which mainly they didn't. And if they did get it, they probably thought that Guilty Pleasures had got there first, which it hadn't. Charlie had. It was enough to make a man sigh, so he did, and the sigh turned into a yawn as he made his way downstairs, glancing through the landing window. The sun was already out, keen as mustard to burn off last night's rain residue; it was going to be another scorcher. Great.

When he was not seething with resentment at Guilty Pleasures, or playing 'I Will Survive' to hen nights, he sort of ran Eclectibles, which was the eBay name under which he sold old vinyl and what, these days, were called 'collectables' but had once merely been known as 'toys'. And if, say, when he'd been eighteen, sitting on his bedroom floor, vinyl all around him, and Michael J. Fox had arrived back from the future to tell him that in his adult life he would be a DJ, playing those selfsame records for money, and not just that, but also *a vinyl trader*, buying and selling those selfsame records for money, he would have jumped up and thanked Michael profusely. Because when you're eighteen, vinyl's all that matters.

But things had changed. Now, neither of his jobs was suitable for a newly crowned breadwinner in his mid-to-late thirties. They might have been, if they'd made any money, but they didn't, so they were silly, like hobbies gone past a joke; as though he'd been on some kind of mild testosterone blocker keeping him perpetually at twelve, an avid collector, a little boy going, 'Got, got, got, need,' poring obsessively over piles of seven-inches, making little displays, collecting, always collecting.

Now there was Mary. Nothing like a baby to show a man his responsibilities.

He padded down the stairs and to the hallway where he stopped for a second in a tired daze, wondering what it was he had been intending to do when he got there. He switched the radio on; it blared ghost-scaring noise and he reached for the aerial, which was dug into a plant-pot, twisted it until the radio made sense.

'. . . accident overnight on the northbound M25,' said Lucy, who did the travel, 'lots of debris. Fire crews with cutting equipment still at the scene. Traffic queuing in both carriageways with people slowing down to have a good old look there.'

Every morning Lucy disapproved of people who slowed down to look at accidents. She sat in her BBC studio, cup of the coffee *du jour* steaming in front of her, and designated every driver going southbound on the M25 a vulture.

But *why* are they slowing down, Luce? thought Charlie. Actually, he found himself saying it aloud. 'Maybe they're slowing down out of fear, or respect, or because there's accident shrapnel on the road.'

Bea would have said, 'Babe, Lucy's right, they're slowing down to have a look, because that's what drivers do at road accidents. It's nice that you're searching for the good in people, but human beings rubberneck – that's what we do.'

But Charlie didn't think he was searching for the good in people, not necessarily. He was just thinking from a different direction, that was all.

He pulled the kettle from its base and took it over to where a mini-Everest of dirty dishes indicated that a sink had once been present. Lifting the washing-up bowl from the sink he was able to find the tap, fill the kettle, replace it on the base, switch it on.

On the side was the cordless phone. He reached for it and pressed last-number redial. Leo's phone was still off. He frowned. Leo didn't have a home phone, just his mobile, and he was like anyone else, sometimes he'd forget to switch it on, or mislay his charger, or accidentally set the phone to silent or whatever. Charlie did it himself and it was sod's law that it always happened just when someone was trying to contact you – your brother, say, worry coiled in the pit of his stomach.

*There's something you should know, mate.*

*People slowing down to have a good old look there.*

# Flowers in the Dustbin

Charlie stared balefully at the dishes, then started to wash up. He made more noise than was strictly necessary. If Bea was awake he wanted her to know what a productive busy-bee he was – doing his fair share, keeping his end up. Sometimes he wondered if anything he did was for real and not some kind of contrived holding pattern to convince the world he was a proper, functioning human being.

All quiet on the upstairs front. Bea and Mary slumbered on as Charlie went through to what was laughingly called his office and sat down at the desk. On it was his Mac, various CD cases, a cup half-filled with yesterday's coffee, and a letter from the Inland Revenue that he picked up. Picked it up like you fiddle with a scab, knowing nothing good can come of reading it for the hundredth time, but doing it anyway. To paraphrase: you owe us money. Great. He returned the letter to the desk, sighed and booted up his Mac, which chimed cheerfully and wheezed a little as various reassuring icons appeared to let him know that Apple Macintosh had his business empire in capable hands. A picture of Mary – the first he'd taken of her – unfurled as wallpaper on the screen, the rest of the desktop furniture arranged itself and he logged on, clicked on his Internet browser and opened eBay.

The account name was Eclectibles. He keyed it in, sighing. It was no way for a grown man to make a living. Not even a secondary one.

Still – there was always that big score just round the corner. Maybe. Cheesy Vinyl was steady and regular, but static. Wearing his Eclectibles hat, however, anything could happen. Some chump, say, who found an original Goldfinger quad poster in his attic and put it up for sale at a quid, and every other collector on the planet apart from Charlie Watson missed it . . .

Meanwhile, back on planet Earth, there was this. He clicked to the Watch folder. Here he kept an eye on various lots coming up for auction; things he thought worth buying to sell on at a profit, either having kept them to appreciate or because they were such a bargain in the first place. In the folder there was something he liked the look of. He liked the look of it a lot. He clicked to it now.

The time on his Mac said 6.02 a.m.; the auction ended in thirty-eight minutes.

It was a Sex Pistols poster. An original. The person selling it, who called themselves 'Urgonaut', hadn't bothered taking a picture of the tiny slug of text at the bottom of the poster but Charlie knew it would say, 'Copyright 1977, Warner Bros Records'. He knew that because all the Pistols posters from that period had this particular bit of text on them. Correction: those Pistols posters printed in America. Because this particular piece had been used to promote the Pistols' Stateside push: the album *Never Mind the Bollocks* and a subsequent tour, which had ended with them splitting. It had a distinctive neon-pink border that framed a grainy, newspaper-style shot of the band. 'Never mind the bollocks,' it said beneath the logo – snarled it, really – 'we're the flowers in the dustbin.' It made Charlie feel 80 per cent more punk just looking at the image.

When he'd finished punching his hand in the air, that was. Because this was an original Jamie Reid-designed Sex Pistols poster, which by Charlie's reckoning made it worth between seventy and a hundred pounds. Bidding was already at ninety-five dollars and, given Urgonaut's unusually honest item description that the poster 'had seen better days', that was about right. So, normally it wasn't something Charlie would have bothered with, beyond checking the price was about market value and moving on to bottom-feed elsewhere.

(6.12 a.m. Twenty-eight minutes to go. Charlie hit Apple-R to refresh the page. Armalite278's bid of ninety-five dollars remained the price to beat. Charlie smiled.)

But there was something different about this particular poster. Something Charlie had seen almost immediately. He'd been sipping a cup of coffee at the time and the cup had stayed against his bottom lip, warming it as he'd stared at the image on the screen. It was one of *those* moments. The kind collectors like him got out of bed for. Because this particular poster was one of a tiny batch printed by mistake and sent out erroneously. Instead of the band featuring Sid Vicious, the band's ill-fated bass-player, it showed Glen Matlock, the bassist Vicious had replaced after Matlock was ousted by Johnny Rotten. Vicious had toured with the Pistols in the States, not Matlock. But this poster clearly showed Glen Matlock. Imagining back to 1977, Charlie could see how the mistake had been made. In those days the Pistols had had two basic poses for photographers: either leaning against a wall, preferably with a guardsman nearby, or wandering through a park looking shabby and vaguely threatening. It was this second pose shown in the flowers-in-the-dustbin poster. There they were, the four Pistols, ambling through . . . difficult to tell, probably Hyde Park, looking highly pissed off and contemptuous of the whole shallow music-industry façade that they secretly hoped would earn them millions. Same pose, same sneer, whatever the line-up. And some poor guy in the marketing department, sat at his desk with a spliff burning in an ashtray, hair in his eyes and an Emerson, Lake & Palmer record jumping softly in the background, had seen four oiks in a park, thought, Must be that one, and sent it for printing. And just a handful *were* printed before some probably much-more-switched-on young punk at the printers spotted the supposedly more-hip record-company guy's mistake and pulled the plug. And that handful had found their way into the world, scattered like seeds across the globe, until a bloke calling himself Urgonaut came into possession of one, kept it in his attic and then, having done a modicum of research on the Internet – ten minutes, if Charlie's calculations were correct – had decided his poster was worth – cool – a hundred quid!

Ten more minutes on the Net and he might well have discovered what Charlie already knew. That the poster, because it showed Glen Matlock instead of Sid Vicious, was worth more than a hundred quid. Much more. Like ten times more.

(6.22 a.m. Eighteen minutes to go. Charlie hit Apple-R to refresh the page. Armalite278's bid of ninety-five dollars remained the price to beat. He smiled again.)

The way eBay works is that bidders can register high bids and the site will bid in increments until that high bid has been achieved. If Charlie now bid, say, a hundred dollars he would be the high bidder, but only if nobody else outbid him before the auction ended, or Armalite278 hadn't secretly registered a much higher bid, its ceiling remaining invisible until Charlie reached it, with eBay automatically and incrementally increasing Armalite278's expenditure along the way.

As far as Charlie was concerned, there was only one way to bid on eBay. Registering your bid early doors was for the birds. Don't let anyone know of your interest, that was the thing. Charlie had a method.

(6.32 a.m. Eight minutes to go. Charlie hit Apple-R to refresh the page. Armalite278's bid of ninety-five dollars remained the price to beat. Once again, he smiled.)

Armalite278, thought Charlie. There were 277 other Armalites ahead of him in the queue.

His method, then. It was a no-lose method. Maybe one day he'd write a pamphlet on it. He opened a separate window into which he keyed in his bid. Seven hundred dollars. His ceiling. He clicked once and the screen asked him to 'confirm bid', which was where he left it, returning his attention to the first window and Apple-R-ing to refresh the page, which told him the auction had six minutes to go.

Armalite278's bid of ninety-five dollars remained the price to beat. Now 5 mins 30 secs. When the auction reached 45 secs left he'd hit 'confirm bid' on the other window and his bid would be registered. If ninety-five dollars was Armalite's ceiling, then Charlie would get a grand's worth of poster for a hundred dollars. The only way Charlie lost was if Armalite 278 had already registered a higher-than-seven-hundred-dollars bid. Or if someone whose balls were made of better steel than Charlie's stepped in at the *very* last second. And if he was outbid at seven hundred dollars, well, no matter, the profit margin was getting low anyway. That was the way he always played it and he prided himself on always winning. The only drawback was that you had to be there. You had to be there in the dying moments to make your bid.

3 mins 30 secs.

From upstairs there was a sound that was unmistakably Charlie's daughter joining the land of the living. A sound like a big flightless prairie bird telling other big flightless prairie birds that it was around, and to pay attention. Sometimes these squawks came in packs of one: a baby's single, loud reaffirmation of existence before falling back to sleep. Charlie cocked an ear, eyes fixed on the Mac. He didn't need to worry; Bea was with her. He was not needed. All was well.

Sometimes, though, they seemed to wake themselves with that first, single noise. The shock of it was enough to set off a string of same-sound squawks followed by a full-blooded yowl, a cry so heartrending that the parental instincts grabbed their goggles and scrambled into action with cries of 'Tally-ho' that drowned out all other reason and logic. He waited to see if it might develop, eyes still glued to the screen. His finger was itchy over that 'confirm bid' button on window two.

'Come on, Mary-Mary,' he whispered to himself. 'Don't be contrary.'

Upstairs, Mary wasn't listening. Her mouth open (he could imagine the quivering bottom lip), the crying began.

2 mins 30 secs. Armalite278 at ninety-five dollars was still the high bidder.

It was okay, though, Bea was with her. Lying beside his screaming daughter, Charlie's poor, sleep-starved wife would sleepily manoeuvre a breast into the screaming child's mouth, Mary would stop crying and the house would be silent again. But she continued to cry and Charlie could picture the struggle in the bed: Mary, just awake and suddenly frantic with hunger like she might never feed again. The scent of breast milk in her nostrils, probably a tiny dot of it on the end of her nose. She'd be truffling at the proffered breast, head going to and fro, unable to latch on and becoming more frustrated as, with each passing second, her last meal was denied her; Bea, trying to soothe with fruitless words, trying not to resort simply to grabbing the child's head and jamming it on to her breast; Charlie downstairs, denying the pantomime above his head (nothing he could do anyway, he told himself), fixed on the screen, autistically Apple-R-ing.

He wasn't sure – was the machine running slowly? Should he bid earlier? At, say, a minute to go, not forty-five seconds? No, he steeled himself, hold the line, *mon brave*, bid early and you run the risk of your price being pushed up. This way worked; it always worked.

At 2 mins the phone began to ring.

'Oh, no.' Charlie's eyes darted to where the cordless should have rested in its cradle, but the cradle was empty, the handset upstairs on the bedside table, a skyscraper rising above a city of crumpled tissues and damp breast pads. Where it was, it rang less than a foot away from Bea, at that moment trying to pacify a screaming Mary. She would, quite literally, have her hands full.

'*Charlie*,' came the shout from upstairs. (*Waah! Waah!* Apple-R). 'Charlie! Come and get the phone.'

He took a deep breath to reply at volume, angling his face away from the screen but never taking his eyes off it. In the dark study his monitor blasted white light on to his face, casting him in the role of the nervous air-traffic controller.

'Just let it ring, Bea,' he called back.

Apple-R. There was a tremor in his voice, he noted. A tiny umlaut of panic.

'What?' (*Waah! Waah!*)

'Just let it ring.' Louder now: hope the neighbours can't hear.

'What?' (*Waah! Waah!*)

'Just let it ring!'

'I don't believe this, Charlie.' (*Waah! Waah!*)

'Just please let the fucking thing ring out,' he said, but this time to himself, Apple R-ing. Then the phone stopped. 'Oh, thank God for that.'

Apple-R. There was one minute left. Exactly a minute. He flexed his fingers self-consciously, like a maestro at his piano keyboard, suit-tails swept back. Normally it took eight seconds to refresh the screen. So, two refreshes before he made his bid, but eBay was running slowly, he was sure of it. Hold the line. Still Armalite278's ninety-five-dollar bid stood. Any takers? Any would-be poachers shooting early? Nobody with Charlie's nerve.

He hit Apple-R, dimly hearing Bea descending the stairs, unconsciously knowing she had Mary in her arms – the careful steps she took. eBay refreshed. Slow. Was it slow? Charlie's hand hovered over the mouse, ready to confirm his bid.

Bea had reached the bottom of the stairs and was standing in the doorway of his study. 'Charlie,' she said, her voice low.

'Not now, Bea,' he hissed. Apple-R.

'Charlie,' she said again, controlled and insistent, restrained emotion lapping at the edge of her voice. Mary snuffled in her arms, unaware either of her father's agitation or her mother's sudden change in mood.

'Please, Bea,' he snapped – forty-five seconds! – and hit 'confirm bid'.

God, it was slow. His instincts had been right. Why hadn't he bid earlier? The bloody thing was running on granny time. He found himself standing all of a sudden, his hands by his face watching the page refresh ever . . . so . . . slowly.

'Charlie, it's your brother.'

'What?' Something about the tone of her voice made him whirl round. His eyes went to Mary first; her little hand was kneading the material of Bea's pyjama collar. Bea stood jogging her, hair unkempt, wearing glasses, face tired, drawn, and now . . . something else.

'What?' he said. 'What about him?'

(*People slowing down to have a good old look there.*)

'I'm so sorry, Charlie . . . There's been an accident. His car. The driver was killed. They think it was him.'

As if drawn by wires his head turned to look at the computer where eBay was waiting patiently to give him the news.

'I didn't get it,' he said. 'I can't bloody believe it. I didn't get it.'

## Fun Times at TGI Friday's

When Charlie first met Bea – what was it, the second or third time they went out together? That transitional date anyway, where talk went from common interests and shared bugbears, and what-did-you-think-of-the-movie and isn't-spaghetti-a-bitch-to-eat, to the bigger issues, parent stuff – they'd ended up at TGI Friday's, escaping the pedestrian blockage of Piccadilly Circus, desperate to find somewhere to eat and thinking anywhere would do. They'd been wrong. Walking into it was like Willy Wonka had lost a fight with Colonel Sanders.

'Are they still together, your mum and dad?' she'd asked, once a grinning waiter had seated them.

They'd been twenty-six then, and it was kind of reasonable to think that both parents would be alive, properly cautious not to assume they'd be together.

'No,' said Charlie, who was in love with Bea then – had been within two, maybe three seconds of hearing her sing. 'No,' he repeated, 'my dad's dead. He died a couple of years ago.'

'Oh, shit, I'm really sorry.'

He was glad she'd said sorry. It seemed fashionable to think of it as an empty platitude, but so what if it was? His father had died. It was nice to say sorry. Kind. Anyway, what were you supposed to do instead? Break wind? No, sorry was the right thing to say, and he was glad she'd said it. 'Thank you. It's okay. People die. It happens.' He sipped from a bottle of Budweiser to give his face something to do. People did die – of course. But not dads. Not his dad.

'What . . . what was it?' she'd asked.

'Paracetamol.'

'Oh . . . God.' In that moment she must have wondered if she was about to take up with a nutter, son of a suicide, bearer of the suicide gene.

'Not . . . like that. He didn't kill himself.'

'It was an accident?' And in that moment she must have wondered if she was about to take up with a family of imbeciles, the kind of people who took accidental overdoses of over-the-counter painkillers.

'Not really, no. He just . . . took . . . on a daily basis . . . an awful lot of paracetamol. More than anybody knew. I mean, we knew he suffered from headaches, we knew he took painkillers for them, but not to the extent he did . . .'

'He was addicted to them?'

'I suppose. To painkillers in general, perhaps. Maybe he just lacked the imagination to cast his net wider.'

'Was he . . . depressed?'

Charlie looked away. On the other side of the restaurant a waiter in a striped shirt, wearing braces covered with badges, began singing 'Happy Birthday' to a girl in Goth makeup, who openly sneered at him. Her mates roared with laughter. It was a wind-up, Charlie realised, watching the waiter go

24

redder and redder. It wasn't really her birthday, but what could he do? Demand a birth certificate. No choice but to sing her the song. What's the betting her mates had told him a joke name?

Was Dad depressed?

What was the pain he was trying to kill? One thing for sure, it came from inside his head. To all intents and purposes they'd been a picture-postcard family, hadn't they?

'He must have been, I suppose,' said Charlie. 'It's just that nobody noticed.'

'Happy birthday, dear . . .' came the singing from across the room, and the waiter paused, and Bea and Charlie looked over, and the Goth girl's mates stared at him, open-mouthed with glee, and the whole room seemed to go quiet, waiting to hear him sing, redder than ever, '. . . *Fanny* . . .' The Goth girl's mates nearly killed themselves cracking up, Charlie and Bea laughed and the waiter finished '. . . happy birthday to you.' The restaurant burst into applause.

# The Day The Cure Sold Out

And now Dad lay in a graveyard in Bentham, just up from Tesco. Their mother lived in Spain with husband number two. Officially she was still recovering from the nervous breakdown she'd had after Dad's death – a full-on twelve-year convalescence. One day Charlie had realised that their father was as neglected in death as he had been in life, so he'd suggested to Leo that they make a yearly pilgrimage to his grave.

To be fair, he'd had the idea at least eighteen months before he and Bea had left Hackney for Bentham, so it wasn't just a memorial of convenience. The plan was for him and Leo to visit the grave on the anniversary of their father's death, give the old man some flowers, say some words (and sprinkle a packet of painkillers over him, Leo had said), reflect on his life, that kind of stuff. Neither of them could ever really understand how their dad had ended up dying; perhaps visiting to his grave would help.

The first year they didn't go. Shamefully, they forgot. Well, Charlie forgot; Leo was unlikely to remember independently . . .

By the time the next anniversary came round, Charlie and Bea had moved to Bentham, Bea pregnant by then. That was why they'd moved, of course, because she was pregnant: the more she looked around her, the less baby-friendly Hackney seemed, and she'd started making increasingly insistent noises about moving out – safer streets, more for their money, a garden, all the usual reasons.

Charlie had resisted at first – his job, his friends were in London; his entire world-view was shaped by the city, it was his natural home and the natural home for Cheesy Vinyl. But damn if that junkie hadn't offered him a blow-job on his doorstep at 3 a.m. The very next day they'd been pushing open the door at Foxtons.

So it was a lot easier to make the first of what he hoped would be many yearly visits to his father's graveside; a lot easier, too, to put the odd bunch of flowers into a little tin vase at the foot of his headstone. Why had he ended up back in Bentham? he often wondered. It was the town he and Leo couldn't wait to leave. Was it partly guilt?

Yesterday, then. He'd used all the technology he had at his disposal to remind Leo that the anniversary was coming up: voicemail, text, email. He'd told Leo he knew it was a hassle getting the train all the way out of Kilburn, but that they could go for a pint afterwards, and Bea would cook later if Leo wanted to hang around and he'd get to see Mary for only the second time since she'd been born. And in his replies to the texts and emails Leo told him yes. Yes, he would come. Yes, he'd see him there.

Never actually spoke to him, though. Leo was kind of elusive that way.

'What time you be here I will pick you up station,' Charlie

had texted the previous day. '12?' Leo had replied, managing to seem vague even on text. 'But will see you at grave.' Charlie was relieved, not exactly relishing the idea of sitting outside Bentham station waiting for his brother to arrive, and he'd sat in the graveyard, holding his flowers like a bloke on a first date some time in the 1940s. Except a bloke with a mobile phone, texting.

'When you coming?'

No reply.

'Where you?'

No reply.

'Where fuck are you?'

No reply.

'BASTARD!'

Even at the time he regretted sending that last one. Trouble is, you can't recall them once they're gone.

But it was typical of him. Typical of the Leo Charlie had always felt short-changed by.

It had started at school. The way it went then was that if you were a girl you wanted an older brother, unless you had one, in which case you wanted a sister – unless you had one; and if you were a boy, you wanted an older sister. At the time, Charlie couldn't get over that his mate Paul Daley had seen his sister Catherine – a sixth-former and *unbelievably fit* – in the nude. God, they were practically queuing up to go round Paul Daley's house when the sun was shining and Cathy might be out with her red bikini on; if the Daleys had had two sons they would have saved a small fortune on Kia-Ora. But Paul Daley was blind to his luck. When they talked about how much they fancied Catherine he used to look at them like they'd admitted spreading dog shit on their toast.

'That's 'cos you don't know her,' he'd say when they pointed out her – to every other lad, anyway – obvious features. And guess what? Paul Daley didn't want an older sister, he wanted an older brother.

And if at their school Catherine Daley was the sister of choice, then Leo was the bloke everybody (but Charlie) wanted as their older brother because he was in a band and sometimes wore a leather jacket and sometimes a trenchcoat. Nowadays he'd be locked up for wearing a trenchcoat, simply as a pre-emptive measure. But then . . . In those days a trenchcoat was the last word in cool. To wear one – to pull it off properly – you had to smoke, swear a lot and do more than your fair share of smirking, three things at which Leo excelled. How cool was he? Put it this way, if you wanted to know how the Judd Nelson character from *The Breakfast Club* would look if you took him out of the movie and set him down in a comprehensive in a small town called Bentham at the very end of the Metropolitan Line – a town that hung on to London's arse like a particularly resilient clinker – then, kids, meet Leo Watson.

Needless to say, Charlie hated him on every level. Girls fancied Leo, they thought Charlie was sweet; teachers got hassle from Leo and they took it out on Charlie even though he was everything Leo was not. He was reserved, considerate, dreamy, awkward around girls – the exact opposite of Leo, the Morrissey to his Iggy Pop. All were qualities that might end up standing him in good stead, given time, but they didn't have much currency in a suburban comp in the mid-eighties.

Okay, one good thing: he never got any grief. Not from the kids, anyway. He could be as reserved, considerate, dreamy and awkward around girls as he liked and nobody was going to put excrement in his bag. Presumably this was because they believed Leo would come after them if they did (and do what, Charlie wasn't sure: Leo wasn't a fighter, he was too cool for that. Get somebody else to do it for him most likely). The reputation was enough. It was a deterrent that had never needed testing. But if Charlie had caught some flak, would Leo have loped forward to defend the family honour? At the time, Charlie had thought not. But his judgement was clouded then. Now, he thought so. Probably. For form's sake, at least.

But as far as Charlie was concerned, Leo had stopped being an older brother – in the proper, moral-guardian, family-loyalty sense – sometime in the early-to-mid eighties. Exactly when, Charlie couldn't be sure. Maybe around the time Charlie'd started taking a different route home from school so that he wouldn't have to pass the lane where Leo and his mates sat after school, rolling joints on guitar cases, strumming chords for adoring fourth-form girls in tight grey sweaters. Maybe from around the time Leo shouted, 'Charlie Watson, leader of the drain people,' at him and his mate as the two of them passed by. He had no idea what it meant back then (except it was rude) and still had no idea (except it was still rude). Why Leo even bothered with him, Charlie never knew. They were in different years, their worlds simply didn't intersect. It wasn't like Charlie ever hampered Leo's style; the days of older brother chaperoning younger were over and had been blink-brief anyway.

('Because he cared about you,' explained Bea, years and years later, one night in bed when Charlie used the cover of darkness to tell her about his school years.

In reply, he snorted, like, *Yeah, right.*

'If he didn't care he would have ignored you,' she insisted. 'You were part of his world and he wanted people to know it.'

'You weren't there, you didn't know him. You don't treat people you love like that. Not at school. At school older brothers protect their younger brothers. Others did.'

'People are different. I reckon by doing what he was doing, he was protecting you. He was marking you. I bet none of his mates took the piss, did they?'

'You weren't there,' he repeated, and turned over. She was right, though: they hadn't.)

But whatever motives lay in the past, at the time it seemed like the only thing they had in common was music, and then only that they were both obsessive about it. Charlie was a chart junkie, poring over *Smash Hits* every week; the seven-inch single was his king and his records were neatly filed away once he'd played them. Leo, on the other hand, was into punk, indie, alternative. His bedroom floor was permanently littered with record sleeves produced on photocopiers, handwritten lyrics sheets, grotesque collages cut from newspapers. Their relationship to music had been crystallised by The Cure. Leo had been a fan. He adored their early stuff: 'Three Imaginary Boys', 'Seventeen Seconds' – dark, boring stuff, Charlie thought. Then they released 'Love Cats', a poppy, jaunty number that Charlie had loved but that to Leo symbolised the moment The Cure had sold out. Charlie wasn't sure if Leo had actually burnt his early Cure albums, but he'd certainly threatened to. They both loved music, sure, but that was like saying Ronald McDonald and Linda McCartney both loved food.

Time, though. Something about it being a great leveller. Leaving school had robbed Leo of some of his Special Powers, and he became just another struggling bloke in a band. Charlie did his A levels and went to university, came out with a degree in media studies and time on the entertainments committee. They both lived in London, where Leo was still a struggling bloke in a band, and Charlie got a job in one of the capital's cooler cinemas, booking cult films, staging all-nighters, putting on audience-participation stuff. Leo still had fantastic girlfriends and impossibly cool mates and was always on the edge of some scene or other, but the divide between them had closed. Slowly, and often without seeing each other for months at a time – often only when they both went home to Bentham – they became mates.

Not great mates. Not ring-each-other-every-day, unbreakable-bond, bemused-jealousy-from-the-womenfolk type mates, but mates all the same. They started liking each other . . .

Then their father died. The grief, the questions, their mother breaking down. Stuff like that can drive a wedge, but not between them it didn't. Yes, there was the odd moment. Charlie thought (well, he *knew*, actually) that Leo ducked out of stuff, could have pulled his weight more. Leo was unreliable, sometimes went incommunicado, would often be pissed. But . . . that was Leo. Everybody got it, friends, family, girlfriends. He was at least democratic.

Each had been left a sum of money exceeding their wildest expectations, and they both invested in property, which was just a fancy way of saying they used the cash to buy flats – no mortgages for them. (And that was the only reason they survived, Charlie, Bea and Mary, the only reason they'd been able to afford Bentham, all thanks to the old man. God, the least Charlie could do was take him the odd bunch of flowers.)

Leo stopped being a struggling bloke in a band and metabolised a lifelong love of Tom Waits into something approaching a career. He became the Tom Waits For No Man Tribute Night, London's best (okay, only) Tom Waits tribute act. Meanwhile, Charlie had met Bea, was dabbling in putting on club nights and, just as the cool cinema closed, launched the Cheesy Vinyl Roadshow. The week that Cheesy Vinyl appeared in *Time Out*, so had Tom Waits For No Man, albeit only in the listings, but even so. It felt like the Watson brothers had arrived. They called each other that day, cracking up because they'd both bought two copies, one to read, the other to keep mint. It only occurred to Charlie after he got off the phone that Leo was in *Time Out* every week – every week at the Lost Oats in Highgate there was a performance by the Tom Waits For No Man Tribute Night. Leo hadn't bought two copies because he was in it – he'd bought two because they both were . . .

Even so, he was still Leo, and he hadn't turned up to the graveyard, and all those past injustices came flooding back, nagging at Charlie until Leo had phoned that evening. He was drunk, stoned, and – wait for it – his flat was on fire.

'You know what's funny about having your flat burn down?' Leo had said.

'No, what?' asked Charlie.

'Nothing. There is nothing funny about your flat burning down.'

Charlie could hear flames in the background, a siren. He imagined firefighters, then realised he was imagining American firefighters. How on earth had American firefighters got in there? 'I don't know what to say,' he said. And he really didn't. Like Bono in 'Do They Know It's Christmas?', tonight he was thanking God it wasn't him; he thought of his own home going up in flames. At least Leo's didn't contain a wife and child.

'I'm sorry,' said Leo. Another siren started up in the background.

'*You*'re sorry. What about? Missing the graveyard?'

'Yeah,' said Leo. Another pause. 'You went, did you?'

'Of course.'

'Of course you did. Well, look, I'm sorry. Stuff.'

'Well, you do have a good excuse – your flat's burning down.' Charlie was giving him a get-out, but Leo wanted to do the whole self-flagellation thing.

'It wasn't on fire then, was it?' he retorted. 'How long do you think it takes a one-bedroom basement to burn, Charlie? It wasn't burning down this afternoon. In fact, if I'd come to the graveyard it wouldn't be burning down now, because instead of getting pissed, smoking a spliff and burning my flat down I'd have been on the way back from Bentham, thinking about getting pissed and smoking a spliff and *not* burning my fucking flat down. I just didn't come, that was all.'

'Why?'

There was a lengthy pause. The noise in the background – it was like Leo was phoning him from a disaster zone, not Kilburn in the middle of summer. Then again . . .

'Look,' Leo had said at last, 'I'm coming over . . .'

He had something to tell Charlie; there was something Charlie should know. He was coming over.

'What?' Charlie had shouted into the phone. 'What do you mean?'

34

But Leo didn't say, called goodbye and rang off. Later, after trying his brother's mobile several times, Charlie had gone to bed, telling himself that Leo wasn't stupid enough to attempt the M25 after a skinful. Not even Leo would do something so idiotic. He'd told himself that and he'd gone to bed.

# Out of the Fire, into the Fire

There was no toxicology report yet. The first order of business was formal identification because the driver (whom the police were 99.9 per cent certain was Leo, since he had died in a car registered in his name, and had been seen by the fire crew making his way to that very car and driving away) was carrying no identification. No, there was no toxicology report yet, but since the Fiat Panda, which was 99.9 per cent certainly driven by Leo, had left the carriageway, smashed through the barrier, tried to mount a built-up police vehicle zone before bursting into flames, was the only car involved, and Charlie had spoken to an obviously inebriated Leo earlier that evening, and Leo was, by his own admission, a terrible pisshead, it seemed fair to assume that when that toxicology report came back, it would tell them that Leo had been blind drunk and run his car off the road.

Charlie had been asked to phone the coroner, who had requested he dig out a photograph and come to the mortuary. He'd been told that this was a formality. Not to get his hopes up. He'd been given the 99.9 per cent statistic.

The photograph, said the coroner, would need to show Leo's teeth.

'Why his teeth?' asked Charlie.

'He was badly burned, Mr Watson. I'm sorry. We may want it for a dental comparison.'

Now he sat in the reception area of the hospital mortuary suite, alone but for chairs: brown plastic ones, school seats for grown-ups. A single poster on the wall advised washing your hands, although there was no suggestion where you might go to do so. And that was it. That was the mortuary suite. Nothing suite about it, thought Charlie, studying the squeaky, rubberised swing doors, behind which, he assumed, was the stock. One of them his brother. Charlie squished his eyes shut and wondered when the tears would come. When their father had died he'd cried almost non-stop for a fortnight. Certain smells set him off, something a TV announcer said. Anything. Perhaps he'd done all his crying then. Maybe there were no more tears in the pot. Nothing left for Leo.

The doors went, jerking Charlie from his self-absorption, and standing before him was an attendant. He wore a white coat and work-jeans, the sort of jeans that had loops for hammers, chisels, power drills. They had turn-ups. Were turn-ups back in? Charlie wondered. Maybe so, but he'd been too busy getting old, moving to the suburbs and having babies to notice. Or perhaps not, and the mortuary attendant had been too busy pushing corpses into cold metal drawers to realise his trousers had crept out of fashion.

But looking at him, no. He was young, bright-eyed, a cult hero. He had hair that belonged in a TV commercial for gel, or clay, or mud, or gum – whatever kids rubbed into their hair these days. He was, Charlie realised, the kind of kid who would have come to see him DJ when Cheesy Vinyl was the talk (well, whisper) of the town. Charlie felt a tiny ping of envy and longing. A message addressed to his heart. Subject: The Rest of Your Life.

'We're trying to effect an identification via a visual dental comparison,' said the mortuary attendant when he'd introduced himself, reaching out a hand to shake and saying, 'Hi, I'm Nick, yeah?' almost apologetically, as though his name, Nick, might somehow be offensive to the recently bereaved.

'Don't you usually use dental records?' Charlie asked. Maybe that was why he couldn't shed a tear, he thought. How could he mourn a brother not officially dead?

'If the subject has them, sure. But if your brother ever visited a dentist during his adult life we haven't been able to trace it, I'm afraid.'

'Okay.' It figured.

Nick-yeah thrust his hands into his white coat, itself a comforting symbol. It meant, somehow, that there was a system, and hands in the pockets meant the system was working. Charlie had felt the same when Mary was born. Like all he needed to do was show up and hold Bea's hand and say the odd encouraging thing. The system would take care of the rest. Same system, different result.

'If that doesn't work we may need to use DNA testing,' said Nick-yeah. 'But first things first, have you brought the photograph?'

Charlie handed over a photograph of Leo. One in which his brother was smiling, as requested.

Charlie said, 'I'm sorry it's so old. We didn't have . . .'

'That's okay,' said Nick-yeah, 'as long as— He hadn't had any major dental work since this was taken, had he?'

'I'm not sure.' Charlie felt a surge of shame at not knowing his brother's dental history.

'Nothing on his front teeth, anyway? For a match. Nothing that might have changed the geology of the mouth?'

'No,' said Charlie, thinking, *Geology?* 'No. Nothing major that I'm aware of.'

'Okay, well, that's great. Um . . . I've got something for you, actually. If you could wait there a minute.' He swished through the doors and returned carrying a brown envelope, which he handed to Charlie. 'Your brother's personal effects – those that were recovered from the body. Anything from the car would be with Highways, although . . . I gather it was pretty much gutted.'

Inside the envelope was a clear plastic bag. In that a bunch of keys, blackened; a mobile, cooked; some change. That was it.

'Anything you recognise in there at all?' asked Nick-yeah.

'That,' said Charlie, pointing at the charred bottle-top opener that was Leo's keyring. 'That's definitely his.'

'Okay, thanks. I'll make a note. You can hang on to it.'

'Does that mean . . .'

'What?'

'Can you tell me? Can you confirm?'

Nick-yeah hesitated, smiling sympathetically. 'A positive identification of the keyring means we're ninety-nine point nine per cent certain that it's your brother.'

'But you were ninety-nine point nine per cent certain *before*,' Charlie snapped, then instantly regretted it, imagined Nick-yeah telling his mates in whatever Hoxton boozer kids with work-jeans hung out in, these days, about the sad git he'd had in the mortuary suite earlier. *Should have seen him.*

*Looked knackered. Thought he was going to have a nervous breakdown there and then.* Because Charlie knew all about places like that. Sure, it was sweetness and light front-of-house. All respectful silence, sympathetic smiles and I'm-Nick-yeah. But backstage, behind those rubber doors, they were playing football, corpses for goalposts. They were giving the bodies nicknames, commenting on their genitalia, taking pictures and posting them on the Net.

Nick-yeah sat down in one of the school chairs. For a mad second Charlie thought he was going to take hold of his hand.

'We can't show you the body, I'm afraid. The manner of death . . .' He trailed off, allowing Charlie to imagine the state of his brother's corpse. He'd seen pictures of car accidents, all that mangled metal. Mangled, blackened metal. A couple of years ago he'd come home drunk – when they'd lived in Hackney, this was – and he'd decided to cook some garlic bread, then fallen asleep. That garlic bread, the next day, was what he thought about now.

'There is something else, though, that might help,' said Nick-yeah, 'providing you're up to it.'

'Sure,' said Charlie, nodding his tired head. 'Whatever.'

He was taken to a viewing room. To his left was the window, a curtain drawn across it. Ordinarily, he guessed, there would have been a corpse on a gurney on the other side of that window. And a still-hopeful relative would have been standing here. Still hopeful, that was, until the curtain was opened. At his feet he saw a wastepaper basket, and he found himself wondering why hospitals don't have special receptacles for catching the sick of those whose relatives have died in grotesque ways. Vomit-catchers. But of course the attendant wasn't about to reach and open the curtain. Because of the manner of Leo's death. The fact that in Charlie's mind's eye Leo now resembled a frazzled garlic baguette; the fact that he had been 'burnt beyond recognition' – one of those phrases you never expected to hear applied to your own life because it belonged somewhere else. On the news. But there it was, red in tooth and claw, elbowing its way rudely into Charlie World. Leo's body was so badly burnt that it was not available to the relatives for visual identification. Christ. One minute you're smoking a spliff and going for a nice, relaxing crap; the next your cadaver's too grotesque for your loved ones to see.

Nick-yeah left the photograph on a table, asked Charlie to wait and walked off on silent trainers. He returned moments later with a black bin-liner – square of something nasty inside – plus a form.

'You have to sign this first,' he said, pushing the form and a pen across the table to Charlie. 'It says you've agreed to view potentially distressing effects. You should maybe read it.' But Charlie had already scrawled his signature and pushed the form back, saying, 'It's just his jacket, though, isn't it?'

'Yes. He was wearing it when he died.'

'So it's just a jacket?'

'Still, it could be upsetting, Mr Watson,' he said, eyes watchful. 'Are you quite sure about this?'

'Yes. Thank you. I am,' replied Charlie, and watched as Nick-yeah donned a pair of surgical gloves then opened the bag and reached inside. Out came irregular sections of leather laid on top of each other. Nick-yeah spread the bag on the table, then held up the first section for Charlie to see. Charlie studied it, nodded, and the attendant placed it to one side and help up another.

Same again, and for a moment Charlie felt still-hopeful – like all those other quivering relatives before him. Briefly he imagined himself saying, 'No, there must have been some terrible mistake because that definitely *isn't* Leo's leather jacket. Leo would rather die than be seen in a leather like *that*.'

Then Nick-yeah held up a portion of the sleeve for Charlie to look at it and suddenly it was Leo's jacket. He had several, but this was his favourite. His favourite because it had military insignia on one sleeve. It had been stitched there by an old girlfriend.

'Is this your brother's jacket?' asked Nick-yeah. Charlie hadn't reacted but Nick-yeah saw something in his eyes die, and recognised it for what it was. 'Take your time,' he added.

'Yes,' managed Charlie at last. 'Well, it's the sleeve of it, anyway.'

'It's from the same jacket. It didn't come off in, um . . . one piece.'

For a moment or so, Charlie thought he was going to have to use the vomit-catcher, but the moment passed.

# When Did You Last See Your Brother?

Detective Inspector Merle opened the security door and ushered Charlie through, saying, 'Just a moment of your time. I won't keep you any longer than necessary.'

There was this to be said for your brother's immolation. Suddenly you got a walk-on part in a Sunday-night drama on ITV. First, the hospital mortuary, now – a week later – the police station. Detective Inspector Merle would like to see him: would it be okay to pop in at some point convenient to him? All sort of – he realised guiltily – exciting: a break from insomnia, nappies and rifling through baby books at 3.20 a.m.

He declined coffee and followed Merle to an interview suite – yes, another suite, he noted – where Merle made a show of leaving the door open. He motioned Charlie to take a seat, then sat opposite. The chairs made scraping sounds.

'Thanks for coming. It must be a difficult time for you.'

'It is, yes,' said Charlie, by rote. He was still wondering when it would hit him. Was he too old, too hard? Had fatherhood re-ordered his priorities to such an extent that they excluded mourning his dead brother?

'He was your . . .' Merle confirmed . . . 'older brother?'

'Yes.'

'By how much?'

'Almost four years.'

'Quite a gap.'

'Well, not really.'

'Were you close?'

Charlie looked at Merle as though the policeman had been reading his mind. 'Yes. Well, no. Perhaps not, as brothers go. I mean, what do you measure it against? I've got a mate whose brother is his best friend. I've got another mate who can't stand his brother. We were somewhere in between. Close, but not as close as we should have been. Not as close as I wish now we had been.'

'Right.'

Charlie wondered whether Merle had a brother – if he was thinking about his brother now.

'Okay, when was the last time you spoke to him?'

'The night he died.'

'Right.'

'I get the impression you already know this.'

'Mobile phone records.'

'Right.'

There was a pause.

'And you check the mobile phone records of everybody who dies in car accidents, do you?'

'No.'

'But you checked Leo's?'

'We were checking Leo's, that's right.'

'You *were* checking them. As in, you were already checking them, prior to his death.'

'That's right.'

Charlie made an exasperated sound. 'Are you going to tell me why?'

'Why do you think?' responded Merle with a tight smile.

'I have absolutely no idea. But I'm more than interested to know what you're implying.'

'Right. Do you know exactly what your brother did for a living, Mr Watson?'

'Yes,' said Charlie, carefully, 'he impersonated Tom Waits.'

'Not especially lucrative work?'

Charlie shrugged. He wasn't about to go into the details of his father's will – it was no business of Merle's.

'What about during the day?'

Again, Charlie shrugged. But he was getting a bad feeling about this. *What*, Leo? he was thinking. What the bloody hell were you up to?

'I'll tell you what he was doing during the day, Mr Watson.' Merle leant forward. 'He was being a con-man.'

# Big, Clever Brother

Charlie looked at Merle and grinned. 'Really?' Madly, he felt a surge of something that was surprise but also, as his imagination went to work, part admiration, part stone-cold envy. Leo a con-man. A fraudster. A scoundrel. A grifter. A *hustler*. 'Really?' he repeated, still grinning.

In return, Merle looked peeved. 'Yes, really, he was quite a guy. Robbing people of their money like that. Getting drunk and going off in his car. Real folk hero.' His expression was granite, daring Charlie to get indignant.

'All right.' Charlie tried to look mollified for appearance's sake. 'Point taken. What sort of . . . what kind of conning are you talking about?'

Merle held up a hand. 'First, you're saying you knew nothing about it, is that right?'

'No,' said Charlie, quickly. 'I mean yes. No, I knew nothing about it. Yes, I'm saying I knew nothing about it.'

'It doesn't surprise you, though?'

'If you told me that Leo was stripping pensioners of their life savings, then, yes, it would surprise me. A lot. But . . .' Charlie found himself staring at Merle, suddenly feeling a little wormy-worm of disquiet at the base of his stomach '. . . but that's not what you're going to tell me, is it?'

Merle waited a long, hollow moment before saying, 'No.'

'And I guess if you told me he was making hundreds of thousands of pounds off it, then that would surprise me, too, but since Leo lived in a basement flat in Kilburn and drove a Fiat Panda, I'm guessing that wasn't the case either, right?'

'Right,' agreed Merle, using the opportunity to punish Charlie further for grinning. 'He was strictly small-time.'

'So . . . What?'

'You've no idea?'

'Is that why you wanted to see me? No. I repeat – I've no idea.'

'He didn't say anything to you before he died?'

Charlie opened his mouth to tell Merle, *There's something you should know, mate*, but stopped himself.

'Go on,' prompted Merle. 'Why was Leo coming to see you so late at night? What did he want?'

'I think . . .' said Charlie '. . . that . . . To make amends. It was the anniversary of our father's death and he'd missed it.'

'And that was what he said, was it?'

'Well, he said lots of things. His flat was burning down. We were supposed to meet that day and he was full of apologies. If you told me what he was doing, then maybe I'd know if anything he said was significant.'

'All right.' Merle leant back and clasped his hands together behind his head. 'Tell me, have you ever heard the name Bryan Smith-Hegel?'

Charlie thought. He considered saying something facetious like, 'Sounds like the drummer in a prog-rock band,' but

47

thought better of it. 'No,' he said, having given the question due and serious consideration.

'What about Matt Clay? They're American, both of them.'

Again, no.

'Right. Well, I wouldn't expect you to. Not unless you were a psychologist, a criminologist or you were pulling a similar scam. Whether your brother had heard of them or not, I don't know. If he hadn't, well, great minds must think alike because they all practised a particular type of con. It doesn't have a trendy name, I'm afraid, so let's just call it the *Dick* Con.' He smiled, with not a trace of humour.

'And what does the Dick Con involve?' asked Charlie.

'Well, like a lot of cons it involves setting up a front company and waiting for the marks to come to you. In this case, it's an investigation bureau. Smith-Hegel did it in a town outside Philadelphia. He had an office above a grocery store, overlooking a petrol station – or gas station, I should say. Very small, very discreet. Clients would visit him there. He was known as a good listener, excellent with customers. Whatever the investigator's equivalent of a bedside manner is, Smith-Hegel had it in spades. A quality he shared, in-cidentally, with Matt Clay, who was practising almost exactly the same con however many hundred miles away in Louisiana. These guys were great with their clients. People left feeling – no, *knowing* – that they were in safe hands. Smith-Hegel – he even had referrals. Can you imagine that?'

'In theory I can,' said Charlie. 'You haven't told me what they were doing wrong yet.'

'Guess.'

'They weren't investigators.'

'Was your brother?'

48

'Not that I knew of.'

'And you would have known, wouldn't you? Him being your brother and all.'

Charlie nodded, wishing he hadn't grinned at Merle just now, realising he was paying for that grin.

'No, they weren't investigators. Listen, pretty much anyone can set themselves up as an investigator – it's not a regulated industry, you don't need a licence or anything. And that's the same in the States. Most people who set themselves up in business, though, they at least try. What Smith-Hegel, Clay and your brother did was simply to sit there, smile, make the right noises, take some money and say goodbye. End of story. Wheel the next mug in.'

'They didn't do any investigating.'

'No.'

'So how did they get the money?'

'All kinds of ways. Take half the money up front and simply not solve the case – sorry, did my best, you know, that sort of thing – or consultation fees, perhaps. Other rackets – Matt Clay specialised in matrimonial cases. He'd take money from the client, then contact the spouse for more, go back to the client with no evidence of infidelity. Thing is, the beauty of this con is that people come into a world they know absolutely nothing about, save what they've seen on TV. The con-man is in a position of absolute power. He can assess each case for what it's worth, take what he can, discard it if he doesn't think he can make it work. So, if the case looks too hairy, he simply turns it down or makes noises about referring it elsewhere. The client appreciates his honesty and goes away with a warm feeling inside – after they've paid the consultation fee, of course. Some cases you can keep clients hanging on indefinitely. Surveillance. You've got men out there, on the clock, right now. Smith-Hegel used to tell his clients that it was unethical to provide clients with surveillance material unless evidence of wrongdoing had been uncovered. Brilliant. Who's going to argue with that? And if they did, Smith-Hegel would suggest they took their business elsewhere. Debugging. "Yeah, mate, you've been debugged. Back again, you think? Tsk. That'll be more money, please—"'

'Sure,' interrupted Charlie. 'But . . . isn't a lot of this investigation work financial stuff?'

Merle nodded enthusiastically. 'Smith-Hegel always referred it. Your brother turned it down. Clay did neither, which was why he got caught.'

'All right, but that aside, I mean, I can see it working for a while, in a limited way . . .'

Merle held up a finger. 'It's low-yield con. Remember that.'

'Yeah, okay, but surely people are going to cotton on? Plus if you're turning down half the clients that walk through your door . . . There can't be that many clients in the first place. Just seems to me there must be easier ways of parting people from their money.'

'Certainly, but this has a low-risk factor. People don't go to the police about dodgy investigators. "My wife's fucking some other guy and now I'm being fleeced by the investigator." It's not a good look. Plus it's difficult to prove that the work hasn't been done, especially if our guy is screening properly. So, low yield but low risk.'

'Right,' said Charlie, who was experiencing a strange deflating feeling. At the mention of the word 'con-man' he'd imagined Leo as a globetrotting Frank Abagnale figure, not presiding over some cheap fibbing with a built-in shelf life –

which wasn't even particularly profitable. He found himself smiling again. He could imagine Leo at it – the whole charm offensive. Yeah, yeah, that was Leo. Not a fighter, liked to think of himself as more of a risk-taker than he actually was. The option of being able to bale out at any time was probably an attractive one. It made sense.

'Were you going to arrest him?'

'No. But we'd begun monitoring him. The file was open . . . and then he died.'

'And how did you find out about him?' asked Charlie.

'Not me. A DC in the division. With a business like this, it depends on keeping the clients coming in. You have to spread your net. Leo was placing adverts in local papers. Naturally he needed to go further and further afield. Somebody saw an advert in one place, then in another, and checked his credentials. He had a little ABI logo on his advert, but he wasn't a member.'

'Ah.'

'That was dumb, actually.'

'Really?'

'Yes. To check that out all you need to do is go to a website. But, then, this is a con that seems to inspire slightly reckless behaviour. Clay was caught because he accepted jobs he hadn't a hope in hell of finessing, the financial ones you mentioned. His lack of work on the cases was always going to be painfully obvious. Dumb, you see.'

'And Smith-Hegel?'

'Also dumb.'

Charlie looked across the table at Merle, but he was thinking. He was imagining a guy in an office, overlooking a petrol – no, a *gas* – station, staring out over the tarmac, waiting for the next client to arrive. More shit to tell them. More flim-flam. More dodging of sticky questions, and excuses. He imagined that guy sick of pretending to be a private investigator; the work was drying up and he was tired of lying. Why pretend to be an investigator? Why not *be* one?

'He took a case, didn't he?' he said, after a pause. Merle nodded yes. 'And it blew up in his face,' added Charlie.

Merle nodded a second time. 'It's why we know about them. They're interesting psychological as well as criminal cases, you see.'

'I see. And Leo – Leo took a case, too?'

Merle looked at him. 'That,' he said, 'I was hoping you might be able to tell me, but . . .' He gave Charlie a look that said, 'Last chance. Tell me now or for ever hold your peace.'

Charlie shook his head.

'Then I don't suppose we'll ever find out,' said Merle. 'If there was a case, the only person who knows whether he meant to take it – or just to take the money and run – was your brother.'

'Why, though?' said Charlie, 'Why would you want to know if he had a case? His death was an accident, wasn't it?' Again that wormy-worm.

'Yes.'

'I mean, the flat. He told me himself he'd set light to it, and it's not like anyone was holding a gun to his head – he was off his face. And then he got in his car. You said earlier that the fire crew saw him get in it, and unless you're going to tell me his brake cables had been cut . . .'

Merle smiled indulgently and shook his head, no.

'Then what? What's the police interest?'

Merle stood. 'There isn't one,' he said, motioning to

52

Charlie. 'As of . . .' he glanced at his watch . . . 'now, my work here is done.'

'Wait a second,' said Charlie, not budging. 'It's not that simple, is it? You don't think it's that cut and dried.'

Merle pulled a face that was almost wistful. 'I'm afraid it is, as far as I'm concerned. Whether you think so or not, that's for you to decide.'

They walked out of the interview suite, back towards reception.

'Did Leo have an office?' asked Charlie, suddenly.

'Oh, yes,' said Merle. 'He had an office, all right.'

Charlie thought of the bunch of keys in the envelope that Nick-yeah had given him.

As he left Merle, he couldn't work out which was worse: that his brother was a low-level con-artist, that the information didn't particularly surprise him, or that, despite himself, he still felt a grudging admiration for Leo, even a bit of envy. His own life was being absorbed into the quicksand of suburban babydom, just one grasping hand still visible (clutching a copy of 'Total Eclipse Of The Heart'); Leo, on the other hand – Leo had been living the life.

## His Blood Ran Cold

Charlie flagged a black cab (driver: racist misery-guts) to Marylebone, then caught the train to Bentham. That night's gig was a Friday wedding, reception at the Ale House, which was an ancient ex-beer-storage facility now used for events, parties and stuff. Charlie had played there before, many, many times; done receptions like this one many, many times. And liked it. The advantage? That you didn't have to set up the rig before lunch. The guests had their din-dins elsewhere – the Dragon's Breath more often than not. Then, once fed, and not so much watered as drenched, they'd get rounded up by the best man with one or more overbearing mothers and herded across the road to where Charlie would be waiting for them, Kool and the Gang already on the decks. They'd file in, and men in suits would do ironic little jigs to 'Celebration'. Later, Charlie would see the same men, sweating, heads down, dancing like their very lives depended on it. Ironic guests were few and far between by the end of the night.

At home he spent about half an hour doing the dishes, cleaning the kitchen, then baby jobs like changing the ster- ilising water and taking a ton of non-biodegradable nappy sacks to the rubbish. He made sure Bea was okay and apologised for having to leave her for the evening. She understood, and asked him how he was feeling; said that he was looking tired. He was fine, he replied, unsure if it was the truth.

'But you haven't . . .' she started. 'I mean, I don't think it's really hit you about your brother, has it? It's not a good idea to bottle these things up.'

He smiled, told her, 'Just you worry about yourself, Bea. I'm fine. Really.'

Next he checked the kit in the van, then ferried three cases of records from the hallway where they were stored because he didn't like leaving them in the van. His vinyl. The vinyl he'd stuck to doggedly while everybody else had made the change to CD decades ago.

Hence the Cheesy Vinyl Roadshow, which did travel, as the name implied: to the Notting Hill Arts Club, to Sunday Best, even to Brixton Academy once, to support a one-album indie hype-flash band whose name he'd since forgotten. And to Turnmills, home of the Cheesy Vinyl mini-residency, the kind of night they called a roadblock. It turned out that the club London had been crying out for was Charlie playing ropy old seven-inches of Three Degrees' songs, 'Centerfold' by the J. Geils Band, Manhattan Transfer, 'At This Moment' by Billy Vera and the Beaters and, yes, 'Total Eclipse Of The Heart' by Bonnie Tyler. The clubbers were a Hoxtonite crowd. They dressed ironically and danced ironically to songs Charlie played ironically but loved, actually, in a way that had nothing whatsoever to do with irony. There was that piece in *Time Out*. Then Guilty Pleasures had sprung up. Then Charlie had moved out of London.

Now, of course, he gigged places like the Ale House, the working men's club, church halls. He still played a lot of the same records, still loved them, but it wasn't quite the same. After all, he'd played the Academy; he knew what it was like to look out over a sea of expectant faces, seemingly stretching as far as the eye could see, and drop 'Total Eclipse Of The Heart'. After that the Beaconsfield scout hut was always going to be a comedown.

Still, he'd clung to the principles, as far as he could. He did have a CD player; he used it to play the handful of tracks that were unavailable on vinyl. But recently there'd been a trend back to vinyl, a move that had warmed his heart. There is something unbeatable, he told people, about the sound of vinyl. It has a depth, a *warmth*, that's absent from CDs. Wow, people said in reply, where did he DJ? Expecting it to be Northern Soul weekenders, or Saturday night at the Jazz Café . . .

The sad thing was, he didn't really need three cases of vinyl. All weddings were different but the same: everybody wanted to hear the same records. Every single time. Maybe they pretended not to, but they did, really, deep down. And Charlie had all those records – and they fitted comfortably into one record box.

It wasn't the quality of the music, it was the predictability. The same requests for the same oldie-but-goldies: 'You couldn't play "Lady In Red" for the missus, could you, mate?' The same tired dive for a tried-and-trusted 'Happy Hour' by the Housemartins after the abject failure of a just-as-boppy but nevertheless strictly-not-on-the-hundred-year-old playlist 'Tallulah Gosh', by Tallulah Gosh. (And he wasn't going to make *that* mistake again.) 'Blue Monday' by New Order, but *nothing else* by New Order. God forbid if you tried. 'Fools Gold' by the Stone Roses – one for the blokes his age – but nothing else by the Stone Roses. Especially not 'I Am The Resurrection'. Quiet word from the bride's mother if you tried, quick crossfade to 'Karma Chameleon'.

'Can't you play something we've heard of?' they might say if something non-prescribed should rear its ugly head. Nothing challenging, mind; nothing that might bring them out in a rash. Nothing they might even *like* if they gave it a chance.

'There was a time nobody had heard of Madonna, y'know,' he'd said, smiling at a professionally disgusted teenage girl once, back in history, when he still cared about his customers' musical tastes.

Nowadays he reacted to the market and didn't play anything new until it had been requested at least twice. He'd also added the odd bout of theatrics to his set. The big pair of comedy lips (proper use: novelty cushion) that he pressed to his face for 'Kiss Me' by Stephen 'Tin Tin' Duffy, the dreadlocks wig for Culture Club, Red Indian headdress and plastic tomahawk for 'Prince Charming' by Adam and the Ants. With a grin that, over time, felt more and more like the face of a man straining away from an electric current passing through his testicles, Charlie donned his outfits, and strummed a blow-up guitar, and led the hokey-cokey, and fended off drunken guests, and introduced the bride's father, and wearily told guests that, sorry, he had to pack up now. And tonight would be no different.

He pushed the last record box into the back of the van, casting a last eye over the rest of the contents: box full of 'gags' (Red Indian headdress etc.), decks, table, amps, speakers, lights. Then he closed it up and, with a last look back at the house, got in and pulled away.

He drove down their road, between its two rows of terraces, and to the junction, where he turned right, aiming across town to its 'old, quaint' section. There was a church, and a river crossed by aesthetically pleasing wooden pedestrian bridges, the green, the Ale House and Alms House, the centrepiece Dragon's Breath pub and hotel, star of many a teatime murder mystery.

And Selina and her friends.

# Selina and Her Friends

They were sitting behind the Old Vicarage – the one that was now offices – on a small piece of green with the river behind it. Contents of the small piece of green: one park bench, five kids, two or more bottles of wine.

They'd spent the day hanging around: three girls, Selina, Carly and Lauren, and two boys, Gavin and Nathan.

The lads wore no tops – just caps and chains. They had lean, wiry bodies and their tracksuit bottoms hung low, exposing boxer-short bands, like the waistbands of nappies. They liked to thrust their hands down the front of their tracky bottoms. They liked to do that a lot. If not rummaging, then the hand would be kept outside but remain at crotch level, worrying at the fabric as though checking for continued penile presence. Some hand movements were even performed from crotch level, as though to benefit midgets. Most came from overhead, though: imaginary guns held to illustrate what might happen; imaginary punches thrown to illustrate what actually did happen; hands held like fish-slices to enforce important points, an angled pointing finger – all of it body language informed by violence, all of it accompanied by voices at top volume, as though they were performing at some kind of circus.

Even with all that treasured testosterone, the loudest and gobbiest among them was a girl, Selina. The one by whom all others measured themselves: 'I never get as pissed as Selina – you ain't never seen me pissed as her.'

'I ain't as nasty as Selina.'

'I ain't got a gob on me like Selina.'

. . . lose me temper like Selina.

. . . make a show of myself like Selina.

Only they said it 'Slinah'.

Selina swore, and spat, and shouted, and smoked, and gave the frightened populace more lip than anyone else. She tried harder than everyone else because otherwise nobody would notice Selina, who didn't have Carly's big tits or Lauren's dad who dealt weed. She had nothing, really, unless you counted a mum who drank and slept, and a dad who was hardly ever there but fucked other women who drank, too, and shouted, sometimes, outside their door late at night.

So she had nothing. Selina was all she had. And she made sure everybody knew it.

When had it become acceptable for girls to spit? wondered unfortunate dog-walkers as they ran a gauntlet of F-words, fight nostalgia, crotch gesticulations and defiant eyes. To swear so much? When had it become acceptable for boys to cup their own balls in public? What suddenly became wrong with putting your hands in your pockets, or folding them across your chest, or perhaps using them to do something constructive? And when, exactly, had kids decided they were going to drink in public? When had they become like that? And now that they were like that, why couldn't they just *fuck off*?

Of course, the kids *were* being circumspect with the booze. Instinctively they knew how to manipulate public response, keeping indignation simmering but never boiling over enough to ring the police, who, anyway, would either never come or simply drive into the pay-and-display, make their presence felt by flashing the blues and watch the kids disperse – problem moved. Later, though – it was teatime now – the kids would have darkness to play with. They'd have dark places to go. So they waited, the boys shouting and gesticulating, and the girls alternating between pouts and doing similar, minus the crotch stuff.

After all, they'd had a busy day of swearing and shouting, and stamping on tadpoles caught with nets stolen from the summertime display at Poundstretcher. They'd had a busy day of being the worst thing about this lovely, sunny Friday, and now they'd earned themselves a bit of kick-loose time. For that they needed dark and privacy. Something was going to happen tonight.

They didn't need to go far to find their fun.

As darkness began to make its presence felt, the boys slapped their football shirts over their skinny white shoulders and the group went across the wooden footbridge, with Selina doing 'Saved-ya!' to Lauren ('Fuck off, Slinah'), and Nathan doing 'Saved-ya!' to Carly ('Nathe, fuck off!') all the way across. They came out by the footpath, then climbed over the stile and walked up the field towards the woods and the cemetery.

Nathan had decided he needed a surface on which to roll a big spliff. Gravestone would do – one of the big flat ones.

They were hard nuts to a boy and girl, so the spooky novelty of being in the graveyard wore off almost instantaneously and, anyway, it wasn't *that* dark – a watery summer dark – and they quickly located the graveyard's only bench, which was in memory of Alfred Hardwick, loving father. Nathan set to work rolling up. Selina sat on the back, feet on the seat. Gavin stood on it, testing the springy bench slats. The two other girls stood, arms folded, looking jaded. Bottles were produced, scrunched packets of fags pulled from jeans. The real drinking began, the proper dope-smoking, none of them little fag-sized spliffs.

The noise levels rose, but there was no one to hear them, maybe the odd dog-walker in the wood at the top of the hill, perhaps an evening runner. The boys drank and posed and strutted while the girls fended off filthy suggestions with fuck-off-peppered replies.

Somewhere between the two, Selina sat on the back of the bench, staring out over the graveyard, bottle of something sweet and five per cent and fluorescent-green in her hands. To her right the woods were a dark shroud, while the hill fell away to the town at her left: the church, the green, the Dragon's Breath. On the still air was a distant thump. There was a party at the Ale House. *Thump-thump-thump*. It was, she recognised, 'Blue Monday' by New Order.

In front of her was the graveyard. There was a watering-can on a hook; a tap there, too, and nearby a litter-bin. Beyond those were gravestones and plots throwing dark shapes at the skyline. Dead people: loved ones who died tragically as infants, or suddenly in their thirties and forties, or peacefully in their eighties, who all kept Jesus company now.

Gav kept jumping to the ground, jumping back to the bench, then jumping to the ground, doing kung-fu leaps.

The first thing to break was the bench. It was bound to, Gavin bouncing on it like that. Even the love of Alfred Hardwick's family couldn't keep it together; it let out a loud crack that rudely penetrated the noise they made.

A second of silence found them staring at Gav, who in turn looked down at the bench. 'Oops,' he said, and raised a bulbous bottle of white wine to his mouth, drank, then stamped down on the slats. Once, twice, three times a lady – until there was an even louder crack. Laughing, Selina reached a foot over and stamped into the hole, and the wood splintered before Gavin bent down to pull up a slat, and Nathan was finding a newspaper that had been left in the litter-bin and they were stuffing it into the cracks, setting fire to the paper.

It had begun. An aluminium flower vase was being used as a football, and then they were jumping from one stone to the next, strewing flowers with their trainers, and Nathan was balancing on a black marble cross, wobbling forward and back, then finding his balance, reaching into his tracky bottoms for little Nathan. The cross was *In memory of a beloved wife, Maura Pryor, who died 28 November 2002 aged 42 years*. Ovarian cancer had taken Maura.

'Give us a suck!' he shouted, cock in hand, to Carly, who screeched, 'Fucking pervert!' and turned her back, arms folded across those big tits of hers.

Nathan started to have a piss but lost his balance, dropping off the cross and finishing against it. He tucked himself back in, took a final swig of booze, shouted, 'Oi!' and lobbed the bottle at Gavin, who moved aside to let it smash against a gravestone, which was *In loving memory of Peter Davis, who passed peacefully into the presence of his saviour, 8 December 1974, aged 64 years.* Peter had died in hospital, his wife by his side.

'Yeah?' shouted Gavin. 'Come on, then, let's have it,' gesticulating from the groin and looking around for something to throw.

Breathless with laughter, Selina suddenly saw a dark shape in the sky and ducked in time to avoid an aluminium flower-pot, feeling droplets of water as it sailed overhead. She lunged for it and threw it blindly back, hearing it clank against a gravestone.

'What you lot fuckin' doin'?' complained Carly – or was it Lauren? The two stood by the bench with studied expressions of disapproval, their arms resolutely folded. Nathan, Gavin and Selina had taken cover behind gravestones, using them as shields to launch missile attacks on enemy positions. Vases and handfuls of decorative gravel were deployed as weapons.

'Fuckin' 'ell.' Gavin stopped short at a monument for *Aubrey Land, died 13 February 1980, aged 78 years, now with his beloved Ginny.* Next to it was another monument boasting the same degree of Gothic opulence, this one for *Ginny Land, beloved wife of Aubrey.*

He reached into the pocket of his jeans.

Finding herself out of ammo, Selina ran across the grave-yard, stooped to pick up a vase and emptied out the flowers and water as she ran. From behind her she heard the *phsssh* of a spray-can and knew Gavin was up to his tricks. Another *ph'ssh* – Nathan had joined him. She smelt paint on the air. Paint and burning bench.

She ran, leaving Lauren and Carly, the boys, the spray-paint and the bench behind her. She was deliriously happy, free as she'd ever felt – as though she might fly – kicking over some flowers left at the grave of *Francis Watson, died 9 July 1994, devoted husband to Joan and loving father to Leonard and Charles.*

She stopped and turned to see the two lads kick over a small concrete statuette (of Winnie the Pooh) Gavin doing one of his kung-fu kicks and falling, then leaping upright with his cap skew-whiff. Seeing them like that, she put her hands to her knees and laughed so hard she thought she might not be able to stop, or might piss herself, gasping to catch her breath.

Gavin saw her, pointed and started to move but bumped into a gravestone, snagging his hip on it, turning and tagging the stone with his spray-can in revenge.

Beside her was a flat gravestone. *Here lies Mark David Slater*, it said. *Died 20 August 1973, aged seven months. Our tiny angel is above us now.* His mother came to the grave three times a week, without fail. She bought flowers from Foster's, the florist between the US Nail Bar and the Early Learning Centre. There was Mark's carefully tended plot, the flowers left the previous day. Such care. Such attention.

And Selina howled at the sky and stamped on it as hard as she could. She scuffed and kicked at the flat stone. She reached down and clawed at the decorative gravel there, sending it flying into the darkness around her. She obliterated the grave beneath her trainers until it was just as shit as her life.

# The Dove

'Hello, son,' said Newlife.

His name was Tom, but Charlie and Leo had nicknamed him Newlife because he was their mother's second husband. They'd called him that, cruelly if Charlie thought about it, for a long time – long before Newlife's business had been smoothly absorbed into a huge corporation and he and their mother had decided to move to Spain. Newlife. One of those shared jokes between brothers. Now, Charlie realised, heart thick and soggy, it was just *his* joke.

Newlife's hand was at his shoulder. It patted until Charlie realised that Newlife was bringing him back gently to the here-and-now.

'Thank you,' he said. He was, as usual, bone tired.

'We thought here, rather than on the M25,' said Newlife, and Charlie glanced at him to see if he was joking. Apparently not.

His mother stood by Newlife. She held a box, inside which was the dove: Charlie could hear it moving, even with the traffic and the far-off sirens – the dirty clamour of Kilburn High Road ona Saturday morning.

His mother threw back her shoulders and met the world bravely, not wanting to let the scum of north London dent her composure. They'd been in the country more than a week but still they behaved like the sun-dried ex-pats they so obviously were, over-tanned and sniffing at the air as though it were toxic, 'keeping their wits about them', because every 'coloured person' was a likely mugger, every discarded chocolate wrapper a used hypodermic, every car horn and overheard expletive a reinforcement of their decision to escape this awful, dirty, asylum-seeker-, single-mum-, dole-scrounger-loving country.

'Hello, darling,' said his mum, and they hugged. Coming apart, Charlie saw tears in her eyes and felt his heart thaw a little. She was suffering too, of course she was. Unfeeling of him to think otherwise. It's just that she had . . . well, Newlife. Things had changed for her. Newlife had taught her the value of the stiff upper lip – and that it was so much easier to maintain one when you had the money to do so.

She withdrew to the safety of Newlife, wrapping herself round his arm like a soldier leaning on a pikestaff. 'Well,' she said, affecting banter, 'he always liked things a bit rough and ready, didn't he?'

Did they really look out of place, or was Charlie casting them in that role? Would she always have looked out of place on Kilburn High Road, even before Newlife? He didn't think so. 'He loved it here, Mum. I can't imagine where he would have been happier,' he said – but did he really know that?

'You did the right thing, moving away when you did,' said his mother, wincing as the air shook with bass from a passing car.

'It's different when you've got kids,' he replied. 'It's okay for some, bringing up a child in the city – plenty do. It just . . . wasn't for us.'

'Well, I think you definitely made the right choice.'

Charlie sighed. 'I'm sure we did.' Then, 'Shall we go?' He looked at Newlife for an answer. Why, he wasn't sure. Maybe because Newlife seemed to be the one in control of General Movement. Maybe just out of politeness.

They walked, turning off the high road and into a residential street where, about half-way along, the house where Leo had lived tugged at their gaze like a facial deformity.

It was a Victorian terrace, the kind that was split into three flats. Leo's was the basement. You didn't need his address to figure that one out: every single house in the terrace was way past its best, but only Leo's was black, its windows boarded up. Charlie could see where the flames had licked at the ground-floor flat above. That, too, had suffered smoke damage: the windows were sooty. Behind those windows he saw light. The family above, he knew, had escaped unharmed, their home barely touched – just left with the smell that won't come out, no matter how much Glade gets thrown its way.

They descended the steps, his mum gingerly. Stoic weeds seemed to have escaped the blaze unscathed. Leo's front door – Charlie could see it had once been blue – had a large bolt and padlock on it. 'Oh,' he said.

'Yes, sorry, son, should have mentioned it,' said Newlife, stepping forward. 'We've put the flat with agents. They'll be, um, doing the necessary refurbishments, disposing of it. Your mother and I . . . we thought, as you had a new baby and everything, that you'd probably appreciate not having the responsibility. I'll meet any fees, of course.'

68

Newlife. This was what he did. He stepped in and sorted. Charlie fought a wave of guilt for ever having thought any bad of him. 'Thanks,' he said. 'Really, thank you. I must admit, I hadn't even thought . . .'

'Of course.' Newlife went to pat him on the back but thought better of it, fishing for the keys instead.

'I can return those once we've finished, if you like,' said Charlie, taking them.

'Okay, son. Appreciate that.'

They nodded manfully at each other, some kind of weird understanding reached. Then Charlie undid the padlock and opened the door.

The smell raced from the open door and ganged up around them, wet and rancid; not the comforting after-smell of a log fire in the morning, but its cruel, acrid nemesis.

'Perhaps you should go in first, Charlie,' said Newlife, glancing meaningfully at Charlie's mother.

*Great*, thought Charlie petulantly, staring down the pitch-black hallway and holding the sleeve of his jacket to his nose. He edged forward, going towards where he thought there might be a door to the living room, where there might be some light.

It wasn't exactly the Channel Tunnel, the corridor, but it felt like it to Charlie. His heart thumped as he shuffled along the soaking floor tiles. Here, a door. The hand not holding his nose fumbled for the doorknob and his legs brushed against something that crinkled like charred skin. He jumped back with a startled sound that prompted Newlife to call, 'Everything all right down there, Charlie?'

'Yeah, thanks, Tom, I think so.' He composed himself, bringing his leg forward to get the measure of the crinkly thing.

A bunch of flowers. That was all it was. Gingerly he gathered them up, then opened the door to the living room. Now there was a new and more evil smell, the sound of dripping water, a claustrophobic blackness undefeated by swordblades of light from gaps in the wooden boards at the window.

'Sod that,' he said to himself, and returned along the passage, realising as he did so that there might have been more light in the hall had his mum and Newlife not been standing in the doorway.

'Did you just swear, Charlie?' said his mum.

He ignored the question. 'I don't think we want to go in there, Mum. It's really not very nice. We can do it here, look. We need to release it out here anyway, really.'

'But I was hoping . . . out of a window.' She looked crestfallen. Perhaps in her mind she'd created a picture. In it she was in an airy, white-painted room with billowy curtains and French windows, the dove flying free from her outstretched hands.

'They're all boarded up, Mum.' He looked to Newlife for support, but Newlife was looking down at Charlie's hands, the bunch of flowers.

His mum noticed them at the same time. 'What are those?' she said.

They were fresh. Sooty, but definitely fresh. Tucked in the polythene was a card that Charlie read out: 'You still owe me a tenner, love S.'

They stared at him as though he'd been speaking Cantonese. 'That's what it says,' he assured them, and repeated it.

'Probably one of those performers,' said Newlife, thinking no doubt of the lookalikes and tribute acts who had crowded the service, all done up in full costume, in tribute. Row upon row of George Michaels, Fab Fours and Madonnas.

'Yeah, maybe,' said Charlie, staring at the card thoughtfully. 'But . . . Probably his girlfriend, actually. He called her Chariot but her real name was Sapphire. That would explain the S.'

# Uncle Leo and Partner

Leo's girlfriend.

Maybe she would know.

Know what, exactly, Charlie wasn't sure. Know what Leo was up to; know what news he'd been planning to break to Charlie the night he died.

But all he had to go on for Leo's girlfriend was a name, and he'd met her just the once, the night of the visit.

It hadn't gone well, that visit. To say the least. Leo (and his girlfriend, don't forget her) had paid an unannounced (and drunken, don't forget drunken) visit to Bentham in the middle of the night – *the night they got home from the hospital with Mary*, don't forget.

The night before, after eighteen hours of labour at High Wycombe hospital, Charlie had got home in the early hours and sent emails to friends and family, the first pictures of Mary, with 'come and see us all soon' invitations included. But he hadn't meant *that* soon. Not the night they arrived home.

'We sail tonight for Singapore.'

Charlie had heard it from outside the window. The unmistakable sound of 'Singapore' by Tom Waits, from the *Rain Dogs* album. The rendition was drunken, but still note and lyric perfect.

'Oh, shit,' he groaned to himself. Beside him, Bea slept, but she wouldn't sleep for long. Not with Tom Waits outside, already on the second or third verse. And it was a fairly salty old song, 'Singapore', bulging with whores and vast amounts of alcohol abuse. Charlie thought of the neighbours. But then Bea stirred by his side, and there was a sound from the crib, a snuffle. Mary had only been asleep – what? Twenty minutes? Bea had not long adjusted the swaddling and placed her in the Moses basket; and just minutes ago, sleep-deprived, hollow-eyed and almost beside themselves with exhaustion, they'd fallen into bed – and now . . .

Now his drunken brother was standing outside the house singing Tom Waits songs at the top of his big fat lungs.

What was Leo doing here anyway? He lived in Kilburn, a long and bumpy trip down the Met line and then some. Leo didn't hang around anywhere outside the M25. The way he told it, Bentham was a nice town but he'd grown up there and had no intention of returning. He wasn't the kind of guy who inspected the bog paper after use. (The implication that Charlie was was left unsaid.) It was far too quiet for him; he needed noise. Chaos was his mistress.

But here he was, despite the never-go-back philosophy. Metaphorically inspecting the bog paper in his home town. And the peace issue was clearly something he intended to address. Now. At volume.

Charlie slid so carefully from beneath the duvet that it barely moved. Baby-in-basket status: fine, sleeping. Wife status: also asleep. He padded to the window, planning to open it, lean out into the warm summer evening and tell his brother to piss off back to Kilburn. But they had double-glazing and window locks, these days – they came as part of the suburban dream – and the key was nowhere to be seen. Instead Charlie pushed his head under the curtain and looked out of the window, helplessly, like a kidnapped child, at his brother, who stood on the pavement below.

Leo caught sight of him and, without pausing, broke into 'Downtown Train', also, if Charlie remembered correctly, from *Rain Dogs*. 'Will I see you tonight?' sang Leo, more loudly, gesturing up at the window now. 'On a downtown train.'

With him was a woman Charlie had never seen before. She sat on the kerb with her back to the house and, from her poise, Charlie guessed her mood was post-anger – resignation, probably. If you signed up with Leo FC you had to expect the odd team outing to strange and faraway places and, let's face it, if you were going to sleep with a professional Tom Waits impersonator, you probably had to expect the odd rendition of 'Downtown Train' into the bargain.

Then Leo burst into 'Rain Dogs', which was definitely from *Rain Dogs*, so loudly that Charlie had no choice but to let them in.

He always had this funny way of hanging his head to one side, Leo did. It softened him. It was a listening look, and listening was something he'd been good at. The bad things about him were legion, of course (though now Charlie found himself remembering his brother's faults with a wry smile, as if death had donned a pair of rose-coloured specs) but so were the good things. Thoughtless, tick, but never maliciously or deliberately so, and always genuinely apologetic if you

74

brought it up; cynical, nasty-mouthed at times, but warm, a protector of those he loved. His love was big, amplified like his voice. And perhaps he was frightened by it – not his voice, although, God knows, everybody else was – but his love. Perhaps the magnitude of his emotion was so big he had to shut it out, and so he became, or seemed to be . . .

'. . . a selfish bastard, you really are. Mary's a couple of days old. Have you seen the time? Are you a vampire? You could come in the daytime, you know. We're half an hour on a tube away.'

'An hour.'

'Half an hour.' Even in his anger Charlie found himself reducing the distance they'd put between themselves and the capital. 'I mean, you know you're not going to get back now?'

'What time does the last train go?'

Sitting at the kitchen table, Leo shook a befuddled head. He was looking contrite, shame-faced – a wee boy who knew he'd done bad things. Still, his voice was as loud as cannon fire among the white goods of their kitchen.

'Keep it down, they're asleep, and it's already gone.'

*This being the sticks*, Leo's eyes seemed to flare and say, even as his head lolled to one side and he asked, 'Is it okay if we stay? Like, er, will Bea mind and stuff?'

Charlie took a pull from his cup of decaf – it was all they had, much to Leo's disgust – and sighed. 'Yes.' he hissed. 'Yes, she'll bloody mind.'

'Oh. Um . . .' Leo was confused that anybody might mind unexpected guests. 'Why? Because, you know, we won't be any bother. We can be out in the morning, first thing. Scouts' honour. We'll make the bed and everything, remove all pubic hairs that may be accidentally left in our

75

wake, make sure we don't leave any trace of our existence. Bea won't mind.'

'It's not just about Bea minding,' fibbed Charlie, loyally. 'It's about all of us. We've got a two-day-old baby in the house . . .'

'And we're hoping to meet that little tot as soon as we can,' said Leo, again too loudly. He glanced at his girlfriend as he said it, and in return she fixed him with a long look and gave him a withering smile. It meant that for maybe the first time since she had entered the kitchen she took her eyes off Charlie – he'd been sensing them as surely as if she was touching him. When she and Leo had come in from the street, she'd walked ahead of his brother, smiling at Charlie as she passed him at the door.

'This is Chariot,' said Leo. 'Chariot, this is my little brother, Charlie. Charlie – Chariot would like a cup of char, and a chair on which to rest her charming charse.'

'Hello,' she'd said, smiling a brothers-in-arms smile at Charlie.

She was Indian, hair bobbed, a tiny nose stud, full, damson lips, and bright, bright eyes, wide and smiling like she saw the joke. Always.

'Chariot?' said Charlie.

She'd gestured at Leo. 'His idea of a joke. It's Sapphire.'

Charlie looked confused.

'Chariot. Sapphire,' she prompted.

'Ah, right.' Charlie had laughed, pointing this-way down the hall, watching her as she walked ahead. She was assured and silent, and there was something about her that rendered the surroundings humdrum and made Charlie feel dull, and grey, and guiltily resentful of the baby paraphernalia that had

76

taken over his home, like an invading army sponsored by Johnson's. And in that instant his life seemed very safe and ordinary. And feeling that – knowing he'd just wished his life different – he'd felt a terrible guilt, sharp as an icicle.

So the two of them stayed, because where else did they have to go? The last train had left and, anyway, Leo was his brother. You don't turn brothers out, not even brothers who come calling at the worst imaginable times. You just don't.

Charlie had schlepped up to the spare bedroom to prepare it for his brother and Chariot, reminding himself that it was Bea who, back in Hackney – pressing home the we've-got-to-move message – had yearned for an extra bedroom. And what was the point of a guest room if you didn't use it for guests, eh, Bea? So be careful what you wish for, because you might just get it.

And having seen them to their quarters, furnished them with towels for the morning, confirmed that Leo remembered the way to the bathroom and assured them that any noise that woke Bea or Mary would cost them their lives, he let himself back into his bedroom. He crept round the bed to his side, slid off his slippers and raised the duvet just enough for a terrified man to slip beneath it. Settling, silent and still, not wanting to breathe until the room had adjusted itself to his presence as if he had been there for hours, he at last closed his eyes.

'What the fuck is going on?' said Bea, from beside him. He felt her beddy breath on him. Her voice was a tired croak.

'It's Leo,' he whispered. 'He was outside. He's with a girl.'

She didn't move. 'He's with a *what*?'

'A girl,' whispering still. 'His girlfriend. I couldn't exactly turn them out.'

'Why are they here?' she hissed.

'I don't know,' he said. 'To see Mary.'

There was a long pause. 'I bet you,' she said, 'that in the morning this is going to turn out to be a nightmare I'm having, and I'm going to tell you all about it and we're going to have a laugh.' She chuckled and fell back to sleep.

Mary woke about an hour later, wet, and they changed her and she wouldn't stop screaming as Bea tried desperately to feed her, and Charlie hoped against hope that Leo wouldn't get up to see if he could help. Thank God for small mercies.

The following morning was a horror film of bad moods, hangovers, awkward silences, forced smiles and torn loyalties.

By mutual consent they decided Leo and friend were going to leave as soon as possible, maybe sooner. There had been one brief, silently livid appearance by Bea, in her dressing-gown, hair bedraggled, limp and greasy, looking what she was: an exhausted woman having the life force parasitically sucked out of her. She'd taken a look at Leo and said hello, half smiled, but a smile like used cooking-oil draining away, and she'd glanced at Leo's girlfriend, and straight away she'd looked at Charlie, who felt transparent and guilt-ridden.

There was five minutes of cooing over the baby, Mary floppy and sleepy, Leo having a hold, Bea trying her best, answering questions about the birth, the odd shard of pride shining through like sunlight from behind badly drawn curtains. But as Leo and his girlfriend fussed over Mary, her eyes met his and they were imploring. *Get them out of here*, they said. Then she excused herself and left to go upstairs. She'd been there ever since, unseen, her hurt a kind of gas that seemed to swirl downstairs and seep into the kitchen where they sat.

'I'm so sorry,' said Leo, when she'd gone. 'This was bad. This was so bad.'

'We're just tired, mate. Really tired. We've got a new baby and we're kind of firing blind. It's all new to us.'

Leo was doing ashamed and apologetic, wearing the look like an old favourite overcoat. Even so, he wanted to be out of this so-uncool situation. He just wanted the awkwardness to end, and Charlie had to agree. He yearned to go upstairs and be with his wife and daughter. Crawl into bed behind Bea, make spoons, close his eyes and sleep. He wanted his home as back to normal as it could be with a new baby in it. He wanted some kind of equilibrium restored. He wanted Leo and his girlfriend out – felt it like a restless leg.

There was silence in the kitchen.

At last she spoke. 'Charlie?'

He looked at her, as though surprised to be addressed by name, here in his own kitchen, by his brother's girlfriend.

'Yes?'

'Is there a downstairs bathroom I could use, so as not to disturb your wife?'

'Sure,' he said, too fast. 'Just off the hall. It's tiny but . . .'

'Thanks. I won't be a moment. It'll give your brother a chance to tell you who I am.'

If Leo was admonished he didn't show it, just waited until she'd left the room and said, 'Sharp, isn't she? She'll end up cutting herself if she's not careful.'

'Are you serious about her?' Ugh. Charlie sounded like somebody's dad.

Leo seemed to ignore the question. 'I've been thinking about having a kid lately,' he said hazily, 'like you.'

'Well. You should. It's great.'

Leo chuckled. 'Didn't work out so well for *our* dad, though, did it?'

79

Whatever his reasons for medicating himself to death, their father had kept them to himself. Over the years Charlie and Leo had had plenty of time to come up with their own theories until they'd run out of them, and gradually the subject had gone from being something they discussed with tears in their eyes, a bottle of wine or two to drown their sorrows, to something they chatted about on the phone, in between how-are-you and how's-things, to something they never spoke about at all. It was inside, though, crouched in there. A vagrant thought, a sticky stain on their souls.

Whatever his father's reasons, Charlie was sure they had nothing to do with parenthood, nothing to do with him and Leo. He'd been a perfect dad. A bit prejudiced, but then dads often are. Not that demonstrative, but then dads often weren't. Mostly, he'd been there. Someone to turn to. Someone at the end of the phone. The pain of that absence had never truly subsided. It probably never would.

'I don't think that was why,' he said to Leo.

'Why, then?'

'We've been through it a million times.'

'Yeah, I know. I wondered, will it make it easier now you're a dad yourself?'

'I suppose so,' Charlie said. 'Things are bound to change.'

'Because you have less time to think about it.'

'Even that's not such a bad thing.'

'I reckon I might do it. Soon. Get married. Settle down – you know?'

'Move out to the suburbs?'

'I wouldn't go that far,' he smiled, 'but just, you know, take it easy, put down roots, meet the neighbours, have a barbecue. Maybe, you know, one day . . . a little baby, a little Leo.' He nodded his haggard head as he spoke. The idealised life he had planned purged his soul.

'That's the hangover talking,' said Charlie. 'You're feeling sorry for yourself. Give it till lunchtime and you'll have itchy feet again. You're not the settling-down-with-babies type, mate. You're not me. You're Leo.'

'Yeah,' said Leo, nodding sadly. 'Yeah, I sure am me.'

At the time, Charlie had wondered what Leo had been doing in Bentham. 'To come see the little one,' Leo had insisted, and Charlie had (albeit with *yeah, right* running through his mind) taken him at his word. Now, though – now he had an idea what Leo might have been doing in Bentham that day.

# Charles Laughton

In the offices of the *Bentham Weekly Chronicle*, 'Bentham's oldest local weekly', it was hot, of course, but not just hot – really, *really* hot.

Charlie stood, almost gasping, needing suddenly to fight a wave of tiredness. A lonely free-standing fan oscillated, recycling warm air into marginally less-warm air. Dotted around the walls were front pages that the *Bentham Chronicle* considered noteworthy: 'New Development for Town'; 'Swimmer Tragedy'; 'Local Band Scores Hit'; 'We're 100!'; 'Adventurer Goes Missing' – that kind of thing. He took a look at the receptionist, who took a look at him, and he went over. 'Hi, do you have someone I could speak to about adverts, please?'

The receptionist smiled thinly. 'Classified or display?' she said testily.

'Classified, most likely.'

'Well, you'll need to know,' smiled the receptionist as though conversing with a retarded child.

'Why?'

'Because if it's classified,' the receptionist smiled, 'then it's me you have to deal with.'

'Right,' said Charlie, smiling back. Anybody glancing through the window would have assumed they were posing for a shot in a promotional brochure. 'All it is – I just need to know whether or not my brother has placed an advert with you. Are you able to tell me?'

'Ah,' she said, enjoying the moment, 'no. I'm terribly sorry, but I can't give out that kind of information.'

'It's classified, is it?'

'I beg your pardon?'

'Never mind.' He glanced at a calendar Blu-tacked to the wall by the reception desk, a single piece of card sponsored by Grangers the Printer's. Not exactly the last word in printing technology but just what Charlie was looking for. Mary had been born in the early hours of 4 of May. That's my girl, he'd thought at the time. May the fourth be with you. Bea had spent just the one night in hospital before she was turfed out, which meant that Leo had visited them on the night of the fifth. It had been a Friday night. If Charlie was right, Leo had combined his brother-baiting and boozing with a visit to the *Bentham Chronicle*.

'If my brother had placed an advert on this day –' Charlie indicated on the calendar – 'when would the advert have appeared?'

She pursed her lips and peered at where he pointed. 'Here,' she said. 'The issue dated May the sixteenth.'

'Thank you.' He smiled. 'Now, if you'll tell where you keep your back copies . . .'

She indicated the window area of reception where there were a raised table and stools, and binders lying on the table. Each had about six months' worth of back copies in them, he found, when he went across to look. She scolded him with her eyes as he moved them from one end of the desk to the other – the end nearest the fan.

He searched back two months, finding the right paper, flipping through the pages, his fingers slowly turning black despite the apparently non-staining ink they were always claiming to use these days – yet one more example of modern life claiming to be something it wasn't. Like those yoghurts . . .

*Ah.*

There it was. He'd been right. He felt his chest vibrating slightly and recognised it for the feeling he used to get when flicking through charity-shop record sections and coming across a ridiculously rare Giorgio Moroder production with a 20p sticker on it – in the days when charity shops were clueless about their stock, this was (never happened any more, of course: the Cancer Research in town even had a Rare section, which took all the fun out of it). It was, he realised, a rush.

Then, chasing that thrill with fresh blood on its fangs, there was something else.

His brother's fraud staring him in the face.

Charlie was looking at an advert for Watson Investigates.

'Good local knowledge,' it promised. 'Discretion. Expertise.' There was an email address but no phone number (which figured. There was no point in undermining your good-local-knowledge claim with an 020 prefix), plus a paragraph covering the kind of jobs Watson Investigates would be happy to look into for you.

Charlie put himself in the place of someone seeing this advert, feeling the hope, and suddenly he felt dirty and wrong on behalf of his brother. This wasn't right, and he understood

Merle being pissed off when he'd smirked. Had Leo been the kind of person who told pensioners he needed to read the meter then, once inside, fished around beneath their mattresses for wads of cash? No, of course not. But still. He had traded in the same emotions: hope, trust. There was no widescreen hustling or grifting going on, just lies. At the bottom of the advert was the logo for the Association of British Investigators, and Charlie thought again of Merle. Dumb move, Leo.

Charlie slipped off the stool, carried the binder to the receptionist and placed it on the counter. She looked at it as though he'd sneezed something on to the desk. 'Can I help?' she asked.

'Yes,' said Charlie, 'hello again.' He smiled. She smiled back. He pressed on: 'Remember my brother who I thought had placed the advert? This is it. I was wondering if you could tell me if there are any more?'

'His name?' She had the inevitable glasses on a chain round her neck and brought them up to her eyes as she squinted at the computer in front of her.

'Watson.'

'Initial?'

'L.'

Tap, tap, tap. She didn't sit down to use the computer, just stood looking at the screen through the glasses, poking at the keyboard as though prodding the corpse of a rodent to check whether it was deceased.

'This placement ran for three weeks in Services Offered,' she said, waving a hand at the Watson Investigates ad.

'Right.'

'Ah.'

'What?'

'L. Watson, you say?'

'Yes.'

'I have an L. Watson who placed a Lost and Found.'

'Really. This one was . . .' he craned to look at the binder '. . . a Services Offered.'

'Oh.'

They looked at one another. Her mouth pursed again.

'So . . .' said Charlie, puzzled '. . . was it the same Watson who placed the Lost and Found?'

'I'm afraid I really can't give you that kind of information.'

'Come on,' prompted Charlie, 'we're almost there. This is my brother we're talking about. He placed *this* advert.' He jabbed at it with a charcoal-coloured finger. 'That's *his* email address. If he placed another advert I'd like to know about it.'

'You're Mr Watson, too, are you?' she said, removing her glasses but holding on to them, like a schoolmarm. That was her all over, thought Charlie: a frustrated teacher.

'Yes, of course I'm Mr Watson also.'

'Well, Mr Watson, why not just ask your brother?'

'Good question. I'll give you three guesses why.'

She frowned uncertainly, then stared down at the binder, sliding it right way up so she could get a better look at the advert and placing a finger to it, wrinkly finger-flesh crowding round the manicured nail. 'This one was placed by your brother?'

'Yes.'

'I remember him.'

*Bollocks*, thought Charlie, heart sinking. If he'd been having trouble with the receptionist he could only begin to imagine the impression Leo had made.

But instead of sending him on his way, she turned her attention to the computer, prodding away at it. Charlie chewed the inside of his cheek, wondering what new horrors she was planning to unleash.

'Yes,' she said, after a short interval of tapping, 'yes, it was the same L. Watson who placed the Lost and Found. His name was Leo, wasn't it?'

'Er, yes,' replied Charlie. 'Yes, it was.'

She looked at him, the use of the past tense obviously not wasted on her. 'The Lost and Found advert is . . .' she was already leafing expertly through the binder, licking her finger, the gesture humanising her, Charlie still trying to assimilate the subtle shift in atmosphere in the room ' . . . here.'

She swished the binder round Charlie's way and pointed at an advert. It was in the issue dated 21 June.

'This one?' he said disbelievingly.

'That one, yes.'

'Reward offered,' it said, 'for information leading to the safe return of a beloved family pet.'

It was a lost dog. For some reason Leo had placed an advert about a lost dog. Well, not 'for some reason'. Presumably because he was involved in trying to find a lost dog. One that was called . . .

No way . . .

Charles Laughton.

# She's Alive!

*Charles Laughton.*

Because . . . When was it? When had they spoken, him and Leo?

'Hey, mate.'

'All right, Leo. You okay?'

'Yeah, hip and moving to the groove. How's tricks in the land of fatherhood?'

'Yeah, good. Miraculous. Spiritual experience. Feel whole for the first time in my life et cetera.'

'Ah. Still not sleeping, then.'

'Not a fucking wink.'

'Not a good time to speak?'

'Doesn't matter, mate, really. The concept of time has ceased to have meaning. What is it you want?'

'Well . . . have you heard of Elsa Lanchester?'

'Elsa Lanchester, the movie star, who played the bride in James Whale's classic *Bride of Frankenstein* for Universal in the mid-1930s?'

'Yeah, her.'

'No, can't say I have. What about her?'

'Ha-ha. Is she collectable?'

'Why do you ask?'

'A mate wants to know. I said I'd ask you – you being the film geek of the family.'

'Thanks. Well, no, she's not particularly collectable by herself. Not like Orson Welles or Marilyn Monroe collectable. But *Bride* stuff is pretty desirable. Wait there, I'm at my computer . . . Okay, here we go. Signed *Bride of Frankenstein* photo, a hundred dollars . . .'

'Doesn't seem too steep . . .'

'Here's something else. A *Bride of Frankenstein* lobby card that went for forty-six thousand dollars at auction. Set a record.'

'Christ.'

'Your mate hasn't got one, has he?'

'No, sorry. What about general Lanchester stuff, not necessarily in *Bride*?'

'I dunno, mate. I'd have to go and look – see what else she was in. She's really just known for that. Well, that's a bit unfair. What I mean is, although she was in plenty of other stuff, she was pretty much defined by that one role.'

'I haven't seen it. What's the big deal?'

'Well, she was the bride created by Baron Frankenstein to be a mate for the monster, but when she claps eyes on the monster, she's so repulsed that she rejects him, and the monster ends up going on the rampage.'

'She rejects him?'

'Yeah. That moment when she spurns the monster is one of the most famous in film history – you've probably seen it, or seen piss-takes of it without even knowing. Then there was her look for the film. Again, it's one of those things that's kind of seeped into the culture. It's become iconic. She had the most amazing shock-therapy hair, with a white streak through it. We used to do double bills of *Frankenstein* with *Bride of Frankenstein* at the cinema, free entry if you came dressed up. We hardly made a bean because everybody came dressed up, and not as the monster, either, but as the Bride. It's one of the most recognisable film images ever. Often imitated but never bettered.

'So, anyway, your bloke's come into some Lanchester archive stuff, has he? What sort? We're talking promotional material here – not, like, personal letters or diaries or anything?'

'No, no, nothing like that. Studio photos and stuff.'

'Well, tell him to let me have a look. I'll see if I can price them for him.'

'Cheers, mate, will do.'

# Rain Dogs *and Other Precipitation*

If Leo had had a mate whose dad had turned up some old shots of Elsa Lanchester, they never found their way to Charlie. That had been the end of it.

Except – drum roll – there never was a mate, was there, Leo?

Apart from what he'd told Leo Charlie didn't know a lot about Elsa Lanchester. Perhaps if he'd been arsed, or a better brother, or not suffering from extreme sleep-deprivation, he would have put down the phone and given it five more minutes on the Internet to see what he could turn up. But he hadn't. He'd ended the call and written a couple of quotes for Cheesy Vinyl gigs. So, no, he didn't know a lot about Elsa Lanchester. But one thing he did know: she was married to Charles Laughton. Right up until Laughton's death, if memory served.

The real Charles Laughton, that was. Not this dog. A dog that, improbably, Leo had somehow been involved in finding. And since Charlie was 90 per cent sure Leo didn't have a dog, especially not one called Charles Laughton – a Spinone, whatever the hell one of those was – it meant that Leo had been looking for a lost dog on behalf of someone else.

*I've got something to tell you, mate*. What? That things had got so bad you were reduced to looking for some sad bastard's dog, which had probably been hit by a car or run off to the dog equivalent of Gretna Green, or just got so pissed off with being anthropomorphised by over-doting owners that it'd legged it for a better life truffling through overturned wheelie-bins at the local dump and howling at parked cars?

Was that what you had to tell me?

Charlie pulled his Motorola from his jeans pocket and flipped it open, wiping perspiration off his forehead, scrolling down the phone book to LeoMob. A small part of him was thinking there had simply been a mistake and that LeoMob and the number in the advert wouldn't tally. That his brother and lost-dog person would be two separate entities.

But the numbers were the same. He snapped his phone closed. It was Leo's mobile number, with 'no questions asked' printed below it – the number you had to call if you knew the whereabouts of Charles Laughton, the clearly pampered but obviously missing and much-missed Spinone.

Was it that? Or was it something else? And why had he wanted to know about Elsa Lanchester?

Was it this, your last case?

Maybe.

As he'd absorbed the advert, a customer had come into reception, bought a paper, passed the time of day (subject: the weather) and gone. Now it was just Charlie and the receptionist again.

Charlie indicated the paper. 'He placed this when?'

'Ah, weeks ago.'

'In person?'

'Not this one, no.'

'But that last one he did?'

'Yes.'

'Any idea why?'

'Your brother had to pay in cash, Mr Watson.'

'Ah.' That made sense. 'But not for this one . . .' He tapped at the Lost and Found. Thinking, Bit more flush by now, Leo? How flush?

'Something's happened to him, then?' said the receptionist. She braced herself for the answer by placing a hand to her chest, as though anticipating heartburn.

'He's dead.' He felt stony saying it.

Her eyelids drooped. 'I'm sorry.'

'Yeah, me too.'

'How?'

'Car accident. Just him. Nobody else involved.'

'I'm sorry.'

'Thanks.'

They had a moment; Charlie wished he hadn't tarred her with the frustrated-schoolteacher brush.

'He was lovely,' she said.

'Lovely?'

'Yes. Lovely. A real gentleman. He had the most wonderful voice.'

Charlie's hand went up to his mouth as though to stifle a cough, but he found himself pressing his fist to his teeth, thinking – this from left-field – that he might be about to cry.

'Thank you,' he heard himself say. 'He would have loved to hear that. He was a singer.'

'Oh? Wasn't he an investigator?'

'Um, yes, he was. As well. He was a bit of both, really.'

'I see. I wish I'd heard him sing.'

'Oh, he was great. I didn't see him enough. I mean, I wish I had now, obviously. He was on every Wednesday night at a pub in Highgate. Only just down the road, really, but you know how it is, and . . . well, I only got there a couple of times. Only ever saw him perform twice . . .' Charlie heard a catch in his own voice and cleared his throat '. . . but great. Both times. Just great to hear. He was a real . . . presence, you know. He had charisma. When you're growing up that's something you kind of resent, I guess. He used to impersonate a singer. Have you heard of Tom Waits?'

The receptionist shook her head no.

'A sort of blues-jazz singer, I suppose. Great gravelly voice. Once heard, never forgotten. Leo's impression was superb. On the nose, it was. With a singer like Tom Waits it can so easily sound like you're taking the . . . mickey, and I think people came expecting a comedy element, like he was going to do Tom Waits singing nursery rhymes or something – as a joke, you know? But both times I went, I mean, he held the room. He did "Downtown Train". You might have heard of it because Rod Stewart did a version, but it's Tom Waits originally, so Leo covered it, and it was brilliant. Brilliant.'

'Can you buy his records?'

'Tom Waits? Sure, yes. I guess you'd say he's been pretty prolific over the years.'

'I'd like to hear him. Can you recommend me something?'

'Well, Leo's favourite was . . . His favourite was *Rain Dogs*.'

Charlie managed to get the words out – then took the tissue the receptionist was offering.

\* \* \*

94

Shortly after Charlie got home – after he'd checked and found Bea and Mary both asleep – he went into the little cupboard where there was a bottle of white spirit, some ancient gardening gloves, an old Waitrose carrier-bag full of matchboxes and a *Yellow Pages*.

Good old *Yellow Pages*. It was not just there for the nasty things in life, like a blocked drain, you could also use it to compile a list of the vets in town. There were four, as far as he could tell.

'Abbey Vets, good afternoon.'

'Oh, hello, I was wondering if you could help me.'

'I'll do my best.'

'Great. What it is – I'm trying to locate the owner of a dog. Quite a distinctive name. Charles Laughton. I wondered if you had that dog on your books at all?'

'Let me check for you.'

She went off the phone – tap, tap, tap – came back. 'Afraid not, sorry.'

'That's quite all right, thank you.'

And he scored through the name on his pad.

He got it on the third try.

'Can I ask what it's regarding?'

'Ah.' He perked up. 'You have it, then?'

'I'm afraid I can't say. Can I ask what it's regarding?'

'Sure. Charles Laughton has been reported missing. I, ah, may have information about that.'

'I see. What kind of information?'

'Um . . .' he screwed up his eyes . . . 'information I can only divulge to the owner, I'm afraid. If you could give me a contact number for them.'

The receptionist paused for a long time. Paranoid thoughts

95

threw tantrums in Charlie's head. Ones like: she's calling the cops on another line.

'Look,' he said quickly, 'this isn't some kind of . . . My name is Charlie Watson. I believe my brother was employed to look for the dog.'

'Your brother was *employed* to look for the dog?'

'I believe so. Unlikely as it sounds. He was, um, an investigator. Unfortunately, he has since died and the only record I have of this particular investigation is the name of the dog and the breed. Obviously there are certain things I'd like to tie up, so it would be extremely useful if I could contact the owner.'

Mary had woken. He could hear her crying in the other room.

'Oh,' said the receptionist. 'I'm sorry to hear that, but I'm afraid I still can't give out contact details of clients.'

'Could you contact the client on my behalf? Ask them to get in touch?'

'Yes, I can do that.'

'Thank you, thank you.' Charlie found himself grinning as he left his contact details and said goodbye, triumphant. That feeling – it beat playing Kool and the Gang.

## Johnson's and Other Lotions

'The dove flew into the flat,' said Charlie, later, across a plastic bath.

Bea put her hand to her mouth, half shocked and half laughing. 'Oh my God.'

'We tried to coax it out, but it wouldn't come. Mum was devastated.'

She reached and pushed a strand of damp hair away from her forehead. She was perspiring. He was too. Another warm and muggy evening: 'Heavy air,' his dad used to say.

'What did you do?' said Bea.

'About the dove? We had to leave it there. Hopefully it'll find its way out of one of the windows.'

'Aren't they boarded up?'

'Well, you know, there's the odd gap.'

'We shouldn't laugh. God, I hope it's all right.'

Between them, Mary was in the bath. She was in *her* bath, which was a plastic tub, boat-shaped. She lay on a bath rest, her head way above the water but still not far enough for her parents, who knelt at either side of the tub, each needlessly reaching to hold Mary's head clear of the deadly $H_2O$.

'She smiled,' said Bea, staring intently at Mary.

'I thought she smiled, too. Maybe she was smiling about the dove.'

'It was probably just wind.'

A spa-like eruption of bubbles followed.

'Not very ladylike,' he joked.

'Don't be silly.'

'We've got a tomboy,' he said, in mock-horror.

'Would it matter if we had?'

'Of course not. No. Of course not.'

Bea reached for the Johnson's dispenser and squished a palmful of baby wash into her hand, then kneaded it into the tiny floaty wisps that passed for hair on Mary's head.

'Ready, Daddy?'

She lifted Mary from the tub, making the appropriate *whee* sound effect, and, in a carefully worked-out move, handed her over the plastic bath to Charlie, who took her, made the appropriate *whee* sound effect, then placed her on a towel on the floor, using another to dry her gently but quickly. Seemingly unaffected by the sudden change in temperature, Mary's head was already moving so that she could drink in the sights.

'Hardly a peep,' said Bea, gleefully.

Mary made a sound, could have been a slightly whingey one. 'Uh-oh, don't speak too soon,' said Charlie, but the whinge subsided. First time out of the bath without crying. They looked at each other, smiling, eyes wide and shiny. Two very tired, ragged people enjoying a silent mini-celebration.

'She's a brave girl, that's why,' said Charlie to Mary. He put his lips to her tummy and blew a raspberry. One of Mary's flailing hands touched the top of his head and he felt as though he had been anointed. Raising himself, he experienced a brief moment of mourning for a time in the future when his baby would be too old to have raspberries blown on her tummy, would probably call ChildLine if he tried.

'Can you do the bath?'

He stood to attend to man's work, lifting the plastic tub and emptying it into the main bath, while Bea reached for a small pile of clothes, a nappy and some moisturiser.

'It's so hot tonight. Can we have the fan in the bedroom?' said Bea, holding the 3-in-1 Baby Miracle Cream.

'It's in the loft.'

'Well, can we get it down?' she asked.

He reached and kissed the top of her head. 'I love it when you say can *we* do something. It means can *you* do it.'

She grinned. 'S'pose it does. You're the hunter-gatherer.'

He thumped at his chest, nowhere he'd rather be.

'Go on then, Rocket Man, go get it.'

'Rocket Man'. It was what she'd sung on the night they met.

It was post-university, post-entertainments committee, but pre-Cheesy Vinyl. He'd been in the middle of a period in his life that at the time had felt scary, insecure and transitional, but now he remembered it as one of the best; wished he'd stopped worrying and enjoyed it. Funny thing: he'd thought he was enjoying it at the time. More than that, he'd thought he knew all about what lay ahead; he'd thought that whatever happened, he'd do it his way. He'd Charlify the world, bend it to his will. But he'd been wrong about that. Because he was an idiot. And anybody who thinks they can get married and have children and scrape by earning a living and be the same person they always were is also deluded. You accept it and move on or, like Charlie did, you mourned it, more keenly sometimes than you mourned your brother.

It was also two years after their father had died. It felt like he'd spent the first year crying, or watching his mother cry, or staring into Leo's tired, empty, defeated eyes over kitchen tables. Going into the second year things had got better. He'd stopped operating on auto-pilot and was beginning to think about himself again. He'd been asking himself what he wanted to do with his life, and since he'd always loved playing records . . .

He'd gone to the cinema manager with the idea. 'Listen, Frank,' he'd said, 'what about using the foyer?'

'The foyer?'

The foyer was this 'inspirational art-deco space', according to some guide or other. And, Charlie reasoned, Frank looking back at him from beneath a wire frame of broken veins, it's hideously under-used. 'Why not . . .' he walked over to the back of the inspirational art-deco space '. . . put a stage here, some decks at the back? Once the late-night show's over we'll have a band, a DJ, something in keeping with the theme of the movie.'

'Like what?' Frank had reasoned.

'Doesn't matter. Just . . . something.' Charlie was already buzzing that Frank hadn't simply told him to bugger off and retired to an office papered with Peckinpah posters to sip vodka surreptitiously from a paper cup.

'All right,' said Frank, 'do your worst.'

So he had.

As directed, they'd put the decks at the back of the stage, and in front of them were the drum riser, guitar amps and a microphone stand ready for the group, who were going to play some Stones and general psychedelic/sleazy 1960s numbers, the idea being to complement the double bill of *Bad Timing* and *Performance*, which would have just finished. After them? Charlie, manning the ones and twos – the wheels of steel – and he reckoned that by the time the 1960s theme had outstayed its welcome, he could get away with some disco, a bit of Carly Simon, 'Bette Davis Eyes' and, of course, 'Total Eclipse Of The Heart'.

The audience had been let in, most of them right-on types in their mid-thirties. Charlie wasn't holding out much hope that they'd be hanging around after the double bill – probably had kids to get home to, frozen placenta to eat, tofu to cook – but, still, worth a go. Plus he got to DJ (and, though, he didn't know it yet, meet his future wife . . .)

Who walked in shortly after *Bad Timing* had begun.

'Oh, sorry, the film's already started,' said Charlie.

'Yes, I know,' she responded pleasantly.

'Well, we have a policy of not allowing people in once the film has started.'

'You're the only London cinema to operate such a policy.'

'That's right.'

'And it was a policy you instigated after consulting your customers.'

'Yes, that's also right.'

'You know how I know all this?'

'Go on.'

' 'Cos I've just had the whole talk from the bloke downstairs, and you know what?'

'What?'

'I told him what I'll tell you, and that's that I'm not here to watch *Bad* bloody *Timing*. I'd rather gnaw off my own leg than watching *Bad* bloody *Timing* again.'

'Oh. Why?'

'Pretentious crap for students.'

'Really? I think it's one of his best.'

'You see? This is the sort of thing I mean. *His* best? Isn't film a collaborative medium?'

All the time she was speaking she was smiling, and Charlie realised that he very much wanted to see more of that smile. Her hair was long, dark and unruly, falling over her face in lazy curls. She wore a large cardigan in the old-bloke style, but beneath that she wore a tight black cotton top, hint of cleavage there, and he found himself raising his chin so as not to seem like he was looking at her breasts, which he wanted to do, very much.

'Um, yes, I suppose it is, but few could dispute Roeg's claim as an auteur,' he managed, feeling as though he was looking down his face at her.

'"Auteur". Something else we've got the French to thank for. Look, sorry, I'd love to stop and chat about the misogynism apparent in Roeg's work, but I have a job to do. I wonder if you could tell me where Charlie Watson lives? I'm in a band that's supposed to be playing here tonight.'

She cast her gaze around the space, taking in the stage and the PA. The roller shutter on the bar went up and a barman (name of George, if Charlie recalled correctly) poked his head out and waved.

'It's me,' said Charlie, waving back at George, then turning to the girl, doing a Spartacus impression, saying, 'I'm Charlie Watson,' half-way to being helplessly, utterly in love for only the second time in his life. Mentally he congratulated himself on resisting the temptation to send her on a wild-goose chase round the cinema, one that would take her through the main auditorium so she'd be forced to watch at least thirty seconds of *Bad Timing*.

'Right,' she said, and held out her hand. 'I'm Bea.'

'Oh,' he said, 'that's a nice name.'

'It's not bad. It could be worse. I'm over here, am I?'

He directed her to the stage. The rest of the band were on their way, she said. She stood at the microphone and looked out over the room. George, at the bar, stared at her, elbows on the counter. From the floor, Charlie watched her. And then, on the pretext of – what? – warming up, perhaps, but really, as Charlie now knew, because Bea had the most beautiful voice, and she loved to hear it, and she loved others to hear it, she began to sing.

It wouldn't have mattered what she sang. Charlie would have fallen in love anyway (and he bet George the barman fell in love at that moment too) but she sang one of his favourites. 'Rocket Man' by Elton John.

He fell. Hard. And he'd never got up again.

## Reality TV, the Graveyard Desecration Show

'I've been learning stuff,' said Charlie to Bea, after the bath.
By now Mary was swaddled and snoozing on the sofa between
them.

'Go on.'

'Quite a lot, really. Don't know where to start.'

'Try at the beginning.'

'Okay. Leo was a con-man.'

'You what?'

'Leo – he was – I mean, I'm not sure if there's a nicer way of
saying it, but he was a con-man. A con-artist. A *trickster*.'

'Well, how do you mean? In what way? Like, was he
fleecing old ladies or something?'

'Christ, no, Bea,' he rebuked her.

'Well, you've just told me he was a con-man, what else am I
supposed to think?'

'I don't know. Paul Newman and Steve McQueen in *The
Sting*.'

'Robert Redford. It was Paul Newman and Robert Redford.'

'*I know*. Listen, I'm the film buff in this family.' She flashed him a quick, victorious smile. 'Or . . .' he searched his internal film guide . . . 'John Cusack in *The Grifters*, or, ah, er, Paul Newman in *The Hustler*. Just not some lowlife.'

'Well, tell me, then. What was he up to?'

So Charlie told her, ending, 'And the night he died, you know he said he had something to tell me? What if that something was to do with a case he was working on?'

'He didn't work on cases, though. That's the whole point, isn't it?'

'Well, here's something else. Leo was *involved* in some way, whether personal or professional, I don't know, or, really, if he was properly involved, or if it was just part of the con . . .'

'But he was involved?'

'Yes.'

'Involved in what?'

'In looking for a dog.'

Bea laughed, then put a hand politely over her mouth. 'I'm sorry. Sorry. I didn't mean to laugh. But how do you mean, looking for a dog?'

Charlie told her about the small ads.

'So maybe he'd lost a dog.'

'*Bea.*'

'Okay. Maybe he was helping someone out.'

'Sure, sure. Maybe. In Bizarro World. But back on this planet he'd placed an advert advertising his services as an investigator in this area, then the next thing you know he's looking for a dog – *investigating*, you might say – in this area. Someone must have been paying him.'

'Who on earth pays an investigator to look for a dog?'

'Somebody with money. The kind of person who calls their dog Charles Laughton.'

'A stupid person with money.'

'Hardly be the first.'

'Right. Plausible. But what makes you think Leo was taking it any more seriously than we are?'

'Nothing. Not really. But . . .' How to explain? Charlie thought he knew. As soon as Merle had told him, Charlie had reckoned he knew exactly how Leo would have felt – the same way that Smith-Hegel and Clay had also felt. The catalyst might have been that pretending to be an investigator paid so badly. It might have been that the work for a pretend-investigator was going to dry up sooner or later. There would have to come a time when you either got out of the game or played it.

But most likely it was that being a pretend-investigator, well, it wasn't like being a real investigator. It lacked that . . .

Thrill.

'He had an office,' said Charlie now.

'*He had an office?*'

'Oh, yeah, it's the kind of scam that calls for an office.'

'Leo "Offices Are Where Souls Go To Die" Watson had an office?'

'Yeah, um, if I could just remind you of the unwritten law about slagging off members of your own family being okay, but nobody else is allowed to do it.'

'Sorry, but still.'

'Well, yeah. He did have an office.'

'Have you been?'

'Not yet. I've got an address. Guy at the mortuary gave me a bunch of keys so the chances are I've got a key as well. I was going to go tomorrow.'

'God.' Bea seemed genuinely impressed, or genuinely

amazed – genuinely something, anyway. 'I don't know what I'm more gobsmacked about. That Leo had an office or that he was tricking people into giving them their money and not getting his head kicked in twice a week.'

Charlie shrugged. 'According to Merle, that's the con. You play the numbers, you assess the form . . .'

'Blimey. You've started talking like an Elmore Leonard novel.'

'. . . and if the job looks like it might involve your head getting kicked in, you pass on it.'

'Still, though.'

'Yeah, still. See, here's the other thing: according to Merle, there are precedents for this particular type of scam. And what happens is that these guys start to believe they can do the job. Instead of just pretending to take a case, they end up taking one properly. Hence, maybe, this dog business.'

Bea thought. 'There are loads of instances of that kind of thing happening. People pretend to be doctors all the time, not a medical qualification to their name. Next thing you know they're removing someone's appendix. They start to believe they really are doctors.'

'And then the shit hits the fan.'

'About that time, yeah. I guess when they're supposed to be removing an appendix and amputating someone's feet instead.'

Charlie considered for a moment. 'Merle thinks there's something strange about Leo's death, I know he does.'

'What did he say?'

'Nothing.'

'So . . .'

'What if Leo had taken a case?'

'The dog case?' Bea was smiling.

'Yes. Or another.'

'What if he had? But wait a sec. Rewind. What exactly *is* strange about Leo's death?'

'Nothing.'

'So?'

'Well, not the death itself, but why was he coming over here at that time of night? What was so important that he had to get in the car, pissed, and come here, over an hour's drive away?'

'Well, babe, haven't you answered the question?'

'How?'

'He was pissed. And people do, um, unwise things when they're pissed.'

Mary stirred and they both looked her way.

'Maybe,' said Charlie, thoughtfully. 'Maybe. But he'd never done that before, had he?'

'Had he ever stood you up on the anniversary of your dad's death before?'

'I know what you're saying, but . . .'

'You know what I think Charlie?' Bea put her hand across the sofa to massage the back of his neck.' She looked at him long and hard. 'You know what I think? I think that it hasn't really sunk in yet about Leo's death. You haven't done your mourning. Your emotions are being misdirected. Keeping stuff bottled up is never good, Charlie.'

'I know,' he said. 'I know. I was in bits when Dad died, and now Leo's gone and I hardly feel anything. It's like getting an injection from the grief-doctor. It's just . . . not there.'

'You see? Not good. The grief-doctor wouldn't be prescribing injections, he'd be advising the opposite. Get it all out, twice daily, after meals. And plenty of rest.'

'But what if there's nothing to get out?'

'Of course there is.'

'I mean, we weren't that close.'

'He was your brother.'

'Even so. Just because a guy's your brother, do you automatically love him?'

'I think so, yes. Blood. Water. Thick. Thin. That kind of stuff.'

'Yeah,' he considered. 'Course I loved him. Course I did. Maybe you're right. Maybe it's all a bit of a smokescreen. You know, I think it might set my mind at rest if I could just speak to his girlfriend.'

'The girl who was here that night? In the kitchen?'

'Yes.'

Bea removed the hand that had been massaging his neck.

'So,' he said, 'that's not a popular idea, then?'


After they had put Mary to bed they sat in the lounge, supposedly watching the television but really listening to her on the baby monitor.

'I think she's going,' whispered Bea, though there was no need to whisper. The cries had subsided to a low yowl.

'I reckon,' whispered Charlie back.

Bea sniffed. 'Can you smell that?'

'What?'

'Pete next door's having a fag.'

'Really?' said Charlie, wearily.

'You've got to tell him, Charlie. Tell him tomorrow. I'm sick of it. I don't want that smell in here when I'm feeding.'

'Okay,' he said. 'I'll have a word.'

They sat and half watched a programme about people buying houses, listening to their daughter quieten down. Before Mary was born they'd often rented a DVD from Blockbuster up the road, the one next to Pricecheck, from which they'd buy a bottle of rosé and maybe a bag of Maltesers or a tube of Pringles (anything but barbecue flavour). Now, any film they rented was interrupted either by Mary or by their own exhaustion; the job of returning it was suddenly more of a chore than it had ever been. So these days they dozed in front of programmes about people buying houses, dimly thinking, Next feed at midnight, one after that at four, the next one just forty short winks after that. Repeat till fade . . .

Beside him on the sofa Bea slept, slippered feet on his knees. A couple on the telly had bought themselves a house in the country, as well as a crash-pad in the city. They looked pretty pleased with themselves, as well they might. A million viewers were testing their gag reflexes, spitting nails at the screen: *two bloody houses*. Reality TV, they called it. Sure.

Charlie removed Bea's feet from his legs and placed them gently on the sofa. Then he walked across the hall to his office. He answered an email from a customer interested in a set of the original Alan Moore run of *Captain Britain* (he checked various comics databases, then mailed back a ridiculous price). He put in a stupidly low bid for an *Apocalyse Now* insert that was ending early in the morning, and he wrapped a Radiohead seven-inch in bubble wrap, then packaged it up ready to send in the morning.

He opened an email, somebody enquiring after an original (i.e., not the reissue) CD of Cud's first album, *When In Rome,*

*Kill Me*, that he'd sold via his seller's shop on eBay. Did he have any more? the sender wanted to know. 'No', he replied, frowning, hating to type the word. First pressings of that album fetched at least forty pounds, a medium-sized trip to Tesco, where every little helps.

Reluctantly, he sent the email.

Next?

An email from someone called Philippa Shaw, who, judging by the name, wouldn't be looking for rare Cud CDs or Marvel action figures. Philippas generally weren't. She would either be interested in some Audrey Hepburn memorabilia for which he was acting as intermediary or, if he was really lucky, the full set of Mr Men Royal Doulton figurines he had for sale in his eBay shop. He'd bought them for seven hundred pounds; they had an asking price of a thousand. That would buy a lot of nappies. Then again: Philippa, Philippa. A little bell was tinkling.

> *Dear Charlie,*
>   *Hello again, it's Philippa Shaw, your brother's agent, we met briefly at your brother's funeral.*

He didn't remember. Oh, God, yes, he did. He recalled that all-too-familiar stab of guilt as she'd introduced herself as Leo's agent, and he'd realised that he hadn't even known Leo *had* an agent.

The email continued:

> *It was very nice to meet you, but afraid my George Michael was somewhat overcome (!) and I didn't have the chance to tell you how devastated I was to learn of Leo's death. I can honestly, hand on heart and without*

*blushing, say that your brother was one of the best clients I have had the privilege of working with in my 15 years of running the agency. His Tom Waits for No Man Tribute was one of our most popular and unique acts. He will be sorely missed by all of the staff at the agency, and by me in particular.*

*The reason I am writing, other than to pass on my condolences, is to remind you about the tribute night we're having in Leo's honour tomorrow evening at the Lost Oats in Highgate. You did say you hoped you'd be able to make it and we would love it if you were able to come.*

Tribute night? The words jarred something loose and he found himself recalling the funeral. In short succession came the memory of his speech at the crematorium; the reception at the Lost Oats; Bea and Newlife helping his mother out, her overcome by grief and red wine; lookylikeys dancing to Abba – most of them had turned out in full costume, bless them – and, yes, the drunken conversation with Philippa Shaw ('Call me Lips'), who had, it was true, invited him to a tribute night in Leo's honour, which he had almost immediately forgotten about because he'd been drunk. Very drunk. Not so much drowning his sorrows as sending out a search party for them; you're supposed to drink to numb the pain – he'd been drinking to hurt the numbness.

There was something else, as well, when the evening had almost died out. The music had stopped, he now remembered. His head had been lolling, falling asleep, a cigarette – he'd given them up five years ago, supposedly – smouldering between his fingers. Suit jacket on. The same suit he'd worn to every wedding and funeral for the last seven years. Black, see. Very adaptable. A bit on the tight side these days, but it had to do.

'Hello.'

He had looked up, trying to bring her into focus. Then, when he had, he'd started and sat upright, rubbing at his tired and drunk face. 'Hello.'

It was her, Chariot. The pub was virtually empty, he'd realised, wondering for how long he'd dozed. He'd looked at her. Plum-coloured lips. Light glinting off a nose stud. She'd smiled.

'Mind if I take a seat?'

'No, no, of course.' He'd glanced at his watch. Mary was staying at Bea's parent's, and his mum and Newlife had booked Charlie and Bea a room in their hotel, a place in Marylebone. Newlife had insisted on paying and Charlie had felt ridiculously grateful, resenting Newlife at the same time. By now the three of them would be in the bar; or, more likely, in their rooms, asleep.

'I was hoping you'd say that,' she'd said, and for the first time Charlie had realised she was holding two bottles of Grolsch, one of which she now offered to him. He had taken it, even though the last thing he'd needed was another drink. But still. It would've been rude not to.

He didn't remember much of that conversation, either. Not actual words and sentences. What he remembered was more of an impression. A feeling that, even though he was happily married and had a newborn, he hadn't fallen completely off the sexual radar. Felt good. Must have been the booze, mustn't it?

'Hello, is that Philippa?' He half whispered it into the

phone, telling himself that he was whispering because he didn't want to wake Bea.

'Yur.' She sounded sleepy and he found himself envying her. In his imagination she lived with three cats and no ties beyond twice-daily feeds and the occasional emptying of a litter tray. She could be a mother of five for all he knew, but that was how she lived in his mind. There, she wielded a fag in a long, ornate cigarette-holder, too. Behind a desk were black-and-white photographs of her clients posing with John Profumo. Maybe. Perhaps.

Anyway. 'Yur,' she said.

'Philippa Shaw?'

'Philippa Shaw speaking.'

'It's Charlie Watson. Leo's brother.'

She fireworked, if there was such a verb, which he sincerely hoped there wasn't. 'Charlie, right. Oh, hello, Charlie. It was lovely to meet you the other night. Oh, but if only it had been under different, less unhappy circumstances. But, I mean, nice to meet you all the same. I sent— Did you by any chance get my email? I mean, Leo. As I said – I think I said – in the email, he was one of the very best.'

'He was a true original,' said Charlie.

'Yes.'

'And I got the email. Thanks very much for that.'

'Great. Great.'

There was a pause. 'So,' started Charlie, 'about the tribute night. I hadn't forgotten. As a matter of fact I've been meaning to ring you. It's very kind of you to invite me, but I'm really not sure I can make it. I'd like to but, um, we've got a two-month-old baby in the house and her sleep patterns haven't . . . well, she doesn't *have* sleep patterns, which means that neither do we have sleep patterns so it's all a bit . . . I just can't really say, you know?'

'Of course, I quite understand.'

'Have you . . . What sort of turnout are you expecting?'

'Well, good. I mean, I hope good. Most of my clients, other performers, bookers, fans – he certainly had his share. I appreciate you don't know those people, but I'm sure they'd absolutely love to meet you. Did you ever meet his girlfriend? She's coming.'

'Um,' he said. 'Really? Well, I'm sure it would be nice to see her again.'

Which it would, of course, to get a lid on those feelings, which, left unattended, might grow into an unwelcome weed in his mental garden. Plus, of course, she should know stuff – stuff about Leo. Two birds, one stone.

'Okay,' he said. 'Well, it sounds lovely. Sorry, did you say bookers?'

'He was very popular with the bookers.'

'Right.' *And this is a tribute to Leo, is it?* he thought. *Not a publicity drive for the agency?* But didn't say. Said instead, 'I'll definitely do my best. Hopefully should be able to make it along for a drink or two. Show my face. Baby permitting.'

They'd just said their goodbyes when he heard the voice from the lounge.

'Charlie?'

He winced. Might she have heard?

'Charlie.' The call came again.

'Just a sec, Bea,' he replied.

'Charlie,' repeated Bea, from the other room. He could hear the news on the television.

'Yeah,' he called over his shoulder.

115

'I think you should come and have a look at this.'

'At what?'

'It's the local news.'

'Oh, yeah?'

'Yeah. Something's happened at the cemetery. The one your dad's in.'

'Really?' But he didn't wait to hear her answer, just pushed back the office-chair-on-wheels and moved to the lounge.

On the TV screen a reporter was talking into a microphone. He stood in front of fluttery police tape wound round trees that Charlie thought were familiar even as his brain was making the connection between that and the words . . .

'. . . scenes of absolute devastation,' the reporter was saying, before the image cut to footage obviously taken earlier.

'Oh, fuck,' Charlie heard himself say. Flowers everywhere, a tipped-over litter-bin. A tiny Winnie the Pooh statuette broken on the ground and a green plastic watering-can pulled from its hook and stamped on, the inevitable bottles of alcopops smashed among the graves. Like it wasn't a cemetery, somewhere you buried your dead to honour them, but outside the Southern Fried Chicken on a Friday night. Fag ends. Empties. People-filth everywhere.

'I'd better get up there,' said Charlie.

# Cemetery Gates

He'd taken the Peugeot, not the Cheesy Vinyl van. Wouldn't have seemed right, somehow. Parked, and about to take the footpath to the graveyard, he saw a reporter and a cameraman clambering into a BMW on the street. For them, the job was done. All the interviews were in the can. Behind them, he realised as he got closer, they'd left a knot of locals waiting to be let in – for the tour. Hard, angry faces.

A uniformed officer was clearing tape away from the scene. Inexperienced, he considered trying to roll it up, presumably to recycle. No dice. Instead he just ripped it away while the group watched him, like it was some kind of inaugural unveiling: 'I hereby declare this cemetery well and truly desecrated.'

They stood by patiently until the officer waved them through, and silently they trooped in.

Like Charlie, others had seen the devastation on TV – no doubt the same pictures had drawn them there. But they were just images. Now, here, Charlie found his fist was clenched, angry. He wanted to hit out. All those empty tabloid words came at him, like, 'senseless', 'mindless', 'moronic' *'animals'* –

the plastic outrage of the supersoaraway*Sun*, the middle-England-baiting rhetoric of the *Daily Mail*. Pathetic, but all of it suddenly making sense as he watched those around him finding the defiled graves of their loved ones.

That feeling came back to him, as though it wasn't a graveyard but a high street; some town centre bruised after another Saturday night of brewery-sponsored fun. It was no stretch of the imagination to picture the kids at play: the baseball caps and cheap gold chains, the harsh, soulless laughter. Charlie wanted one to be here, now. Didn't matter if it was one of the actual culprits or not. Any generic loudmouth yob would do. Any kid drinking and swearing on a train platform. Gobbing on the pavement outside For-buoys, gathered outside Threshers. Just one. So he could smash his fucking face in.

And that was before he reached his father's grave. *Francis Watson, died 9 July 1994, devoted husband to Joan and loving father to Leonard and Charles.*

At least it hadn't been sprayed. There was that. Charlie stooped to pick up the metal vase that he had filled with flowers a few days earlier – the same flowers now trodden underfoot. It was dented, almost crushed, as if someone had stepped on it. He closed his eyes for a moment, fighting the anger. Then, opening them, he replaced the vase at the foot of his father's headstone. The decorative marble stones on the grave had been disturbed by some-one running across it, and he reached down to smooth them over.

Not far away, he noticed now, there was a much larger grave. Two, in fact, one next to the other, shaped like a small double crypt. A tall man was standing before it – lean, silver hair, sunglasses and a suit. He stood staring out over the cemetery, on his face an unreadable expression.

He was staring at something. Rather, someone. About twenty-five yards away. A woman, with long, straight, greying hair. She knelt by a grave, hands working as though trying to make sense of a jigsaw puzzle. It was difficult to see but Charlie thought the grave looked too small to be an adult's plot. A child's, then. Her child's, perhaps. Flowers had been kicked off, scattered stones surrounded it and, as he watched, the woman scooped up handfuls of stones, replacing them, head bent.

Charlie looked back at the silver-haired man, who was transfixed by her. For a moment or so he watched them both; her, oblivious to the attention. And then she stood and looked up. She had pale, sunless skin. High, well-defined cheekbones. There had been something there once, Charlie thought, but life had had other plans for what beauty she'd once possessed. Defeat was sculpted into those once-fine features.

She caught sight of the silver-haired man.

For a second they gazed at each other, and Charlie felt something old and terrible pass between them. Then the well-dressed man's head dropped and, thrusting his hands into his pockets, he turned away from the grave and walked towards the cemetery gates. And was gone.

Over the way, the woman knelt again, hair falling over her face, and Charlie decided he'd seen enough and he, too, turned his back on the desolation and took the footpath back to the Peugeot. He went home.

Just above the graveyard there was a maintenance clearing. In it was parked a red flat-bed Toyota truck, an upturned

# Twinkle, Twinkle

The next morning Charlie woke to an empty bed and an almost silent house.

For a moment he was transported back to a pre-Mary time, when Bea had caught the daily commuter train into London to spend her days marshalling rooms full of telephone marketeers. Work she hated, though it paid well. Work she'd been happy to give up.

On the days when duty had pulled her in at ridiculously early hours, Charlie had lain in bed like this, delaying the moment he had to get out of bed and begin the day's Cheesy Vinyl/Eclectibles business. He'd lie listening to the sounds of nothing, feeling bad that he didn't even have to get dressed to start work, while she had to make the soul-destroying trek into town. But not *that* bad: they'd each made their choices, after all. Shouting at row upon row of bored students wearing headsets might have been acceptable to her, but he'd forgone the nine-thirty-to-six life. Not for him the daily drudge of a servile corporate drone, wage slave for some faceless billionaire. He'd opted out. Brave Charlie.

Or stupid, arrogant Charlie, depending on how you looked

at it. Certainly if you viewed it from the perspective of a man whose house was filled with useless tat he worked hard to sell at insultingly low profit margins; and who played 'Relax' by Frankie Goes to Hollywood to halls filled with drunk people, also for insultingly low profit margins.

*He* wasn't a corporate drone, oh no.

'We need to talk about whether I go back to work or not,' she'd said, on an almost daily basis. 'I'm worried about money.' She was willing to, that was the thing – which made it all the more important to him that she didn't.

'All you need to worry about is getting sleep and making sure my little girl's taken care of,' he'd say loftily. 'Let me worry about the money.'

Duty made him cast aside the duvet now, and he pulled on his dressing-gown and deliberately avoided seeing himself in the mirror as he went downstairs in the direction of soft music coming from the lounge.

'Hi, Bea,' he said, yawning.

'Hi, babe.' She looked at him with tired eyes, her skin pale. She was drained. On her lap, resting on a strange, U-shaped pillow that looked like an escapee from an old people's home, was the source of all their problems and the receptacle of all their love and hope for the future.

'What you doing?' he asked Bea, satirically, voice low.

'Baking a cake.'

'Cool.' He smiled at her, then smiled down at Mary. 'Look at her,' he said. 'Butter wouldn't melt.'

'That's a shame. I need it for the cake.'

He laughed.

She smiled, too, whispering, 'I think she might be dropping off.'

'Any problems?' he asked.

'Well, you remember my nice soft nipples?'

'Yes.'

'Good. Because I don't. They look like something you'd expect to see growing on a butcher's nose. Understandably, Mary's not a thousand per cent keen on sucking them. Imagine having to drink a glass of beer through a pine cone that squealed in pain every time you put your lips to it.'

'Yeah,' he said. 'It sounds hideous.'

'It could be worse, I suppose. She got an hour's sleep earlier. An hour. Fancy that. A whole hour. After I'd changed her and hung her bedding out to dry and put a new wash on I was able to get a good thirty seconds myself. I'm hoping to snatch a quick quarter of an hour if she drops off again. What are your plans today?'

He winced inside. He wished the answer could have been, 'Staying here and helping you.' But it wasn't.

'Well,' he began, 'I've got things to do, Bea.'

She took it well. Just a slight lowering of the eyes, body that seemed to crumple a tiny bit.

'Then, um, later, there's a tribute thing on for Leo that the agency is giving for him at the Lost Oats. His agent got in touch about it and I said I'd poke my head round the door. You know, it seemed like the polite thing to do.'

'Of course.' She smiled weakly.

Charlie's soul tied itself in knots. 'I won't be late,' he said.

'Don't worry about us,' she said. 'Really. You go. We'll be cool.'

'About ten,' he said. He smoothed her hair and kissed it, burying his mouth in her soft, beddy smell. 'Just let me get this over and done with, then I'll be here to mop your fevered brow and fetch you dry sleepsuits and all that other stuff.'

She looked up at him. 'Don't. Worry. Do what you gotta do.'

As he grabbed his stuff to leave, she was singing 'Twinkle, Twinkle Little Star' to Mary, and he hung around in the hall for a moment or so, just to hear her.

## The Nose Job

Barry left Gemma and Kev, and, draping his T-shirt over his shoulder, began the walk home. He had on trainers, a rolled-gold chain, a baseball cap and three-quarter-length training pants, worn low so that if you looked closely you could see a tuft of his pubic hair. There was a vehicle following him, but he didn't notice it: he was too busy being Barry, walking his granny-scaring, miscreant walk, looking shifty if police cars went past, even though he was doing nothing illegal. It was a demanding job being Barry; still, a popular career for the kids round here.

He darted across the station car park and took the foot-bridge over the line, gobbing on to the tracks below, hocking another and gobbing it on to the walkway – a little green egg for someone to see. He was thinking about Gemma, and how, when she'd gone to the toilet in the rec, Kev had leant over from his swing and told Barry that they were going to run a train on Gemma, and that she was up for it, *right up for it* were his exact words.

Barry was getting a chubby just thinking about it. Running a train on Gemma. Right up for it, she was. Cool.

'All right, mate.'

He was dragged from his erotic reverie by a bloke leaning on a red flat-bed truck parked just where the footpath ended at Shuttock Close.

No, not a bloke, not any old bloke. Joe Parks.

Joe Parks was older than Barry and his mates. Maybe three years above at school. He had blond hair, blond eyebrows. His hair was cut US-buzzcut style, gelled upright on top, shaved at the sides. He had grown-out, last-decade razorcuts shaved above the ears – ears that boasted piratical gold, hoops, bought from a shop in the Arndale, High Wycombe. His cheeks were large, puffed, as though recently punched. They seemed to swell on his face, narrowing his eyes to slits.

What did Barry know about him? Same as everyone else. That Joe Parks was a contractor working on the parks. That he drove a red flat-bed Toyota truck. That he talked about guns and knives and murder a lot, and liked to describe porn scenes he'd seen on the Net, ones where the woman was hurt, got punched or spat on. That he dealt drugs – coke, mainly – and was always hinting at other, even shadier business concerns. That you didn't buy gear off him if you didn't need to, because going to Joe Parks meant having to sit in the Toyota hearing about guns and knives and porn. And he might hold a new knife he'd bought to your throat and wait till you were beginning to sweat before he revealed that he was just pulling your leg. That because his eyes were permanent slits, he looked at the world as though he despised it, always. That he was a nutjob. That he was a fucking psycho.

Joe Parks wore jeans and was bare-chested beneath his fluorescent waistcoat. There was another bloke sitting in the truck. Barry nodded in reply to Joe Parks's greeting, went to move round the van up Shuttock Close towards home.

'You got a light, mate?' Joe Parks pushed himself off the truck, smiling easily, at the same time rummaging in his jeans, presumably for his fags.

Barry shook his head, no, heard the passenger door of the truck go, and registered the second bloke getting out. Not good. 'Nah, mate,' he mumbled, trying to maintain a presence, making to go past.

The second bloke moved round the truck.

'Yeah, you have,' said Joe Parks. He indicated the fag-packet-shaped bulge in Barry's training pants.

'Not a lighter, though, mate,' said Barry, not wanting to back down.

'All right. No worries. Er, tell you what? Do you want to earn a quick bit of cash?'

'No, cheers, mate, gotta get off,' replied Barry.

The second bloke moved closer and suddenly Joe Parks was wearing a bored-of-this-now expression. 'Get in the van,' he told Barry.

'Fuck off,' came back Barry.

Joe Parks gobbed on the pavement.

Then, snake-fast, he stepped forward and shot out a hand, grabbing Barry's ear, wrenching it, twisting.

Barry screeched. He screeched 'like a bitch getting ass-fucked', Joe Parks would later say.

Barry continued screeching. Somewhere inside he couldn't believe it was possible to wrench a human being's ear so hard without pulling it off. He'd had his ear twisted in the past, but other attackers had been bored amateurs compared to Joe Parks. This took him to a pain that went beyond wounded pride and wanting to fighting back to just *stop*. Pain so bad that whatever it took, it had to end. Now.

He dropped to his knees. Joe Parks punched him in the throat. Barry collapsed to the pavement, bare chest grinding into stones and fag butts and gob. Served him right.

As Barry writhed, Joe Parks and his mate looked at each other across the top of the van, then up Shuttock Close. The violence had been quick, almost silent apart from Barry's cry, and the van had screened them from the houses. With a nod, Joe Parks motioned his mate to keep an eye on the footpath entrance. His mate jogged round to loiter there as Joe Parks knelt down to Barry.

Barry, who coughed and spluttered, was trying to get his hands beneath himself as Joe Parks grabbed his ear again.

'Who did the graveyard?' said Joe Parks.

'What?' managed Barry.

'Which of you fuckwads did the graveyard? Was it you?'

'No.'

'I need names.'

'Fuck off. How would I know?'

'Was it you? Were you one of them?'

'*No*.' Barry bucked and panicked.

Joe Parks considered it, and believed him. 'Then gimme names, cocksnot.'

'Fuck off,' insisted Barry.

Joe Parks released Barry's ear with a final twist, looked around, fished in his pocket for his Clipper. He knelt on Barry's neck so that his head was fixed, then held the lighter beneath one of his nostrils. 'Names.'

'Fuck off,' gasped Barry, less certain now.

With good reason – Parks lit his Clipper.

Barry screeched again.

With the smell of burnt nose skin and nostril hair still hanging in the afternoon, Barry told Joe Parks the names. He gave Joe Parks names, descriptions, anything the fuck he wanted.

Later, when they'd left Barry in some nettles, and Joe Parks had given his mate Jude the twenty pounds he owed him for helping him out on the job and sent him on his way, he made a call on his mobile phone. 'Mr Land,' he said, 'I got the names of the fuckers who did the graveyard. What you want me to do now?'

Listening, he smiled, feeling his cock through his tracky bottoms.

# When Doves Cry

Charlie pulled a torch from his rucksack, clicked it on and unlocked the door to his brother's flat. 'Coo,' he called into the corridor.

How did you summon a dove? The other day his mother had stood with her back to Leo's charred flat and said a short prayer before sweeping her hands into the air and grandiosely granting the dove its freedom. But instead of flying off into the sky like the good approximation of a human soul it was supposed to be, the dove had unexpectedly set a course directly behind them, going back into the dank and unwelcoming hallway of Leo's flat – where, of course, Charlie had left the living-room door ajar.

They had put their heads into the doorway. 'Coo,' they had said, hoping to entice it out.

But it hadn't worked then, just as it had no effect now.

'Coo,' said Charlie again, to be on the safe side.

Next, with the torch lending him backbone that had been sorely lacking the day before, he made his way along the corridor to the living-room door. Chariot's flowers were where he'd left them in the doorway; he shone the torchlight on them. An extra night without water and they looked even more sooty and sad. Now he pulled a handkerchief from his pocket – brought especially for the purpose – and held it over his nose as he reached for the door handle, pushed and went inside.

The room seemed to move wetly around him, as though moisture in the walls was shifting. The carpet, thicker in here, squelched as he took a couple of steps into the lounge, his eyes adjusting to a new level of dark. The handkerchief was clamped to his nose and mouth, but even through the cotton he could smell the room, evil with smoke-stench – the smell of old, burnt flat. Life, when it goes up in flames, doesn't burn like freshly collected wood in a kitchen range. The fire sets free the stink of decades: the dust, the sweat, the piss – everything ingrained in its past. And, God knows, Leo had past to burn.

Charlie coughed into his handkerchief, trying to control his stomach.

'Coo,' he said, through the fabric, thinking: Lost, one white dove, although having spent the night in here it was likely to be off-white by now. Lost: one white dove. Could pass for raven. Last seen flying in the wrong direction into Kilburn flat.

He looked at the front window of the flat: at least one of the panes was smashed, and most had cracks, but there was no way Mr Dove could have found his way through, thanks to the boards that denied both exit and light. He shone the torch round the room, picking out the television in the corner, a large bookcase to the left, then Leo's stereo area, where his most precious records were neatly indexed, plus his pride and joy, his one-thing-I'd-save-from-a-burning-flat purchase: the Nad stereo. Like everything else it was blackened, and charred, and wet. From the front snaked a melted cable to a pair of expensive headphones on the floor, also melted. That was something Charlie did know of his brother: Leo had bought a new pair of headphones because he didn't want to bother his neighbours, and could Charlie help him get a bargain pair off the Net? Charlie had found him a set on eBay and pointed him in the right direction. Hardly the greatest favour in the world, but still. Thinking about it made Charlie wonder if he had been such a bad brother after all. Maybe not.

The armchair. He played the beam of torchlight over it. Here was where the fire had started.

It faced towards the TV, the small table beside it bearing a scalded can of Tennents. This having been the core of the fire, the armchair was virtually unrecognisable. Brown fabric had seared away to reveal a frame beneath. He let the torch rest on it for a moment, imagining his brother sitting in it in the way he had seen him, always a fag and a drink on the go on the table beside him, always something on the Nad – usually Tom Waits, sure, but give him his due, Leo occasionally indulged his guests and varied the programme a little. Only a little, mind. You came in here and part of the deal was that you spent your time under scrutiny from Tom Waits on the walls – the signed copy of *Swordfishtrombones* was framed and hung there still – as well as listening to him and, of course, conversing with his slightly drunk but never less than entertaining impersonator . . .

He cast another look round, at the peripheries of the room where the fire hadn't quite spread but which were still wet and black and like something from a nightmare. The curtains, the nets, the TV and video.

He reached for the lager tin, gave it a little shake. There was fluid inside, probably water from the hoses. Not like Leo to leave any spare beer lying around . . .

'Hello there, Mr Watson, you've come to return the key.'

The estate agent stood from his desk, his ponytail bobbing behind him. He wore stubble, shirt open two buttons at the neck. Charlie imagined he was a renegade among estate agents. A real maverick.

'You released the dove all right?' asked the estate agent. 'That's a touching tribute, doves. He flew away, did he?'

'He did, thanks, yes. It was really more for my mum, you know, something she'd wanted. She'd have liked to do it at the service, but the funeral directors had run out of doves.'

'Ah, I see,' said the estate agent, unsure if he was having the piss taken out of him.

'No, honest,' smiled Charlie. 'It's true. Deranged but true.'

The estate agent made heard-it-all-now hands. His name, according to a plaque on his desk, was Dave Rogan. The two of them laughed a little. Charlie handed over the keys to the flat and thanked Dave Rogan for allowing him to borrow them. In his pocket was a copy he'd had cut at a while-you-wait place not ten minutes ago, a copy he thought he might need in order to return to Leo's flat. Not for the dove: he'd found that, or it had found him. Just as he was leaving it had appeared from somewhere, flown through the door and out, and Charlie had watched it go, the dove finally doing what his mother had wanted it to do. 'Coo,' it had said.

No, he wouldn't be returning for the dove, but because something in Leo's flat didn't gel.

## Some Kind of Bluetooth

Next to the UK Supermarket on Kilburn High Road – a shop so bursting with stuff that customers had to turn sideways to pass each other in the aisles – there was a doorway. On the doorway was an entry panel. There were just the two floors, but it looked as though the building contained several offices. Did, or had: it was difficult to tell whether the various businesses with their names by buzzers were current or not. Solicitors, insurance brokers and Leo Watson.

Charlie looked at the small bunch of keys, inserted a couple before he found a match, then pushed open the door.

Stepping inside, he stared at his feet and the junkmail pooled around them, the free newspapers. Not exactly a thriving hub of the Kilburn business community, then. A generous passer-by had posted an apple core through the letterbox; it gave the tiny foyer a ciderish smell. Charlie nudged it into a corner with his foot and was about to close the door behind him when a man stopped him, stepping into the lobby himself. A shortish man, shorter than Charlie at least, he lugged a small drag-along vacuum-cleaner as well as a plastic carry-all almost overflowing with tins of polish and yellow dusters.

From the clues at his disposal, Charlie guessed the man was a cleaner.

The cleaner thanked him. He called Charlie 'sir'. Charlie followed him up the stairs and on to the landing. At the end of the corridor was an office, on the door a home-made sign, letters scissored from newspaper: LeO wATSoN InVEStigatOr.

How did you play it, Charlie wondered, if you were setting up a business front? For any other scam it would probably pay to make the operation look as slick and professional as possible. But not for this one. When you walked into Leo's office you had to be *hoping* for results, not expecting them. That way you weren't going to be asking awkward questions when they didn't happen.

Still, though: yet another reason why the operation was low level, low yield. Yet another reason why Leo might have taken a case, an easy one, perhaps. Something he thought he could handle. A missing dog, say. With a case like that, it wasn't as if you could go wrong. Where was the precedent? Who in the history of investigation, save perhaps Ace Ventura, had ever been asked to find a lost dog? If you lost a dog you rang the local kennels, spoke to the neighbours. You walked around calling its name for a couple of hours. You didn't hire a detective.

The cleaner stopped at Leo's door, placed the carry-all and vacuum-cleaner on the floor and rooted for keys.

He turned as Charlie said, 'Excuse me.'

'Yes, sir?'

'You're here for Leo's office?' Charlie indicated the door, trying to keep the incredulity from his voice.

136

'Until such time as I'm informed to the contrary.' He looked Charlie up and down. 'Would you be the deliverer of said news?'

'Um, I don't think so. I'm Leo's brother, Charlie.' He stuck out his hand, feeling ridiculously formal.

'And my name is Terry,' said Terry, shaking it. 'First, before we go any further, let me extend my deepest condolences to you and yours. Your brother was a true gentleman. One of the good guys.'

'Yes. Yes, he was,' said Charlie, thinking he liked that about Leo. *One of the good guys.* Thinking that he, Charlie, wanted to be one of the good guys as well.

Terry smelled strongly of aftershave. A sweet, heavy scent, something that was properly intended to be worn after dark, and then only in the imagination – or in a television commercial *circa* 1982. If the office building had previously boasted a fusty, sunlight-on-dirty-windows smell, it now smelled of eau-de-whatever, the eau of Terry's battle against his advancing years. Nestled above one fat fleshy earlobe was the plastic sci-fi lozenge of a Bluetooth earpiece, and Charlie noticed that he favoured the other ear when speaking or, more to the point, listening. These, though, were merely accessories to the main Terry-feature, which was his hair. Innocent hairspray had died in the upkeep of what was – there was no nice way of saying it – a bouffant so tall and springy that Charlie had to restrain himself from reaching out to press it down and go '*boing*'.

Terry smiled at him. 'If memory serves, I believe you and your good lady wife have just had the prognosis of a newborn.'

'A baby, yes.'

'Yes, a baby,' smiled Terry indulgently. 'I know exactly what you're going through. Myself and my missus have three of them, for our sins. Three girls.'

'Right.'

There was a pause. Terry cleared his throat. 'I've seen to it that the requisite standard of cleanliness has been maintained since your brother's, ah, accident. Until – how should I say? Until further notice.'

'Right,' said Charlie.

'So,' prompted Terry, 'I now look to you to provide the further notice I require.'

Charlie looked blank.

'Do you still want me to clean for you, in other words?'

'Oh. Um . . . Well, no, not really.' He realised that he hadn't given the office a thought. Presumably Newlife hadn't known about it either or, no doubt, the proper channels would already be open. 'I guess it's rented, is it, the office?'

'It is, sir, yes. I work on a sort of permanent freelance basis, you understand, nominally employed by the freeholders but retained at the discretion of the individual office tenants, of which I'm pleased to say your brother was one.'

Charlie wasn't sure he understood. He gave a pained look.

'Your brother bunged me a tenner to clean up every now and then, sir, in other words. Those being layman's terms, so to speak.'

Charlie nodded. 'I see. And how often was that?'

'Bit ad hoc, sir. I tended to give him a knock every Monday or so. Whether he wanted the clean seemed to depend on whether or not he had the cash in his wallet at the time. But if he had the money, he took a clean. Now, I'm no charity case, you understand, but if it weren't for the continued support of

138

your brother and those of his ilk, I dare say things would be very different for me. A total good guy.'

'Right . . . Right. Did you ever see any of his clients?'

'Can't say I did but, then, I'm very discreet.'

'Okay. The thing is, I suppose the office reverts back to the agents at some point.'

'I imagine when the rent doesn't appear, sir.'

'Right.'

'So . . .'

'I won't really be needing your services any more. Sorry.' Charlie managed a sympathetic grimace.

Terry drew himself up. 'It's not a problem, sir. Not a problem at all. It's simply a case of providing me with the notice I require.'

'Come again?'

Terry smiled as though he were explaining something to a special-needs kid. 'As any other employee, I need a period of notice, sir.'

'Right. What sort of notice?' Charlie was thinking that their definitions of the phrase ad hoc were from different dictionaries.

'Well, as it happens, I do have other work lined up, so shall we say a week? Vis-à-vis, I'll clean today at the usual rate . . .'

'Which was?'

'As I said, sir, ten pounds. And if you'll be good enough to grease my palm with notes of paper I'll be on my way with further condolences and fond farewells.'

'Right. Okay. Sounds fair enough.'

Just then Terry held up a finger to signal no more conversation, then started talking to himself. For half a second

139

Charlie thought Terry might be a dangerous schizophrenic, then realised he was speaking to someone on his Bluetooth.

'Hello, love,' Terry was saying. Charlie wasn't quite sure of the protocol. Was he expected to stand there or leave? He opted for looking down the corridor, as though there were something important in that direction. Suddenly he knew what it would feel like to be a ghost.

'Yeah, yeah,' Terry was saying, 'I'm at Leo's office now . . . Well, no, as a matter of fact, his brother's in attendance.' Charlie smiled at the mention. 'We have reached an agreement regarding the cessation of my employment that would seem to be of satisfaction to both interested parties.' He winked at Charlie, who looked down the corridor again, wondering what the exact terms of his arrangement had been with Leo. Something he could guarantee had never been written down.

'You're a disc jockey, are you not?' said Terry. By now he'd found Leo's key and turned to the office door, was unlocking it to go in. 'A club in town, ain't it?'

'Used to. Now it's more weddings and stuff. That, and I run my own Internet business.'

The door to the office swung open. Terry motioned Charlie through.

Charlie's first thought was, It's one thing having a home-made sign on the door. This is bloody ridiculous. Everywhere was chaos. And not, it quickly became clear, contrived-to-look-that-way chaos. Not Leo being untidy-Leo either.

There was a desk along one side of the room, an office chair behind it. Facing that was another chair, no doubt where Leo's clients had once sat. Both oozed foam through slashes in the fabric. Two filing cabinets in the corner of the room had each been emptied, their contents, meagre as they were, ditched on the floor. On Leo's desk stood a computer and telephone, both relics, as though rescued from a skip after an office clearance. The desk drawers had been pulled open and the contents dumped on the floor. Again, there wasn't a huge amount to dump.

Behind him, Terry had walked in and was looking round the room, whistling softly.

'I'm afraid this is going to be more than a two-hour job,' he said. 'You, sir, have been burgled.'

## Staring at an Empty Screen

Charlie looked around the office, feeling a ferocious cocktail of wrong emotions: guilt, that something big had been going on with his brother and he didn't have the faintest clue what it was; violation, because, Christ, somebody had burgled his brother's office. And worry. Because someone had burgled the office, and he had no idea why. But he'd bet his entire vinyl collection that it wasn't for Leo's crumbly old PC or his half-empty jar of Nescafé, neither of which was missing anyway. It was for some other reason.

And he thought about Leo missing their dad's anniversary, the phone call, the flat. Something was wrong with that picture.

Terry turned to him. 'We're agreed that this is more than two hours' work, sir, just to be upfront about it?'

'Wait a second,' said Charlie. 'Nobody's cleaning anything. We've been turned over. We should leave it for the police.'

'Not that I've checked, sir, but I'm fairly sure office cleaning doesn't feature on their list of duties.'

'Yeah, yeah, you know what I mean. For fingerprints and stuff.'

Terry laughed. 'When was the last time you were burgled, boss?'

'Um, never. Why?' said Charlie, feeling somehow ashamed of the fact.

'Well, the police don't send Dixon of Dock Green round to instigate a thorough investigation. You'll be lucky to get PC Plod yawning into his lapel, and unless you've just been alleviated of the family silver or a bunch of diamonds, or you're a drug-dealer or an asylum-seeker, they ain't gonna be taking much notice. *Fingerprints?*' he scoffed.

Terry was right. Of course he was right. Charlie stared around, feeling helpless, impotent – exactly the way he'd felt at the graveyard.

'All right. Do you know what's been taken?'

'Not a lot, I dare venture,' answered Terry. 'There was no such thing as a safe or a petty-cash tin. About the only thing of any value was the computer, and that's still here.'

Charlie glanced over to the desk. The computer. The one that looked like a rescue job. He moved over to the desk and booted it up.

It was empty. As in, it had nothing on it. The documents folder was empty, the schedules were untouched, the email nuked of all content.

Someone, maybe Leo, had stripped it down, taken off all trace of life, left it a plastic husk on the desk.

# Fight, Fight, at the Tribute Night

On the blackboard was written:

> The Look Again Lookylikeys and Tribute Acts Agency pays
> tribute to Leo Watson and his Tom Waits For No Man
> Tribute Night.
> R.I.P. Leo.

Below the wording, itself a tribute to the word 'tribute',
was a telephone number. Below that, stuffed into the little
wooden trough that usually held chalk, was a stack of
promotional leaflets, one of which he now took. It was a
leaflet advertising the agency. It folded out into several
parts and inside were woefully bad versions of George
Michael (round-faced man with stubble), Elton John (bloke
in bad wig, sunglasses, oversized jacket and crucifix earring), Geri Halliwell (large woman in Union-flag dress) and
more.

Charlie stood in front of the blackboard for a moment or
so. There were two steps down to the function-room door
from behind which boomed a track off *Mule Variations* that
he recognised but couldn't quite put a name to. He could smell

the fag smoke and booze and even a hint of dry ice from events long ago, all – to him, anyway – comforting smells.

But not comforting enough to banish his nerves, and he found himself wanting a cigarette; even pressed the side of his jacket as if there might be a packet in there, overlooked for the last five years or so. He folded the leaflet he'd taken from the trough in the blackboard, stuffed it into his back pocket, stepped down towards the 1970s double doors, pushed them open and walked in.

The room was exactly as he had imagined it would be. Any gentrification that elsewhere gave Highgate its much-prized village status had taken one look at this room and decided not to bother. Here, there was patterned red carpet, flavoured with thousands of fag stubs and discarded chewing-gum, dotted with furniture built some time in the early 1980s, probably to the sounds of Dollar from the factory tranny.

A set of decks presided over a grimy-looking dance-floor, and Charlie instinctively found himself comparing the rig to his own. It didn't fare too badly, which was more than he could say for the DJ: a kid, sitting, looking bored, smoking. Charlie damped down a surge of irritation that was as much personal as professional.

There was a crowd, such as it was. Most of the tables at the sides of the room were taken. His eye went to a table full of lookylikeys, not far from the decks, in particular the Geri Halliwell from the leaflet. Either she hadn't been at the funeral or she hadn't been in full Spice regalia as she was now. The whole caboodle. Dress as seen on TV, red hair, over-excited lipstick. With her was a group of other looky-likeys, all in uniform.

Suddenly she looked up, brightened on seeing him, then

stood and tottered over on what looked like genuine Spice Girl platform boots. 'I'm sorry, but we don't really have any call for a George Clooney lookalike,' she said, and smiled. 'We tend to concentrate more on the musical side.'

'Oh,' said Charlie, 'I think I'm more Mickey Rooney than George Clooney.'

'Not a bit of it.' She held out at a hand. 'It's me, Philippa – but you can call me Lips. I wasn't dressed like this at the funeral.'

'Ah,' said Charlie.

'Let me introduce you.'

So she did. Charlie met virtually everybody who appeared on the Look Again books, and then some. They nodded and smiled and went to the bar to get drinks, which Charlie drank, and after a few he found himself in earnest conversation with a Diana Ross, before Meatloaf wobbled up with a tray of tequila slammers for the table, and then, when they were gone, with a loud, almost angry tribute to Leo, another round of tequila slammers turned up, and Robbie Williams opted out of his, so Charlie had two, and then some more beers, because (a) it would have been rude not to, and (b) it helped him loosen up in front of all these people he didn't know, and (c) his brother was dead, and if you couldn't get pissed when your brother was dead – had burned to death in his car, like a *cake* or something – then when could you, eh? *Eh?* And (d) because why the hell shouldn't he get pissed? Since when had his name changed from Charlie Watson to *Husband-Father* Watson? Since when had his entire sense of character and self been defined by his domestic status? Eh? *Eh?*

'Do you . . .' Charlie said later. How much later he wasn't

sure: the DJ had played most of *Mule Variations* and some of *Real Gone*, plus a few other bits and pieces before moving on to *Closing Time*, Tom Waits's début, a melancholic, piano-bar album. 'Do you represent DJs?'

Geri, sorry, Philippa – *Lips* – gestured across the table at Boy George, who didn't notice; was too busy chatting to a woman whose name Charlie hadn't caught but who might have been Debbie Harry (the twilight years). 'He does the occasional bit of DJing. Why?'

'Because that's –' said Charlie – 'what I do.'

Philippa, very gently and with great sensitivity, removed his hand from her arm. 'Of course. Leo said you were a wedding DJ.'

'And I run my own Internet business . . . Um . . .' He stopped. 'Sorry, is every song going to be by Tom Waits?'

'Well, it *is* Leo's tribute. He was a huge Tom Waits—'

'He did listen to other stuff, though, you know. I mean, he wasn't totally defined by Tom Waits. That wasn't all he ever listened to.'

'What else did he listen to, love?' she asked him softly. 'Tell me. I'll get the DJ to put on something different for you. How would that be?'

'I don't know.'

'What? Sorry, darling?'

'I don't know what else he listened to.' Which was rubbish. Of course he did. Leo had liked jazz. Charlie couldn't stand jazz. He used to say, just to wind Leo up, that 'Bette Davis Eyes' by Kim Carnes was light years better than anything Miles Davis had ever done; that he'd take Sonny and Cher over Sonny Rollins. 'Are you *on crack*?' Leo used to say, in mock-horror. Laughter.

'I don't know what else he listened to,' wailed Charlie now. And he dissolved into tears.

'Darling, darling,' Philippa said, putting an arm round him. 'That's it, you let it out if you want to.'

They'd come, the tears, at last. But why here, now? He felt ashamed, frustrated.

He tried to stand, was aware of Philippa saying, 'I don't think you ought to . . .' Then heard the wet-wood thunk of a pint glass knocked over on the table, the flurry of movement as the gathered lookylikeys stood to avoid split beer. Dimly he thought that if he ignored the spillage it might not really have happened. But who gave a fuck? Because his brother was dead and all they could do was sit around talking about . . . about the . . . *price of fish*.

Somebody put a hand on his arm to stop him but he was moving towards the deserted dance-floor where he began a lone, jerky dance to what was probably the slowest track off the slowest Tom Waits album. He became aware that he was the only person dancing to the world's most maudlin song, stopped, then marched towards the table where the DJ sat.

'Let's have some Donna Summer,' he demanded. ' "I Feel Love". The fifteen-minute version.' Somewhere inside – a place that knew he was falling, and falling hard – he believed that the disco thump of 'I Feel Love' would redeem him; that lookylikeys would crowd to the dance-floor and clap him congratulations on the back, and his drunken crying and his dancing alone to sad songs would be forgiven and forgotten.

'No,' said the DJ.

'What?'

'I said, "No." '

'Okay, then, the edit.' He curled his lip to let this pup of a

DJ know what sloppy seconds the edit of 'I Feel Love' was compared to the full majesty of the quarter-hour version.

'No,' insisted the DJ. 'I ain't got it.'

A potent brew of outrage and disbelief foamed within Charlie. 'But you must have "I Feel Love" by Donna Summer. Every DJ has "I Feel Love" by Donna Summer.' Most did not have the fifteen-minute version that he had, true. The fifteen-minute version he never got to play but packed anyway – the original Casablanca twelve-inch, this was. And he would have kissed the bride or the groom, the best man, whoever – a warty dog, even – if they'd asked him to play the fifteen-minute version. But it had never happened. So he had to settle for playing the edit instead. But he always had the edit to play. Everyone had at least the edit to play. Everyone, apparently, but this clown. This *noob* who didn't even stand up behind the decks, who *sat down*, like it was some kind of relaxing evening out. Sat down.

So Charlie said the words. He said, 'You're a DJ. Do you know what business you're in? Do you?'

The DJ shook his head no and squinted at Charlie through cigarette smoke, reaching to stub out his cigarette in a small tin ashtray that rested on the decks. *He had his ashtray resting on the decks.*

'Well, I'll tell you!' shouted Charlie.

'Leave it, mate, yeah?' said the DJ.

How many times had Charlie said it to Bea, even believing it himself? How many times had he said those exact words, packing the Red Indian headdress he would wear for playing Adam Ant, blowing up his inflatable hammer, loading all those record boxes into the van even though he only needed one, the one with Dexy's Midnight Runners and 'Happy

Hour' by the Housemartins inside. How many times had he said – as he said now – 'You're in the entertainment business'?

The DJ smirked. There was a hand on Charlie's arm. He felt Lips by his side and heard her say, 'Charlie, come and sit down. Please.'

'No. This guy – this fucking *noob* – needs to learn a thing or two about being a DJ. He needs to know, first, that he's in the entertainment business, and second, he needs to make sure he's packing some fucking Donna Summer. No Dexy's either, I suppose.'

'Look, mate, give it a rest.'

'What about Kylie? "Better the Devil You Know". "Love Machine" by Girls Aloud. Have you got the one that goes, "Klingons on the starboard bow, Klingons on the starboard bow".'

The DJ leaned across the decks. 'Just fuck off, will you, mate?'

Two things happened simultaneously.

First, Philippa Shaw snapped '*Jason*, in the way you might if your son was doing some DJing for you at a tribute night and had just been rude to the brother of the deceased.

And at the same time Charlie punched him.

It was a terrible punch. Charlie was no pugilist. His fist was barely clenched. It was a lash-out more than a punch; a Wetherspoon's bitch-fight blow, its impact surprise more than pain. Still, it was enough to galvanise Philippa's son into action, and he sprang over the decks and Charlie tried to duck too late to avoid Jason's fist catching him beneath the eye.

It was to Jason's credit that he was still using vinyl. Perhaps the world of DJing – the entertainment business – wasn't completely lost to him after all. But as he dived over the decks at Charlie the needle skittered across 'Closing Time' with a screech like agonised livestock, and anyone in the lounge who was not already aware of the fracas by the DJ decks suddenly got wise.

And then there were lookylikeys all round them, pulling them apart. Lips in the middle, frantically trying to keep her son from killing Charlie, who was trying to reach Jason with his fists and feet.

There was shouting, 'Cut it out,' 'Hey, hey,' and someone shouting, 'Donna Summer,' over and over in a voice he recognised.

And then, just as he thought things could get no worse, he woke up in Chariot's bed.

# The Worst Feeling in the World,
## to the Power of 1000

It took Charlie a horrible moment to realise he wasn't at home. And these were bad times, but that second of sick realisation went straight in at number one – that moment of knowing he was not at home.

Last night he'd been drunk. Scratch that, *very* drunk. Which was bad. There had been a fight. Which was also bad (but he'd deal with that later). Still, these two things were nothing – *nothing* – in comparison to the fact that he hadn't made it home. Because if he'd been at home he could have battled through the physical and mental pain, told the right white lies, helped Bea care for Mary knowing that Bea had more pressing concerns than Charlie's late night, his alky breath and whatever other trophies he'd brought home. He would have kissed his wife and daughter because they were the two most obliteratingly precious things in his life, and everything – relatively speaking – would have been all right.

*If* he'd been at home.

He was in a flat, he could tell. Something about its feel. The sense of enclosure. He was in a flat somewhere in London, not his semi in the suburbs.

It was almost silent in the room, dead still. From outside he could hear traffic noise muffled by double-glazing. Apart from that, just the sound of her sleeping.

It was Chariot. She lay with her back to him – a black vest top on – but he could tell it was her. He knew the hair; the scent was the same. He didn't recall seeing her at the tribute the previous night but, then, he didn't recall much of that at all. What little he did remember was coming back to him in terrible strobe-light bursts. Flashbacks of flying fists, Boy George clutching a ripped-off hair extension, one hand over an injured eye, Ant and Dec shouting at each other, Diana Ross, her head in her hands, and somebody repeatedly shouting '*Donna Summer*' like a disco version of Dustin Hoffman in *Rain Man* . . .

Oh yes, that was him: Charlie, who now had a pavement-breaking machine pounding away in his head, whose mouth tasted like rats had been vomiting in it, whose skin felt wrong and second-hand, as though he'd just bought it at a car-boot sale.

He wiggled his toes. No socks. Feeling with his hand he confirmed a similar lack of jeans, but – and here was the good news – he did appear to be wearing his boxer shorts. He tried to remember which pair he had on – please not the ones with Wallace and Gromit on them – but could not. Upper body now. The last time he'd been a functioning human being he'd been wearing a T-shirt beneath a short-sleeved shirt, and he'd thought he looked pretty dapper when he left the house. Now, nothing.

He slid stealthily from beneath the duvet. The movement reminded him of trying not to disturb his sleeping wife and daughter, and what he felt wasn't so much a twinge of guilt as a sonic charge – delivered to his scrotum, travelling up to his heart and detonating there.

For a second he sat on the side of the bed in the silent room and massaged his eyes, pushing them, like doing that might squish away the agony and shame, pushing until his eyeballs hurt. The floor felt unfamiliar beneath his feet. Instead of carpet, a copy of From Birth to Toddler and a small stack of Record Collector magazines, there was laminate flooring. The kind of flooring young women preferred. Probably from Ikea. Probably everything in the flat would be from Ikea apart from the electrical goods and a lava lamp. He turned to regard her back for a moment, seeing its curves and wondering briefly what was going on beneath the duvet – what she wore – then cast his eyes round the room in search of his clothes.

Over in a corner of the room was a chair. His shirt hung over the back. On the seat were his jeans and T-shirt, folded, socks rolled up into a little ball. His desert boots were there, too, stowed beneath; like the rest of the set-up, neat, considered, the work of someone taking care. As in, not done by Charlie in the throes of passion. As in, put there by Chariot, who had considerately undressed the near-comatose Charlie, before allowing him to sleep in her bed.

'We didn't fuck, if you're wondering,' she said from behind him. Her voice was sleepy.

He started. Her choice of language did something to him he preferred not to name. 'I'm sorry,' he said, very quietly. It was all he could think of to say.

'You're sorry we didn't fuck?'

'No,' he said, too quickly. 'I'm just . . . sorry . . . about everything.' He scuttled over to the chair, hooked his jeans off it and started dressing.

Without moving, she said, 'That's quite all right, you know. It was kind of fun, certainly for a Tuesday. Better than *EastEnders*. What's your thing with Donna Summer, anyway?'

'Oh,' he said, mortified. 'I just like the record, that's all.'

'Well, yeah, I gathered that. You told the whole of High-gate.'

He groaned, then coughed and remembered smoking last night. 'Was I much of a problem?' he asked, dreading the response, feeling like shit. He pulled on the T-shirt and felt dressed at last.

'Not really. I went out with your brother, remember. Compared to Leo you were a walk in the park. You don't sing, which is a real benefit. Plus you fell asleep straight away. You really needed your sleep, didn't you? If I was giving marks for hassle caused I'd give Leo an eight and you a six.'

'I didn't . . . try anything?'

She sat up, the duvet at her waist. One strap of her vest-top had slipped from her shoulder, inevitably. She looked from beneath mussed-up hair at him. 'No,' she said. 'Must be losing my touch.'

He laughed and looked down at his T-shirt. There was a small spot of blood on the chest. 'Oh.'

'I don't think it's yours,' she said. 'Either Ozzy Osbourne or one of Ant and Dec, I reckon. Not sure which. Can't ever tell the difference – between Ant and Dec, I mean.'

He stepped outside the room to let her dress, which involved pulling on a pair of jeans. She joined him in the lounge and they sat on the sofa, which was new, she explained, otherwise he would have slept on it. Over his blood-splattered T-shirt he'd put on his short-sleeved shirt. In the fight it had lost two buttons and now gaped open at the neck. Bea had bought him that shirt, telling him how nice he looked in it. He had a feeling that that particular beautiful moment was not going to be one they revisited in their dotage.

'Dec is the shorter of the two,' he said.

'Yeah, but how do you remember?'

'Um, either you have a baby, go out less and watch a lot more telly,' he said, 'or you remember that Dec is closer to the deck. See?'

'But Ant could be the smaller of the two. Like an ant.'

'Yes, but that's not how it works. Sorry.'

'Oh. Okay.'

There was a silence. He felt terrible on every level.

'Do you miss him?' he said, at last.

Chariot sighed. 'I was already missing him,' she said, looking away, at the television that wasn't on. On top of it, he noticed, stood a lava lamp.

'Oh? How do you mean?'

'Leo and I had split up.'

That came as a surprise. He wasn't sure why, but it did. 'You left him?'

'He left me.'

That came as an even bigger surprise.

'See what I mean?' She laughed, without humour. 'Losing my touch.'

'Why? I mean, what did you do?'

She stood. 'I don't know.' Without looking at Charlie she stood and went to the kitchen – more of an alcove than a room. 'Do you want a cup of coffee?' she called.

'Thanks, yes.' He followed her to the kitchen where she stood unscrewing the lid from a coffee jar.

'Really, though. Why did Leo leave you?'

'You mean, "If it's not a personal question, Sapphire, do you mind if I ask why Leo left you? Like, really, why did he leave you?"'

'Sorry. Yes, that's what I mean.'

'Same answer. I don't know. He never said. There was no letter, email, text, or even – God forbid – a conversation. He just stopped talking to me.'

'Leo? He never stopped talking to anyone.'

She didn't bother to laugh. Not even to be polite. 'Well, he stopped talking to me. He didn't answer the phone. He didn't reply to his mail or reply to his voice messages or respond to texts. I was trying, you know, different avenues of communication, in case one or the other had fallen out of favour. But he was ignoring them all. From me, at least. If I went to his flat, he didn't answer the door. I went to his office, but he was never there, always working from home. And when I went there, well, like I just said, he didn't answer the door.'

'How did you know he was there, at home?'

'He wasn't at the office.'

'Working from home, I mean.'

'Terry told me. Have you met Terry?'

'Er, yes, I have.'

'Great hair, isn't it? Well, Leo told Terry he was going to be working from home. Anything he was doing, he was doing it from the flat.'

Suddenly it struck Charlie that she didn't know – Chariot didn't know the truth about Leo.

'What work was this, do you know?' he said cautiously.

'I don't, no. Cases, I suppose.'

'You don't know what cases?'

'Well, no, he wasn't speaking to me,' said Chariot. 'He'd put an advert in your local paper. It was something from that, I think.'

Charles Laughton, thought Charlie. By now, Chariot was spooning coffee into mugs, the kettle boiling away. Everything in her kitchen was neat and new. The fridge had photographs stuck to it with magnets. Charlie saw Leo. One of him by himself, gurning into the camera. Another, of him and Chariot together, taken at a pub – the Oats, probably.

'On the subject of people splitting up, have you checked your phone?' she said. 'I think you'll find you have a lot of missed calls. I'm sorry, but the bleeping was beginning to drive me nuts. I used all my expertise as a fully qualified Carphone Warehouse phone trainer to switch it to vibrate.' She handed him a cup of coffee. 'Which reminds me, I'd better get ready for work.'

Half an hour later, and to add to his problems, the caffeine had begun to make him shake. She'd walked him to the tube and now they sat together: him shaking, her slightly amused at him shaking. Beside him was one of those blokes who thought shifting even a tiny bit to give Charlie room made him look like a loser. So he'd done the opposite, subtly digging his elbows into Charlie's sides. His legs, already wide apart on account of his obviously gargantuan scrotum, seemed to spread even wider. Being squashed exacerbated Charlie's hangover, which was bad. The paracetamol had turned and fled at the sheer size of the headache squatting behind his eyes; he had begun to leak tepid, itchy sweat all over, but particularly from his hairline, so every now and then he needed to palm away the wet from his forehead. And he felt tired. Really. Very. Tired. Any sleep he'd had was just alcoholic downtime; it didn't count as rest. It hadn't even blown the froth off his exhaustion – had only made it worse. He wasn't merely tired, he was exhausted. He felt truly wretched.

Opposite them a man was eyeing her up. Too-short trousers, grey shoes, the type of bloke who bought the *Sunday Sport*. And *Sunday Sport* guy was eyeing up Chariot because she was devastating. She was funny, and dry, and smart. She was a limited edition in its original gatefold sleeve. Near mint. And – what? Leo had thought he could trade up?

'You didn't fall out at all?' he found himself saying now.

Despite the long silence she twigged instantly what he meant. 'No. He just stopped calling. Stopped speaking to me. I thought things had been going great, you know, the odd drunken episode aside, but . . .'

'That was Leo.'

'Right. You kind of sign up for it.'

Then he said, 'Did you know he'd been burgled?'

'Burgled?' said Chariot. 'Did they get anything?'

'Not really, no,' he said, lost in thought for a moment.

*Leo was burgled.* By a couple of scrotums wearing hoodies, probably – most likely and almost certainly. Any other explanation belonged on *Taggart*. But still. Still.

Everywhere Charlie went, nothing seemed to fit quite right.

## Home, Shame, and Don't Spare the Horses

On the way home he had the train carriage to himself. He supposed the railway company resented having to lay on entire trains to ferry losers like himself out of London in the morning. They liked the inbound commuter trains, packed full of drones bleakly writing each other emails, or reading Dan Brown novels, or working on Sudoku puzzle number 423. Or just staring out of the window, empty-eyed, and wondering where on earth it had all gone wrong.

There was a notice saying, 'Please do not place feet on the seats.' You shouldn't need to tell people not to place their feet on the seats. It was kind of obvious. Still, he guessed the sign was there to give passengers something to refer to – so they could indicate it when asking a yob to remove his feet from the seats, like, 'Look, it's a rule.' Not that they would, of course; they'd be too wary of being stabbed. Perhaps the sign should say, 'Please do not stab people who ask you to remove your feet from the seats.'

On arrival Charlie dragged himself out of the station feeling as if he'd gnawed off his own leg to escape a man-trap. The street outside went about its business oblivious to his physical and mental agony, and he watched it for a moment: the Booze 4 Less shop, Tandoori Knights, Southern Fried Chicken. A car blasting music. A kid gobbing on the pavement. It was home, he supposed, and the transport links were good.

Half a mile away, his wife. There had been fourteen missed calls on his mobile – some kind of record – and four voicemails, starting angry, then getting worried and becoming frantic.

After leaving Chariot he'd sent a pathetic text message telling Bea he'd missed the last train home and was going to stay the night with one of the Wee Davey McBowies. Only ten hours too late; he was going to blame its late arrival on 'the network'. Lies and more lies.

At Marylebone station he'd bought some cheese and onion crisps. A jumbo pack from the station shop. 'Would you like to purchase a half-price bar of chocolate with that?' the assistant had said, indicating a pile on the counter.

No. Sod off. He'd taken the crisps and wolfed them, waiting for the boards to announce his train. Now his fingers – not just his fingers, his whole hands – stank of cheese and onion crisps. Worst flavour for that, cheese and onion, worse than prawn cocktail, even.

Wiping sweat from his forehead with cheese and onion fingers, he began to make his worthless way home, wishing something would happen on the journey so that he might die a hero's death.

But it didn't. He turned into Candle Street. There was a sunny afternoon stillness about the place. His van and the Peugeot were outside the house, as they should have been. From somewhere there was the sound of a lawnmower, a crash and clink as somebody else discarded their empties in a recycling bin.

Opposite their house a man in a fluorescent sleeveless jacket sat in a red flat-bed Toyota truck, apparently reading something. He glanced up as Charlie approached and their eyes met. In his diminished state, Charlie felt as if he was being judged. Sure enough, the workman smirked a little and inclined his head in greeting, looking back at whatever it was he held – a newspaper.

Charlie fished for his keys and let himself in.

It was as still in the house as it was out. An awful silence. God, if only he could have been welcomed by the sound of laughter, Mary gurgling happily, the windows thrown open, a cool breeze . . .

Just off the hall, the door to the lounge was open. Inside, the room was dark, curtains closed. Bea lay on the sofa with Mary on her chest, Mary asleep, snoring softly. Bea had placed one hand over Mary's ear to prevent the noise of the front door waking her, and now she stared over the head of her sleeping baby at Charlie, who stood in the doorway.

She looked wiped out. Hollow eyes red-rimmed with lack of sleep, worry and fear. Bird's-nest hair. Face a picture of fatigue and now, seeing Charlie, something else – something on the borders of hatred and outright terror, as though her world, made of straw as it already was, had just been blown away by the big bad wolf.

He wanted to go to her and hold her tight. To say he would never leave her again, and for it to be the truth.

On a table pulled up to the sofa he saw a cup of tea long gone cold, an empty glass, their cordless, her mobile, plus the baby apparatus – wet wipes, sick-stained swaddling blankets,

Infacol, a muslin cloth, a bowl of sterilising water, feeding bottles, teats – that spoke of a long, terrible, sleepless night of new-baby panic, every action chased by the same questions: Am I doing it right? Is she okay? What does she want? *Why won't she sleep?*

All of this endured alone by Bea, the person he loved most on the planet. He wouldn't wish it on his worst enemy.

Now she stared over the top of their sleeping baby's head at him with haunted eyes and whispered, 'Where the fuck have you been?'

'I'm sorry,' he whispered back, 'I'm so, so sorry.' He wanted to move to her – more for his own comfort than hers he shamefully knew – but she stopped him, holding up the hand that wasn't protecting Mary's ear. '*Don't.* Just. Where. Have. You. Been?'

'I'm so sorry,' he pleaded. 'I was at the thing. It was. I let my emotions. I got. Really, I missed my. Bea, can I get you a glass of water?'

She nodded a resentful affirmative, desperate for a drink – desperate enough to allow Charlie to fetch it for her.

'I can't believe this, Charlie,' she hissed as he brought it back. 'You went and got pissed and stayed out all night. I didn't know where you were or who you were with.'

He prayed for his face to betray nothing.

'Or when you were going to be back. You didn't answer your phone. I was frantic, Charlie. And the whole time Mary just would not settle. I can't – I don't know if we've got the wrong size nappies because she keeps waking up wet and I'm running out of sheets and her mattress is sopping. She's been crying *so much*, Charlie, and she won't take any boob, and she won't do *anything* but cry.'

Her eyes were shiny. There was a catch in her voice so heartrending that Charlie felt himself pulled to her as though on rails; had a need to gather her up that was so urgent it was like a physical event. Again, the hand. No.

'Why didn't you call me?'

'I tried,' he started.

'No.' Her voice broke and she was crying. 'You didn't try.' She indicated the telephones on the table. 'If you'd tried you would have reached me. I wasn't out clubbing, Charlie. I've been in here all night, and apart from speaking to my mum I was available the whole time.'

'You spoke to your mum?'

'I needed help. I needed support.'

'Did you tell her where I was?'

'I didn't *know* where you were.'

'Did you tell her that?'

'No.' She looked away. 'You don't deserve it, but no. The first time I told her you were working. The second time I told her you were sleeping, that it had been a tough gig.'

'I'm so sorry,' he said, his voice only just above a whisper.

On Bea, Mary shifted. Bea went double-chinned, straining to look at her baby, who slept on.

Bea glared up at him. Behind the exhaustion he could see fight. 'Where did you stay?'

'With one of the guys out of a band. The Wee Davey McBowies.' He tried a weak, isn't-that-a-funny-name smile and found it didn't fit.

She was shaking her head. 'A call. One call. That's all it would have taken. I would have been upset, you'd have had to face some music and it wouldn't have been pretty, but I wouldn't have been half as upset as I am now. Do you know how upset I am?'

'I can see you're upset,' he said.

'There are no words to describe it. You're supposed to be the *one* person I can rely on. This —' she glanced down at the sleeping baby – 'this is so hard,' her voice broke again, 'and it gets a million times harder if I'm here trying to do it on my own.'

'I'm really, truly sorry. I can't tell you how bad I feel.'

'How bad *you* feel?'

'Sorry. Sorry.'

'How bad *you* feel?' Now she was crying, and Mary was stirring on her as though aware of her mother's anguish. 'Get out, Charlie.'

'Please, Bea . . .'

'Just. *Get. Out.*'

He left, barely noticing the red flat-bed Toyota truck still parked on the road outside.

# Land, Ho!

Charlie walked, glistening in the heat. For everyone else, the day had brought out summer accessories in force. Men wore their jackets on their thumbs, or not at all, or not even shirts. Girls shimmied in summer skirts that sat on the hip and shifted left to right as they walked. On the roads, music blasted from the windows of metallic-purple cars with tinted windows and unnecessary roll-bars; women who lived for the description yummy-mummy drove Land Rovers filled with genetically perfect children and shiny-coated pedigree dogs; open-top cars were manned ostentatiously by power-suited people on mobile phones.

Charlie was none of these things. He wore yesterday's clothes and last night's shame.

But he was thinking as he walked, the hangover doing bad stuff to his mind. Resentful stuff.

Fuck's sake. He would have got home last night – no problem – *if* they'd still lived in London. *If* Bea hadn't insisted they move.

After all, they'd moved out because she wanted to. ('I don't want to bring a child up in London, Charlie. I'm sorry. It may be all right for other people, not for me.')

He could see her point, but London was his home and the home of Cheesy Vinyl. In other words, he had made sacrifices. Like a good soldier, he'd fallen into line for the good of her because she insisted it was for the good of their unborn baby. He'd smiled and said, 'Great,' when she announced plans not to return to work.

The thing was, this move. It was supposed to make things less expensive than living in London. They had a nice house now. The extra space she said she couldn't live without. The suburban dream. Except their more-expensive suburban dream house had pushed the mortgage repayments into a scrotum-tightening new band. And heating and lighting the suburban dream was a hell of a lot more expensive, because there was a lot more of it. The suburban dream's council tax was more than twice that of Hackney. The tube trip that used to cost Bea a few quid a day now cost more than five times as much. Hey, that was one less cost since she'd stopped work, of course, but it was also one extra person to feed, clothe, buy pushchairs and decorate rooms for. Because that the other essential ingredient of the suburban dream, and whoever said life was cheap never drove all the way to Milton Keynes to try to get the best price on a pushchair.

All of this he'd taken on the chin.

He'd stayed out one night, and the shit had hit the fan. He'd stayed out one night – at his dead brother's tribute night, for fuck's sake – and she'd thrown him out of the house.

He reached the station, touched his Oyster card to get through the gates and sat down on a bench, waiting for his train. He was going back into London – home. He was going shopping. For records. He was going to Haggle Vinyl on Essex Road, to Selectadisc on Berwick Street, Rough Trade in

Covent Garden, Sister Ray, the Music & Video Exchange, Mr Bongo and Vinyl Addiction. He was going to eat a fucking big burger and then he was going to see what was on at the King Charles or the Screen on the Green. Fuck her. Couldn't win either way. Might as well be hung for a sheep as for a lamb, or however the saying went.

His phone rang.

Rather, it vibrated in his pocket. He stood to retrieve it from his jeans, not recognising the number as he flipped open the handset. 'Hello?'

'Hello, is that Mr Watson?'

The voice was well-spoken. Good pronunciation. All of a sudden he was alert, thoughts of running away to London forgotten. 'Yes, that's me,' he said.

'My name is Jane Land,' came the voice. 'I had employed your brother to look for my dog.'

## Lanchester, So Much to Answer For

'Um . . . I was very sorry to hear about your brother,' she said. 'Very sorry indeed.'

Charlie tried to paint a mental picture of her and came away with something out of an Agatha Christie novel, complete with fretful fingers at a string of pearls. 'Thank you,' he said. 'That's very kind of you.' Unconsciously he adopted a plum to speak to her.

'I always found him very helpful indeed. He was trying to find Charles Laughton.'

A train was pulling in. To escape the noise, Charlie let himself out of the gates and stepped out of the station, away from the obligatory scrotes smoking outside the entrance.

'I see,' he said, trying to bring his thoughts into line, 'that's nice to hear. Really, um, very good.'

There was a pause.

'The girl at the vet's said you wanted to speak to me,' said Mrs Land.

'Yes, well, yes, I do. I don't know where to start, really. Could we meet, do you think? There are some things I was hoping to ask you.'

'Well, I'm not sure. What sort of things?'

'Just a few quick questions – about Leo?'

'What sort of questions? I'm really rather busy.'

'Well, it would be better if we could meet. I'll only take a couple of minutes of your time.'

'Um . . . Well, we could, I suppose. It's a question of where . . .'

Seeing something, Charlie stopped short. 'Mrs Land?'

'Yes.'

'Are you anything to do with Land Associates?'

'Why do you ask?'

'Just that I'm looking at a sign for Land Associates, the estate agents. I wondered if you were something to do with it.'

'I am,' she said. 'Or, rather, my husband is. He's Byron Land. The company was formed by his father, Aubrey. It's they, really, who are Land Associates. I'm just the person who stands on the left-hand side of the photograph when they're giving money to charity. Mostly I get cropped out.'

'Oh,' Charlie laughed, though he wasn't sure if he was meant to. 'That happens a lot, does it?'

'Well, they give a lot of money to charity. Aubrey died of cancer four years ago and the Aubrey Land Foundation was set up by Byron to distribute funds to worthwhile cancer charities, so every now and then we have to hold one of those giant cheques for the cameras.'

'Well, I'm fairly sure I know the Land Associates office. We could meet there, if you like.'

'No,' she said quickly. 'Byron's there at the moment. One of the rare occasions he's decided to go in, funnily enough.'

Right, thought Charlie. Interesting.

'In fact,' she continued, 'it would be better if you could come to the house.'

'I can, yes. Is it nearby?'

It was. But first he popped home, letting himself in quietly and breathing a sigh of relief whe the house was silent. He had apologies to make, sure, reparations to pay and quite rightly. But now was not the time. Now he needed a quick spruce-up before going to see Jane Land.

Bea and Mary were out, gone for a walk, seeing Bea's mate Sarah and her kid – whatever. Be thankful for small mercies. He grabbed a polo shirt and a fresh pair of jeans, looked at himself in the mirror and decided he would have to do.

They say it's possible to drive anywhere in Los Angeles within twenty minutes. In Bentham you can walk anywhere within twenty minutes. So, eighteen minutes later, after taking a short-cut up a footpath, Charlie was feeling poor and insignificant, but marginally less scruffy than he had been earlier, among the luxury homes of Armitage Avenue.

It was a private road. He could tell because it didn't have pavements, just grass verges, each neatly tended as though trimmed with nail scissors. And the road wasn't road-coloured: it was an aesthetically pleasing rust-red, all the better to complement the insanely expensive homes hidden behind skyscraping hedges. Like the verges, the hedges were neat. They were trimmed and square – nothing show-offy like swans or leaping fish: these people didn't need gimmicks; didn't have to try. At the top of the road, as if it was sitting at the head of the dinner-table, was the Lands' home. Their hedge was interrupted by a wrought-iron gate behind which

he could see a gravel driveway, some kind of fountain orna-
ment and, further back, the house.

He walked towards it; was glad to reach the gates having
been given the once-over by a woman in a passing Range
Rover.

'Hello,' he said into the intercom, aware of the camera,
wishing he'd fiddled with his hair and wondering if he looked
as hung-over as he felt. 'It's Charlie Watson. I'm here to see
Mrs Land.'

'This is Mrs Land.'

'Oh, hello.'

'There's a pedestrian gate.' A bleep sounded, a clunk as the
gate unlocked. 'Just push it. I'll meet you at the front door.'

He pushed, went through, crunched over the gravel, past
the ornamental fountain, climbed the steps to the front door,
which opened as he reached the top.

'Hello,' she said. 'Please excuse the attire. I'm going for a
run shortly.'

He thought back to the image of her he'd formed on the
phone: his imagination was laughably out of date. She wore a
Nike baseball cap, some kind of zip-up top. The cap was
pulled low, peak arched. Below it, shoulder-length black hair
framed a strong face, sun-browned, full cherry lips. Either she
wore no makeup or it was applied to make it look that way.
All there was to indicate her age – late forties, Charlie was
guessing – were the crows' feet round the eyes, accentuated by
her tan, and a touch of hardness to the face. The zip-up was
slightly undone so that he could see a V-neck T-shirt and the
rise of her breasts, and he couldn't help but wonder if she'd
had them done.

She led him along a corridor, wooden flooring – but not

Ikea-wooden like Chariot's flat; this was the real deal – and to the kitchen, where she waved Charlie to a stool at a central table; above it hung kitchen utensils, which she brushed with her hand, letting them clink as she went to the side and began to fill the kettle.

'Tea?' she said.

'Whatever,' said Charlie, looking around. 'Whatever you're having, I mean.'

'I'll be having water,' she said.

'Actually, water's fine. It's a hot day.'

The water came from a dispenser set in the door of a brushed-aluminium fridge – the kind that had two doors and room for a small family. It struck Charlie how quiet it was in the kitchen, in the whole house. CharlieWorld always had music playing, a TV on, Mary crying, cars passing, kids shouting in the street. In this house it was as though the outside had been denied entry. The mortuary had had more life.

'Here,' she said, coming to join him at the table and giving him the glass of water. She sat. 'Once again I'd like to say how sorry I am about your brother,' she said, eyes wide and sympathetic, holding his. 'Do you know – I mean, are you able to say what happened?'

He told her. Not the full, uncensored director's cut. He left out Leo doing a dump, for example. Just the short version: fire, car, M25.

She nodded sadly, holding his gaze. 'I see. I'm sorry.'

'Thank you. I'm just trying to . . . Well, I'm trying to build up a picture of what he was doing before his death. And one of the things that came up was that he was looking for your dog. Is that right?'

173

'Yes. Charles Laughton went missing while out walking with my husband. I had hoped a private investigator might be able to bring some experience to bear in locating him.'

*Experience?* Charlie almost winced.

'Right,' he said, choosing his tone carefully. 'And that's all there was to it? Nothing else?'

'What else would there have been?'

'Well, um, was there a suspicion of foul play? A ransom note or anything?'

She laughed indulgently. 'No, Mr Watson.'

'Okay, but it seems a little unorthodox to hire an investigator, that's all. With the greatest of respect, a lost dog – they run off all the time, surely?'

'I see,' she said, frowning. 'Is that what you needed to talk to me about? To tell me that Charles Laughton has run off, as dogs invariably do, and that paying someone to tell me what you've just told me for free was an act of folly on my part?'

'No, it wasn't.'

'Then why did you need to speak to me?'

He took a deep breath, not knowing quite how to answer and not sure, even, what the answer was. Then he said, 'What was the connection with Elsa Lanchester?'

'I don't follow you.'

'Well, in real life Elsa Lanchester and Charles Laughton were married.'

That laugh again. 'I know that, Mr Watson.'

'Right. How come?'

'I'm still not sure I follow you. It isn't a secret that Elsa Lanchester and Charles Laughton were married. Why on earth should I not know?'

'Okay, let me put it this way. Not long before he died, Leo

asked me if I knew anything about Elsa Lanchester. I sometimes dabble in film memorabilia and he wanted to know
whether or not she was collectable.'

'Is she?'

'She can be. He told me that he was asking for a mate. Was
that mate you?'

She shook her head no.

'Then why?'

She stood. 'Follow me, Mr Watson.'

They left the kitchen, walked back down the hallway
towards the front door, and for a moment or so Charlie
thought he was going to be asked to leave until she opened a
door he hadn't even spotted, ushering him through and
following.

They were in an office. Huge. At one end was a desk and
leather chair; above them was a portrait.

'That,' said Jane Land, pointing at the portrait, 'is the dear
departed Aubrey Land. Byron's father.' Charlie glanced at the
portrait, but his attention had already been diverted by
something on another wall.

'And that,' continued Mrs Land, 'is Byron's little wall of
devotion to Elsa Lanchester.'

It sure was. He had glossies. Eight-by-ten studio stills that
seemed to tile part of the wall. How many? Charlie didn't
count; neither could he place the majority of the films. In some
she stood with Charles Laughton, and – yes – she had made a
bunch of films with him, that was how they'd met. There were
several from *Bride*; at least two of her standing in the full
Bride get-up. In the middle was a close-up, a shot of her face
and hair. Her lips were pursed and chocolaty. Sharp eyebrows
lifted into the edges of that iconic hair. Eyes blazed. She

wasn't a beauty, but she was beautiful. It was signed across the bottom: Elsa Lanchester.

'Blimey,' said Charlie.

'You're impressed, then?'

'Um, sure. A signed still of Lanchester in *Bride* must be worth – what? A grand? Things of this vintage go for about three hundred pounds even without the signature. It's a find. Your husband would have been pleased to get it.'

'I'm sure he was thrilled.'

Charlie cast his eyes right. More Lanchester memorabilia. There was a British quad for *Bride* – one with 'The Monster demands a mate!' across the top – and he was about to get very excited until he realised it was for a re-release. Even so. What? A grand? Two? There was a one-sheet for *Rembrandt*. An insert for *The Bishop's Wife*, another one-sheet, this time for Come to the Stable. That must have been a re-release, too, because it included the information that Lanchester had been nominated for the Best Supporting Actress Oscar.

'Best Supporting Actress. I never even knew she was nominated. Bet she didn't win, either,' said Charlie.

He turned to Jane Land, indicating the *Bride* poster. 'Look at that. She played the title role in *Bride of Frankenstein* but didn't get top billing. Karloff did. The one role for which she'll be known for ever and she didn't get top billing – always the bridesmaid, always the Bride.'

'Very good, Mr Watson.'

'Thanks. If I ever write her biography, that's what I'll call it.' He paused. 'So this is the Elsa Lanchester connection, then?'

'Yes.'

'So Leo was asking on behalf of your husband?'

But he knew immediately that wasn't the case. Why would an obviously seasoned collector of Elsa Lanchester memorabilia be asking his wife's dog-finder about prices? Answer: he wouldn't be. Leo was either asking on behalf of someone else, or because he wanted to know himself. Something about Byron Land had piqued his interest. What?

'He must have been, I suppose,' said Mrs Land, clearly not interested in why Leo had been asking about her husband's collection. 'Come,' she said, 'we'll go back to the kitchen.'

They returned along the hallway and sat down, where Charlie asked about Charles Laughton. Sipping her water, she told him.

Charles Laughton. Breed: Spinone Italiano. That's the breed that looks like it's got a beard. Six years old. Favourite food: poppadums. Went absolutely mad for them, apparently. He was a pedigree registered to Mrs Jane Land, who bought him from a breeder in Windsor. Mrs Land had the documents to prove it, if he wanted, which he didn't, but if he had, they would have given him the names of both of Charles Laughton's parents, their aristocratic names, their pedigree lineage. Primrose Mistress by Tibbett and Hartley Shortcake on Rye, or something. Suffice to say, they were pretty impressive-sounding names. And if he'd thought calling a dog Charles Laughton was a touch on the posh and pretentious side (like, what's wrong with George, or Champ, or – Charlie had thought about this one – Batman?), it turns out Charles Laughton was only his given name, supplied by Mrs Jane Land 'because I thought it would annoy Byron'. His real name was Mortlake of the Mist by Cobbets Twice.

Charles Laughton had cost Jane Land a thousand pounds.

A grand, thought Charlie. Christ. A grand would pay his mortgage for the next couple of months. A grand was like passing Go for Charlie.

Charles Laughton had been chipped. If you were rich and had a grand to spend on a dog, whose main purpose seemed to be to irritate your husband, you didn't just leave it to chance that he might wander off and find himself a more harmonious home. You got him chipped. Which meant that if Charles Laughton turned up at any of the places doggies usually turn up, like with vets, breeders, the RSPCA or concerned old ladies, they could check for a chip, and a serial number embedded in the chip corresponded with a number that held details of Charles Laughton, his home address and telephone number. Owner and pet would soon be reunited.

But he had to turn up at one of those places first for the chip to do its job. And he hadn't turned up at any of those places, otherwise Jane Land would have been contacted. There had been no ransom note, which was why, when she saw Leo's advert, she'd decided to give him a call, she said, because her prime suspect was not a dog-napper, blackmailer, or even the suspicion that Charles Laughton might have met another dog and they'd run off together. Prime suspect was her husband, Byron Land.

Jane Land and Byron Land were not exactly hearts-and-flowers. There was no reading between the lines on this one. No subtext. As far as Charlie could tell, they hated each other's guts. So that meant that Jane Land hated Byron's collection of Elsa Lanchester memorabilia, and Byron Land hated Jane Land's desire for a dog, and subsequently hated the dog, and subsequently hated it even more when she called it Charles Laughton. Thinking about it, Charlie didn't see the big problem. Seemed like a nice tribute to him. But to Byron? To Byron the name was hemlock. He absolutely *hated* that dog. Apparently.

But here was the thing. There must have been something about the dog. Byron, who, remember, despised it and loathed its name, had been taking Charles Laughton out for walks. Usually Charles Laughton would go out on runs with Mrs Land, but lately, or in the couple of weeks leading up to his disappearance, Byron had been offering to take him out. Hadn't said why. Just that he enjoyed the walk. Why not? she'd thought. She was glad of the rest, glad to have them both out of the house. So she let him. Then one night – Friday, 2 June, to be precise – Byron had returned from his walk, and Charles Laughton had not. Where had he been taking the dog on those walks? She didn't know. But on that particular night, Byron had said he'd let Charles Laughton off his leash in Tennant Park. Thrown a stick, something like that. Charles Laughton had been off, running, chasing, exercising, whatever, and he'd gone into the little spinney along the side of the park . . . and never returned. And although Byron had spent half an hour or so calling him, 'Charlie! Charlie! Here, boy!' whistling for him and jangling the leash, he had disappeared.

'And how did he seem?'

'How do you mean?'

'Was he upset, contrite, what?'

They'd argued, of course. Couples like Byron and Jane Land hardly needed a thousand-pound thoroughbred supposedly beloved pet to go missing before they could get stuck into one another. So they had, and Byron had retreated to his study, his default residence in the Land domicile, apparently, and the last thing he'd said to her before turning his back was, 'I bloody hated that dog anyway.'

Making him top of Jane Land's Most Wanted list. According to her, he'd either put paid to the dog completely, sold him, or given him away to spite her. Which was why, when she had seen Leo's advert in the local paper – the final ad of its three-week run, if Charlie's mental calendar was correct – she'd contacted him.

He had, to all intents and purposes, taken the job.

Why?

'Do you mind my asking how much you were paying Leo for this?'

'Not really. Four thousand pounds.'

Charlie was glad he didn't have a mouth full of water at that moment.

## Hungover in the Library

Four thousand quid. Four *thousand*.

So that was why Leo had taken what sounded like the world's dumbest job. Because someone was offering him four thousand pounds and, really, for that kind of money, why on earth turn it down? The four thousand had been for the return of Charles Laughton or proof that Byron or someone else had been involved in his disappearance. But Leo was getting two thousand just to look. Christ, all he needed to do was put out the feelers. As long as Jane Land *thought* he was looking, the money was in the bag. Leo had absolutely nothing to lose. Perfect.

But still.

Still.

Something wasn't quite right.

After he left Jane Land, Charlie went to the library, where a pound bought him an hour on the Internet. The computer room was empty, and with good reason. The heat was up to old-people's-home levels, the sun beating down on windows without blinds to deny it entry. Charlie sat, feeling droplets of perspiration tickle his hairline, telling himself that at least the sauna conditions might sweat out his hangover.

He keyed 'Byron Land' and pressed return. Nothing. Well, nothing of any use. Lots of entries for Byron the poet, and things to do with land, and Australian professors, and genealogical trees of Byron Lands living in Cleveland, Ohio, and a couple of short entries in the online edition of the *Bentham Chronicle* about Byron Land's good works, but nothing of any interest to Charlie.

He keyed in Land Associates. The first entry was for the branch in town. It was a good site, expensive-looking, but obviously not designed by people wearing low-slung jeans. It was the kind of site Newlife would approve of. Land Associates, it said, below the company logo. Below that was a menu of the many things Land Associates could do for you: estate agents, commercial agents, planning and development, surveying, land agents, property management, grounds maintenance, residential management, new homes.

And then – from nowhere – it hit him.

The timings. They were wrong.

Charles Laughton had gone missing on Friday, 2 June, and Jane Land had seen Leo's advert in that week's paper. Friday, 2 June had rung a bell with Charlie, and that was because he'd done a gig that night.

He remembered it well. It was an eighteenth birthday, a booking he had taken reluctantly because it was a parent booking, and parents should never, under any circumstances, be allowed to book DJs for their kids' birthday parties. Charlie had tried to explain that he was more, you know, a wedding DJ. 'But it says "ex-London DJ" in the *Yellow Pages* ad,' the kid's mother had insisted. There was even a rather impressive quote from *Time Out*. How to explain that Cheesy Vinyl needed a context. That Cheesy Vinyl imported to the suburbs and played to a room full of eighteen-year-olds just became Shit Vinyl. Fuck-off-mate Music.

So, yeah, he remembered that booking, that night, that date. He remembered because it had gone every bit as badly as he'd feared. He'd left 'Isn't She Lovely' at home, and had not bothered with the box of gags, obviously. He'd tried to make himself into Hip Kids' DJ. And they were having none of it. The requests for records he didn't have were soon replaced by phalanxes of lads bawling at him from the dance-floor. There was a fight; a girl puked over his mixer. By 11.30 p.m. he was packing up and virtually tossing his gear out through a fire escape. A second fight began. There were kids out cold. Kids with their tongues down each other's throats. Monged-out kids. Punchy kids. Very, very drunk kids. Puddles of vomit and lager. The odd, forlorn party balloon, probably inflated by a well-meaning grandparent. He caught sight of the mum and dad on his way out. They were watching the carnage with mouths open. They looked like coma victims who'd been woken up just in time to see the end of the world. The father gazed, shocked, at Charlie, who mimed, 'Will call you.' Somehow – he could see it in the guy's eyes – he blamed Charlie.

He remembered the night Charles Laughton went missing, in other words. And it was *after* Leo had rung him about Elsa Lanchester.

## Lies and a Lobby Card

Standing in front of the Land Associates office brought back a sour memory of him and Bea going in during their house-hunting days. It had been the estate-agent equivalent of accidentally walking into an obscenely expensive clothes shop and realising you don't belong, then trying to withdraw with dignity intact. In the case of Land Associates they'd had a look at the properties on the wall but decided to ask anyway. Hey, perhaps they'd have other, more affordable properties that weren't displayed.

The agent had asked their price range. She'd smiled con-descendingly when they told her. They had skulked out, feeling poor, each dreaming of a time when they'd win the lottery, return and wipe that smile off the estate agent's face – a bit like that scene in *Pretty Woman*.

Now he pushed open the door feeling not-much-more hopeful. He didn't recognise the lone estate agent who sat behind the office's one desk. He gave her the once-over. Young. Glossy. The type to look down her nose. Charlie's heart sank. 'Hello,' he said.

She stared at him.

'I was wondering if I could . . . um, see Mr Land, or . . . arrange an appointment to see Mr Land.'

'What is it regarding?' she said, clearly knowing that, whatever it was, she could deal with it.

'Um, well, it's about his interest in Elsa Lanchester memorabilia.' She looked taken aback and Charlie had to suppress an urge to go, Ha! 'Plus my brother, who was . . . doing some work for his wife.'

She stared at him carefully. Her jaw moved slightly, and Charlie realised she had some gum in there. He wondered if she'd have kept it there if Mr and Mrs Richpants had been coming through the door, not just him.

'I'll ask,' she said, picking up the phone. Then, 'Mr Land, there's a gentleman to see you in the office. Name of . . .' She looked enquiringly at Charlie, who told her. 'Watson,' she repeated, 'Charlie Watson. He'd like to have a word. About Elsa Lanchester. Also about his brother.' She listened, said goodbye, then indicated a black leather sofa. 'He'll be down in a moment.'

Charlie sat, the sofa deflating as he did so, and waited.

Byron Land took ten minutes to make the journey from the first floor to the ground floor. When at last he arrived, Charlie recognised him immediately: tall, lean, silver hair, sunglasses. It was the man he had seen at the cemetery, the man who'd been watching the woman at the child's grave.

If he recognised Charlie also, he made no sign, walking forward, pulling his hand from his pocket to shake. 'Mr Watson,' he said, 'I was sorry to hear about your brother.'

'Thank you.'

He didn't look particularly sorry. Instead, Byron Land wore an air of distraction that, Charlie soon learned, was almost permanent. The other long-term inhabitants of his face were the glasses. They were brown-framed, the lenses slightly orange. Below them, Byron Land's face was lined, stretched, as though it was fixed into a permanent howl. There was something skeletal about it, right down to the colouring.

'Please come this way.' Land led Charlie past the agent and to the back of the room where a flight of stairs went up to the first floor. Here, a door opened on to an office that took up almost the entire floorspace; low ceiling, exposed beams. It felt cavernous, as though there should be five or six desks inside, not just the one – a mammoth affair at the back of the room: a mahogany-flavoured swimming-pool of a desk. As well as that there were two sofas – same sort as downstairs, the deflating kind.

'I was in a meeting when you rang,' said Land, indicating a man who was sitting in one of the sofas. He was older than Land, late sixties even, but had a sort of outdoors appearance about him. Black suit, unbuttoned jacket, one arm across the top of the sofa. He looked the sort who only needed to glance at the sun to tan and, sure enough, his skin was brown, leathery, Clint Eastwood-approved skin. 'This is Timson,' continued Land. 'He manages the grounds-maintenance side of the business. Timson's worked with the family longer than anyone cares to remember, so – don't mind him, in other words.'

Charlie wasn't minding him. What Charlie was minding was the framed picture on the wall above Timson's head: a *Bride of Frankenstein* lobby card.

A Bride of Frankenstein *lobby card*.

'Wow,' he said.

Land's eyes went to the card. He stood there a moment, as though allowing Charlie to view it.

186

'You've got a *Bride of Frankenstein* lobby card,' said Charlie. 'Is that an original?'

'Yes, of course,' replied Land, attempting to arm-sweep Charlie into a chair.

'That's worth around thirty grand. Well, I don't know about the condition, but one went for that not long ago.'

Land smiled patiently and motioned to the chair. With a backward glance at the *Bride* lobby card Charlie sat down. 'You're a collector, I gather.'

'That's why you're here to see me, isn't it?'

'Yes. Yes, it is. Partly . . .'

'Partly?' queried Land.

'Yes.' Charlie reached into the back pocket of his jeans and pulled out his wallet – an ageing surfer-type thing, with rippy Velcro. He felt vaguely adolescent opening it in front of Byron Land and the Clint Eastwood lookalike, but still. From it he extracted one of the cards he'd had printed up in the early days of Eclectibles, leaned forward and handed it to Land. 'My card,' he said.

'Yes, I can see that. Eclectibles. What's that?'

'I deal in collectables. That sort of thing.' He gestured at the lobby card and immediately regretted it. Land's face twisted into the briefest, snidest smile. 'Well, obviously not quite at this level but that *sort* of thing. I don't know if you know, but as posters and lobby cards are becoming more and more pricey, the biggest growth area in the market is action figures, and for a lot of collectors coming in at the bottom, it's a good way to build up a collection.'

'I see.' Land was watching him carefully.

'And there may be a Lanchester opportunity coming up you might possibly be interested in.'

'Ah.'

'Which reminds me . . .' Charlie felt like he was fumbling, and probably was, but soldiered on. 'You met my brother, Leo, I understand. I wondered, did he ever ask you about Lanchester memorabilia? Did he ever mention me at all?'

Land glanced over Charlie's shoulder at Timson, a look passing between them that Charlie could feel more than see.

'Your brother came to ask me about my wife's dog.'

'Charles Laughton?'

'Charles Laughton was its name, yes.'

'Was?'

'Are you trying to be clever, Mr Watson?'

'No. Not at all. I just thought it was funny your wife called the dog Charles Laughton?'

'She thought so. Have you spoken to my wife?'

'Yes. Yes, I have. That's how I was able to trace you.'

'And why did you want to trace me?'

'To tell you about this Lanchester opportunity coming up.'

'Or to ask me about the dog?'

'My brother is dead, Mr Land,' said Charlie, sensing something now: that Land had invited him in not because he wanted to hear about Elsa Lanchester memorabilia but because he wanted to size Charlie up, wanted to get the measure of him, 'and the last case he was working on before he died was your wife's missing dog, so you'll have to forgive me if I seem interested in that. Wouldn't you, if it was your relative, want to know their final movements?'

Again, that glance over to Timson. 'I'm not sure. Unless

you thought . . . Your brother's death was an accident, was it not?'

'Oh, yes. Beyond a shadow of a doubt. Even so . . .'

'Quite. Well, you're absolutely correct. He did come to ask me about my wife's dog, who *is* called Charles Laughton, present tense, I sincerely hope, but no, he didn't mention Elsa Lanchester, or you. Why do you ask?'

Now Charlie tried to picture Leo in this office. How had he been sitting? Did he take notes? Perhaps he had one of those little dictaphones and stood it on the desk. Perhaps he just lounged back in his seat and took it all in. Or lounged back in his seat and took nothing in, knowing he planned to do nothing about it – all part of the con. Or all part of something else?

'Just that he mentioned her to me. He seemed interested.'

'Did he?'

'Yes.' Charlie was watching the other man carefully. 'He seemed to want to know a bit about her. Probably because he saw that.' He waved at the lobby card. 'That's all it was, I suspect.'

'Yes, I'm sure that's what it was.'

'A bit of background, perhaps.'

'I'm sure.'

There was a pause.

'Now,' said Land, 'why don't you tell me about this Elsa Lanchester opportunity I might be interested in?'

The meeting was all but at a close, both of them knew it. Charlie spun a story about having an inside man at McFarlane Toys, who were, he lied, about to embark on a very limited-edition run of *Bride* action figures, with Lanchester the rarest. He could, he fibbed, get Land's name down on the waiting list, and named a ridiculous price. Land said he'd think about it, and Charlie stood, shook hands and, with a last look at the lobby card on the wall, found himself being escorted from the office by Timson, who remained silent, wafting aftershave as he gestured Charlie out.

# Flowers for a Conscience

He went up the hill and into town where, between the US Nail Bar and the Early Learning Centre, he found Foster's florists. A girl with an inevitable tattoo on her exposed lower back served him with two bunches of flowers, and he took them back down the hill, where the footpath behind Tesco led him to the graveyard. He walked over to where he'd seen Byron Land standing by a memorial, the last time he'd been here. *Aubrey Land, died 13 February 1980, aged 78 years, now with his beloved Ginny.* His father's grave; next to it his mother's. The yobs had given it a going-over. A green spray-can X had been drawn on it, and below that a dot. It didn't mean anything. It was – those tabloid clichés again – 'mindless vandalism'. Little fuckers couldn't even be bothered to write their own names.

Charlie stood at the grave for a long time: Aubrey Land and his wife, Ginny. Stout pillars of the community in life; shat on by bored youngsters in death. Then he went to sit on a bench in the graveyard, the one that had not been burned. It was in the shade but warm, and he thought he might fall asleep there. But sleep had been such a rare visitor to casa Charlie recently it had forgotten the directions. Instead he sat and thought.

First about Leo, Jane Land and Elsa Lanchester. Then about Chariot. The image of her back, the vest top, the mocking way she had about her, as though she was enjoying some private but entirely spiteless joke. She'd make you feel special, amusing, witty, the centre of her world. She could be addictive.

In other words, she wasn't the kind of person you dumped. That's what you're saying, Charlie, isn't it? Those tiny fronds of jealousy are not about having Chariot, but having her, then letting her go.

*If* that was what he did.

Because, aside from supposedly dumping Chariot, Leo had been engaged in some other odd behaviour. Working from home (apparently), looking for a lost dog (nominally) and, of course, getting burgled.

He glanced around the cemetery then fished out his mobile. Finding DI Merle's card he called the mobile number on it.

'Hello,' said Merle.

'Detective Inspector Merle?' said Charlie, talking quietly out of respect for those around him.

'Yes. I can't hear you very well. Might be a bad line.'

'It's Charlie Watson,' he said, louder. 'Leo Watson's brother. We met the other day.'

'Yes, yes, I remember,' said Merle. 'Just a moment.' The phone came away from Merle's mouth and Charlie heard him talking to a colleague. Terry had been half right, of course. Why bother reporting a burglary these days? Especially a burglary in which it seemed nothing had been taken. Still.

'Sorry about that,' said Merle. 'How can I help you?'

'It's Leo,' started Charlie. 'His office, actually.'

'Right. The office in Kilburn?'

'That's right.'

'What about it?'

'It's been burgled.'

'When?'

Between them, Terry and Charlie had managed to work out when the intruders had struck, and it had been after Leo had died. Charlie told Merle.

'Okay. Anything taken?'

'This is the thing. Nothing taken that we could work out between us, no. Nor was there any sign of a forced entry.'

'How do you think they got in?' asked Merle.

'Maybe they had a key,' suggested Charlie.

'If someone lets themselves in with a key and doesn't take anything, we don't tend to class that as a burglary,' stated Merle.

'They could have easily picked the lock. He didn't have the best lock in the world.'

'Okay, right. Leave it with me.'

After saying goodbye Charlie sat back on the bench and mentally apologised to the dead for talking on his mobile phone. First they get desecrated, then some git's yakking into his phone. There's no respect any more. Sorry.

He picked up his flowers and did what he had come to do. He made his way over to his father's grave. There, he remembered the crushed and dented vase. The last time he was here he'd replaced it at the foot of the headstone and there it was now, buckled and sad.

He should have bought a new one. Charlie Watson: mid-to-late thirties, professional fuckwit; specialist subject, letting down his loved ones. He reached for the metal vase, tears pricking his eyes, hating himself and the little bastards who had stamped on his father's flowers. But mostly hating himself. He put as many flowers as he could into the newly snug vase and kept the rest to add to the bunch he'd bought for Bea. Now he straightened and glanced round the rest of the graveyard.

Just a couple of days after the desecration it looked as it usually did. Whoever had tidied it up had done a good job. Unless you knew where to find it, there was precious little evidence of the crime: a tiny piece of police tape still tied to a tree was all that remained of any investigation. They would probably never find those responsible, and people would tut about that, but they didn't really care – not really – because it wasn't the specific kids they were interested in getting, the actual culprits, but the generic society-going-to-the-dogs bogeymen; in this case, drunk kids. Any kid would do, just as long as he or she was loitering outside Londis and wearing a baseball cap. Nobody cared who, or why: they just wanted labels and stereotypes to fear.

Charlie turned to head for home – so lost in thought that he forgot about the second bunch of flowers, leaving them behind on the bench.

## Joe Parks, Rennaissance Man

Sitting in his red flat-bed Toyota truck, fluorescent waistcoat over bare chest, smoking a cigarette and massaging his penis through his jeans, Joe Parks watched Charlie leave the grave-yard.

Almost twenty years ago Joe Parks had beaten a bloke half to death for having an earring, screaming 'Poofter' over and over as he repeatedly drove a steel-toe-capped Doc into the man's face, his body, his groin. As a final gesture, Joe Parks had reached to pluck out the offending earring, which had torn his victim's earlobe into two bleeding fillets.

The intervening years had seen Joe Parks change his mind on earrings. He now had two: one gold ring in each ear. He also used to hate men who wore hair gel. The lucky ones, he'd hoicked a green into their hair. The unlucky ones had gone the poofter route. But Joe Parks had changed his mind on gel, too, and now scooped it generously into his hair each morning. He looked at it in the rear-view mirror as he picked up his mobile phone from the passenger seat. He turned his head this way and that to admire the earrings, which did, he was always pleased to note, make him look like a pirate.

'Yes,' said the voice at the other end of the line, and he gave that person an update on the bloke he'd been following.

He finished the call, then peered out of the window towards Tesco at the bottom of the hill. Funny that he'd followed the bloke here, really: it'd meant he'd parked the Toyota where he usually did when he was working at the graveyard – the graveyard he'd just had to clean up. Which reminded him of his other job at hand, that of finding those spunk-rags and making them pay. Hardly a job, really; it was more like a pleasure.

Casting a quick look round, he got himself out of his jeans, massaged himself to erection, jammed a thumb over the end of his cock and smelt it. Before he could go the full distance the phone rang, and he pushed himself back into his jeans as he answered it. 'Yeah.'

'It's Jude.'

Jude, his partner – in the cop sense of the word only, mind – who sometimes worked with him on the parks, who was helping him with a little job. Jude was not as well known around town as Joe Parks, and Jude, while not quite blessed with the looks of his namesake Law, also had a way with the ladies. Which was why Jude had been given the job of snaring Carly.

'All right, Jude?'

'Yeah, all right, Joe.'

'You got her?'

'Yeah, I got her. She's having a piss.'

'You got your phone?'

'Yeah, course.'

'I hope you've already got some good footage.'

'I have, mate.'

'With her well on for it?'

'Fucking gagging.'

Joe massaged himself through his jeans again, smiling. 'Where are you, then?'

Jude told him.

'I'm on my way.' Joe Parks checked he had enough battery left on his mobile phone – didn't want it running out right in the middle of an important shoot, like – then gave himself a last squeeze and started up the Toyota.

## The Stupid Thing, Part One

Later, after a night of careful, delicate making-up, Charlie slid into bed, as unobtrusive as a bookmark. Beside him, Bea stirred. an arm came snaking over his chest, and he felt forgiven, began to drift off . . .

'Charlie?'

'Sorry, did I wake you?'

'I was already half awake.'

'Oh?'

'Worrying.'

Outside a car passed, music thumping. Headlights lit the room momentarily.

'What were you worrying about?' he said.

'Mary. I worry so much about her. I worry so much I can't think straight. She's hot and whingey. She won't settle. I think maybe she's got a cold coming on.'

'Could just be the colic?'

'No, it's different.'

'Let's see how she is in the morning.'

'I suppose.' There was a pause. 'There's something else I'm worried about, Charlie.'

He squeezed his eyes tight shut. 'What's that, babe?'

'You.'

'Me?'

'I read in one of the books that men, when they become first-time fathers, they react in strange ways. They have male crises. They do strange things.'

'Like what?'

'Buy fast cars, look at weird pornography . . .'

'Christ, what were you reading?'

'All it was saying was that they can react against fatherhood. You would talk to me, wouldn't you, if you had . . . I don't know . . . urges?'

'Urges?'

'Or feelings. For other women.'

'God. *God*. Bea, I would never . . . Never . . .'

'You wouldn't go off and do anything stupid?'

'No, of course not.'

'Promise?'

'Promise.'

But that night, he went off and did something very stupid.

# The Stupid Thing, Part Two

And the reason he did that stupid thing was because it finally came to him – the thing that had been niggling him since the visit to Leo's flat.

Mary woke up at midnight, almost on the dot. It began with a whine that woke them both, and they lay there, breath held and listening, as though they'd been disturbed by the sound of glass smashing downstairs. Except all ears were trained on the baby monitor, which sat, still and silent, a plastic instrument of torture. She whinged again and the monitor's warning lights described a green arc. She whinged again, louder, and the green lights became red lights, and then she was wide awake and screaming and Bea's hands went to her face as she moaned the long, slow moan of a woman cursed never to rest.

'Leave her,' said Charlie, uselessly. 'Maybe she'll go off again. You know what your mother says . . .'

But the volume and pitch of the crying cancelled out parental advice. Bea threw back the covers, 'She's maybe hot,' unfolding her legs from the bed. 'Perhaps I'll put a lighter blanket on.'

She moved into the hall and Charlie closed his eyes, daring to believe that a new blanket would do the trick, have the desired effect and Mary would sleep the four hours until her next feed – that they could all sleep the four hours until her next feed.

'Charlie,' called Bea from next door.

He pulled himself from the bed and zombie-walked to Mary's room: the Moses-basket-on-a-stand they'd bought from Babies R Us, the polka-dot wallpaper, teddies on every available surface. Bea had her back to him, facing Mary on the changing-table.

'She's woken up soaking. I need wet wipes. There's a packet in the kitchen. Can you go and get them for me?'

He headed downstairs, resisting the impulse to check an eBay auction, went back up with the wet wipes where Mary was still crying and Bea was changing her, trying to calm her at the same time. 'It's okay, it's okay, my baby, Daddy's coming with the wet wipes. I'm sorry you were wet, baby. We'll just get you dry and then you can have sleeps . . .'

And Charlie allowed himself to dare believe that they'd get Mary dry and then they'd all have sleeps.

But she didn't quieten. They swaddled her and put her back down and still the monitor lights were red, and Charlie couldn't see it, but he felt Bea wrestling with the desire to go straight back in there; knew she'd also be fighting the guilt she felt about putting the baby into her own room so soon. And Mary kept crying, until once more they were driven from their beds to next door, where the tiny scrap – that little smudge – had fought herself out of her swaddling, and lay there red-faced and bawling. Bea picked her up and she didn't quieten. They checked the room thermometer and argued about the reading. They tried winding her. They gave her Infacol. They argued about whether a dummy might work. They offered her boob, and water, and would gladly have offered to sacrifice a cat if they thought it would send her to sleep. They tried rocking her, and cooing, and putting her down while a CD of gentle wave noises played in her room, then hoovering, because a book had said that sometimes helped. But the book had lied, so it was a stupid book. And then they tried bickering again, and then full-scale arguing, because surely not everything Charlie suggested was rubbish? *I mean, come on. Surely it's worth trying the dummy?* Then Bea tried sobbing, and Charlie switched to placating and hugging, until it was 2 a.m., and, as if in the middle of a battlefield, Bea grasped Charlie by the shoulders, saying, 'You've got to take her.'

*Oh, Christ, post-natal depression*, he thought. A future of hysterical outbursts flashed before his tired eyes: of Bea accidentally going to the supermarket in her nightclothes, trying to kill herself with an overdose of Calpol.

'Take her in the car,' she pleaded. 'That'll settle her. She always sleeps in the car. Just so she can get a bit of sleep. And just . . .' Charlie could see the defeat in her eyes – her shame that her limit had finally been reached '. . . so I can get some sleep.'

So he took Mary, grateful for something to do, distraught to leave the comfort of home and the promise of bed, thin though that promise was. He pulled a zip-up over his pyjama top, left the bottoms on, looked at his hair in the mirror and decided not to bother. He laced on a pair of trainers and, dressed as if he'd just discharged himself against Matron's wishes, he placed Mary in the baby seat of the Peugeot (still

feeling suddenly awake – charged, even. '*Fuck, yes.*'

He should have gone all the way round the roundabout and headed for home. Instead he took the slip-road for the M25, because suddenly he needed to see Leo's flat one more time.

The motorway was empty, a ghost road. Forty minutes after leaving home – an all-time best – he pulled up outside Leo's flat and let out a long sigh. Status: Mary still asleep; the street deserted and silent. Opening his door as quietly as possible he got out on to the pavement and gazed through the rear passenger window at his sleeping daughter. She looked angelic: a little puff of golden hair already going curly (and God knows where she'd got that from: neither Charlie nor Bea had curls), tiny mouth pouted slightly and moving almost imperceptibly. As he watched she shifted and he caught his breath – *please-please don't wake up* – but her head moved to the other side, one tiny fist flexing a little, as though she dreamed of grasping something, and she stayed asleep. He glanced behind at the flat, then back at Mary. There was no way he could leave her here. Taking her in meant removing her from the warmth and comfort of the car and into a fire-damaged midden, but still – he couldn't risk leaving her; what he was doing was dumb enough without making it worse. So, he opened the door with the care of a bomb-disposal expert, unplugging the baby seat, each plastic click sounding like a mortar attack. Baby seat out and on the tarmac (Mary status: fast asleep), he reached in and found her blanket, which he draped over her, doing his best to tuck it in. Then he closed the door and went to the boot where – oh, thank you, sweet Jesus – was the present he had laughed about when Bea's mother gave it to them for Christmas. Yellow plastic box. Black writing that said *Emergency Kit*. Contents, one first-aid box, one cellophane-wrapped blanket, one collapsible warning triangle and tonight's star prize: a torch. A tiny torch, sure, and testing it the beam was truly pathetic – a statutory-requirement light at best, but a torch all the same. Thank the Lord for Bea's mum.

Thank Him, also, for Dave Rogan's key, which Charlie used to open the flat. Feeling like a burglar, he looked guiltily around, then picked up the baby seat, switched on the torch and let himself in.

Christ, the air in here must be bad for Mary. The damp. The dead, smoky, toxic air. Cold, too. He felt the chill through his pyjama bottoms and went to Mary, rearranging the blanket around her for maximum warmth. Now, wanting to make it quick, to get out of there and return his baby to the good place, he went to the middle of the living room, where the scorched chair sat, and shone his torch at the stereo.

I'd save Mary, he thought. The first thing I'd save from a burning flat would be Mary. Well, Mary and Bea. But assuming Bea wasn't out cold and could find her own way to safety, it'd be Mary.

What would you save, Leo? Don't answer that, I already know, you told me. Your one-thing-I'd-save-from-a-burning-flat was this: the Nad stereo.

Which was still there.

Well, that was what you always said, anyway. And it would have figured in the top five, for sure, even if in the (ha-ha) heat of the moment you'd decided to leave it in favour of the irreplaceable signed copy of *Swordfishtrombones*, which you'd had framed and which hung on the wall.

Also still there.

As a matter of fact, that whole alcove, filled with stereo, vinyl and Waits souvenirs – the Royal Albert Hall programme, for God's sake – was practically undisturbed. Moist, of course. Blackened, yes. But otherwise not touched.

So? What? He took nothing?

You're Leo. You're pissed. You've dropped a spliff and, presumably, walked away without knowing it. You've gone for a crap.

Charlie made his way through a small hallway where there was a bedroom in the minimalist, mattress-on-floor style, plus the bathroom, a tiny affair with a dwarf-sized bath, basin, toilet, all in pea-green. The toilet lid was up. Charlie peered in, shining the torch downwards. Sure enough, there was a bed of wet tissue in the pan, thankfully hiding whatever horrors lurked in the waters beneath. He toed down the lid and flushed away Leo's final crap. 'Don't mention it, mate,' he murmured, turning and leaving.

Right. So, no doubt, your relaxing crap was interrupted by the smell of burning coming from your living room, so you wipe, stand, waddle a couple of feet, then pull up your trousers and exit the bathroom (leaving the toilet for your brother to flush some time in the future).

You hurry through to the living room and – *whoosh*! Your armchair's burning. What next?

To the kitchen. Charlie checked on Mary and walked through. Like everywhere else it was dark, smelly, smoky, the windows sooty. He opened the fridge door, had a moment of weirdness at the lack of internal light, no humming sound. Just the fridge and the odd bit of food going mouldy and one lonely tin of lager. But opening the fridge is not what you'd do if your armchair was on fire, is it? No.

Shining the torch around the kitchen Charlie caught sight of something on the floor. Of course. The washing-up bowl. Your chair's on fire, what do you do? You fill a washing-up bowl with water. One load. Splash. Then back for a second.

But your chair was manufactured some time in the 1970s, when it was practically the law to make chairs using mankind's most flammable materials. Same goes for your carpet, and they're going up like a dog – woof! – and there's nothing you can do about it. The fire's moving more quickly than you and a washing-up bowl can possibly cope with.

Charlie walked back to the living room, trying to think like his brother. The room was silent. Just the sound of him and, he realised, his daughter breathing. Which stopped him in his tracks. Should he be able to hear her breathing like that? Was she breathing too hard? Was that a rattle in her chest? The wet, the cold – what if she got asthma? Did you 'get' asthma, or did it come in the same pack as the rest of your genes? He wasn't sure. Plus she'd been in the car seat all this time. He'd forgotten about that. How long were they supposed to sit in car seats before they got a hunchback or some lifelong curvature of the spine?

So, what then, Leo? You've got to get out, right? And you're suddenly faced with the kind of decision that only a few unlucky people ever have to make. You, and celebrities answering questions in Sunday supplement questionnaires: what are you going to save from your burning flat?

Charlie swung the torch round the room. Street-lamps pushed measly slices of light through the gaps in the window boardings, bisecting the room. He cast the torchlight over to the corner of the room where the television stood.

Okay, the TV. Why was Leo's chair facing the television?

Never was a piece of furniture more unloved. It sat there in the corner, out-of-date and shunned. It had a brown cabinet – *a brown cabinet* – although it was slightly charcoal now, of course, but still, that was how old it was; the video hardly more modern, not a Betamax, but that kind of era. May even have been top-loading.

He went across to the TV and video unit, noticing for the first time that it was slightly skew-whiff in the corner. It had been moved at some point; he could see from little indents in the carpet. As far as Charlie knew, firemen didn't rush into burning flats and look for sockets to plug stuff into, so the only person who would have moved it was Leo. Something behind it, then?

Charlie knelt down, peering round the back of the television.

The first thing that struck him was how few leads Leo had back there, certainly compared to CharlieVille, where a mini-mountain of cable seemed constantly on the verge of achieving full sentience, taking over the entire house, going on the rampage and swallowing Bentham whole.

The second thing that struck him was that there was a video-camera back there. It seemed to be lodged on top of the video-recorder shelf of the cabinet, where it had been merci-fully protected from the firemen's deluge. Some kind of connecting cable led from it to the back of the video.

'Yes,' hissed Charlie. Again, that almost electric surge. '*Yes*,' he repeated, reaching for the camera. He couldn't quite get to it. He stood and moved the TV unit some more.

Behind him, Mary snuffled. 'Just a minute, baby, just a second.' He glanced towards the seat where she slept. And she slept. Wasn't this some kind of record? Almost a shame Bea wasn't there to witness it.

On the other hand, what if there was something poisonous in the room that was making her sleep? Some kind of chemical released by the Bay City Rollers-era carpet? Harmless to adults but like Agent Orange to tiny, vulnerable baby girls.

'Just a moment, baby. Daddy's almost finished.'

Placing the torch down he brought the camera to him. The lead sprouted from a 'video out' socket. He got down on his stomach and stuck his head into the well behind the TV, using the torch to track the cable from the camera to the rear of the video-recorder, confirming what he was already beginning to suspect.

*Yes.* Again, yes. The jack went into an 'aux in' socket.

Which meant – he scrambled out from behind the TV and round to the front of the unit – that Leo had been making a copy of whatever was on the camera. That was why his chair faced the TV. He wasn't watching it – not the telly, anyway. He'd been watching whatever was on the camera. Charlie crouched down to the video. No, it wasn't a top-loader, it was the postbox type. He pushed his hand in. Empty.

That was what you took, wasn't it? The thing you saved from your burning flat. The copy you'd made.

Charlie looked behind him. Leo must have given up on dousing the chair. The fire would have been getting too strong. Instead he'd scooted over here. The obvious thing to do was take the camera, but the camera was out of reach behind the telly. Maybe it had been on top of the TV and fallen down the back. So Leo had ejected the copy and taken that instead. And the copy had burned in his car.

But the original?

Charlie turned the camera over in his hands, finding the eject button. *Chunk.* The casing seemed to divide in half and there was the tape. Leo had even written on it: 'Land original'. Charlie closed the tape door, found the flip screen, clicked it open, then hunted for the on/off switch. He switched it on. The bleep sounded like Krakatoa in the room, and the tiny monitor lit up, all systems go. He turned the camera over, looking for the play button, pushed it. It whirred mechanically, engaging the tape. Charlie realised that his breath was held. There was a battery icon in the corner of the screen and he winced – it was red: no little power bars. It was so on-its-last-legs that it had a strike-through line across it and it was flashing, just in case you hadn't got the message that the battery was low.

Any second now it would shut off. Any second.

'Okay,' said Leo, from the camera, and hearing his brother's voice floored Charlie for a moment. 'We're here on, uh, Crosby Street and the time is, uh, seven twenty-four p.m.'

The screen showed Byron Land was walking along a pavement on a street much like Candle Street. It looked as though he was being filmed from a car, parked on the opposite side of the road, because now he drew level and, blissfully unaware that he was under surveillance, walked past, the camera following him. The frame adjusted and improved as Leo moved the camera, less concerned about being seen now that Byron had his back to him, able to focus on the woman Byron approached, who was walking in the opposite direction. They both had their eyes fixed on something else, and there was a moment of surprise as they saw one another. They stopped, two or three feet apart.

And the tiny red battery icon flashed furiously. The camera bleeped angrily at the outrage and shut off.

Charlie stared at the empty screen, still shocked by hearing

Leo; his brother's voice had come at him like a baseball bat out of the dark.

At the same time he was trying to process what he'd seen. Several things. The first was that Charlie had recognised the woman Byron Land had been meeting. It was the woman from the graveyard. The long, greying hair. The high cheekbones. She was even wearing the same clothes she'd had on the other night: a shawl, peat brown and threadbare, jeans, plimsolls. Definitely her. Charlie had also noticed that Byron Land had been walking a dog, a Spinone, and the tape had a time code. Charlie hadn't had time to assimilate the exact date, but he'd seen that it was in May. And Charles Laughton had gone missing in June. Which meant either that Leo was some kind of psychic, or finding her missing dog hadn't been the only job Leo was doing for Mrs Land.

That was it, wasn't it? Jane Land had told Charlie a big fat lie, and that was why the dates didn't tally. Leo had been spying on Byron Land because Jane Land thought he was having an affair. And, by the look of things, he was.

Charlie slung the camera over his shoulder, grabbed the baby seat and let himself out of the flat.

# The Stupid Thing, Part Three

It was 3.10 a.m. Mary still slept. He checked his phone. No messages, no missed calls. He imagined – no, he hoped and prayed – that Bea was still asleep; that the only thing that could possibly wake her was Mary, and Mary was with him. He allowed himself to believe he was working in free time, dead time – time she wouldn't notice gone.

'One more thing, baby,' he said to his sleeping child. 'Then we'll get you home. Promise.'

He clicked the car seat into the back of the Peugeot, then let himself in. The camera – its secrets hidden by the flat battery – he stowed in the glove compartment. Behind the wheel he took a deep breath of oxygen that felt heavy in his desperate-to-rest lungs, then keyed the ignition. Next stop the office. Leo's burgled office. He checked Mary, checked his phone. It was still dead time.

Minutes later, and he was pulling up to the kerb outside the office building. Check Mary, check the phone. Out of the car and unclip her seat, speaking to her all the time, 'Not long now, baby, not long now,' because the books said babies slept more soundly if they could hear the voices of their parents. It was a subliminal, instinctive, pack-like thing. They felt safe and protected. Silence meant danger. Maybe the books were right for once: perhaps the constant movement and talking were keeping Mary asleep for what was proving to be a marathon session. Must mention it to Bea.

Then again, maybe not.

He let himself into the building, up the stairs and into Leo's office. Terry had started to tidy it, then left, claiming he had another job to go to, and that he'd finish next time, 'if that is amenable to you, sir'. It had the whiff of a scam, but at the time Charlie couldn't be bothered to challenge him so he'd left it. Consequently the office had a schizophrenic half-messy feel about it. He walked in and set Mary down, able to work by the glow from the street-lights. Now, moving quickly, he traced the computer's power leads to source and yanked out the plugs, brought them above decks to gather up, placing the keyboard on top of the monitor, then gazed at the whole set-up, looking from that to Mary, still sleeping.

That was a lot of stuff he needed to carry. Okay. Better get on with it. He grabbed the car seat and deposited it outside the office door, then returned for the computer. Christ, there was a lot of it. His Mac at home was pocket-size by comparison. This one had a huge screen, big as a portable TV, plus a separate CPU and keyboard. Charlie placed the screen on the CPU, the keyboard on the screen, gathered up the cables as best he could and hefted it from the desk, managing – just – to carry it from the office and into the corridor.

Outside the office door he placed the computer on the floor, caught his breath and turned to lock the office – not that that seemed to make any bloody difference. He took up the car seat and moved it along the corridor to the top of the stairs, then went back for the computer. Abandoning the idea of carrying it, he hunkered down, scooped it to him and dragged it along the corridor to the stairs, trying doggedly to keep it all together.

Which was why he didn't see the policeman standing in the hallway, watching this strange, determined, beetle-like thing moving towards him. A thing so engrossed in the effort of moving that it didn't even realise it had company until the policeman switched on his torch.

Charlie stopped, turned and looked up, dazzled and panting, at the policeman, who said, 'Nice jim-jams, mate.'

# The Stupid Thing, Part Four

It was 4.22 a.m. and Charlie thought that if he didn't sleep soon he'd die. Detective Inspector Merle returned to the interview room and said, 'Right, I've had a word with the desk sergeant and you're free to go. We're not even going to caution you for wasting our time.'

Charlie looked at him, tried to suppress a wave of anger and found he was only half successful. 'Sorry? You caution *me* for wasting *your* time. Look, I was visiting *my* office. My office that I'd entered using *my* keys, and I was taking *my* computer, only to find myself in the back of a police car and sitting here for the last hour. Exactly whose time has been wasted?'

Indignation wasn't a good look for Charlie. Mary had woken up. And how. She'd started screaming in the police car, then continued screaming in the reception area at the station.

Now she slept again, only pacified by Charlie's finger in her mouth, the car seat on the desk between him and Merle. A couple of minutes ago he'd tried to remove the finger but she'd started crying again, so now he sat attempting to occupy the moral high ground in his pyjamas, with his finger in a sleeping baby's mouth.

He hated her being there. It was that that angered him – more than being arrested on suspicion of a crime he wasn't committing, more than having to endure endless comments about his pyjamas, more than having his sleep delayed while they contacted Merle to verify his story and get him released – having his baby contaminated by this room, where rapists and killers had told their stories, where cold-eyed child molesters claimed they'd been led on, where PCs looked the other way.

Merle nodded slowly. 'Mm, I can see why you might be angry. There you were, a man who lives about an hour's drive away, just casually dressed in your pyjamas – as one does – deciding to remove a computer from an office in the early hours of the morning. Complete with sleeping infant. Oh, and carrying nothing that could really be described as proper identification. Now, why would anyone be suspicious of that kind of behaviour? Stupid us. We really do leap to the most ridiculous conclusions, don't we? Not to mention, of course, that you yourself had reported a burglary at that very office earlier the same day. Sorry, the previous day. So, before you get all I-know-my-rights about being asked to explain yourself, why don't you, um, explain yourself?' He smiled, leaning forward. 'Come on, Mr Watson, I'm all ears.'

'Look,' said Charlie, 'we've just had a baby. You keep odd hours when you've got a newborn. I was driving to get her to sleep. It was as good a time as any.'

'To do what?'

'To collect the computer.'

'For what?'

'I'm sorry?'

'What was wrong with the computer where it was?'

'I want to check it at my leisure. At home. As you say, I live some way away.'

'And why do you want to check it?'

'I should have thought that was obvious. Leo was my brother. Checking his computer is like going through his stuff, isn't it? It's what you do when you – when your brother dies.'

'Is it?'

'Yes.'

'Okay, I can accept that. I can even accept that you needed to do it in the early hours of the morning and in your pyjamas, which are very nice, by the way. Thank God you don't sleep naked, eh?'

Charlie bridled. 'Right. Well, now that's straight, I'll get on my law-abiding way, shall I?'

He stood up, ready to go.

'The thing is,' interrupted Merle, 'while I can accept all that, I need a big pinch of salt to do so.'

Charlie sat back down.

'Because whichever way you look at it – and, sure, you can give me all that stuff about keeping strange hours and it might look reasonable on paper – but in the here and now, when I've been woken up at gone three in the morning, and you're sitting there in your PJs, it looks awfully strange. It looks like you're behaving in a very suspicious and furtive manner. Do you understand?'

'Yes,' said Charlie uncertainly.

'Good. Because what I have here is a little bit of thread. By itself, it's just a little bit of thread. But now I want to start pulling it. What am I going to unwind?'

Charlie stared at him. Merle smiled back. There was a long pause.

'I think . . .' started Charlie, then stopped. *There was something on that camera.* Leo had been doing more than just searching for a missing dog. If Charlie's guess was right, Leo had already been on the Land payroll when the dog went missing, already had a case to solve. And correct him if he was wrong, but it sure as hell looked like Leo had been asked to keep an eye on Mr Land. Who by? That would be Mrs Land, then.

Even so, none of it amounted to anything worth telling Merle. Not yet, at least.

'Listen, he'd been burgled. I wanted to make sure that if they struck again, they wouldn't get the computer. That's all.'

Merle seemed to have located something stuck in his teeth. A bit of peanut, perhaps. His mouth stretched as his tongue hunted it out. 'You think that the burglary's suspicious, do you?'

'Aren't all burglaries suspicious?'

'Don't piss about. You know what I mean.'

'All right. Well, it is a bit odd, yes.'

'I had a look into it,' he said. 'Your late brother's office wasn't the only one broken into that night. In fact, all three offices on that floor were burgled.'

'Oh.' But Charlie was thinking. 'They could have done that for a reason,' he said. 'To draw attention away from Leo.'

'Maybe. Did they take anything from your brother's?'

'No.'

'Was there anything to take?'

'No, I don't think so.'

'Look, Charlie,' said Merle. He seemed to have dislodged whatever it was in his teeth that had been bothering him. 'Do you know how many fires are caused by stoners?' Charlie shook his head no. 'Lots. Lots and lots. They fall asleep. They go shopping and forget they've left some chips on. And it's a sad fact of life that people get into cars when they're wasted and have accidents. And it's an equally sad fact of life that offices – especially offices in places like Kilburn – are burgled all of the time. I'm sorry, Mr Watson, but these things happen.'

Was that it? wondered Charlie, as Merle spoke. Was it just the case that these things happen?

They gave him and Mary a lift back to the Peugeot and he retrieved the computer and put it in the boot, furiously rubbing exhaustion from his eyes before setting off for the M25 and home, finally getting there at just gone 5.30 a.m., when he silently unclipped Mary's car seat, took her to her room, swaddled her and, gently, as if she was an unexploded bomb, placed her in her crib. Not daring to breathe he closed her door and tore off his denim jacket, just his pyjamas beneath, and then, with the stealth of a Ninja, crept into bed. For a second he felt something that was as close to pure bliss as he'd ever felt. His baby asleep next door. His wife slumbering beside him. As he drifted, at last, to sleep . . .

The monitor burst into life as Mary awoke. Starving hungry. Bea stirred. And a new day began.

# Tesco and Other Journeys

Charlie sipped a cup of tea, his hand shaking slightly.

'I'm worried about her breathing,' whispered Bea, Mary asleep on her lap. 'Listen.'

He was standing in the doorway of the lounge. They listened as Mary's tiny breath seemed to rattle in her chest. Guiltily he wondered if last night's (or, rather, this morning's) trip had anything to do with the definite (bronchial?) wheeze they could both hear.

'I'm sure it's nothing,' he said weakly.

Bea looked doubtful and they gazed at Mary whose mouth moved, tongue lolling to the front. They both thought they might die of love.

'Perhaps we should take her to the doctor,' said Bea, and Charlie tried to seem accommodating even though what he thought was, *God, please, no, not the doctor again.*

'Okay, Bea,' he said. 'Let's keep an eye on it.' Then, 'Look, would you be okay for a moment or so? I've got to check eBay.'

He let himself into his office and fired up the Mac.

'Why haven't you got a PC?' his mate Victor had asked him once.

'Because I like Macs best,' he'd said in reply, smiling what he hoped was an enigmatic, you-could-never-understand smile.

'You say you like them best because you're a ponce,' said Victor. 'They're expensive. A designers' machine. Culty. Media people and creatives have them – the rest have them because they want to be media people and creatives and it's the nearest they can get.'

He'd said it seemingly without malice, as though he was stating a simple fact, rather than voicing an opinion that ate into Charlie's entire sense of self-worth. Charlie's enigmatic smile had remained stitched on to his face, a queasy shadow of its former self.

Charlie answered some emails. A request for a quote – wedding, of course. An assurance that the CD of 'First And Last And Always' by the Sisters of Mercy would be sent out the next day (total profit: seven pounds. Wa-hey). Then he wrote an email to Philippa Shaw, thanking her for a great tribute to Leo the other night and apologising for his bad behaviour, which, he assured her, was an aberration: he didn't usually punch DJs while screaming 'Donna Summer'. He wasn't really himself at the moment. He sent it.

Next he went to the car and fetched in the camera, checked it over to confirm that – yes – he definitely needed a charger, then searched eBay. There was one for sale, of course – everything was for sale on eBay. Even better, this seller had included a Buy It Now option, so Charlie could hurdle the bidding and get the charger double-quick. He clicked to buy, then paid, asking the seller to despatch the charger today, adding a little white lie about an imminent holiday to speed things up. He hid the camera beneath his desk and returned to the lounge, where Mary had been installed in a tiny bouncy chair from Mothercare, one with an arch of toys, a tinny electronic kiddy-tune playing.

'Babe?' he said.

Bea was half asleep, her dressing-gown in disarray around her. She'd been lying watching Mary. Just watching her. 'Yuh,' she murmured.

'Do we need anything from Tesco?'

'Yeah, loads. Are you going to go?'

'I thought I could, yes,' he replied. 'Unless you fancied a trip out?'

She pulled herself up to sitting, rubbed her eyes. 'I can't. Got loads of washing to do, and I've got to do some expressing for bottles.'

Which was a bad-weather warning for Charlie. Expressing meant bottles he would have to give to Mary in the early hours of the morning. Expressing meant seeing his wife's breast sucked into a strange shape via what looked like a transparent plastic air-horn. 'Okay,' he said, trying not to blanch visibly. 'Is there a list?'

'On the fridge. Oh, and can you make sure the nappies are Tesco's own? They're the only ones that fit.'

He grabbed the list, marvelling, as he often did, at his wife's capacity to store all this stuff: to remember to write lists and know what brand of nappies to buy; feeding times and the number of millilitres needed for each bottle; bedding, and what creams to use where, and what gripe-water was, when to wind and which teat on which bottle worked best. What he felt in those moments was an intense pride, and love, and a crushing sense of inadequacy. He stuffed the list into his pocket and left for the car.

At the end of the road he should have turned left for Tesco, but instead he turned right. For Victor.

Victor was a mate because he, too, was a DJ and he, too, did weddings. Charlie liked to think of himself as different from Victor because Cheesy Vinyl was a concept, an idea, because Cheesy Vinyl had been in *Time Out* once and because he had played Brixton Academy. But, really, there was no difference between the two, which was why they were able to help each other out with bookings occasionally, recommend each other, that kind of thing.

Victor answered the door wearing a Pink Floyd T-shirt and a pair of jogging bottoms that, Charlie guessed, had never jogged further than the fridge and back.

'What are you doing here?' he said, pushing hands through Castrol GTX hair. 'It's early.'

'Sorry,' said Charlie. Then, 'Actually, it's not that early.'

'Well, it is for me. I had a gig last night. Working men's.'

'Oh yeah? How'd it go?'

Victor turned and Charlie followed him down the hall to the kitchen. 'Pretty shit, all told,' said Victor, 'but there were no fights, at least, although I almost decked a guest.'

'Really?'

'No, not really, but he was one of those types – you know? The sort who looks down his nose at you because you're playing Doctor and the Medics and not Basement Jaxx or something. He's coming up to me asking for such-and-such a white label like he thinks I'm some kind of idiot, like he thinks I don't even know what a white label is. But no, "Sorry, mate" – you have to be polite, don't you? – "I don't have any white labels. I know what white labels *are*, thanks, because I was going clubbing when you were still eating your own shit, but I have *CDs*, and they're full of tunes that everybody else but you likes to hear at engagement parties. Because this is not Pacha or Peach, this is the engagement of Julie to Arthur we're celebrating here, and Julie's parents have paid a lot of money not to hear the hardcore mix of the Prodigy's latest single. They want to hear 'A Little Bit Of Monica', the theme tune to *Friends*, 'I've Had the Time of My Life' from the Flashdance soundtrack, 'Wonderful Tonight' by Eric Clapton. Now, I know I'm going to get a reaction from every single one of those tracks if I play it because – let's make no bones about it – *that* is what I do. I make people at weddings happy. *That* is my job. And you, Mr Mixmag –" not you, Charlie, the guy at the party I'm talking about – "fine, you sneer all you want, but I'm a wedding DJ and proud of it. I'm proud that when two people have the best day of their lives I'm there to provide the soundtrack. It's not about the money. It's about that special feeling. About making people happy. These famous DJs, they get thousands of pounds for a sunrise set on Bondi Beach and that. But can Paul Oakenfold lead the hokey-cokey? Could Fatboy Slim help locate the owner of a brown Daihatsu at eleven o'clock at night?" '

'We're in the entertainment business,' agreed Charlie.

'Absolutely right. Cup of coffee?'

Victor worked in IT.

'No thanks, mate.'

Victor made himself one, chatting as he did so, then turned and said, 'Listen, I was very sorry to hear about your brother. Very sorry indeed. If you need any help with bookings . . .'

'Thanks,' said Charlie. 'I should be okay. I haven't got a lot on, anyway.'

'I've been waiting for an opportune moment to give you my commiserations. In our line of business, wasn't he? An entertainer?'

'Yeah, he was,' and Charlie reflected that, yeah, Leo was. All of Charlie's talk about being in the entertainment business, and so was Leo. Only Leo got to be Tom Waits, and he probably didn't even own a Bon Jovi record.

'Well, it's doubly sad to lose one of our own,' said Victor, shaking his mane sadly. 'Anything I can do to help, just ask.'

'There is something you can do to help, actually.'

'Oh? I mean, Oh. Great. Fire away.' He looked concerned.

'It's his computer . . .'

'Ah.' Victor held up his hands, like, *say no more*.

'The thing is, it looks like it's had a load of stuff wiped, and I know, obviously, that it's not "Goodnight, Vienna" when it gets wiped. I mean, that's how they got Gary Glitter and stuff, isn't it? You can get stuff out of the cache, can't you?'

Victor nodded, pro face on. 'That's one way of doing it, yes.'

'Would you take a gander at it?'

'Of course. Not a *problemo*. Bring it round.'

'Actually, it's in the car.'

'Right,' said Victor. 'Well, let's bring her in.'

The pair of them got it out of the Peugeot's boot and sat it on the sofa in Victor's front room, where they stood looking down on it. Once it had been cream, now it was brown. Once it had been a proud lion at the cutting edge of technology, now it was so out of date it made Victor's sofa look hip.

'Looks fairly straightforward. And what is it you're hoping I can find?' said Victor.

'Dunno. Anything, really. Emails especially.'

He was remembering Leo's advert in the *Chronicle*. No phone number: just an email address.

'All right,' said Victor. 'Leave it with me.'

'Uh . . .' Charlie grinned sheepishly. 'When do you think you might get round to it?'

Victor chuckled. 'Tell you what, I'll have a look today. How does that sound?'

'Brilliant. Cheers, mate. Really appreciate this.'

And Charlie was already moving out, saying his goodbyes and walking to the Peugeot, where he pulled out his mobile.

Thank God she'd given him her number. Thank God he didn't need to race down the A40 again. He dialled Chariot.

'Hello?'

'Hi, is that Chariot?'

'It's Sapphire, Charlie. Only your brother got to call me Chariot.'

'Sorry. Ah, Sapphire.' He pictured her, then screwed up his eyes to chase away the image. Bad image. 'Can you talk?'

'Not really. I work in a mobile-phone shop. We're not supposed to talk on the phone.'

'Sorry. Sorry. Very quickly, then. Well, first, thanks very much for the other night. I really, really appreciate what you did for me.'

'You're more than welcome. Was everything all right at home?'

'Oh, yes, of course. Fine, thanks. Fine. Um, you mentioned, the other day, that Leo had picked up a case from his advert in our local paper.'

'Yes.'

'Do you know what it was?'

'Um . . .'

'Was it a missing dog?'

'Oh, no. It definitely wasn't a missing dog. Missing husband, I think.'

He felt a thrill, hand tightening on the phone. 'How do you mean?'

'I mean playing away, being unfaithful. It was a cheating husband. More than that I couldn't say.'

'Right,' he said. Thinking, *And that cheating husband wouldn't be Byron Land by any chance, would it?* 'Thank you.'

'Why do you ask?'

'Ahm. Well, I'm not sure. It's just that I thought one thing and now it's turned out to be another. I'm just trying to, you know, piece together what Leo was doing when he died.'

'Great. Well, listen, if I can be any help, just shout, y'hear? Let me know how you're getting on.'

'Thanks,' he said. 'Thanks. I will. Definitely.'

He punched out of the call, felt galvanised. Next stop Tesco.

Which smelt of baking, and Charlie realised he hadn't eaten for what felt like days, so he added a batch of Krispy Kreme doughnuts to the trolley, then saw how much they cost and looked left and right before returning them. He made sure he bought Tesco's own-brand nappies, paid a girl who gazed right through him, as if he didn't even exist, and drove home. Mission Accomplished.

A red flat-bed Toyota truck was parked in the street. As he drew the Peugeot to the kerb Charlie glanced inside, but the man with the flourescent jacket wasn't in it. Then, as he retrieved his shopping from the boot and made for home, he saw him. Same guy, same jacket. He was standing at Charlie's front door.

A sharp dart of unease. Charlie quickened his pace, arriving at the house as his front door closed and the man with the fluorescent jacket turned away.

'Can I help you?' said Charlie, hoping he sounded more commanding than he felt, the shopping bags having an unhelpful, emasculating effect.

The man smiled. But a bad smile, mocking and insolent. A pub-car-park, broken-Becks-bottle smile. 'You're all right, mate,' he said. 'Just having a natter with your missus. Nothing important, like.' And he made to go past. Then, 'Oh, congratulations, by the way.'

'On what?'

'On the kiddie. Little girl, isn't it?'

Charlie looked at him.

'Can't say I envy you, mate. Must be a worry, eh?'

Then he was off down the pavement, heading for the Toyota, sauntering, looking back at Charlie and grinning as he opened the door and stepped inside.

'Who was that guy?' said Charlie, in the house.

'Oh, some contractor. For the council, I think.'

'Did he say he was from the council?'

'Um, I'm not sure. It was something about trees. They're going to be doing some tree-lopping, so he was telling everybody on the street.'

'And that was what he wanted?'

'Yes. That was all he said. Why?'

'I dunno. He seemed . . . Did he ask about Mary at all?'

'No. He talked about trees, Charlie, why?'

'He mentioned her. Outside. Why would he do that?'

'Probably saw the pushchair in the hall. Probably just being polite and passing the time of day.'

'Yeah,' agreed Charlie, 'That was probably it.' And it was another of those explanations that sounded good, but not if you were there. Not if you had the evidence of your gut to back you up. That pub-car-park smile. *Must be a worry, eh?*

He unpacked the shopping, then looked out of the front window, straining to see the red flat-bed Toyota truck. Still there. He needed to go upstairs to see whether it had an occupant, and it did. Not much house-to-house visiting going on there.

# How Clare Grogan Dates You

Later, they both smelled the cigarette smoke at the same time. Charlie sighed, pulled himself out of the sofa.

'Hello, mate,' he said to Pete, who stood outside his front door, smoking. Charlie closed his own front door behind him.

'Hello, lad,' said Pete.

Pete wasn't what you'd call the life and soul. He carried the constant demeanour of a man who had always been expecting disappointment, and had not been disappointed. Off-white hair topped a life-weary, lined face that wore a permanent expression of tired resignation. All Charlie knew of him was that he used to work for a company that made hinges, and had been there all of his working life, and when he retired, the lads in the factory thought it would be great fun to buy him a blow-up sex doll as a leaving present. He was married to a woman called the missus, who did a lot of gardening and some volunteer work; he disliked the usual *Daily Mail* roll-call of minorities and managed to introduce this prejudice into almost every conversation, no matter how fleeting or mundane; and he smoked – but because the missus didn't like him smoking in the house, he did it outside his front door, and because his house was joined to theirs, the smoke travelled somehow into the Watsons' hallway, where it entered Bea's nose and could, if she was in a bad mood, turn her into Lizzie Borden.

'Your missus tells me your old man's buried in that grave-yard that got vandalised,' said Pete.

'Yeah, mate, yeah,' said Charlie, shaking his head sadly, toeing a little pebble with his trainer, then kicking it off the pathway on to the pavement. He wondered how Pete saw him and Bea. As strangers, probably. Londoners who'd left the city and moved here to make use of the good transport links, in the process helping to push property prices out of Pete's reach so that if he and Mrs Pete wanted to move they couldn't, while also filling the streets with God-awful four-by-fours. Just such a couple lived on the other side of Charlie and Bea. They were Gareth and Francesca, and they'd got married after Gareth went down on one knee and proposed to Francesca in a hot-air balloon in Africa. As with Pete's prejudices, this was something Gareth managed to introduce into most conversa-tions. They both worked in the City, drove to the station in separate cars. They left the house each morning with car keys in their mouths, jackets half on, briefcases under their arms and always, but always, muttering into mobile phones tucked into their necks.

'Your dad lived round here, then?' asked Pete, perhaps revising his opinion of Charlie and Bea.

*Lived around here, worked around here, medicated himself to death around here*, thought Charlie, but said, 'Yes, he did live round here. We all did. This is where I grew up.'

'Right. Right.' Pete nodded slowly, gazing out over the street, his eyes seeming to fall on Charlie's Cheesy Vinyl van.

'The van okay there?' said Charlie.

'Yeah. Yeah.'

'I mean, it's not spoiling your view or . . . You would say if . . .'

'Yeah, yeah. Course.'

'Because, you know, obviously, as neighbours, we all have to . . .'

'Did you go up there?'

'Sorry?'

'To the graveyard?'

'Oh, yeah, I did.'

'Was it bad?'

'Oh, you know, it was pretty bad. Thankfully, Dad's grave wasn't really damaged. Just one of those pots a bit dented. There were others a lot worse.'

'Saw it on the news.' He blew smoke. 'Little bastards. Ought to be dragged out into the street and shot. They know who it is, you know, the Old Bill do. Should round the lot of 'em up, put 'em up against a wall.'

'Hmm,' said Charlie, hoping to sound noncommittal. Part of him agreed, another part thought didn't want to open a can of worms by saying so. It would be 'do-gooders' next. After that, gays and lesbians. He had a feeling that shooting would be too good for the lot of them.

He glanced up and down the street, looking for the red flat-bed Toyota truck. No sign of it.

'Have you been in all day today, Pete?' he asked.

'Yes, lad. Spent a bit of time in the garden. Drove the missus up to Age Concern. Apart from that, yeah, why?'

'Did you have a bloke come to the door about tree-lopping? Guy wearing a fluorescent waistcoat?'

'Can't say I did. Not planning on hacking them down, are they?'

'Don't know,' said Charlie, distracted. 'I was wondering myself. Bea spoke to him but he didn't seem to give her much detail. Just that they were planning on doing some work.'

'Well, she's got more important things to worry about, I expect,' said Pete.

'Yeah,' said Charlie, thinking about worry, and how it was beginning to dig a trench in his stomach, settling in there. Of course the guy hadn't been house-to-house, he'd only visited Charlie's.

Pete reached forward and stubbed his cigarette out on his front wall, which was studded with black circles from fags past. He dropped the butt into a plant-pot, shooting Charlie a look that said Mrs Pete might have a thing or two to say about him dumping fag butts in plant-pots. Charlie didn't see much of Mrs Pete, but she was the sort who always had a weed in her hand: just spotted, immediately rooted out.

'Right,' Pete was saying, 'best get back in. That telly won't watch itself.'

'Oh. Just a moment, Pete.' Now was his chance.

'Yes, lad.'

'Um . . . I was wondering . . .'

'Yes, lad?'

'Do you know anything about the Land family?'

Pete sniffed a bad-smell sniff. 'The Land Associates lot?'

'Yes. Them.'

'What about them?'

'Just, I don't know, who are they? What do they do?'

Pete thought. 'Well, Aubrey Land was the head Land there. He was mayor for a time, and when he wasn't mayor he was leader of the Tories, or chairman of the Rotary Club or chief Freemason or whatever it is that type gets up to. One of those blokes every time you opened the paper there was another picture of him. Always opening carnivals, his big face in the paper every bloody week.'

'You didn't like him?'

'Didn't like seeing his gob over breakfast every week. That's why I stopped getting the paper. Bloody rag. Got to give him his due, though. He started Land Associates. I remember when it opened. Titchy place where Twynham's newsagent is now. Just got bigger and bigger. Christ knows, must be worth a fortune.'

'I reckon,' agreed Charlie. 'What about his son?'

'Byron Land?'

'Yes.'

'Waste of space, from what I hear. Took over the business but does eff-all. Aubrey had a right-hand man that basically runs it. The kid's just a puppet. Although he probably thinks of himself as being a figurehead, knowing him.'

Charlie smiled inwardly at the description of Byron Land as a kid. The right-hand man had to be Timson. Charlie thought of him in Byron Land's office, relaxed and watchful, and Byron with his glasses and haunted visage, trying and failing to appear calm behind his desk. He wondered if Aubrey had secretly preferred Timson. Perhaps not so secretly.

'Did you tell him?' said Bea, when he'd let himself back into the house.

'Kind of,' he said.

'You didn't, did you?'

'Look, he's our neighbour. You can't just steam right in

234

there. We'll be ostracised by the community. Mary will grow up friendless and alone.'

'So what did you say, then?'

'I . . . Well, I'm playing the long game. I sowed the seeds to tell him another time. It's a two-stage operation.'

'I trust you. Thousands wouldn't. Oh, Victor rang. Wants you to ring him back.'

'Did he say what he wanted?'

'No. Just for you to call him back. Booking, maybe?'

'Let's hope so.'

'Fingers crossed, babe.'

He left Bea in the lounge and went to find the cordless, dialling Victor and ducking into his study at the same time.

'Hey, Victor,' he said, when it was answered.

'Tell me something,' said Victor, who liked to think of himself as too left-field for pleasantries, 'why have you got me looking through your brother's computer, and why has somebody tried to wipe everything off it?'

Charlie sat down hard in his office chair. 'So they have?' His elbows went to the desk.

'Well, yeah, they have,' replied Victor.

'And did they do a good job?'

'Nope. They just hit delete. A lot of stuff's still there – if you know how to look, which I do.'

'So, not done by a professional?' *Maybe done by Leo, then.*

'I wouldn't say so, no.'

'And what did you find?'

'A lot of gibberish. Most of the retrieved stuff comes up as gobbledegook. I could dig deeper . . .'

'Any movie files?' Charlie was thinking of the camera. Had Leo transferred footage to his PC?

'Didn't find anything like that – what sort of movie files are you expecting to see, then?'

'Steady – not what you're thinking. What about emails?'

'Yeah, I was coming to that. Got almost all his emails.'

'Really? Could you forward them to me?'

'Consider it done. But, first, what's all this about?'

'Dunno yet. Can I tell you later?'

He ended the call feeling a rush of something that was two parts jubilation, three parts fear.

It felt good. It felt like being alive.

*Ping.* An email arrived and he clicked to it, but it was from eBay, the seller of the battery charger telling him it had been despatched. The rush feeling intensified. There was something on that camera, he knew it.

Then, *ping*.

And his email window was suddenly busy. 'Fetching 120 mails,' it informed him as they started to arrive, all forwarded from Leo's machine. They were junk, spam. Junk-spam and spam-junk. Some from Sapphire Desai – Chariot. Then more junk and spam – offers of Viagra and GREAT stock options – then, among the deluge, one from Jland101.

Jland101. Jane Land. Surely. It was a Hotmail address and Charlie clicked into it:

*Dear Mr Watson, I saw your advertisement in the Chronicle and there is a private and sensitive matter I wish to discuss with you. I wonder if you could call me at your earliest convenience on the mobile number below? Please verify you are speaking to me, Jane Land, before identifying yourself. I need hardly tell you I require the utmost discretion. Many thanks.*

Below that a mobile number.

Charlie's heart was racing, his mind doing dodgems. *A private and sensitive matter.*

He checked when the email was sent: 18 May. Yessiree, Bob, it was sent *before* the dog disappeared. That settled it: Mrs Jane Land was wearing the horns.

Charlie exhaled, thinking, Lying cow. She'd seen Leo's advert, all right, but not the third one, the first.

'Bea,' he called softly, over his shoulder. There was no reply, just the sound of the TV – it worked overtime, these days.

He pushed back his chair and went to the lounge, glancing in at the kitchen on his way. While he'd been talking to Victor and checking his brother's emails, she'd done the dishes. Now, though, she lay dozing in front of the television, the baby monitor silent on the coffee-table. Status: mother and baby asleep. On the TV a couple were debating whether to buy a Bugaboo pushchair, or one that was seven hundred pounds cheaper. 'I'm sorry, but it's the Bugaboo or nothing,' squawked an over-accessorised woman.

'Bea,' he repeated, even more quietly, just to check she was asleep. Satisfied, he returned to his study, picked up the cordless, dialled.

'Mrs Land,' he said, when she answered.

'Yes?'

'It's Charlie Watson.'

'Ah, hello.'

'I'm sorry to bother you again but . . .'

'Yes?'

'There was something else, wasn't there? Something other than the dog that Leo was looking into for you?'

'I don't know what you mean.'

'You contacted him prior to Charles Laughton's disappearance, Mrs Land.' Instinctively he'd lowered his voice. 'I've got access to Leo's records.' He cleared his throat. 'His emails.'

'I see.'

'And I wondered about that private and sensitive matter you'd asked him to look into.'

Her voice was taut. 'What about it?'

Heart thumping, he said, 'Could we meet, perhaps?'

'I really don't think so. I've already said everything I've got to say . . .'

'I may have some evidence. Something you may be interested in.'

She lowered her voice. 'Okay, yes. When?'

'Tonight?'

'Yes, I can see you tonight.'

'Bea,' he said. 'Bea?'

On TV the couple had opted for the less expensive push-chair. Not much of a programme if they didn't take the financial experts' advice, guessed Charlie. As soon as the cameras stopped rolling they probably dumped the Mothercare model and snapped up a Bugaboo anyway; told their dinner guests what 'fun' it had all been.

'Bea?' he repeated, and she stirred, opened her eyes and checked the monitor.

'Everything all right?' she asked.

'Yes, fine. She's asleep still.'

'Good.'

'And guess what?'

'What? Oh, Victor?'

'Yeah. Came through.'

She beamed. 'Excellent.'

'Yeah, he's in a fix. Birthday party at the Conservative Club.'

'Great,' she said. But her smile was tired and lonely.

A short while later he was carrying his record cases from the hall to the van, having to go through the charade of preparing for a gig.

'Have you got your box of gags?' said Bea from the doorway of the lounge.

'Yes, thanks,' he replied, barely able to look at her for guilt.

'And you've got "Happy Birthday" in your box?'

'Check.'

'The Altered Images version or the Stevie Wonder version?'

'Both. Just in case.'

'Well done.' She laughed. 'How old is the birthday boy?'

'Er. God. Forty, I think.'

'Hm, forty. Could be Stevie or the Altered Images. Tell you what, best stick with the Stevie Wonder version unless he seems like a particularly young forty.'

'Good advice, Bea.'

'You'd be lost without me.'

'I would. I would.'

'Are you all set, then?'

'Yeah, I think. Pretty much.'

'Then come and get a hug. Free while stocks last.'

He moved over to her, and they cuddled. 'I'm so proud of you,' she said into his shoulder, nuzzling, 'my hunter-gatherer.'

'I'm proud of you, too, Bea,' he said, feeling like scum.

# A Calippo, Some Racist Abuse . . .
## Oh, and Twenty Embassy

Years and years ago it had been an Esso garage, and Charlie remembered that attendants used to come out and serve the petrol and his mother had said, 'Could you fill it up, please?' And the person using the pump either dispensed the petrol as if the people in the car did not exist, staring off into the distance, or chatted to his mum through the window or, sometimes, grinned at Charlie in the back seat, tapped on the window, made funny faces at him.

Now it was a BP. And nobody came out to your car any more, but you could withdraw money from the cash machine, or buy a cup of coffee that was inexplicably described as gourmet, or choose from a selection of magazines all with Jennifer Ellison on the cover, or buy a muffin, or a Will Young album. Or, of course, get your car washed.

Only you couldn't. Not tonight. The car wash was closed for repair, and they were very sorry for any inconvenience that might cause. It would have been annoying if Charlie had driven on to the forecourt hoping for a wash 'n' wax, but he hadn't. He was due to meet Jane Land, and she'd told him she'd be parked in the bays by the car wash.

There was just one vehicle there, a Land Rover Discovery. In it Jane Land, once again in running gear.

She nodded. The passenger window slid down with a purr that must have cost, and she leaned over the seats to speak to him. 'You'd better hop in,' she said. There was an expensive clunk as the central locking disengaged. He climbed up and used a moment of silence to marvel at how high the Land Rover seemed. No wonder these things were so popular with the status classes. You could look down on everyone – literally.

There was a scent in the car, familiar.

Beside him, Jane Land stared straight ahead.

'Thanks for seeing me,' he said at last.

'I couldn't not, really, could I, as you seem to have cottoned on to my little secret?'

'I'm not trying to pry,' he said. 'It really came about as a result of . . .' He paused, thinking, then added, 'Looking through my brother's records.'

'I see. And this evidence you referred to?'

'Yeah,' he improvised, 'it may be something or it may be nothing. If it's something then I promise you'll be the first to know about it, but for the time being I need to clear up a few details.'

A group of kids sauntered on to the forecourt. Three lads and two girls. The usual assortment of caps, bare chests, polyester-wear from JD Sports and jewellery off the Shopping Channel. Two of the lads held tins of lager. All of them were talking loudly, one louder than the others, telling them to piss off as they laughed at her, probably at something she'd said or done. A joyless, overloud, look-at-us and we-don't-give-a-fuck laugh. Charlie wondered if kids like that ever got over themselves. If they ever simply became bored of being repellent, or forgot about it.

'Okay,' said Jane Land, from beside him. 'What do you want to know?'

'Right. First, what exactly was Leo investigating for you?'

'Don't you know?'

'You suspected your husband of having an affair?'

'Yes. Present tense. I *suspect* him of having an affair.'

'Okay. Do you have your suspicions who it might be?' He was thinking of the woman in the snippet of tape he'd seen. The graveyard woman.

'No. I have no idea. All I can say is, I hope she knows what she's taken on, whoever she is.'

'Why?'

'God, where do you start? He's a confused person, Mr Watson. For years he lived in fear of his father, who was a thoroughly vile man, and I think the trauma of his childhood and early adult life has remained with him. They're like part of his DNA that he can't escape. He's troubled, Mr Watson. Very troubled.'

'Troubled? And how does that manifest itself?'

'My husband relies on prescribed drugs. Prozac, Seroxtat, whatever. I suspect he may also be dependent on illegal drugs. One, at least – cocaine.'

'Okay. What makes you think that?'

'I've found residues.'

'Right,' said Charlie.

A Volvo drove on to the forecourt and pulled up at a pump. The driver had got out before remembering his petrol cap was on the other side. He slapped his forehead theatrically – for the benefit of those watching, really –

then got back in to manoeuvre the car. There was a sudden explosion of shouting as the kids came out of the shop having stocked up on crisps and Calippo lollies and having, no doubt, made the cashier's life hell. 'Paki!' one shouted and they dissolved into fits. Funny word, that: Paki. Charlie glanced at the man on the other side of the Mini-Mart window – an Indian guy, who watched the gang leave with an unreadable expression.

'Okay, what makes you think he's having an affair?'

'His behaviour mainly. Recently – I should say about three months ago – he began going out in the evenings a lot. Almost nightly. As I told you the other day, he would take Charles Laughton for long walks.'

'And that was unusual?'

'Any exercise Charles Laughton had was running with me.' She indicated her clothes and Charlie processed an image of her jogging, faithful Spinone by her side, as in a tampon commercial. 'Never with Byron,' she continued. 'Then, suddenly, he was taking him out every night, including the one Charles Laughton disappeared.'

The kids had made their way to the edge of the forecourt, to the pavement, still shouting and screaming, two of the lads having a play-fight as one tried to dig his knuckles into the head of the other. 'Fuck off. Fuck off.' Even in the costly, climate-controlled and hermetically sealed environment of the Land Rover he could hear them. Their voices bounced around the forecourt canopy, the acoustics tinny, dehumanising. He wondered if these were the kids who had stamped on his father's grave. Maybe. Maybe not.

'Was there anything else?' he asked Jane Land, dragging himself back to the matter at hand.

'He was making phone calls. Many more than usual.'

'You overheard?'

'No. He spent a lot of time in his study. What he was doing in there, I've no idea. I should say a mixture of avoiding me and knocking back whatever sedatives he'd managed to lay his hands on.'

'So how did you know he was making phone calls? Presumably he could have been doing anything.'

'Our house is slightly too big to physically walk the distance when you need to speak to someone at the other end of it, Mr Watson, so on the occasions I couldn't avoid having to converse with my husband, I called his mobile. In the last few months it was often engaged.'

'And the land line?'

'I think he just used his mobile. If you were having an affair, wouldn't you?'

'Yes,' he agreed. 'I suppose I would.'

Then something caught his eye. Hers, too. The group of kids. One second shouting and trying to knuckle one another, the next gone. Almost as though someone had lobbed a hand grenade into their midst, they had darted off in five different directions. Something they'd seen. Something that had scared them. And scared them more than a mum or dad, who probably didn't give a shit what they did anyway; much more than a policeman or two for a bit of verbal sparring and maybe even a dramatic arrest. It was something that had *really* scared them.

A red flat-bed Toyota truck drew into the forecourt, upturned wheelbarrow in the back, like the fin of a shark.

Charlie froze: found he wanted to push himself back in his seat so he couldn't be seen. The car-wash bays were to the rear of the petrol station, not exactly prominent. But there was his van, with Cheesy Vinyl written on it in letters big enough to read from space.

But the lettering was on the side. There was no reason the guy in the flourescent jacket would even see it unless he decided to mosey on over to the air-and-water station.

*And anyway.*

Anyway, what was Charlie scared of?

Problem: he didn't know. That was the problem. There was nothing wrong, nothing to be scared of, on paper. So how come he felt a churning in his gut every time he saw the truck and its driver? How come what he felt was fear? For himself. For Bea, and for Mary. And the way the kids had reacted, he wasn't the only one.

The Toyota's door opened and out stepped the guy in the high-visibility waistcoat. He glanced towards the car wash, seeming to clock the Land Rover. Charlie found himself shrinking into the seat. Just his luck that she'd had to back in. But it had been just a glance – perhaps a reflection off the windscreen would favour Charlie – before he was yanking the petrol pump from its holster as if it was a hostile force, then turned his back to them as he filled up.

If Jane Land sensed Charlie's unease she said nothing about it, commenting instead on the kids' sudden scram: 'What's got into them, I wonder?'

'Hmm,' said Charlie.

'Probably police they want to avoid,' she said.

There was silence in the car. Charlie watched as the high-visibility guy dispensed himself petrol. His back was still to them, eyes on the little numbers clicking round. He finished, and without looking back towards the faulty car wash, he replaced the pump and swaggered over to the Mini-Mart.

'Mrs Land?' Charlie said at last.

'Yes.'

'What are the repercussions of your husband's affair being exposed?'

'What do you mean?'

'I mean, how far would he go to stop you finding out? Or to stop it being made public?'

'I'm sure he'd do what he could. Why?'

'Up to and including threatening somebody?'

Jane Land laughed, turning to meet Charlie's serious gaze, then stopped. 'Look, no. It's an affair, Mr Watson. When I divorce him it will cost him a lot of money. A lot. I promise you that. But it's money he can afford. He'll pay it, hate me, and life will go on. It's certainly not worth risking jail over.'

Charlie looked at her. 'You said yourself that he's confused. "Troubled and traumatised", you said.'

'Well, yes,' she admitted. 'But not *that* badly. No, it's not possible.'

Charlie could see the guy in the fluorescent jacket through the window of the Mini-Mart. He was looking at the magazines, the top shelf where they were stored in plastic wrappers.

'You're sure?'

She made an exasperated sound. 'Of course. I mean, who the hell would he go to? He's a Rotarian, Mr Watson. He used to be a councillor. For the Conservative Party. He just doesn't know the kind of people you might ask to do something like that.'

'Okay,' agreed Charlie, thinking, *Really? Is that right? So where does he get his drugs from, then?*

## No Ordinary Vauxhall Corsa

Joe Parks inspected the photo he'd taken on his phone – the photo he'd just taken of the bloke and Mrs Land at the petrol station. Tell you one thing, he was glad he'd decided to go for the multimedia phone now. Who knew it was going to come in so handy?

Now, though, he had things to do. He had an evening to spend on Joe Parks stuff before the night went black and he went to work. So, he paid for his petrol, calling the cashier a Paki under his breath, loud enough for him to hear it, not loud enough so anyone else could, and returned to the truck, glancing at the Land Rover as he got back into the Toyota. Grinning to himself, he performed an unnecessary wheelspin pulling out of the forecourt. It was a nice wheelspin. Nice and noisy. But nothing like the spins he could do in Betty.

Betty had pride of place near the bins in the quadrant of his block. No fucker dared mess with her because she belonged to Joe Parks, and if they touched her – if they so much as laid a finger on her – he'd kill them, no doubt.

She was a Corsa, but no ordinary Corsa. He'd modified the engine with a J&R induction kit and fitted seventeen-inch

BSA chrome-alloy wheels. He'd decluttered the body by junking the factory badges and door strips so it was nice and smooth. He'd gone with low, low suspension springs, added a wide arch kit, a silver metal flake paint job, installed racing seats and harnesses, changed the numberplates into a difficult-to-read font, had 'Betty' painted on the nose along-side a decal of a big-chested bird with long legs, ripped out the rear parcel shelf and installed a completely new ICE system, whose crowning glory was a thousand-watt active sub that could actually make your chest rattle when it was playing, and lots, lots more little modifications, including some plastic fingers that poked out of the boot so it looked like someone was stuck in there.

And what he liked to do in Betty was drive around, be seen. He hardly ever used her for business. That would taint her. He didn't even like carrying passengers in Betty. But what he did like was the looks. He liked the looks he got when he strapped himself in and drove around town with the stereo on, that stereo saying 'Here is Joe Parks' just as effectively as an air-raid siren, but an air-raid siren at impossibly low frequencies. For a while he'd had tinted windows, and at first he'd liked the feeling of privacy they gave him. He could touch himself as he drove, or make wanker signs at the pigs without them pulling him over. But the thing with tinted windows was you could see out of them but nobody could see in. And what was the point of that? Joe Parks wanted to be seen.

When he got home to his flat, he changed his jeans, fixed his hair, sprayed on some Lynx, then pulled on a T-shirt. It had an arrow printed on it that pointed to his crotch, with the words 'Ladies! Free face-cream dispenser here!' printed on it. It was his favourite T-shirt.

Next he booted up his PC and ran the cable from his phone to the USB port so he could upload his footage of Carly to the site *Porn.You.US*. The thing with *Porn.You.US* – or PYU, as its regulars knew it – was that you had to upload your own porn in order to remain a member of the community. It worked on a ratio system, downloaded to uploaded. Joe Parks clicked to the upload form and entered a description of his footage, keying, 'Unwilling teen takes it and likes it from two guys.'

Then, *Amend description*.

'Unwilling teen SLAG takes it and likes it from two guys.'

*Amend description*.

'Unwilling teen SLAG takes two cokes and likes it.'

*Amend description*.

'Unwilling teen SLAG takes two cocks and LOVES it.'

Post file.

He clicked to upload the footage of himself and Jude with Carly, so members of *Porn.You.US* could download it and even add their own comments to the thread. 'Excellent footage!' and 'Gr8 2 C a new gurl on the site!' and 'Fresh blood always appreciated. Thx!'

And Joe Parks's ratio would improve, enabling him to download even more porn. And so it went on.

Next, Joe Parks let himself out of his flat and took the stairs to the forecourt where Betty was parked. Some kids nearby watched him get into her and clip himself into the racing harness.

He started her up and blatted the accelerator. The noise was like thermo-nuclear war. He whipped her round in what was almost a handbrake turn, then, for the benefit of the lads, let rip with an ear-splitting wheelspin and tore out of the forecourt. The lads watched him go, thinking what a wanker he was.

For the next hour, Joe Parks drove round town, the stereo rumbling like an earthquake. He drove past Woolworths and slowed down for the benefit of girls in school uniform, who looked him over with a mixture of interest and contempt. As an elderly lady using a walking frame negotiated a pedestrian crossing, Joe Parks revved his engine loudly, the modified Vauxhall Corsa edging forward impatiently. And the elderly lady thought what a wanker he was.

Joe Parks drove on, keeping an eye out, because you never knew. Then, as he drove round by the leisure centre, he caught sight of a familiar profile by the railings, back to him, talking into his mobile, and he smiled, driving past and glancing in his rear-view mirror to see whether Nathan had spotted him. He hadn't. Was still talking on his phone. Out of sight, Joe Parks pulled into one of the customer spaces outside Only Kitchens and got out of the car, circling back on foot so that he'd come on Nathan from behind. He flexed his fist.

Little fucker had a ponytail.

One thing Joe Parks hated was blokes with ponytails.

# A Little Extra Oomph

'How come you were so early last night, anyway?' said Bea, smiling down at Mary in her arms. It was – Charlie checked – 5.25 a.m., and his day had begun with a yowl from next door that took the red dots of the baby monitor to meltdown. They'd both scrambled to the baby room and Mary had stared at them resentfully from her Moses-basket-on-a-stand, face puce, arms free of the swaddling and flailing angrily. Moments later they all lay in the bedroom, peace restored, Mary calm and feeding happily, her eyelids half closed, contented, sated. Phew.

Charlie's own eyes had been closing again when the question came.

'Oh,' he said. 'Yeah.' Thinking, *Damn.* He'd thought she was out of it when he got home last night, so dead to the world that he could maintain the illusion of a whole night's work. He thanked the God of Spousal Fibs that he hadn't already incriminated himself with a lie. 'Well, there was a bunch of kids in and a fight started so they shut the bar down and the party ended early.'

'Oh? Somebody take exception to "The Birdy Song"?'

'Even I don't play "The Birdy Song", Bea. Dunno what it was about. One moment a full dance-floor, the next pandemonium. I had to defend myself with my inflatable hammer.'

'It's always handy to have an inflatable weapon in case something blows up.'

He laughed. 'Quite funny, really, aren't you?'

'I have my moments.'

He looked across at the two of them. 'Bea?'

'Yuh.'

'There's something not quite right about Leo's death.'

'What do you mean?' she said carefully, eyes on him.

'There's just a few . . . inconsistencies.'

'Like?'

'Well, he was burgled.'

'Right. And?'

'It's a bit odd that he dies and then gets burgled, isn't it?'

She shrugged. 'Happens in a place like Kilburn. It's why we moved out of London. Did you tell the police?'

'Yes, I did.'

'And?'

'They said other offices in the building had been burgled, too.'

'Ah.'

'Yes.'

'So, not just Leo's, then?'

'No. I know, it's not . . . There are other things.'

'Come on, then, Inspector Morse, what other things?'

'I met his cleaner.'

'Leo had a cleaner?' The surprise jerked her nipple away from Mary's mouth and for a moment or so Mary was sucking air, one tiny hand pawing at Bea's breast before mouth and nipple were reunited.

'Yeah, he did.'

'He had a cleaner to clean his office that wasn't really an office? Are you sure the cleaner was really a cleaner and not just pretending to be one?'

Charlie laughed. 'Well, he had all the kit. And there was definite cleaning activity taking place. Anyway, Leo hadn't been going into the office. He was working from home.'

'What? Pretending to work from home? Or had he taken this case, the dog one?'

Charlie could see that Bea was only just hiding her bemusement; he knew how it sounded to her. 'I don't know, but either way, being at home's not going to help, is it? I mean, what I'm saying is, I don't think he was working from home.'

'So what was he doing?' asked Bea.

'I dunno. Avoiding his girlfriend, maybe.'

'That girl he came here with?'

'Yeah, that's the one,' he said.

'The one you were keen to speak to?'

'Well . . . yes.'

'And did you?'

'No,' he lied, 'not yet.'

'Why do you think he was trying to avoid her?'

'Well . . . he'd finished with her.'

'According to who?'

'Terry,' he fibbed.

'Right.'

'You don't find that surprising?' he asked.

'Find what surprising?'

'That Leo had finished with Chariot?'

'No. Why would I?'

'Ahm, well, didn't you think . . . I mean, didn't you think he was punching above his weight there?'

She looked across the pillows at him. '*You* obviously did.'

'Um. Well, yes. I mean, you could see. She was . . .'

'What?'

'Pretty. You know. Attractive. She was, you know, a better-looking example of a woman than Leo was a man.'

'Is that so? Is that why you're so keen to hook up with her again?'

Charlie could barely speak with his foot in his mouth. 'No. No, of course not. But . . . Didn't you think?'

'No. I thought she was okay-looking. Nothing particularly special. I thought she liked herself a lot, and I thought she gave me the skunk-eye in my own kitchen, and I can quite understand your brother dumping her, actually. What I'm struggling with is my husband describing her like she's Kilburn's answer to Kate Moss. Did you *fancy* her, Charlie?'

'No.' But the denial was too quick, too sharp, and high-pitched enough to shatter crystal. It betrayed him.

'You fancied her.'

'No. She was just . . . I thought Leo had done well for himself, that was all.'

Bea shifted Mary on her lap. '*Done well for himself?*'

Charlie could see that she was starting to get up. 'Where are you going?'

'I'm going is where I'm going. She needs changing.'

'You're in a mood.'

'Wonder why.'

'But – look –' he went to get up to follow her out of the bedroom 'what if he hadn't dumped her? What if? Or . . . or

. . . what if he'd dumped her but not because he didn't want to be with her any more. Maybe he finished with her because he thought she might be in some danger if he didn't.'

She turned in the doorway and put her free hand over Mary's ear. 'Bollocks, Charlie. What if he just dumped her because he saw the same nothing-special sort of girl the rest of the world apart from you saw, and the relationship had run its course? Try that, if you can keep it in your pants.' She turned and marched out of the bedroom.

Nice one, Charlie, he thought. Diplomatically handled.

Perhaps everything added up. He'd been knocking on the door marked 'Conspiracy' when he should have been ringing the bell of the one marked 'Dumb-ass Accident'. Maybe every clue was, in fact, a banana skin. Leo had died because he was a fuckwit who smoked too much weed; Charlie was trying to give his brother's death some greater meaning. A little dignity.

Or, worse, give his own life a bit of extra oomph; put back the excitement that seemed to have bled from it.

The battery charger turned up mid-morning. 'Package for you,' said Bea who, with her tone of voice, informed Charlie that she hadn't forgotten about their earlier conversation. No way, chum. There were a few cups of tea to fetch before that little talk became water under the bridge.

He grimaced, thanked her, and was silently grateful for his job, which sent him strange-shaped Jiffy bags on a daily basis. It meant an already-tetchy wife wouldn't quiz him about this one's contents, and he could legitimately disappear into his study, work out which jack met which plug and leave the camera to charge while he did the washing-up.

It took him two hours to do that, then the hoovering, then

some dusting, then some more hoovering because he'd forgotten that you should do the hoovering *after* you do the dusting because when you dust – especially if your pleasant suburban home is as dusty as theirs was – you tend to dislodge lumps of dust, big as Christmas-card snowflakes, that settle on the carpet. Which you then have to hoover again.

While he was doing this, Bea took care of feeding, changing and putting Mary to sleep, then set herself up with the iron in the spare room, a pile of baby clothes beside her.

And the camera charged.

He came up the stairs to hear her singing – the click-and-drag sound of the iron, her singing softly above it. For a second he felt a sense of bliss and wonder as pure and keen as coming upon a deserted tropical beach. Not 'Rocket Man' (he requested it so much that she only sang it on special occasions), but 'Love and Affection' by Joan Armatrading. Almost as good. He stood and listened, and she probably knew he was there, but neither said anything.

Why did he need more *oomph* than this?

He went into the bedroom, glanced out of the window, looking unconsciously for the Toyota truck with the upturned wheelbarrow. No sign. Was that another banana skin? A red herring? A nothing that he'd promoted to the status of something?

He went back downstairs. Closing the door to his study, he checked the video-camera. The finicky battery icon showed half full, but it wasn't like he wanted to watch *The Deer Hunter*, just whatever happened next in *When Byron Met Graveyard Woman*. He flicked open the camera's screen, found himself swallowing a dry, jagged swallow, and pressed rewind.

The tape rewound. Not far. The other night Charlie had seen only about thirty seconds of it. Now he watched again, hearing the same words from Leo: 'Okay. We're here on, uh, Crosby Street and the time is, uh, seven twenty-four p.m.' They still took his breath away.

On the tiny screen Byron Land was making his way along the pavement, Charles Laughton at his side, shiny-coated, rank with pedigree and breeding. Now here came the woman – the graveyard woman – and the two seemed to notice each other, like two people under the influence of an extra-terrestrial tractor-beam.

'Hello,' said Leo, his voice jaunty on the tape. He had every right to sound pleased with himself. How long had he been following Land? Charlie checked the time-code on the screen: 30 May. He'd been on the case for a matter of days – days spent cramped in his Fiat, no air-conditioning, suffering in the heat, following Byron Land so his wife's solicitor could hang him out to dry. Getting him on tape meant payday, didn't it?

Maybe not, because these two didn't greet each like lovers. Not even like friends. The camera hadn't picked up expressions – they were too far away – but still . . . There was coldness in their body language.

'Nice to see you, too,' said Leo sarcastically, echoing Charlie's thoughts. Charlie smiled.

A car passed. Byron Land looked into the road and for a moment the image was lost, presumably as Leo lowered the camera or withdrew into the car.

Land, who had his back to the camera, seemed to sag on seeing the woman. There was, in that moment, something intensely human about him, as though he, too, lived beneath a weight and in that second the pressure of it was too great even for him. He took off his sunglasses. The hand not hanging on to Charles Laughton's leash was at his side, palm upturned, a beseeching look about it.

Only Charles Laughton seemed unaffected by the gravity that had settled around his owner and the woman. He bounded up to her, went on to his hind legs, forelegs pawing at her as she softened visibly. Youth and light came to her face, strangers there, and she bent to take Charles Laughton's paws in her hand. Then, the greeting over, Charles Laughton panting happily at her feet, she stood and looked towards Byron Land.

She stared at him. Said nothing. Nothing Charlie could see anyway. Then Land seemed to be saying something. His arm was moving and he was stepping forward, gesticulating at a house to which her gaze was drawn, and suddenly Charlie understood. It was the house.

There was something significant about it.

Was it hers?

Either way, they had both found their way there. And now she was talking. She was shouting, in fact. Shouting with her hand held out to the house, fingers splayed as though firebolts might shoot from her fingers and set it alight, burn it from her thoughts. Land was moving towards her, trying to pacify her it looked like, wanting to hold her. And Charlie saw the human being again, recognised in Land the need to reach out and comfort. Saw himself in that movement. Land was trying to calm her down, trying to talk to her. Pleading.

'Not playing ball, is she, mate?' said Leo, on the tape. He said it thoughtfully. Whatever he was seeing had been new to him, too.

Now, on the tape, Byron Land was trying to make a peace-offering.

'Gotcha,' said Charlie, because the peace-offering was Charles Laughton. Byron Land was holding out the leash to the distressed woman. He was imploring her to take it, and she seemed to hesitate – she definitely considered it, a move that, judging from Charles Laughton, would have made all parties happy.

But no. No, she wasn't accepting the dog. Not now, any-way. She turned, waving him away and pushing aside his outstretched hand.

Perhaps Charles Laughton sensed the pair were about to go their separate ways. Having cocked a leg at a tree, he'd resumed his position at the woman's feet, but now he stood, bouncing on his front paws as though he were trying to attract her attention. As though he were saying, 'Don't go. Don't leave me with this bloke who doesn't really like me, and his stupid wife who only bought me to spite him and treats me like a cool jogging accessory. Take me with you.'

She bent to him, nuzzled him a little, straightened and said one last thing to Byron Land before she turned and walked away.

'Nice one, guys,' sighed Leo, on the tape. He sounded displeased, and Charlie could understand how he felt. Not exactly cast-iron proof of a playing-away situation there. Quite the opposite. Hardly tasty nourishment for Mrs Land's solicitor.

Still, though. Byron had been trying to give her the dog. She hadn't taken it, not on that occasion. But . . .

'You've got the dog, haven't you?' said Charlie to the

graveyard woman, as she walked away. 'He gave you the dog, didn't he? Not that night, of course, but three days later, on the Friday night.'

On the screen Byron Land watched her go. Then he turned and he, too, walked away from the house, in the opposite direction to the graveyard woman.

For a moment the screen went black as the camera was placed in Leo's lap. There was the sound of the Fiat starting up. Music began. Tom Waits, of course. The camera was picked up and Leo pointed it at his own face.

Charlie caught his breath. The goatee beard, the smile, the hair at odd angles and the heavy-lidded eyes so he always looked stoned or sleepy, whether he was or not. His dead brother stared back at him from the screen.

'Okay, Mrs Land,' said Leo, on the tape, 'since you already know who your husband is and where he lives, what say we follow his friend, yes?' He nodded the camera in reply. 'Good idea. Let's go.'

Recovering, Charlie said, 'You'd better get a move on, then, mate.'

Leo stowed the camera on the dashboard so that it was pointing forward, still filming as the Fiat pulled away from the kerb. Charlie could hear him singing along to 'Blind Love', a track off *Rain Dogs*. Note-perfect, of course. It occurred to him that Bea had always been the resident singer in his heart – her voice could do strange and liquidy things to his insides – but all that time there had been another great singer in his life. He'd just never got round to noticing properly. He said a silent sorry to his brother.

The car came to a junction.

Leo tutted. He stopped singing and Charlie heard the creak

of leather as Leo moved in his seat, presumably looking left and right.

He's lost her, thought Charlie. She got to the junction and he didn't see which way she went. Leo, you doughnut.

Then: 'Gotcha,' said Leo, on the tape, and Charlie heard the *tic-tic-tic* of an indicator, saw a car pass in the road before the Fiat pulled out, going left, turning into the road.

Which, with a shock that had him sitting upright in his seat, Charlie recognised. His exhausted brain was fighting to place it even as Leo, on the tape, said, 'Fuck.'

Yes, Charlie was thinking, leaning forward, 'fuck' was right because the street – it was . . .

He was sure of it.

It was Willow Street.

The car had stopped. Leo had picked up the camera from the dashboard – the woman forgotten – and he was aiming it at a row of houses. A row of houses on Willow Street, which was just round the corner from the house where Byron Land and the woman had just met.

The row of houses on Willow Street.

'Fuck,' said Leo again.

Because Willow Street was where Charlie and Leo had once lived, years ago. And now Leo trained his camera on one house in particular.

It was, wasn't it? The house the Watson family had lived in, all those years ago, in the early 1970s.

# 1973

'You're quite sure you don't need your lawn doing while I'm at it?' he said, sarcastically.

She looked at him over the top of her sunglasses and took a sip of soporific, sun-warmed lager. 'You can do the lawn next time you come.'

'There won't be a next time,' he said, 'if you're going to work me like a dog when I visit.'

'Ah. Well, now it's my turn. After all, it's normally *you* working *me* like a dog.'

*Double-entendre.* She licked her lips saucily. He ignored her, turning back instead to the paddling-pool. 'That's it, then,' he said.

'One more bucket,' she wheedled. 'Go on. And is it warm enough?'

'All right,' he agreed. He'd picked up his jacket and slung it over his shoulder but now he replaced it on the grass, thinking, Mow the lawn, that was a good one. The grass was parched and brittle, in a heat-induced coma. Any mower action would more than likely kill it off for good. Plus, he had a feeling the Qualcast he'd glimpsed in the shed had been one that relied not on electricity or petrol but on someone big and dumb enough to push it.

He picked up the bucket, went to the kitchen and refilled it, moving his sunglasses down his nose to gaze out at her through the kitchen window.

He would have done it, though, if she'd asked. Would have broken his back pushing the lawnmower. Would do anything for her, including packing her up in the car and taking her away. Away from this clingy, deadening town, her husband and his hardened, waxy husk of a heart. And away from . . . Yes, even away from *him*.

Soon he would. Whatever it took.

Water overflowed from the bucket so he emptied some down the sink, then carried it back outside, watching her as he crossed the dying lawn and poured it into the paddling-pool.

'That really is it now,' he said, putting the bucket down.

She looked up, one hand reaching to steady Mark, who was on the verge of falling. Tutting archly, she said, 'Well, I suppose it'll have to do.'

'That's it for today. I'll get back to work.'

'Suppose you better had,' she said, her head resting back on the sun-lounger.

He dropped to his haunches. 'You know . . .' he started.

'That you really love me?'

'Yes,' he managed, hating how she made him feel. 'You have no idea how much.'

'If you ever have a kid,' she said – he bridled, about to say something, but she continued – 'you'll know what love means. What you feel for me, it's just a dress rehearsal, a pale imitation. There's nothing I wouldn't do for Mark. Nothing.'

'There's nothing I wouldn't do for you.'

She smiled. Indulgently. 'You'd better get to work.'

Feeling flustered, frustrated, his words thrown back in his face, he stood, knees crunching as he did so. 'I'll see you, then,' he said.

'Don't take everything so seriously.' She smiled as he turned to go.

He sighed. For a second he stood there, wondering if there was anything more to say, then, having decided there was not, he left, going to the side of the house, unlatching the gate, moving through the access alley, past the dustbin and giving a quick look left and right before he went out on to the pavement, walking quickly, head down. He had been walking for a long time, a good five minutes, before he turned, retracing his steps, back along the street, to her house . . .

# The House on Willow Street

'Fuck,' said Leo for the third time.

Charlie watched his old house on the camera screen, thinking, *Is it? Is that really our old house?*

Charlie's phone started to ring, and from above he heard Bea's footsteps as she went to fetch it, answered it. 'Hello?' He heard her say, voice muffled. 'Oh, *hello*,' she said, and began to chat.

He rewound and paused the tape. A fuzzy frame. An image of washed-out green and dark brown; of brick and trees.

That was all it was – nothing special, just a terraced house. And it probably looked like every other terraced house within a hundred miles of the M25. Except it didn't, because Charlie recognised it. Even though they'd moved out when he was too small to remember much.

Moments later, he dashed up the stairs, was on their landing and hunting for what they called the loft-pushy thing – a pole with a little hook at the end.

Their old flat hadn't had a loft. Well, originally the house would have done, but the loft was home to a couple of Italian language students the whole time they'd lived there. When they'd moved to Bentham he'd decided that it was good to have your own loft. Having your own loft was one of those life-markers that meant you were getting somewhere. He'd climbed the steps and marvelled at the apparent space up there. Even wondered about getting it converted, perhaps sticking a couple of language students in it.

Now he jabbed at the hatch with the loft-pushy thing. The door dropped open and he hooked the steps, which slid down obediently. Climbing into the roof space he looked around. There was no room for language students in here any more: it was piled high with boxes full of books, records, CDs, and what he called his stock – cardboard cartons filled with action figures, tubes with rolled-up posters inside.

And it was hot. Roiling hot. Instantly, skin-prickingly so. No sooner had he stepped through the hatch than sweat was sluicing down his forehead. He was wiping it from his eyes as he clambered over a box marked Marvel Collectors' Editions, a folded-up picnic table, two suitcases that, he thought idly, were probably only good for chucking, although they wouldn't fit in the wheelie-bin, and the refuse-collectors lived up to their name by refusing to collect anything not in a wheelie-bin, so that meant a trip to the dump, and he hated going to the dump, which meant the two old suitcases would stay in the loft for the foreseeable future . . .

And there it was, the box he was searching for. The one marked 'Dad's Stuff. NEVER THROW'. A strip of curling packing tape tore away easily and he wiped the sweat from his eyes as he peeled apart the cardboard flaps to look inside. Collected in there were the last of his father's personal effects, the stuff Charlie couldn't bear to throw

266

away. It was a job he'd been left to do by himself, Leo too busy impersonating Tom Waits, their mother too happified by Prozac to care. So what was in there was Dad's stuff seen through Charlie's prism. His wallet, the one he'd carried for as long as Charlie could remember; his address book; his diaries, in them not daily entries but notes of work meetings, people's birthdays and the little notes Charlie used to leave his dad as a surprise, mostly forgetting he'd even written them until Dad got home from work and said, smiling, 'Got your note, Charlie. Made my day. I think Batman's cool, too. So does everyone else at the office'; his dad's watch, of course, the same watch Charlie used to live for winding up; the paperweight Charlie had made him at primary school, a stone with 'Dad' painted on it, which was then glazed under adult supervision; and . . . photographs. A set of photographs so precious and personal to his father that there had been no other home for them but in this box. To have placed them among the other family snaps would have been like cutting their roots.

They'd moved into Willow Street a year before Charlie was born. That was in 1969 and Charlie's only memories of the place were fuzzy, vague impressions. Shoes in the hallway. A rotary washing-line, their mother on tiptoe.

They had left in 1973. They'd moved to Evening Row, a nicer street, a bigger house. And it was there that Charlie and Leo had grown up, gone to school, sulked sullenly in bedrooms reading comics, played records on hand-me-down music centres, fought over the TV remote, played Swingball in the garden, brought girlfriends for spurious homework sessions, smoked cigarettes by the back door when Mum and Dad were out and dreamed of leaving for London, where the streets, if not paved with gold, were paved with the vinyl that was unavailable in their local record shop.

And throughout all of those years there had been the photographs. Every summer Dad would say, 'Right, it's July. You know what that means?' And they'd groan, because that was what they always did when it was photograph time. Because they'd have to troop out and stand as a tight little family unit, urging him to get on with it as he snapped away, saying, 'To your left a bit. Get in closer. Look, I need to get the house in as well and I can't do that if you're all spread out. Come on, come on, show a bit of interest.'

Year after year, the photograph of the family. Sometimes he stood them in the garden. Sometimes – if they were really unlucky – he made them go out to the front. Sometimes he'd forget, and they'd do it another month. The odd year shuffled past without anybody noticing. One year – 1982, was it? – they'd been dragged out in their pyjamas on New Year's Eve. 'Almost forgot,' said their dad, doing a theatrical phew-wipe of his forehead as they trooped back inside and to bed.

Brushing sweat from his eyes, Charlie slipped a thick wodge of photographs from their paper wallet. The different picture sizes and photographic paper used over the years gave the pile an uneven, collected-together feel, but the images were near identical. In the top one, Charlie was – what? Nineteen? He turned the picture over to read the date his father had written carefully on the reverse. Yes, nineteen. Mum, Leo, Charlie, the house.

The next one was the previous year, and so on, and so on. Charlie wiped more sweat out of his eyes and realised he was crying, too. His life in stills, year before year, a slow-moving movie in which he and his family aged in reverse. His clothes went from sober, Gap-bought Everyman wear to fashion-chasing gear to baggy sweatshirts to his charity-shop era, then his Smiths phase, complete with quiff; he could date the year he first heard *Unknown Pleasures* from the clothes and the studied, withdrawn pose; *Never Mind the Bollocks* had come into his life and he stood with the merest hint of a sneer, his hair gelled fiercely into spikes. Ill-advised beards came and went, a hard-won earring, until he was a child again, his clothes became sober and he'd insisted on holding talismanic objects for the pictures. In one he grasped a fishing-rod. In another, *Mad* magazine, a Spider-Man comic, a copy of *The Lion, the Witch and the Wardrobe*. And then he was four, and he was sitting on a beloved trike, sun-hat pulled low over his eyes, and Leo wore shorts and a T-shirt that said 'Ant Man' on it, and their mother wore huge, hooped earrings, and a short, stripy summer dress. And then he was three, and they had reverse-moved house. Now the three of them stood in front of their home in Willow Street, and Charlie caught his breath.

He knew, of course, that it would be the same house. Hardly needed to check, really. The innumerable times as a kid that he'd looked at these selfsame photographs, watching the collection grow and listening to his dad give an almost identical commentary each time. It was the house on the tape.

A drip of sweat, or possibly a tear, fell on to the photograph and Charlie used the hem of his T-shirt to wipe it away. He fell back to his haunches, the wad of photographs in his hand. Then he replaced them in the paper wallet, put it back into the box marked 'Dad's Stuff. NEVER THROW', and pulled the curling packing tape back over it to seal it.

Decades' worth of photographs showing the three of them, Mum, Leo and Charlie. Dad hadn't been in a single one.

He thought for a moment, then went to another box: '1980s TV Action Figures'. But the 1980s-TV-action-figures box had no 1980s TV action figures inside it. Despite his lofty hopes of letting them age like fine wines, they'd all been sold for quick cash. Instead the box was full of Freddy Krueger figures. Oh, and some *Nightmare before Christmas* characters. Hardly rare, the box had another quarter-century to go before it could expect fine-wine status. He scooped up a Freddy Krueger and climbed back down.

'What you doing?' asked Bea, watching him descend.

'I had a request for a Steve Austin but,' he brandished the figure, 'no Steve Austin figures left, worse luck.'

'So you thought you'd try to entice him with Jason?'

'It's Freddy Krueger, actually. And, er, no. This is for someone else. In fact, I'm going to pack it up and get it to the post office, if that's okay. See if I can get it out today for him. Is that all right?'

'Yes,' she said, drawing out the word with mock long-suffering. 'You can get me a couple of bits from Tesco while you're at it.'

'Sure, sure, whatever. Let me get this packed up. Do me a list.'

'Are you all right?' she said, seeing his face.

'Yeah,' he said, looking away. 'Touch of hayfever, I think.'

'Right.'

'Who was that on the phone?' he asked.

'Ah. It was work. They want me to go in and see them. Talk about going back – part-time.'

'Oh.' Charlie's shoulders slumped. 'You don't have to go back to work,' he said. 'I'm sure we can manage.'

'It's just a chat,' she said. 'See what the options are. You'll have to look after Mary while I'm gone, okay?'

'Sure, sure,' he said. 'Whenever.'

'It's the day after tomorrow,' she said.

'Really? Right, right.' But he wasn't paying attention.

He returned to his study, where the video-camera sat patiently on his desk, awaiting his return. It was paused. He rewound, watching them again, Byron Land and the graveyard woman.

Who was she? Why was she meeting Byron Land here, at that house, just around the corner from where we used to live?

You knew, didn't you, Leo?

*I've got something to tell you, mate.*

You knew.

# The Girl with the
## Inevitable Lower-back Tattoo

'Here.' Bea pushed a list written on the back of an envelope into his hand. It said, 'Bread × 2, sweetcorn, avocados (nice ones), pears.'

'Great,' he said, pushing it into his back pocket. He was trying to keep his hands busy so Bea wouldn't notice they shook. Ever so slightly. With excitement or apprehension, he wasn't quite sure which.

'Aren't you going to do your joke?'

He forced a smile. 'What joke?'

'Where you go, "Can't I get horrible avocados? Do they have to be nice?"'

'Oh. Sorry, yeah.'

'Just test them before you buy them.' She mimed a person testing an avocado in Tesco. 'Don't get them if they're too hard or too soft.'

'So they have to be just right?'

'You're learning, Buster. Get this one right and I may even let you loose on mushrooms.'

He picked up the Freddy Krueger figure.

'Don't you have to wrap them before you post them?' she asked.

'Oh.' He looked down at Freddy, who snarled menacingly back, one deadly glove raised. 'Oh, yeah, sure, but I'm out of bubble-wrap so I'm going to have to do it at the post office.'

''Kay. Well, don't be too long, we'll see you in a bit. Remember . . .' She repeated the avocado mime.

'What? To check my testicles?'

'Get out.'

Moments later he was pulling himself into the Peugeot, thumbing open the electric windows. He looked up and down the road searching for the red flat-bed Toyota truck.

He pulled away from the kerb, heading towards the grave-yard.

Behind him, Joe Parks started Betty. He was in his civvies today, wearing tracky bottoms and a polo shirt with the collar up. From the ashtray of Betty poked a little souvenir of the other day: Nathan's ponytail. Joe Parks hadn't been too careful when he was hacking it off. Like, you could still see some blood on it.

Charlie parked behind Tesco and made his way up to the graveyard. At the top he stood puffing slightly and wafting his shirt to get some air round him. Status: another hot day. What are we? Lizards? he thought.

Okay. The artist formerly known as Graveyard Woman. Who the hell are you? Have you got Charles Laughton? Are you now or have you ever been bedmates with Byron Land? All these questions and more circulated in his head.

The graveyard was empty – well, apart from him and a load of dead people. During his Smiths phase Charlie had hung around in graveyards, pretentious little git that he was. But graveyards don't mean anything to you when you're fifteen, try as you might. Life's too reliable then. Swallowing a grape whole won't kill you, falling up the stairs won't put you on life support.

He walked over to the monument for Aubrey and Ginny Land.

The night after the graveyard desecration Charlie had seen Byron standing there, and over the way, Graveyard Woman. They'd looked at each other. They'd had a moment.

The slime-green spray-can spore was gone, cleaned away, the Lands restored to their former glory. Charlie stood there, just as Byron Land had that night, and looked over to where Graveyard Woman had been.

She had been standing at a grave just over there.

He walked towards it.

*Here lies Mark David Slater*, it said. *Died 20 August 1973, aged seven months. Our tiny angel is above us now.*

For a long time he gazed at the inscription, then pulled out a small notebook and made a note of it.

There were flowers in a vase, a new one. Left recently, he guessed. They were still in their crinkly wrapping, a red stripe on the plastic that he recognised from his own purchase the other day. Foster's the florist. The girl with the inevitable lower-back tattoo. And if he'd come here hoping to find a clue as to how he might find Graveyard Woman – the woman who was probably Mark Slater's mother, who was somehow connected to Byron Land and now, if Charlie was right, had Charles Laughton – this was it. He turned and made his way back to the Peugeot, not noticing that, further up the hill on the maintenance clearing, a figure watched him: bare-chested, high-visibility waistcoat on the ground at his feet.

'Hi,' said Charlie to the girl with the inevitable lower-back tattoo.

'Hi,' said the florist, smiling.

'I was wondering – I've seen some flowers I liked up at the graveyard, and I was hoping you could tell me what they are.'

She looked taken aback. 'Sure,' she said. 'What did they look like?'

He made a show of checking around the shop. 'Oh, crumbs. Now I'm in here they all look the same. The flowers were definitely from here because they had your wrapping.' He gestured at a pile of cellophane squares on the counter, the red stripe running through them. He pretended to look some more, then said, 'Um, I tell you what, I saw a lady with them. I bet she comes in here all the time. She's quite distinctive. Um, she's got greyish hair. Long. I think she wears, like, a shawl.'

The assistant was nodding as he spoke. 'Yeah,' she said, 'I know her. She comes in here quite a bit, yeah, and she usually buys . . .' she moved to the opposite side of the shop, indicated a striking, purple bunch of flowers . . . the remembrance bunch. Surprised you didn't recognise them.'

'Oh, God,' said Charlie, 'couldn't see for looking. I'll take a bunch. How much are they?'

She told him and he dug for his wallet, following her to the counter. 'Does she come in here a lot, then?'

'Yeah,' said the florist. 'For her son, I think.'

'Right.' Charlie nodded. That was what he'd thought – she was Mark's mother. He added, 'The flowers I saw her place were on a grave for a little boy – a baby. He died in 1973.'

275

'Really?' The florist didn't look especially moved. 'That's . . .'

'Thirty-three years ago.'

'It's a long time, innit?'

'It's a long time to be grieving.'

The florist nodded. 'She hardly says a thing. I don't reckon I've spoken more than three words to her ever.'

'Right,' said Charlie. Then, 'Has she got a dog, do you know?'

The florist looked at him. 'Why?'

'She had one with her at the graveyard, you see,' said Charlie, levelly. 'It was a great-looking dog, real Crufts material.'

'Right. Um. She'd probably tether it outside here. It's not like she comes in talking about pets and stuff.'

'Sounds like she's not your most popular customer.'

The florist laughed, expertly lassoing the bunch and sealing the deal with a single strip of tape. 'No, it's not that. She's just . . . Oh, I don't know. It's just that it's not healthy, is it? I mean, get *on* with life, you know?'

Behind them, the door went. It opened with a musical *t-ting*. The florist glanced up. Her eyes widened and Charlie hardly needed to turn round to know who had walked in.

But he did, anyway.

For the first time he got a good look at her. And, for a moment, it seemed odd, as though somebody famous had walked in. Up close there was something less beaten about her than he'd imagined. The shawl, for example. It wasn't quite the badge of victimhood it looked from afar. Beneath it she wore a man's suit jacket, which had seen better days. Beneath that, a grey T-shirt, with jeans and plimsolls. Somehow the look suited her. Just feet away for the first time, he was able to have a guess at her age and went for early fifties.

For a moment or so she stood in the florist's doorway and stared at Charlie and the girl behind the counter, and it was as though she knew they'd been talking about her, but didn't care. She regarded them with a bored expression. There was, Charlie realised, something magnetic about her – an apartness. You might mistake it for slight hostility – the florist clearly did – but it was more than that. It was a kind of brittle weariness.

She frowned and dipped her head so that her hair fell over her face as she turned towards the bucket where the remembrance flowers were kept. Charlie shared a glance with the florist, then paid, took his flowers and went to the door. There, he paused, wanting to turn, to speak to her.

But to say what? 'Hey, you'll never guess. My brother was filming you because Mrs Land thinks you're shagging her husband. Don't suppose you could give me the definitive answer on that, could you? And while we're at it, what's the significance of that house you were meeting outside? I'm particularly interested, you see, because it's quite near where we used to live . . .'

Instead he pulled open the door – *t-ting* – and stepped outside into the remorseless sun. There, tethered outside, was Charles Laughton. Yes.

So Land had given the dog to Graveyard Woman. A present for his mistress.

With a backward glance, he got into the car. He found 'Mr Blue Sky' by ELO on a homemade CD marked 'Cheesy Vinyl Faves (Vol. 2)' (in Bea's handwriting, not his, because his own handwriting was illegible), and turned it up loud as he headed towards Tesco, his hands drumming on the steering-wheel, head nodding. As he drove, then as he was shopping, he thought about Mark Slater, Graveyard Woman, who might be his mother, Charles Laughton, Byron Land and the house on Willow Street, slotting pieces into the jigsaw, plucking them out and trying them different ways.

## Plastic-covered Book on the Parcel Shelf

'Where's the little red book?' said Bea, the next day.

'What little red book?' asked Charlie, who was holding the gatefold sleeve of *Around the World in a Day* by Prince, undecided whether to pack it in his box, because he didn't – believe it or not – have 'Raspberry Beret' on seven-inch (which was a shame, because it had a great picture sleeve) but the track did appear on *Around the World in a Day* and he'd like to include it in a set at some point, or whether to put it on eBay.

'The little red book they gave us for Mary,' said Bea.

He slid the album back into its clear protective sleeve and replaced it in the rack – that decision would have to wait until later.

'Uh,' he called, 'has it got a kind of plasticky cover?'

'That's the one.'

'On the parcel shelf of the Peugeot. Why?'

She appeared, pulling her hair into a ponytail and winding a scrunchy round it. 'Because, my love, we have to take Mary to the surgery today and get her weighed. I say "we", I'm hoping you'll be able to join us?'

'Yeah,' he said, 'Yeah, of course. That'd be great.'

'Excellent. That means you can take Mary while I have a look for something to wear to my work thing tomorrow.' She stuck out her tongue at him. 'And we can – I don't know – go for a walk or something, like normal families do.'

'That sounds great,' he said, feeling his phone buzz in his pocket and pulling it from his jeans. Bea was making her way into the kitchen and he watched her – she was wearing combats, which always had an effect on him – as he opened the phone, vaguely registered a London number and said, 'Hello?'

'Hello there, this is Sapphire Desai and I'm calling from the Carphone Warehouse.'

'Oh,' he said, 'um, actually, I'm very happy with my current contract.'

'Really? You sure I can't interest you in three million minutes of free call-time, twenty billion free texts and a new handset developed by NASA that normally retails for eight thousand quid?'

'Hello? Who is this?'

'It's Sapphire. *Chariot*, you dingbat.'

'*Oh*,' he said.

In the kitchen, Bea glanced his way, brow furrowed, like, *Everything all right?* Charlie waved that it was, making the kind of face you reserve for when telemarketers call.

He headed for the sanctuary of his study. For a second he felt guilty. Then decided he had no reason to feel guilty. Then remembered he had every reason to feel guilty.

'Hi,' he said, 'how are you?' He pushed the door behind him, casually not quite closing it but not leaving it open either.

'I'm okay, I think,' she said. 'Better than you, it seems – you sound weird.'

'Oh, it's just . . . You know,' he took a seat, 'trying to keep my head above water.'

'Any news on the Leo stuff you asked about?'

'No,' he lied, 'not really.'

'And you've fully recovered from the other night?' She chuckled.

He tried to ignore how the sound of her chuckling made him feel. 'Yeah, just about. I'm really sorry, you know, to put you to all that trouble, and for generally being annoying-drunk-bloke.'

'That's all right,' she said. 'It was nice . . . It was nice to have the company. Really nice.' There was a pause. 'It was really nice to meet you.'

He cleared his throat. 'It was good to meet you, too.'

For a moment or so, he wondered if the line had gone dead.

'Well, good, I'm glad that's out of the way,' she said. 'Um . . . The reason I was calling is because I have some of Leo's CDs. I dunno, about fifteen of them, all classics, according to him, jazz stuff he loaned me in a bid to turn me into the perfect woman. But the thing is, it's that kind of jazz that sounds like someone having a fight with a saxophone. I really, really cannot understand why anyone would even consider it music, much less want to listen to it out of choice, so, I thought . . . rather than have them sit here and get the piss taken out of them by my Moby CDs, maybe they'd be happier with someone who might appreciate them.'

As it happened, she'd described exactly how Charlie felt about jazz, and he found himself smiling. 'After all,' she added, 'he did say that no home should be without these albums. So, er . . . maybe yours is the home that shouldn't be without them.'

'Okay,' he said, 'I mean, if you're absolutely sure you can bear to part with them.'

'Oh, it'll be a wrench, I assure you.'

'Then thanks, it'll be nice to have them.'

There was another pause. 'I could send them,' she said, 'or if you're . . . I could take them into work for you to collect or . . . one evening . . .?'

'Right,' he said, forcing the word out. 'That's . . . Okay, I'm not quite sure how I'm fixed. Probably evening is best, though.' I'll phone you.

After he ended the call, he wiggled the mouse of his Mac and went into the email application. All Leo's emails were there; he'd created a separate folder called 'Leo's Mails' and dumped them in it, most still unopened. He went to that folder now. There were three – no, four, five from Sapphire Desai.

He opened the most recent one. It had been sent, he checked, two days before Leo died. 'Leo,' it said, 'please, please get in touch. Love, C, xxx'

That was all.

The next one, a similar tone. The one before that contained more detail, something about a misunderstanding over whether or not one of them liked gherkins, and was it that? She couldn't believe he'd finished with her over something as trivial as gherkins, but whatever it was, please could they talk about it?

No, Charlie couldn't believe he would have finished with her over gherkins; he couldn't believe that Leo would have finished with her at all.

He clicked the emails closed, feeling bad for having looked at them.

'Hey, you almost ready?' There was a knock-knock at his study door, which swung open. He turned. Bea stood there, hair successfully tied back. Most of it, anyway; strands fell across her face. He wasn't sure whether she let them come free of the scrunchy deliberately, but he loved them, the little escapees that seemed to frame her features.

'Yes, ready, babe,' he said, rising from his chair, kissing her.

## *Back in the* Bentham Chronicle

They waited in the surgery, then went into a room with around ten thousand other babies and their parents. All were naked, all were screaming. The babies, that was. Efficient nurses made efficient gestures, semaphoring instructions to parents, who reacted as though they had been drilled for that very moment. Everybody seemed to know what to do, except Charlie, who hung back, feeling hopelessly out of his depth, once again in awe of his wife, who flashed him an exasperated look before taking Mary to one of the weighing stations.

'How old?' said a nurse.

'Two months,' said Charlie.

'Ten weeks,' corrected Bea.

Mary was a good weight, they were told. The picture of health. Their little red book was filled in and they left, with Charlie feeling odd about the whole experience.

'That was a dystopian vision of the future,' he said to Bea when they were outside, wheeling the pushchair along the pavement.

'Did you think?'

'Didn't you?'

'No, I thought we were going to get our baby weighed so we can be certain she's not malnourished, but if you think it's indicative of a brutal, oppressive state regime, I guess there's not much I can say about that.'

'I didn't say that,' he said. 'I suppose it's just . . .'

He tailed off. Bea was laughing. 'Only you, Charlie! Suddenly going to the doctor's is a glimpse of a totalitarian future.'

He laughed. 'Yes, I know. Stupid.'

'Or . . . maybe it's not a bleak version of our collective future,' she said. 'Maybe what you're scared of is seeing your own.'

'*No*,' he said, but it sounded weak even to him.

Cars passed. On their left was the leisure centre. A group of kids by the railings were fighting over possession of a mobile phone – some message they all wanted to see. Shouts and screams.

'Ooh, he doth protest too little,' said Bea. 'You're having second thoughts about having kids, are you? 'Cos I gotta tell you, Charlie, it's a little bit on the late side for that.'

'It's adjusting, that's all it is,' said Charlie.

'Uh-oh,' said Bea. 'Told you. That article I read. Remember? You start going all weird. You're not looking at S&M on your computer, are you?'

'No, no,' he said quickly. 'It's just – don't you mourn what you had before? When it was just the two of us and we had London, and I was DJing and you were singing. Back then,' he sighed, 'it feels like I had what I wanted. I had it in the palm of my hand. I was the person I always imagined I'd be – but for five minutes. I didn't have time to sit back and enjoy it before it was all-change, you know?'

'There was quite a lot of "I" in that, Charlie.'

'Yes, yes, there was. I'm sorry.'

They walked on, in silence. He wasn't sure what he expected her to say. What *could* she say?

In the end what she said was, 'We're coming up to the high street. There's a couple of places I want to look in for outfits.' He looked blank. 'For tomorrow?'

'Oh, yes, of course.'

'Right. How about we meet in half an hour outside the card shop?'

Moments later, Charlie was wheeling Mary into the reception area of the *Bentham Chronicle*. He parked her near the fan, grateful for the air wafting across his back as he waited for a receptionist to appear.

'Sorry,' said a girl, walking through and taking a seat, a different receptionist from last time he'd been there. 'I'm trying to stay out the back whenever I can. It's cooler there. How can I help?'

She had flushed, hot cheeks. She looked behind him at Mary and made the appropriate clucking sounds. He did the relevant dad-face in return.

'It's about an obituary,' said Charlie.

'Okay.' She reached across the desk for a form.

'No, not placing one, I was hoping to look at one from years ago.'

'Depends how long,' she said. '*Chronicle*'s been going almost a century and a half. We don't have copies going back that far.'

'Nineteen seventy-three?'

'Can do.' She smiled. 'Do you know the month?'

Now he pulled his notebook from the back pocket of his jeans. Memo to self. Don't put notebook in back pocket of jeans in this weather. The pages were moist already. 'August,' he said, finding the page.

'Take a seat and I'll bring you the binder.'

She returned with it, looking even hotter than before. Charlie took it and leafed through to the first paper in July. He checked his damp pad again: Mark had died on the twentieth.

Charlie flicked to the relevant date.

'Tot Dead in Pool Tragedy'.

It was the front-page story.

'Christ,' he said.

'Everything all right?'

He gathered himself, called back, 'Yes. Yes, thanks.'

He had been seven-month-old Mark Slater. The mother was twenty-year-old Susan Slater. The father, who had been out at work at the time, was twenty-four-year-old mechanic Geoffrey Slater. They lived on Crosby Street.

Crosby Street. Of course. The house on the film where Byron and the woman had met. There was a photograph of it on the page, the same house, time-warped back to 1973, the nose of a parked Cortina visible.

Beyond their names, the story's details were sketchy. Police were trying to piece together the events surrounding the drowning, but the mother, a secretary, who had been spending her day off in the garden with her son, was too distraught to speak and currently being comforted by her husband, a car salesman.

A neighbour had been alerted to the tragedy by Mrs Slater's screams.

That neighbour had been Charlie's dad. ' "I was just about to go back to work after my lunch," said Francis Watson, an insurance broker, "when I heard this terrible commotion from the garden area. I went to see what the problem was and saw Susan by the paddling-pool. She appeared to be trying to give Mark the kiss of life and shouted at me to call for an ambulance. It's an absolutely horrific thing to happen. They are a lovely family, and perfect neighbours." '

When he spoke to the reporter from the *Chronicle*, had he been wearing the watch Charlie used to love winding up? Did he have his worn old wallet in his back pocket? Charlie had never seen his father cry. Never seen him more than mildly perturbed. How had he looked then? He imagined him drawn, grey-faced with shock, standing at the door of the house talking to the reporter.

She'd been on her day off from her job as a secretary, repeated the paper, which had gone to her employers for a quote: ' "Susan is a wonderful employee, and we're all very shocked. Our thoughts are with her and her family at this time," said Aubrey Land, chairman of Land Associates.'

Hello?

She'd worked for Land Associates. How old would Byron have been at the time? About her age? Definitely old enough to be learning the old man's trade, to be working in the Land Associates office. To be getting friendly with the staff.

How friendly? How friendly that, decades later, he'd be compelled to walk past the house where she once lived and her son had drowned? How friendly that he'd *give her his wife's dog*, for God's sake?

Charlie flicked forward to the following week's paper, and

there was another, again on the front page: 'Mother Charged With Son's Death'.

Twenty-year-old Susan Slater had been charged with criminal neglect, it said. She had appeared before magistrates and been bailed to show up at the Crown Court, bailed until . . .

Here the binder finished. He stood. 'I'm sorry,' he said, to the receptionist, 'but do you have the rest of the year anywhere?'

She looked at him, shiny-faced, the fan clearly doing little to cool her. 'You're joking.' She smiled.

'No. I'm sorry. Is it – I mean, if it's high up or heavy I can always help you down with it.'

Her smile widened. 'And that's exactly what he said, too.'

'Who?' said Charlie.

'Customer I had a while back. He wanted the nineteen seventy-three binder, the August one. I go off to the storeroom, almost fall to my death and break my back at the same time, then, like you, he wants the rest of the year.'

'Do you remember what he looked like?' said Charlie, who already knew what she was going to say.

'Yeah, sure, I do, actually.' She seemed to blush even deeper. 'He was nice-looking. Not from round here. He was about your height, had dark hair, kind of messy . . .'

'A goatee beard.' Charlie stroked his own chin, slightly unnecessarily, that being where goatee beards are usually kept.

'Yes. You know him?'

'He was my brother.'

'Was?'

'Sorry,' he said. 'I'm afraid he was killed in a car accident.'

The receptionist stared at him, mouth open. Charlie sensed the fan oscillate across his back, felt the breeze like a kiss.

'I don't know what to say,' she said at last. 'Other than . . . I'm sorry. I only met him the once, but he seemed like a nice guy. A really nice guy.'

'Well, he was, I suppose.'

'*And* he offered to help me get the binder down.' She smiled.

He nodded an of-course, checked that Mary was okay, then followed her behind the desk and into a corridor. In the storeroom, she indicated the binder. 'It's a job for a stool, really.'

'Well,' said Charlie, reaching, 'I've been called worse.'

She chuckled, taking the leatherbound book from him.

'Did he say what he was doing?' He said as they retraced their steps.

'Some research, he said.'

Charlie put the binder down and leafed forward to the date of Susan Slater's Crown Court appearance. Nothing in that edition; must have missed their deadline. He turned his attention to the following week; it had been a short trial, because by the next edition it was already over.

'Mother Jailed Over Tot Death', was the headline. Again, it was the front page. She had pleaded guilty to criminal neglect after admitting that she had drunk two tins of lager before placing the baby in a paddling-pool and then dozing. She had awoken to find Mark face down in the water. The judge in his summing-up had said that no punishment he could impose would ever be as harsh as the daily knowledge that her actions had led to the death of her child. Therefore he was going to be lenient with his sentencing. He gave her twelve years.

Twelve years.

Charlie's head dropped. How long ago was it that he'd read about a couple whose child had died? A four-month-old baby girl. The couple had given her tea instead of milk. They had never sterilised her bottles. They refused to co-operate with social services. When the child was admitted to hospital she had a fractured jaw, wrists and legs. But with no evidence to prove that they had inflicted the injuries, all they took from court was a dressing-down and community-rehabilitation orders. They walked free on unfractured legs, and the father used his unfractured wrist to punch the air with jubilation. Charlie had wished a slow death on him. He'd hoped that one day somebody would grab his wrist and yank it so hard that it broke. He'd hoped that one day when his body cried out for water someone would feed him bleach.

Susan Slater, meanwhile, had got twelve years. She was not punching the air in her picture: she looked like a woman about to serve the first twelve years of a life sentence. She looked as if she had been stamped on and left to die in the gutter.

The story was continued inside, and now he turned the page to a photograph of Susan and Mark Slater, taken in joyful times.

If there had been any doubt that Graveyard Woman and Susan Slater were one and the same, there wasn't now.

She had been pretty, thought Charlie. At that age, she looked like . . . She looked like Elsa Lanchester, he realised suddenly. It was in the eyes, the full mouth, those high cheekbones and the hair that seemed to want to frizz away from whatever was holding it in check.

What had come first? he wondered. Byron Land's interest in Susan Slater, or his interest in Elsa Lanchester?

Okay, let's think about this. They'd worked together, that

was how they met. They were having an affair. Charlie thought of the beseeching Byron Land on the tape. He loved her. But something terrible had happened that split them apart. Her son had died and, for her, there was no more Susan and Byron, there was just that – losing her son. Prison. The eternal grieving.

But not for Byron. He'd never stopped loving her. He can't see that, to her, coming back to him would be like cheating on her grief. Years pass and he tries to forget her, even gets married. But his life is passing and it's a life without the only woman he's ever loved. Does he see her one day? On her way to the florist, perhaps? And it begins again. He pleads with her. He phones her. He finds out she visits the house on Crosby Street and starts taking the dog for walks, hoping to bump into her. For crying out loud, he even gives her the dog. But still she refuses him. And he medicates himself against the pain.

So, sorry, Mrs Land, there *is* no affair, just a lonely, lovesick man, slowly killing himself.

But now the twenty-eight-million-dollar question. Did any of this involve the Watson family? Or was it just a coincidence that they were neighbours? A sheer fluke that they should move out the same year.

He put a shaking hand to his forehead, closed the binder and slid off the stool. What had Leo uncovered? Come on, come on.

'Everything all right?' said the receptionist, watching him.

'Yes, thank you. Yes.' Thinking. 'One last thing . . .'

'Yes?'

'My brother. Was he looking at anything else while he was here? Was there anything else he asked about?'

She thought. 'Yes, there was one thing.'

'Yes?'

'He wanted to see an advert for a car dealership.'

'Really? Do you remember which?'

'I will if I see it.' She reached for a recent copy of the paper and flicked through. 'Got it,' she said after a moment or so. 'It was Slater's of Rickmansworth.'

'Right,' said Charlie, slowly, trying not to show the charge of excitement he felt. 'You wouldn't happen to know who owns it, would you?'

Her face darkened. 'Yes, he comes in here quite a lot. Especially if there's been a problem with the ad. Geoff Slater.'

As in Geoffrey Slater, who in 1973 had been a twenty-four-year-old mechanic. The bereaved father of Mark.

Charlie had Leo's next move.


With ten minutes to spare before he met Bea outside the card shop, Charlie left the *Chronicle* office, gave a *Big Issue* saleswoman the last of his change and found a bench by the war memorial. He parked Mary and pulled out his mobile.

Somebody had written 'Jenni suck cock' on the bench in black marker-pen, he noticed. Good for you, he thought. Well done. Future generations can now enjoy the fact that Jenni suck cock . . . 'Hello, could I speak to Detective Inspector Merle, please?'

'Might be out,' said a bored receptionist. 'Want his voice-mail?'

'Yes, okay, that's great, th—' But the bored receptionist had transferred him, disappearing to brighten someone else's day, and he was listening to Merle's voicemail greeting.

'Mr Merle,' he said, when it had finished, 'it's Charlie

Watson, Leo Watson's brother. I know we've sort of had this chat before about Leo's death, and, um, the last thing I want you to think is that I've got an overactive imagination, and I appreciate everything you've said about the cause of death, but it's just that I've found out that – well, you remember the missing dog? That wasn't Leo's only case. He was doing – I don't know what you'd call it – an unfaithful-husband case. And there's, kind of, other stuff as well. Um. It's all a bit . . . well, nothing kind of quite *gels*. I was wondering – perhaps if you could return my call? I'd really like to talk it over, and . . . sorry if you think I'm being a pest.'

He ended the call.

## Freddy Krueger, Bastard Son of a Thousand Maniacs

As they put Mary to bed that afternoon, Charlie glanced at his watch. 'Listen,' he said, 'there's a bloke at the golf club who's been wanting me to come and see him about a possible booking. He wants to meet me face to face so . . . I've already left it a bit too long, actually, and I think I might get off there now, if that's okay?'

'Really? Bloke at the golf club? What sort of do are they planning on having up there? Aren't they all about fifties nights and stuff like that?'

'Yeah, yeah, I think, but . . . I don't know, really.'

She looked at him for a long time before she said, 'Charlie, what was Freddy doing in the car?'

Christ, of course. Krueger was in the boot. He'd been in the boot since Charlie tossed him in yesterday. When it came to folding up the pushchair and popping it in the back of the Peugeot, Charlie had winced inwardly at the sight of Krueger, one menacing gloved arm raised. He didn't think she'd noticed . . . but, well, he was wrong about that.

'Oh,' he said, faltering, 'I got down there and realised I'd forgotten the bloke's address.'

'Right,' she said, nodding. 'Just surprised to see him, that's all.'

They kissed and said goodbye, and Charlie left, thanking his lucky stars she'd fallen for it.

Knowing, of course, that she hadn't.

It had turned out that Slater's of Ricksmansworth were regular advertisers. The flushed receptionist had pointed out an advert to him, with a line-drawing map showing the dealership 'conveniently opposite Rickmansworth station!', and it was there that he headed, making the journey in under ten minutes, just one possible speed-camera infraction. He'd have to wait and see about that.

Slater's was a Ford garage, a big set-up that swept round a turn in the road, all tall glass and gleaming cars – with the exception of the old, blue and not-very-clean Peugeot that Charlie steered on to the forecourt and parked. He checked his watch. Had to make this quick.

A kid with glossy, spiky hair approached him, looking pointedly at the Peugeot. He had a thin face, was only just out of school. He clapped his hands together as he approached, like an old pro. 'Can I help you at all, sir?' He glanced at the Peugeot again, as if it was quite obvious that Charlie needed a lot of help, and if he had any say in the matter, it was going to be the kind of help that Charlie needed finance to pay for.

'Actually,' said Charlie, 'I was hoping to speak to Mr Slater. Is he around?'

Warning klaxons sounded in the kid's head. Like, Uh-oh, we got a complaint. 'Can I say what it's regarding, sir?' he said, his smile firming a touch.

'Is he in or not?'

'I'll need to know what it's regarding first, sir.'

'It's a personal matter.'

The kid looked at him, no smile at all now. 'Then can I say who's asking?'

'Yes, my name's Watson. Charlie Watson.'

'Okay,' said the kid. 'If you'd like to wait there, I'll see if he's in.'

He was. A minute or so later a man emerged from behind glass, came walking across the forecourt to where Charlie stood.

Like the rest of the world Geoffrey Slater seemed hot, but he wore a double-breasted suit anyway, buttoned over shirt and tie. He walked with his hands in his pockets, trying to be casual, making sure Charlie knew he was being carefully appraised as he strolled up. His greying hair was cut short, his chin bounced slightly as he walked, and his eyes were hard and watchful. As he came closer Charlie saw a Rotary Club badge pinned to his tie, just below the knot. Other details: a tiny fragment of tattoo that only just protruded from beneath his shirt collar, otherwise buttoned tightly – to hide the tattoo, probably – and ears that bore puncture marks from earrings past.

Geoffrey Slater stopped opposite him, his face relaxing into folds. 'What can I do for you, Mr Watson?' he said – growled it, really.

Charlie wasn't sure what he'd expected of Slater. A smaller, more bruised person, perhaps. All he knew was it wasn't this. Slater looked like a man whom life had at first viewed with indifference, then changed its mind. What was Mark to him? A forgotten setback?

'You're Geoffrey Slater,' said Charlie, 'the owner?'

'I am, yes. But I gather you're not here about cars.' The eyes were unmoving.

'You used to live at Crosby Street, number twenty-one?'

Geoffrey Slater glanced behind him. He reached and wiped a film of sweat from his forehead, glanced at his hand as if expecting to see something there, before thrusting it back into his pocket. Charlie felt a drop of perspiration run down his own face, as though in response.

'Why would you want to know that?' asked Slater.

'My name's . . .'

'Watson, yeah.'

'And we used to live in the next road.'

Slater leaned forward so that his stomach was almost touching Charlie's. Even though he wore jeans and T-shirt, and Slater was in a double-breasted suit and a tattoo-hiding collar, Charlie felt by far the warmest, the sweat now running freely down his temples.

'Bully for you,' Slater said.

'I was wondering – hoping, actually – if you might re-member something about that period.'

Slater looked away, smiling. The tattoo folded into itself momentarily on his neck. 'You know,' he said, 'you're the second *Watson* wanting to know about my previous where-abouts, did you know that?'

'Ah. My brother Leo,' said Charlie. 'Did he come to visit you? A month or so ago?'

'He did indeed.'

Charlie swallowed. This wasn't right. Leo had come to see him about Mark – *about the death of his son* – and Slater was smiling like he'd just been given a free burger and fries. 'I wondered if you could tell me – what did he come to see you about?'

Geoffrey Slater rocked back on his heels. 'Oh, he had a lot of questions.' He gazed across the forecourt. 'Wanted a lot of answers.'

'What did you tell him?'

He turned his head back to Charlie. The smile remained. 'Why don't you ask your brother?'

'I can't. He's dead.'

And at last the smile faltered, the eyes narrowed. 'Really? What happened?'

'Car accident.' Charlie watched Slater's face carefully. 'But there was something he was looking into before he died. Which is what I want to ask you about.'

'What was it?' said Slater.

'Don't you know? Didn't he tell you when he came?'

'Don't fuck with me, boy.'

That was nice. Long time since anyone had called Charlie a boy.

Slater looked left and right, checking there were no customers, before he spat, grinding the spit into the tarmac with a polished shoe. 'Listen,' he said. 'Anything I wanted to say to you lot I already said to your brother. If he went and died, well, that's your tough shit. But I'm done answering questions about things that happened over thirty years ago. There ain't nothing in it for me. There ain't nothing in it for you. Go home, watch TV, walk the dog, whatever. Just do it away from here. And take that fucking horrible old banger off my forecourt while you're at it. You're making the place look a mess.'

Charlie nodded slowly. 'Sure, sure. Fair enough. The thing

299

is, though, Mr Slater, there's an awful lot of weird stuff going on. Stuff I can't make head or tail of. I was trying to make sense of it all and I was hoping you could help me. I suppose,' here he gave a theatrical sigh, 'I'll just have to tell the police what I already know and see if anything's of interest to them.'

The P-word seemed to have the desired effect. Slater pursed his lips, regarded Charlie for a moment. 'All right,' he said, after a pause, 'I'll tell you what I told your brother, but tomorrow. I'll meet you at midday. Do you know Richardson's Garden Centre on the A40?'

Charlie thought, remembered seeing signs for it. 'Yes.'

'They've got a little coffee shop. I'll see you in there.' He began to walk away, then stopped. 'And one more thing. If I were you I'd wait till midday tomorrow before you do anything or speak to anyone else, especially the police. Whatever it is you *think* you know, it can wait until then, don't you reckon?'

And he was walking back across the forecourt, his hands in his pockets. Charlie reached out to the Peugeot for support. He dragged open the door and pulled himself in, wanting to be anywhere but there. As he drove home, he was constantly glancing in his rear-view mirror.

He needn't have worried. As he drove up, it was on his street – the red flat-bed Toyota truck – parked a few doors from his house. He could detect a figure inside, but the distance and the sun made it impossible to see more – to judge whether the man was just sitting, eating a sandwich and reading the *Sun*, or if he was staring intently at Charlie.

'I'm back,' Charlie called to Bea as he let himself in. He glanced at the Toyota down the road before closing the door.

If it was here, it couldn't have been anywhere near Slater's garage in Rickmansworth, surely?

There was a muffled response from a bedroom: 'You all right?'

'Well,' he said, climbing the stairs, 'if I told you I was tired would you say I didn't know the half of it, and that I should try breast-feeding if I want to know the true meaning of tired?'

'Something like that.'

'Then I'm fine.'

He walked to the spare room from where, if he craned forward, he could see the red Toyota. He was only just in time: it was on the move, pulling away from the kerb and coming down the street, towards their house and on to the junction at the end. As it passed, the driver, his high-visibility jacket on, looked up at the window, his eyes finding Charlie's. For a moment the two men stared at each other. Then the truck was gone.

He'd been holding his breath. Now he let it out.

'Hey, Bea,' he called, watching the Toyota pull out on to the main road. 'I've just spotted that tree-lopping bloke in the street. Not seen him, have you?'

'Yes, he's doing the rounds again.'

'He's been here? At the door?'

'That's right. Not twenty minutes ago.'

Again, he felt a mix of relief and fear. If the guy had been on the street twenty minutes ago, he hadn't been in Rickmansworth. But what had he been doing here?

'What did he want?' he called, trying, with a degree of success, to strike a casual note.

'Um, to tell us that the work might be put back, subject to a planning decision, and that they were sending out consultation documents. He seemed to think we were signed up to receive that sort of thing by email. Are we?'

No, of course they weren't.

'Yeah,' he said, leaving the bedroom, heading for the stairs. 'I registered us at the council website so we'd get stuff by email rather than in the post. All part of a move to a Utopian paperless society.'

'Really? Still seem to get loads of stuff from them.'

'That's the council for you,' he said.

He checked the email. There was nothing. Not yet, anyway.

# The Night Visitor

It was later. Much later. Joe Parks had slept, messed about on his PC a little, watched a bit of TV and changed his clothes. New outfit: black combat trousers, T-shirt, black hooded top. From the bed he picked up his balaclava and tried it on, admiring himself in the bedroom mirror. Also on the bed was a diving knife he'd bought off the Internet. Part-serrated blade, a wicked curve at the point. He rolled up a leg of the combats and strapped the sheath to his leg, then reached for the knife and held it to his face, admiring the combination of knife and balaclava in the mirror. He bared his teeth, turning the knife so it caught the light, then slid it away, pulled off the mask and stuffed it into the map pocket of his combats. He checked his watch. It was 2 a.m. All the good boys and girls would be in bed. Time to go to work.

He couldn't take Betty. She was too recognisable. Instead he used the red Toyota, a much more common vehicle. Still, he made sure to park it a few streets away; didn't want anyone putting two and together. He stepped out of the truck and breathed summer night air, his heart bopping away nicely.

That was good: you needed the adrenaline. Knowing how to control it was the thing. He walked along the street, keeping the house in sight. Semi-detached, so there was rear access through an alleyway to the side, and he glanced up and down the road – lightning fast – before ducking down it.

He steadied his breathing and listened. What for, he wasn't sure. Any indication that someone might have heard or seen him, perhaps; it was a hot night, people had their windows open. Maybe they couldn't sleep and were sitting in the cool breeze from a half-open window, smoking a fag, wondering about that noise from the street.

But he had been almost silent, and there was nothing but the sound of distant traffic, the faint rush of a plane overhead, climbing on its flightpath.

From his combats Joe Parks pulled out the balaclava and slipped it on, adjusting it around his eyes and mouth, sticking his tongue through the mouth hole and tasting the fabric. Moving quietly now, like a panther, a Ninja, a ghost-pirate boarding at the dead of night, he crept to the back of the house and the tiny garden there. A washing-line stretched from one fence-in-need-of-creosote to another, pairs of boxer shorts and a T-shirt hanging from it, the night painting them the colour of spent charcoal. The back door led straight into the kitchen. Joe Parks knelt below it and raised himself up very slowly, peering through the window. The kitchen was empty. He could see dishes piled in the sink; moonlight shone off a white fridge-freezer. An inside door led into the hall and that, too, was empty. Everyone was asleep. No one fetching a glass or water, no one deciding to watch a bit of early-morning TV. All were in the Land of Nod.

But not Joe Parks, who had a large flat-head screwdriver in his pocket ready to work into the door frame if necessary. But only if . . .

The ski mask split into a smile. His tongue appeared, as it sometimes did when he was excited. Someone had thoughtfully left a kitchen window ajar, the one above the pile of dirty dishes, and he rose to it now, pulling it open further, steeling himself against a squeak, which never came. It opened gratifyingly wide – wide enough to allow Joe Parks to enter – and he pulled himself up into it, feeling the weight on his upper arms, suddenly reminded of pulling himself out of a swimming-pool, his arms failing and dropping him back into the water, the girls laughing. But that memory was from another time, before Joe Parks had started working out. Now his arms never failed when he got out of the pool. The girls didn't laugh. And pulling himself up into the fuckwit's kitchen window was a doddle.

More of a doddle than getting in. The sink and worktop made a porcelain assault course. Cups and plates shifted treacherously together as he found a spot for one hand, then another, inching his body on to the windowsill and dragging a knee through until he was perched, like a big black parrot in a balaclava, half on the sill, half on the counter, but inside the house, controlling his breathing and, once again, listening. Nothing. He jumped, prepared to hear the treacherous shift of crockery behind him, but there was no sound.

He stood and walked to the bottom of the stairs where he cocked his head and listened. Then he began to ascend.

The thing with stairs was that all the squeaks were in the middle, where years of being walked on had made them tetchy. So Joe Parks used the edges, walking slowly but surely, testing each step before he applied his full weight, all the time listening and peering up ahead of him. In the kitchen he had had the benefit of moonlight through the window; there was a large window on the landing, but curtains kept out most of the light. Should have brought a torch, he mused, but it wasn't a pitch-dark night, the curtains were flimsy and cheap, and his eyes soon adjusted to the new gloom. He was a wraith, a Ninja. You never saw a Ninja with an Ever-Ready.

Reaching the landing he surveyed the doors. One was open; inside, dark shapes of Royal Doulton and a little skyline of an electric toothbrush and snub-nosed roll-on deodorant against a tiny frosted-glass window. That would be the bathroom, then. Seeing it, the dull threat of need-a-piss made its presence felt. But he knew that was because he was nervous, and you had to use those nerves, use the adrenaline, make it your bitch. He turned his attention to the second door on the landing now, this one closed. He crouched, pulled up his trouser leg. Finding the handle of the diving knife with fingers that, he realised, were trembling (use the adrenaline), he released it from the sheath. He stood. Then, very, very gently, he grasped the door handle, levering it slowly down, all the time expecting a squeak that never came, until he was easing the door open and stepping through.

There was enough light through cheapo curtains to let him know he was in a child's bedroom. No – correction – a baby's bedroom. In the middle of the room stood a cradle and he walked to it, stared down at the swaddled baby inside. For a moment it seemed to open its eyes to look at him, and he had a horrifying vision of it waking and screaming and him having to shut it up, but its head moved and its eyes stayed closed. Joe Parks gazed down at the sleeping baby for a moment or so. He let his knife hand relax into the cot so that the blade met the cotton of the swaddling cloth and he looked at the blade and the cloth, the baby asleep, oblivious to death's proximity. He drank it all in and, for a moment or so, Joe Parks felt light-headed and giddy; his eyes seemed to milk over, his breath was hot and wet on the sodden fabric of the balaclava. Then he remembered the job at hand, and he turned, went out of the room, leaving the baby still sleeping behind him.

# The Night Visitor, Part Two

'Charlie.' Her voice was harsh and hushed. She sounded spooked, as though she'd heard something from downstairs. But he knew from experience that it wouldn't be a noise from downstairs. It would be something she'd remembered at dead of night that must be shared that instant. Had he changed the timer so the water heater would come on? (Yes, he had.) Had he rung the insurance broker back about the mortgage redemption period expiring? (No, he hadn't – he was putting off that thrill for the time being.) Wasn't he supposed to have a tax bill that needed paying round about now? (Yes, funnily enough. Now, please go back to sleep, Bea. We need to sleep.)

But she said none of those things.

Again: '*Charlie*.'

'Yurnh,' he groaned, throat dry and rusty.

'I just heard something.'

He turned, whispering, 'What?'

'A noise.'

'Mary?'

'No. A noise from downstairs.'

'Really?'

'Keep your voice down.'

'Why?'

'Because there might be someone down there.'

'It's probably just something falling off the worktop. Is the washing-machine on?'

Their Hotpoint was a seismic force. Worktop-slides were known to occur.

'No.'

'Still, though.' He thought of the piles of dishes he'd turned his back on when they'd trudged to bed. 'I'd better go and look. There might be a mess to tidy up.'

'What if there's someone down there?'

'They can help.'

'*Charlie.*'

He'd swung his feet out of bed and was scratching his head, searching the floorboards. 'I need my pants,' he said.

'Why?'

'Because I don't want to disturb the burglar.'

'*Charlie!*'

Chuckling, he located his boxer shorts, stepped into them and opened their bedroom door.

He went out on to the landing. There was never anybody there, that was the thing. In his adult life he'd had to go and investigate strange noises – what? Ten times in total. And there was never anybody there. It was something shifting, the aforementioned worktop-slide; once a picture dropped off a wall because he'd done a half-hearted bit of DIY.

It was a win-win situation for a bloke, he mused: there was never any danger, but you still got to feel like a hero.

Mary's door was closed. He thought of checking on her but decided against – didn't want to disturb her. He clicked on the hallway light, dazzling himself, suddenly feeling naked and vulnerable. He padded downstairs into the kitchen on to cold floor tiles. They'd left the window open. Correction, *he* had left the window open. And he decided to keep that particular piece of field intelligence to himself rather than risk the wrath of the Bea-hulk. He closed the window and thumbed the lock. Looking around, the sink was in the same shameful state he'd left it, nothing disturbed. It was the same story in the lounge, his study. Whatever the noise was, it was ancient history.

He looked out of their landing window, wanting to see the garden lit by moonlight, but seeing only himself reflected: bloke in boxer shorts.

Then he let himself back into the bedroom where Bea, clearly beside herself with fears for the safety of her beloved, lay snoring, mouth open. He watched her for a moment, removing damp strands of hair from her forehead, for no reason other than that he wanted to touch her. Then he got back into bed and was soon asleep.

## The Night Visitor, Part Three

Joe Parks stepped out of the baby's bedroom and into the hallway. His tongue flicked from the soaking mouth hole of the ski mask, his fingers flexed and tightened on the handle of the diver's knife. There was silence. He could smell the house. It smelt of cigarettes, babies, boiled food, old carpet. Above that, there was a sharper, keener scent: the smell of his own fear and excitement. He grasped a door handle and, very, very gently, leaned into the door, easing down the handle, holding his breath. Then, very, very slowly, he slipped into the bedroom.

The room admitted him silently. His eyes adjusted, taking in the bed in the middle of the room. He held the knife, flexed his fingers, licked his lips.

And in one fluid but almost casual movement, he flicked the light switch, strode to the bed, sat down and held his blade to the throat of its occupant. 'Hello, scumbag,' he hissed. 'Guess who?'

Gavin knew exactly who it was. For him the world was abruptly and rudely lit up, and he had a second of flashback to the times his mother – before she left, this was – would bustle angrily into his bedroom and whip open the curtains, throwing them apart with a force that often yanked them from the runners, calling, 'Get up, before I get you up.'

Only it wasn't his mother now, and there was no indignant screeching from the room next door, where she would have done exactly the same thing to his older sister. This was Joe Parks.

Even though Gavin had expected Joe Parks to come for him, and that it would be soon, and he'd been carrying a kitchen knife around for that very reason, he had never expected Joe Parks to turn up here. With his new baby sister sleeping in the room next door, and in the room on the other side her mother, a girl who'd only been two years above him at school, lying in bed, arms round his snoring father, who thought every day was Christmas Day.

Gavin had expected Joe Parks in the street, in the rec, in the pub. Not here.

He saw Parks's lips stretched away from his teeth beneath the balaclava. He felt the knife at his throat, then a warm, almost pleasurable sensation at his groin as his bladder emptied.

'You've been expecting me,' said Joe Parks.

Gavin whimpered. With the blade at his throat he dared not move. He knew not to shout or scream, and Joe Parks knew he knew, which was why he didn't hold a hand over Gavin's mouth. Instead he reached to Gavin's bedside table and picked up the kitchen knife that, some three hours ago, Gavin had removed from his sock before kicking off his trainers, jeans, boxers, getting into his nice, safe, comfy bed.

The bed that Joe Parks now sat on, like a dad imparting fatherly wisdom. A knife-wielding dad in a ski mask.

Joe Parks admired the kitchen knife. He held it alongside his diving knife so that Gavin could see the two together; so Gavin could see what a pathetic, useless weapon he had chosen to defend himself against Joe Parks. Then he placed it back on Gavin's bedside table, smiled and broke wind. Still with the diving knife at Gavin's throat, he used his other hand to scoop fumes up to Gavin's nose.

'Jesus,' said Joe Parks. 'Almost followed through there.'

Gavin tried not to breathe as Joe Parks wafted the air a bit more, enjoying the smell of his own fart. When the moment had passed he said, 'You did the graveyard, didn't you?'

Gavin shook his head, no, but the man smiled. 'Yeah, I know you did. And the thing is, apart from upsetting me, because I was the one who had to clear up your party, like your fuckin' *butler* –' He jabbed the knife and a tiny lozenge of blood escaped from a nick on Gavin's neck – 'you upset a lot of other people into the bargain. And not all of those people are going to be the type to practise Christian forgiveness and turn the other butt-cheek, know what I mean? Could be that someone wants to get even for what you did to the grave of a loved one. You know Byron Land?'

'No,' managed Gavin.

'Tosspot. Land Associates. I work for them. And Byron Land is most upset about what you did to the graveyard. He's got personal reasons for being pissed off about it. So he's asked me to give you a message.'

The diving knife stayed where it was at Gavin's throat. Joe Parks picked up the kitchen knife from the bedside table and inserted the tip into Gavin's nostril. Gavin whimpered a second time. Joe Parks opened up the nostril with the knife.

Blood squibbed from Gavin's nose. At first it felt like

someone using their finger and thumb to squeeze and pull at his nostril. Then there was a splash of warm blood across his cheek, the pillow beside him suddenly scarlet. His mouth stretched wide in silent agony and Joe Parks stepped off the bed, allowing Gavin's hands to come to his tattered nose, blood seeping from between the fingers.

Joe Parks glanced behind him at a plastic chair in the corner, the kind of chair that looked like it had been stolen from a dentist's waiting room. It had Gavin's clothes strewn across it. Joe Parks picked out a football shirt, balled it up and tossed it across to Gavin.

'Stop the bleeding,' he whispered, 'I've got something to show you.'

First he unzipped his hooded top and dropped it to the floor. Beneath it was his third-favourite T-shirt, which he'd had printed up at EZ-Print. It was a photograph of himself, wearing his ski mask. Gavin stared disbelievingly as Joe Parks gestured at his own chest with the blade of the knife, snickering quietly. 'Cool, eh?' he said.

Gavin snivelled.

Joe Parks moved the tip of the knife to point in his direction. 'I said it's cool, yeah?'

Reluctantly, Gavin nodded.

'But that ent what I got to show you.'

Joe Parks moved across to where the wounded Gavin sat. He was in no hurry: Gavin wasn't going anywhere. As he moved he took his mobile phone from his pocket before he settled back on the bed, bringing the diving knife back towards Gavin's neck – Gavin who tried to edge away, still holding the balled-up football shirt at his nose.

'Aw, *fuck*,' said Joe Parks, voice rising. 'What the fuck is this? Have you fucking wet yourself?'

'Sorry – sorry,' Gavin said. His wound made him sound blocked up.

'These are D&G, these jeans,' lied Joe Parks indignantly (he'd bought them from Primark). 'They're dry-clean only.'

'Sorry,' repeated Gavin, wanting Joe Parks to keep his voice down; wanting the bleeding to stop, the pain to subside. Wanting, more than all of that, the day to come when he took a hammer to Joe Parks's head.

'You're paying for the fucking cleaning,' hissed Joe Parks, jamming the blade edge against Gavin's neck.

'Yes, yes,' agreed Gavin.

Beneath the ski mask, Joe Parks smiled, lips stretching away from teeth. 'Good,' he said. 'Good, good.' He twitched the knife, Gavin's neck tautening and lengthening in response. He noticed Gavin's earrings, a diamond cluster in each ear. Expensive, maybe. He produced his mobile phone, flicked it open and keyed a button, accessing a menu, talking at the same time. 'What you do in this life has consequences, mate. You can't just go round being a toerag all the time. And the reason you've got a fucked-up nose is because of what you did. That's called justice. Your mates have been learning the same lesson. Especially Carly. You know Carly, doncha, mate? Sweet as. You and her got history, I hear. Why don't I show you the fun me and a mate had with Carly?'

So he did. Lounging on Gavin's bed, knife at his throat, he angled the phone to let Gavin see the Carly footage.

'Good stuff, innit?' whispered Joe Parks after three minutes twenty-three seconds had elapsed. 'There should be more but I ran out of memory. Shame.' He looked at Gavin and Gavin looked back. Joe Parks tensed the knife. 'Don't go giving me fucking daggers, boy. Don't even think about it. And don't think this is the beginning of something either, because it ent. You better consider yourself lucky it's just your beak I'm clipping. You better know that anyone ever comes for Joe Parks he'll be waiting for them, and whatever they got, he got two of. Now, before I go, I got a question for you.'

Gavin stared at him, then flinched as the knife jabbed again. 'What?' he said. 'What question?'

'You ever heard of Mark Slater?'

Gavin shook his head slowly, watching Joe Parks over the top of the bloodied football shirt.

'He was a little boy that drowned years and years ago. He drowned in his paddling-pool. Ring any bells?'

Saying nothing, Gavin shook his head, no.'

'His little grave is at the far end of the cemetery, the opposite end to the entrance, and someone gave it a right going-over. They really ripped into it. Now, Carly gave me a good idea who it is I should be looking for, but being as she was in the throes of ecstasy I wanted independent confirmation.' He leaned forward, bringing his face close to Gavin's.

Gavin pulled away from the lips and teeth and the ski-mask, wet glistening in the fabric.

'Who did Mark Slater's grave?' whispered Joe Parks.

Gavin shook his head but got a prod with the knife in response.

'There ent no such answer as no. Who did the little one's grave?'

Gavin let out a whinny, the knife digging into his throat.

'It was Selina, wasn't it?' smiled Joe Parks. 'That was what Carly said. Selina. Bitch vandalised her own half-brother's grave. It was her, wasn't it?'

He prodded with the knife. Gavin snivelled, nodding – yes, it was Selina.

## Multimedia Speakers

The first thing he thought when he woke was, Geoffrey Slater. Meeting Geoffrey Slater today. With it came a quickening of the pulse, a sense that he was close now.

At his side, Bea moaned and stretched. He felt her body tighten and flex against his. He luxuriated in the moment. 'Sleep, baby, sleep,' she sang, muffled by the duvet, to the tune of 'Cry, Baby, Cry' by the Beatles. And Charlie luxuriated in that moment, too.

So, status: not such a bad night. A marathon sleep-session from Mary (up there with the night he took her to Kilburn, but that was their little secret). The monitor had woken them up at – he glanced at the phosphorescent lights of the clock-radio, which had been sent to them free by a catalogue about a decade ago and had remained their bedside timepiece ever since.

'Seven twelve a.m.,' he said. It counted as a lie-in.

'That's good,' said Bea beside him, and they each allowed themselves a second of believing that it marked the dawn of a new era. No more 5.18 a.m., the old 4.49 a.m. a thing of the past. From now on they were going to sleep like normal people.

Bea made to get out of bed, then stopped. 'Hey, do you hear that?' she said.

'What?'

'Nothing.'

'Blimey.' He raised his head from the pillow to check the monitor, like perhaps there'd been a sudden power-cut. But no: the monitor go-light glowed green. The only change was the red lights. As in, there were none. Mary had stopped crying.

Bea swung her feet back into the bed.

'That's a first,' said Charlie.

'She's gone back to sleep.' Bea turned to snuggle into him, and the feeling of her there was blissful. 'Perhaps I'd better go and check,' she said after a moment or so.

'No,' he said, not wanting her to move. 'She's cried herself back to sleep. Let's just enjoy the lie-in for once.'

So they did. They lay there, not really sleeping, not really awake. Snoozing, napping. And they were magicked back to a pre-Mary time when they'd dozed weekends away, when the only thing driving them from their bed was hunger, or the telephone, or the woman who collected the Kleeneze catalogue, who always looked so peeved that they hadn't ordered anything.

'You know what?' he said at last.

'Yuh.' She spoke from her snuggle-position at his back, her voice muffled and indistinct.

'A cup of tea would be nice now.'

'Yeah, I'd love one, thanks.'

'Let me go, then.'

She made a fake-tantrum noise but released him anyway. He got out, found his jeans, pulled them on and pushed a hand

319

through his hair, then headed down the stairs. At his study he paused to boot up his Mac and, too late, turned to lower the volume on the multimedia speakers.

But the expected orchestral boom from the Mac never came, and he realised the speakers were turned off.

Funny. There was a titchy thumb-switch on one. He never used it, preferring to toggle the volume, but he obviously had last night because this morning the speakers were off. Perhaps he'd knocked the switch when he packed up last night. He thumbed it and a little green light came on – his life was ruled by little lights, it seemed. It wasn't easy to do. Well, not so easy you could do it by accident, jog it with a mug or a paperback book. He looked round the study. Everything was as he'd left it. He hunkered down and peered beneath his desk and, yes, the video-camera was still there, still plugged into the mains, dutifully charging away. He flicked open the screen and pressed play. There was Susan Slater walking off, Byron Land turning away. It was in exactly the same place he'd left it.

You're being stupid, he told himself. Most likely Bea had switched them off, probably because something random had started playing from a website and she'd killed the noise. The only other explanation was someone else – someone booting up in the middle of the night, who had switched off the speakers so nobody would hear them do it. Because they wanted access to his computer.

He opened the email application. Its window bounced into the screen and the hundreds of emails forwarded from Leo's machine were still there, most of them bolded-up and unread.

What else? He flitted the mouse pointer round the screen, unsure what he wanted to see. Evidence that somebody had been poking around on his Mac? Proof that he was being paranoid?

There was nothing. The emails were as he'd left them. When he double-clicked the Internet application there was nothing there either. He even checked the browser history, as though any phantom intruder might have settled down to look for pictures of Jordan in the nude, but no, zilch. And he had a feeling that when he asked Bea if she'd switched off his speakers, she would say, 'Oh, God, yeah, I forgot to say. Can you make sure your computer's shut down if you're going to bugger off? Bloody thing.'

From upstairs he heard a familiar sound and his heart lifted: Mary, announcing that for her and her parents the day had begun, and she'd like attention, please, now, if you don't mind. Above his head – thump, thump – Bea's lie-in interrupted, her feet meeting floorboards. She'd be finding those slippers again. She'd be getting out of bed and going to Mary's room where she'd pick up that little scrap from the Moses-basket-on-a-stand and soothe her, tell her it was all right. Mummy's here. Daddy's downstairs.

He walked through to the kitchen, looked at the kettle level and added water from the tap, glancing up at his reflection in the kitchen window.

Which was open.

At that moment he heard a *ting*, the sound of an email arriving on his computer in the other room. He froze, staring at the open window.

The open window that he'd closed a matter of hours ago.

Slowly, calmly, he placed the kettle back on the worktop and clicked it on, then walked to the bottom of the stairs. 'Bea,' he called.

'Yeah?' she came back.

'Everything all right up there? Mary all right?'

'Fine, yeah. Why?'

'Just checking. Oh, and another thing.' He tried to sound as casual as possible. 'I've got a bone to pick with you.'

'What bone?'

'You left the kitchen window open last night.'

'Did I?'

'Yeah. You trying to get us killed in our beds?'

'Well, you were the last one down, remember?'

'Was I?'

'Yeah, so if anyone should have checked it was you.'

'All right,' he said jauntily. 'You're forgiven. This once.' He saw himself in the reflection of a photograph that hung at the bottom of their stairs, one of him and Bea taken at a wedding. The man in the picture was pissed and happy, Bea looking beautiful, leaning forward to give him a kiss and unintentionally showing plenty of cleavage; the man in the reflection was a man wondering how their kitchen window had opened itself.

He walked quickly to his study, sat down, jiggled the mouse to lose the screensaver and clicked to the mail application.

The new mail was from someone called Your Mate. It came from one of those free webmail addresses. Difficult to trace. You'd need the IP address, for a start, which is like the DNA code of the source computer. This one had probably been opened in an Internet café or a try-hard branch of Top Man, so even the IP address wouldn't help.

Charlie swallowed hard and opened the message. Inside was a picture taken on a mobile phone. It showed Charlie talking to Jane Land in her Land Rover, the meeting at the

322

petrol station, the picture clearly taken from inside the Mini-Mart. Of course. Your Mate and the driver of the Toyota were one and the same. At the time Charlie had dared believe the man hadn't seen them. He'd been wrong about that.

Beneath the picture were the words: 'We know what you're doing, and now its time to stop.'

Charlie hit reply: 'Who are you?'

He sat back, clicking Get Mail, clicking it again and again until the computer pinged and there was another message from Your Mate.

'I'm your mate!' it said.

'Were you in my house last night?' he typed, sent.

He clicked Get Mail – clicked it and clicked it – breathing heavily. He imagined the guy in front of his own computer, high-visibility waistcoat on, waiting for Charlie's response.

He clicked Get Mail again. Clicked it and clicked it. There was the ping of a new message and he opened it.

It was another picture taken on a mobile phone. The image was dark and fuzzy, and for a moment or so Charlie struggled to decipher it, the details accumulating slowly: polka-dot wallpaper, the teddies, the chest of drawers they'd bought from Ikea that Charlie had nearly destroyed in attempting to assemble it.

It was a photograph of Mary in her cot.

'*Charlie!*'

It came from upstairs.

On the way up he tried to jump three steps and fell forward, hands friction-burning on the carpet, scrabbling upright, thinking, *God-no-please-not-Mary*, reaching the landing and lurching into Mary's bedroom.

Mother and child stared at him as if he were mad.

'You all right?' asked Bea.

He stood, dazed, catching his breath.

'Babe?'

'Yes. Sorry. I'm fine. Haven't woken up yet.'

'Know how you feel but, listen, I've left the wet wipes downstairs. Lounge, I think. I've got toxic nappy from hell here. You wouldn't go and get them for me?'

'Everything's all right?' he asked.

'Well, no, not really,' she said. 'Bad nappy. Can't you smell it? Wet wipes. Please. Pronto.'

He did as he was told, fetched wet wipes and took them to Bea, once more scanning Mary's room as though he was expecting to see the man in the high-visibility waistcoat lurking behind a fluffy bunny.

Then he was hurrying back downstairs, pausing to scoop his mobile phone from the side in the kitchen, then sitting down at the computer, jiggling the mouse. The screensaver flicked off and the picture sent by Your Mate was once again centre-screen.

He clicked reply and typed, 'How did you get in?'

'You left the window open,' came the reply. 'Everybody's leaving their windows open in this weather.'

Christ, he'd been in the house when Charlie came down and closed it.

*Ping*. Another message arrived. 'PS Nice boxer shorts.'

'So the object was to scare me? Get my email address? Anything else?' he typed, and sent.

Click Get Mail, click Get Mail.

*Ping*. 'The object was to make sure you leave certain people alone. The object was to make you see how easily I can get to you.'

Okay, arsehole, thought Charlie, opening his phone, you just made a big mistake. Big fucking mistake. He scrolled through to Merle's phone number. 'Who do you want me to leave alone?' he typed and sent to Your Mate.

Click Get Mail, click Get Mail.

*Ping.* 'Byron Land.'

Charlie smiled, dialled the number. 'Hello, could I speak to Detective Inspector Merle, please?'

'Not in yet,' snorted a receptionist. 'Want his voicemail?'

'Er, no, not yet,' said Charlie quickly. 'Could I take his email address? Somewhere I can forward emails that are potentially evidence of a serious crime?'

'I'm sorry?'

'What's his email address? Just, please, can I have his email address?'

The snorty receptionist read it out to him and he took it down, his pen hand shaking as he wrote.

'Don't forget to tell Mr Land how you implicated him in a break-in and threatening behaviour, will you?' he typed and sent to Your Mate.

Moments later. *Ping.* Another message. He opened it. 'Your email address is on the back of your van.'

Charlie looked at the message. Felt a sudden disquiet.

Moving quickly, he selected all of the emails from Your Mate and clicked forward, keyed in Merle's address and sent. The email application did a *phwoosh* to indicate the message had gone.

'So what did you want on my computer, then?' he wrote to Your Mate and sent.

*Ping.* New message: 'Your IP address.'

For a moment or so he dithered, his mouse dancing round

the screen. He knows your IP address. Okay, not the end of the world, you've still got your firewall, he told himself. As long as the firewall's activated you're protected.

*Ping.* Another message. 'Plus I disabled your firewall.'

Charlie went cold.

Then it all happened at once. *Ping.* The emails he'd forwarded to Merle arrived back: 'Messages refused by outgoing mail server'.

Shit.

And *ping*, a new message from Your Mate.

'Consider yourself hacked,' it said.

And suddenly he was being asked if he really wanted to delete all messages from all mailboxes and he was moving his cursor to say no – no, he didn't want to delete anything – but the yes button clicked itself and he watched, helpless, clicking frantically, as a little bar moved across a tiny window and his emails, all of them, every single one, drained from his machine.

# The Garden Centre

He tried restart. It powered down and up again and he opened the mail application, thinking his messages might miraculously have restored themselves. But no. The window was empty. '0 messages,' it said at the top. All of them, gone.

*Ping.* A message arrived. 'By the way, my mate Gavin will tell anyone who's asking that I spent all night with him, helping him after his accident. And I wore gloves and I didn't nick anything or even break in, technically speaking. Just thought you ought to know in case you were thinking of going to the pigs. Consider yourself unhacked.'

The message deleted itself.

'0 messages', it said once again at the top.

Charlie sat back in his chair and sighed. Whatever it was Slater had to tell him, Byron Land didn't want him to hear it.

The morning was an agony of clock-watching. Charlie tried desperately to maintain a normal-Charlie face as he took the bulk of parental responsibilities, simultaneously making supportive noises as Bea prepared for her trip into town.

All the time thinking of Your Mate, Geoffrey Slater, their

house on Willow Street and the little boy who had drowned in 1973.

'I'm strangely nervous,' said Bea, towel on head. 'I haven't been into town for God knows how long. All those people. I'm not acclimatised.'

'You'll be fine,' he said. He was lying on the bed, Mary across his chest.

'This is only the second time I've ever left Mary.'

'She'll be fine, too.'

Bea left the room. He let out a silent sigh, kissed the top of Mary's head, tried not to let his mind wander.

'What if they don't want me to come back?' she said, not long later, wearing a skirt now, hair still wet.

'They will.'

'It would be a bit embarrassing, though, wouldn't it? I mean, I'm sort of expecting they'll want me back.'

'If they don't want you back, don't go back.'

She looked at him, head to one side, towelling a rope of hair. 'It's not that easy. I *want* to go back, Charlie.'

He remembered popping in once and finding his way to her floor, another of those moments when he'd been awestruck by his wife. She moved through ranks of kids who should have been bored rigid and resentful, hating every second of their soul-destroying, spirit-crushing jobs, and would have been, too, if not for Bea. He'd never thought a headset could look sexy until he saw one on his wife; never thought a floor full of people jabbering into them could be an exciting, inspiring place to work until he saw his wife marshalling her staff. He watched as she moved through them, cajoling, piss-taking, joking, pointing, rebuking, giving advice, stepping in to help and being – clearly – *fabulous* at her job. If she arrived home exhausted, now he knew why. She was constantly on the move; she seemed to juggle a thousand things at once and, in the relatively short time he watched, she never lost her composure and never seemed in less than total control. She thrived on it, he could tell. *Bring it on*, her expression seemed to say.

'Ah, you caught me on a good day,' she said later, when he told her that he'd been watching, and how bloody sexy it had been seeing that side to her. 'Usually I'm a complete mess.'

So, yes, he understood exactly why she wanted to go back. Not for the money (though it would help, of course) as much as for her, for that person Bea was when she didn't have a disgruntled wedding DJ and a baby to look after.

He helped her choose the blouse and told her she looked beautiful when she tried it on. She did, although she was right: it did pull a touch at the chest. Then he ran her up to the station, and made more right noises when she told him she might do a bit of shopping after the meeting, if that was all right with him.

He drove away from the station, parked in the pay-and-display, got out. Mary gazed curiously through the window at him and he drummed his fingers on it, something to amuse her while he waited and watched. He was waiting to see if a red flat-bed Toyota truck would appear.

One did not. Maybe Your Mate had decided to give it a rest, the message having been hammered home.

Relaxing slightly, Charlie climbed back into the car, kissed Mary's nose, then checked her nappy just in case. She was clean. Clean and serene. 'Okay, baby,' he said. 'Let's go and see where Daddy used to live.'

Funny – he'd needed to go on the Internet to check where

Willow Street was. Well, not *funny*, exactly: they'd moved when he was a tot so why should he have been able to find his way there without help? Just weird, he supposed. Weird that you'd ever need a map to find your home. He wondered if one day Mary would be checking a map to find her way back to Candle Street. If she did, he hoped it would be out of curiosity, a desire to explore her past. Because she *wanted* to. Not for the reasons Charlie did now.

He felt nothing as he drove into Willow Street, counting the numbers until he found the house he used to live in. Again, what had he expected? Some kind of residual memory? A generic old-house nostalgia, like the way you feel when you go to a school – any school? But, no, there was none of that, he was just on Willow Street, and like any other street it was difficult to park along. Charlie waited for two laughing girls in an open-topped jeep to pull out of a space, spent a millisecond envying their life, then reversed in, killed the engine and looked over to the house where he used to live.

On the tape it had been like any other terraced house in a row of terraced houses. That was how it was in the flesh, too. No blue plaque on the outside saying, 'Charlie Watson, creator of Cheesy Vinyl and owner of his own Internet business, was born here in 1970', just bricks and windows and a door.

It was a rental property now. You could tell because there was a to-let sign outside.

The agent was Land Associates.

He got out of the car, grinning through the window at Mary, who looked for a moment as if she might be about to burst into tears. Then he jogged across the road to the house and stood outside. If he looked to his right, there was the junction with Crosby Street. In fact, there was just one house between the Watsons' old home and the junction.

He glanced at the car and trotted up to the junction, checking the house numbers on Crosby Street. There was number twenty-one. Standing at the intersection of the two roads he could just about see both houses at once: the Watsons' and the Slaters'. Not exactly neighbours – there was no reason why his family should know theirs. They lived on different streets, worlds apart. The houses themselves were miles away, might as well have been in different towns for all they had in common. The gardens, though. You couldn't see it from the street but he'd bet his entire collection of the *Amazing Spider-Man* that the gardens were practically nudging each other.

He walked back to the car, Mary regarding him as though she was peeved to have been abandoned. He got in, throwing a last look at the estate agent's sign: Land Associates. Figured.

'Okay, darling,' he said, pulling his seatbelt across his chest. 'Let's go and see what the nasty man has to say, shall we? Almost time for your bottle, too . . .'

Maybe it didn't matter, he thought as he drove. Whatever Slater had to tell him, it involved events from decades ago that, until recently, had meant nothing to Charlie, that he'd lived quite happily without knowing about. Isn't the present so much more urgent than the past? Perhaps he ought to turn round, forget it.

A sign told him that Richardson's Garden Centre was fifty yards on the left, and that he should indicate now, so he did.

## Falling Asleep, Waking Up

There was no particularly surprising reason why Susan Slater hated sleeping. Just that one day, a very hot summer's day in 1973, having drunk two tins of lager – the small sort, not the huge three-quarter-pint things you see in the shops, these days – she fell asleep.

Nodded off.

Snoozed.

And when she woke, her son Mark was face down in his paddling-pool, having toppled over and been unable to push himself upright again, those motor skills being insufficiently developed. He could eat grass and put a little wooden block to his mouth, and he could grasp one of her fingers, but not that.

Which was the not-particularly-surprising-reason why Susan Slater hated sleep. Distrusted it. She had fallen asleep and her son had died.

Sleep was no one's friend in prison, either. She lay awake when the lights went out and all she heard was people crying. In films the tough women tell the crying women to shut up, but they don't in real life. In real-life prison when you fall

332

asleep you do it to the sound of women crying. So she hardly slept.

And now she hardly slept because – because she was punished every day for the things that had happened back then, and sometimes she thought that was exactly how it should be.

She poured two fingers of vodka into a tiny glass and drank it straight back. Paul wasn't in. She hadn't seen her boyfriend for two days now. She wondered whether he had gone for good, but found that she didn't care, which was probably how he liked it. For Paul, Susan had been like a project. Often he would talk of how he had 'taken her on', as though from Christian goodwill – as though he was doing not just her a favour but the whole world. When he came home he smelt of other women and she found she didn't care about that, either, even when he'd admitted that he slept with other women, purring that he had *needs*, as though she were a sexless cripple. Which, in a way, she supposed, she was.

The booze landed in her throat and she felt it flow across her shoulders, relaxing them. She poured another two fingers and drank that, too, knowing that another would make it three, and three was too much. This shot found its way to her eyelids, which dropped as though weary. She smiled a thin, dreamy smile and rocked back on her heels, enjoying the vodka hit.

She did this in the kitchen. Mostly she did it in the bathroom, where there was a bottle of Smirnoff and a mug with Time for Tea! on it stowed behind the water-heater. Today she did it in the kitchen because not only Paul was out but Selina too.

She shrugged on her jacket, wrapped her shawl round it. She looked in the mirror and flicked some hair from her face.

Was it wrong to think, Not bad for an old bird? She did, anyway.

'Come on, Charlie,' she said to the dog. 'Let's go and see how Mark is today.'

To Charles Laughton the words meant walkies, and he wagged his tail happily.

She stopped off, as she did two or three times a week, at Foster's, wordlessly picking a remembrance bunch from a tall metal bucket and taking them to the counter, her purse already open.

'*Three times a week*,' Paul used to say. 'Baby, I'm really not sure we can *afford* flowers three times a week.' He'd say it smiling, a watery smile that got sloppy and unpleasant when he was nasty-drunk. Which wasn't often, to give him his due: he was a happy boozer, mainly.

She'd met him not long after she'd got out of prison. Susan was trying to rebuild her life; they'd given her a house, were trying to fix her up with a job, reintegrate her into society, give her back everything she'd had before the day she'd fallen asleep, when she'd had a job, a husband, a son, a lover, friends and admirers. Coming out, her life was reduced to a single person: her mother, who was in a home. She would visit her at the Gables, the old lady staring ahead wordlessly, slowly being eaten by a degenerative disease. Residential support worker Paul Philips was one of the few human beings she spoke to.

She let him take her out. She let him fuck her. They moved in together. It was hardly Mills & Boon but somehow they seemed to fulfil each other's needs. Paul was caring, but he liked to spread that caring around with whoever was available. He was gregarious and sociable, the life and soul when it suited him, which was often. A Susan at home suited him. His

334

project. But an uncomplaining, unquestioning Susan. An inert project.

So, '*Three times a week?*' he'd said at first, years ago, before they'd had Selina, even. Yes, she'd told him, three times a week, and Paul wasn't stupid: he understood. He knew that forking out for flowers three times a week was a small price to pay for having an inert Susan around the place. Besides, his own job prospects had improved – he'd moved into care-home management. It meant he worked longer hours, of course, meant he needed to make sure the staff were kept happy with motivational nights out. 'Them's the breaks,' he said.

In return he was as generous as he could be. Selina never went without – trainers, iPods, she was always after something new – and Susan got her flowers three times a week.

'Had a chap in the other day,' said the florist now. 'He'd seen you buying those. He wanted to know what they were.' The girl smiled. 'P'raps we should put you on commission.'

She forced a smile in return, not daring to open her mouth in case the girl smelt the vegetable-scent of vodka on her breath. She thought she saw her grimace as she turned to snip a length of ribbon from a wall-mounted roll.

Outside the shop, she retrieved Charles Laughton from the lamp-post and, with him straining ahead, made her way to the graveyard, once more tying the lead, this time to the post on which hung the watering-can. She sometimes wished she had need of the can, but Mark had stones. For some reason she would have liked to add it to her ritual.

She knelt before the grave, took the old flowers from their vase and replaced them with the new ones. What she always did was take the old flowers to one of the other graves, the ones that were never visited as far as she could tell. She imagined that if anybody ever visited them they'd wonder about the flowers; they wouldn't know it was Mark sharing his gifts, like the good little boy she would have brought him up to be.

With the new flowers nicely arranged in Mark's vase, she sat back on her haunches and brought her shawl round her. She didn't notice the figure who walked into the graveyard, weaving between the graves towards where she knelt. It was only when the person stood directly behind her that she turned and looked up, squinting and shielding her eyes to see.

'Selina,' she said. She felt irritated. Selina and Paul: this wasn't a place for them, nor did she ever want it to be. This was a place for her and Mark. 'What do you want?'

As her eyes grew accustomed to the glare she could see that Selina was crying. Her head was low. She looked out from beneath her fringe – not at her, Susan realised, but at Mark's grave.

'Selina? What do you want?' said Susan, a heaviness in her chest. Her daughter was in trouble again. Her selfish, selfish daughter.

'Mum,' snivelled Selina, and something in her voice chipped away at the thaw within Susan, who got to her feet, wrapping her shawl round her. She peered beneath her daughter's fringe.

Then Selina did something neither of them had done in almost a decade. She threw her arms round Susan, who stood for a moment, taken aback, her own arms by her sides, hands kneading the shawl. Then, very tentatively, she returned the embrace, putting her arms round her daughter.

'Mum,' said Selina again. Her head was buried in Susan's shoulder.

'Yes.' Susan reached up a hand to smoothe Selina's hair.

'Mum, there's something I need to tell you.'

# Geoffrey Slater, Fool for Love

Geoffrey Slater was already in the coffee-shop. He stood as Charlie approached, manoeuvring the pushchair between the tables.

'There's an outside,' said Slater, who wore the same double-breasted suit as he had the previous day. The Rotary pin, the tattoo. 'Thought we could talk out there.' He looked pointedly at Mary. 'See you've brought company.'

'All right with you, is it?' said Charlie.

'Yeah, mate,' said Slater, chuckling. 'It's all right with me. As long as she doesn't cut up rough.'

They made their way outside, Slater seeming not to care how incongruous he looked, his self-important hands-in-pockets waddle, the suit. Retirees stared over their teacups at him, all straw hats and bony knees in shorts, the sun seeming to shine right through them. A waitress followed them and they asked for two coffees. Moments later she reappeared with a tray.

Slater picked up his cup and blew gently on it. He made a face as Charlie reached to take Mary from the pushchair.

'I've got to feed her,' said Charlie, in response. 'Otherwise she'll start shouting the place down.'

The bottle was still warm – he'd deliberately overheated it before they left home. He tested a drop on his tongue and Slater made another face. Charlie offered the bottle across the table to him and he sneered some more. Now Charlie brought it up to Mary, watching her for a moment, her contented little face.

'When you're ready,' snapped Slater.

'Okay, I'm ready.'

'You'd better fire away, then.'

And now, after all this, Charlie's mind went blank. 'God,' he said, 'I don't know where to start. What about . . . Why don't you tell me what you told my brother?'

Slater smiled. 'I told him what he wanted to know.'

'Which was?'

'He wanted to know if my ex-wife was sleeping with Byron Land.'

'And what was your answer?'

'That yeah – yeah, she was.'

'In nineteen seventy-three?'

'Well, yeah,' laughed Slater. 'She was sort of indisposed after that, really, what with being in prison.'

'And Mark?'

'What about him?'

'What happened to Mark?'

Slater looked surprised. 'Mark drowned. Glug-glug-glug. Your brother already knew that.'

There was a pause.

'He wasn't your son, was he?' said Charlie.

Slater chuckled. 'Your brother'd worked that out, too. You're not slow, you lot, are you? Pathetic, but you ain't slow. The graveyard was vandalised the other day, wasn't it?'

'Yes.'

'They get his, do you know?'

'Yes, they did.'

'Good.'

Charlie's hand tightened on the bottle. He looked around the patio. Everybody else here was enjoying a pleasant afternoon of garden centring. The old dears catching up, two mums over there in the corner, probably sharing baby woes. Only him, Charlie, having his nose rubbed in filth. 'He was Byron's kid,' he said.

'In one.'

'Why didn't you leave her?'

Slater lowered his eyes.

'You didn't know he wasn't yours?'

The eyes stayed lowered. He frowned as though resenting how the memory made him feel. For the first time since Charlie had met him, Slater seemed almost human.

'You *did* know?' pressed Charlie.

'No,' said Slater, looking up now. 'Not for sure. I didn't . . . The thing is, with Susan, she had me, you know.' He held up his hand, cupped. 'I was just a grease monkey when we met. She came to get her car done. No, it wasn't to get her car done – she'd run out of petrol, right outside the station this was. That was her thing, Susan. Always running out of petrol. I've never run out of petrol in my life, mate. Have you?'

Charlie thought a second and shook his head, no.

'It's a woman thing, innit, running out of petrol? Used to fucking . . .' He shook his head. 'But she just laughed about it, always. She drove a Mini in those days. I worked at Hallam's garage. It was where the junior school is now, at the top of the hill. You know it?'

'Yes,' said Charlie, who thought he probably remembered the garage. A sorry selection of Austin Maxis and Vauxhall Chevettes on a tiny forecourt, the wide-open maw of the unit where cars went for surgery and a selection of men in grey overalls outside, smoking and sipping from thermos cups. Or was it that exact garage? Maybe it was just an assembled image of Any Garage, *circa* 1970.

'Me and another bloke, Derek – ended up working for me, he's dead now, even then he was the resident old geezer – we gave each other a look, like, "Hey up." She was a looker. I mean, not drop-dead, but you noticed her because she had this way about her, like she thought everything was a bit funny, know what I mean?'

Charlie nodded, thinking that he did; thinking of Bea when he'd first met her – then of Chariot.

'When you got to know her she wasn't like that, really. She was actually a bit shy, not at all sure of herself. But the way she came across was kind of piss-takey. It's difficult to describe . . .' He looked annoyed at having to dredge her up, the essence of her. 'Like life just kind of bounced off her.

'We pushed her up the hill, me and Derek, round to Hallam's. She just took it in her stride. We had birds come on to the forecourt all the time. Cars were shit in them days, always breaking down. And most of those women would be flustered and dithery and full of apologies and thank-you and giving us tips out of their purses and making sure they mentioned their husband every other sentence. Like we'd be pouncing on them if we didn't know they was married. Not her. None of that. Didn't have a husband to mention, of course. But either way she was . . . Oh, I don't know . . .'

Slater did a kind of shrug. 'She was a bit different, anyway.

341

Her own person. I thought so – at the time. Turned out to be just like any other bird, of course, one eye on the next chance, you know what they're like.' He looked at Charlie, who didn't respond. 'Well, you've been lucky. Way I see it, they're all on the climb.'

'And what heady heights Susan reached,' said Charlie.

'Yeah, ha. Shit happens. Sometimes, if you're lucky, shit happens to shit people.'

'Happens a lot to her.'

Slater smiled as though his point had been made for him. 'I asked her out that day. Her brake pads were gone an' all so I changed them.' He smiled. 'I was a right little grease monkey in them days. Bet you wouldn't know the inside of an engine if it bit you, would you, mate?'

'If I ever get bitten by one, I'll let you know.'

Slater chuckled. 'What do you do for a living, then?'

'I'm a DJ,' said Charlie, feeling as if he was admitting it.

Slater leaned back, slapped his thighs and laughed a nasty, harsh laugh, shouting it to the sky. A table full of oldies stopped their conversation to stare at him. 'A DJ,' he said, composing himself. 'A fuckin' *DJ*. You went to university, did you?'

'Yes, I did.'

'Thought so. Had grants in them days, didn't they?'

Charlie nodded.

Slater grinned. 'So when I was working, paying my taxes like a good little boy, they were going to pay for your education so you could learn to be a DJ.'

'I didn't learn how to be a DJ at university.'

'Really? That was God knows how many years and God

knows how many thousands of pounds well spent then, wasn't it? What *did* you learn?'

'Well, I learned how to avoid miserable twats like you, for one thing.'

Slater laughed, but not quite the heaven-splitting roar of last time. 'Didn't do you much good, then, did it? Because here you are, spending a beautiful day like this with a miserable twat like me. What went wrong, eh?'

Charlie stared at him with what he hoped was disgust, shaking his head. But the gesture was feeble, the raw nerve exposed and bleeding.

'Well,' sniggesed Slater, 'if I ever need someone to put some records on I'll be sure to give you a call.'

'Right,' said Charlie. 'You do that. In the meantime, you and Susan . . .'

'We started seeing each other, yeah. She came back for the Mini after I done the brake pads, and I asked her out. Never shat myself so much in my life as then. Most times when I asked a bird out, the words would be out my mouth before I even thought about it. I was cheeky like that in them days. I asked girls out for the hell of it. With her I knew she was coming back and I knew I was going to ask her. I had time to get nervous, so by the time she comes back I was bricking it. I had something funny to say. I can't remember what it was, but it made her laugh. That was the other thing about Susan back then. She'd laugh at stuff. Any joke you made, she laughed. I thought it was just me but she did it with all the blokes. Makes you feel special – till you realise.' He squinted and looked away. 'After that I couldn't wait to marry her, you know? I made all the right noises around me mates, like you do – ball and chain, life sentence and all that – but the truth

343

was, I could not *wait* to marry that woman. I thought that once I married her she was mine. She'd never be able to get away. Thing is, I didn't want to change her, not like a lot of blokes who get married. I wanted her to stay Susan for the rest of her life – but be mine.' He broke off. 'Have you met her?'

'No. I've seen her, but not met her.'

'Changed now, of course. Lost her looks. Drinks a bit, apparently. Lives with some do-gooder on the Eastern Estate. They've got a kid together. Right tearaway, I hear. Things have changed for her. But back then . . . She was . . .

'See, a girl like Susan. When you meet someone like that, your life changes. You can't go back to living like you lived before, and you kind of know that, so you do your best to keep it safe, and that's what I was doing. That's what I was doing with my . . . with my love –' he glanced at Charlie as if expecting to see him smirk – 'which was why I couldn't wait to get married, to try and . . .' He formed his hands as though he were holding a box. 'But Susan – there'd always be some bloke sniffing round. With a woman like that you just hope they'll never sniff back. All you can do is hope.

'Then she started work at the Land place, January nineteen seventy-two. I remember – I took the Christmas tree down the day she started – I remember that. Fuck knows how long it took for Byron Land to start sleazing around. Not long, I bet. He was just starting himself, same age as Susan, learning the ropes from his old man. His old man was twice the man he'll ever be, I'll tell you that much . . .'

'She started an affair.'

'They started fucking, yeah.'

'You knew?'

'Sometimes, with stuff like that, you ignore what's going

on. You accept lies that you know are lies because you want them to be true. She got pregnant and I was still kidding myself, like a twat. I decided the kid was mine and that was that.'

'Until?'

'The day he died. She told me that night. In hospital. They took her in for the shock and she told me. I never saw her since.'

Charlie looked down at Mary, who had now fallen asleep, the bottle slipped from her mouth. He placed her in the pushchair, carefully pulling the straps round her arms. She snorted, seemed about to wake up then fell asleep again, head lolling. He pulled the sun visor down and checked her feet were in the shade before he turned back to the table. 'I'm sorry,' he said. 'That must have been heartbreaking.'

Slater sniffed. 'Yeah. Course. But it ended up being the best thing that ever happened to me.'

'The Lands paid you off.'

Slater chortled. 'Oh yes. What do you think bought me the dealership? The house in Rickmansworth?' He fingered the Rotary pin on his tie. 'What do you think took me up in the world? Aubrey Land didn't just pay me off to save his son's blushes, he made me one of his own. I shouldn't have to pay for his son's mistakes, he said.'

'So he paid you to keep quiet,' said Charlie.

'They still do. It was all worked out with loans. Keeps it above board.'

'Plus you can't just take the money and decide to talk anyway. The pay-offs ensure your continued silence. Or did. But you've made your money now, and the loans are a drop in the ocean for you, or maybe you've even paid them off, and you don't need their money any more, so you've decided to start talking?'

Slater was grinning, shaking his head. 'Nah, you're barking up the wrong tree, mate. You're right about the money. Course I don't need it. But do you think I'd want to get on the wrong side of the Lands? I own the leasehold on the dealership. Guess who owns the freehold? Guess who owns the field behind my house? If you've got a field behind your house, they probably own that, too. The Lands have got outline planning permission on sheltered accommodation for the field behind my house. They could knock a quarter of a million off my property if they wanted. They could decide to redevelop my dealership if they wanted. They could turn me inside-out overnight without even trying. So if you think I'd do anything to upset the Lands, my friend, you've got it wrong.'

Charlie felt frozen in time, knew that it was coming. The answer. 'So why are you telling me?'

'I'm telling you because you need to know that there's a time to ask questions and there's a time to shut the fuck up and let the past stay in the past.'

'And why would I want to shut the fuck up?'

'Because of your old man.'

## Sins of the Fathers, and All That

Charlie's head dropped. Anyone watching would have come to the conclusion that he'd just been informed of the death of a relative. Finally he raised his head. 'My father took money too, didn't he?'

Slater nodded, proud of his juicy secret. 'Sorry, mate,' he said. 'I'm sure you were hoping it was just a coincidence that you lot all moved out to the nice part of town not long after Mark died. Kid's hardly gone cold and you lot were trading up. I suppose you thought Daddy'd saved his pennies. Because he was the frugal sort, of course, always went home for lunch, which must have saved a couple of bob. But lunch is when Byron Land and my wife used to do their fucking, so maybe he saw some comings and goings, your old man. What do you reckon?'

'Shut it.' Charlie stood up abruptly. The gentle hubbub of conversation on the patio seemed to tail off. Slater smiled up at him.

Charlie sat down. 'Listen, you,' he hissed. 'Don't. Ever again. Drag my father down to your level. My father never blackmailed anyone. He wouldn't have known how.'

'*Known how?*' laughed Slater. 'What's to know? Blackmail's easy. A word in the right earhole, a little wish list. The trick is not to get too greedy. Keep them close, let them think they're keeping *you* close. And as long they keep their side of the bargain, you keep yours.'

'That's you. He wasn't like you.'

'Was he twice the man I am?' sneered Slater.

For a second, Charlie thought he'd actually do it. In that moment he imagined himself diving across the table and sticking one in Geoffrey Slater's ugly, stinking mouth.

Maybe he would have done if his mobile phone hadn't vibrated in his pocket. Once. Twice. Not a message, a call, and he reached into his pocket for it, holding Slater's gaze as he did so.

Beamob.

'Hey, babe,' he said. 'How did it go?'

'Is everything all right? Mary okay?'

'She's fine. She's had her lunch.'

'Is she in bed now?'

Charlie glanced at Mary, snoozing in the pushchair. 'Yeah,' he said. 'She's sound asleep. Might take her out this afternoon. Anyway, how did it go with you?'

'Oh, yeah, it went well, thanks. I told them my proposal and they didn't pull any faces or anything, so we'll just have to wait and see.'

Slater was looking at his watch.

'That's fantastic, babe,' said Charlie. 'Ah, I think just heard something from the monitor, I'd better go.'

'Right. Don't let her sleep too long. She only needs an hour or so or she won't go down for her mid-afternoon nap.'

'Will do, Bea. Take care. Enjoy your shopping. I'm glad it went well at work.'

He ended the call.

'That the missus?' said Slater.

'Yes.'

'She any idea what kind of family she married into?' He snorted. 'You're dropping like flies, you lot.'

He ignored it. Let the abuse pass into him and out again. White noise. 'My father wouldn't have blackmailed anyone,' he repeated levelly.

'Maybe he didn't need to.'

'What do you mean?'

'I mean, not everybody's a go-getter like me. Maybe they came to him, made him an offer he couldn't refuse. What would you do, mate, someone comes along and offers you enough money to get your company out of debt, move house, provide for your family? All for not mentioning certain facts to the police.'

Charlie thought about it. What would he do? 'Did *he* know the baby was Byron Land's?' he asked.

Slater shook his head, no.

'Then what? He knew Byron Land had an affair with your wife? And that was it? That was enough for the big pay-off?' Charlie was thinking madly. 'No, it wasn't enough, of course not. There was more than that, wasn't there? You knew the kid wasn't Byron's. He didn't. But he knew something else. Something just as damaging.'

Slater was nodding. 'Yeah, he knew something else. The Lands weren't spunking up all that cash just to spare Byron's blushes after he fucked the office girl – some affair that he could have said ended months ago. He could have brushed that one off, no harm done. It wasn't like he was married or anything. A baby, though, that was different. That was worth keeping quiet. So they paid me. And what your dad knew was worth keeping quiet, so they paid him.'

'What did he know?'

Slater beckoned him across the table, leaning forward. Charlie glanced at Mary, checking she was still in shade, and leaned forward too.

'That Byron Land was there that day,' said Slater.

'The day Mark died?'

'The very day. Normal service was being resumed. She'd hardly popped Mark out and Byron Land was back, snuffling around. God knows why. Must've had a fanny like a wizard's sleeve.'

'He was there, at Crosby Street? With Susan?'

'Yup. And that's not all, my friend. Not only was he there that day, but he left and then he returned.'

'You were at work?'

'Yeah, working my arse off like a good little husband and father. But not your dad, remember? Home for lunch, your dad, and who should he see in the neighbour's garden but my wife and Byron Land, and not long after, little Mark's gone glug-glug.'

'Who told you this? Aubrey Land?'

'Aubrey? Nah. He worked on a strictly need-to-know basis, did Aubrey.'

'Byron, then?'

'Bryon's a basket-case, my friend. He took a holiday from life a long time ago. What I hear he can barely get out of bed in the morning. It's Timson who runs Land Associates. No, Byron didn't tell me anything. Somewhere in his mind he probably thinks it never even happened, and that he dreamed it all. It was your dad who told me, actually.'

Charlie looked at him.

'He came to the showroom,' continued Slater, 'the old one on Hill Street. Guess who owned the freehold on that one? Anyway, he come bowling up in his Granada . . .' Charlie squeezed his eyes closed. He remembered the Granada. Burgundy. Mum had said it was too big.

'This wasn't long before he died, as I recall. He was ill, you could see it,' continued Slater. 'He didn't have long for this world, looking a bit yellow round the edges. He was pissed, too. But I suppose if you're going to have cirrhosis of the liver, you might as well enjoy it, eh?'

'Don't push it,' said Charlie. 'Just don't, all right?'

Slater licked his lips. 'Anyway, he comes on to the forecourt shouting the odds so I took him into the office before he ended up telling the world. That's when he talked. He'd seen Land that day, he said. Did I know that my son's blood bought all this? The dealership, he meant.'

'Byron went back in,' said Charlie, more to himself. 'What for?'

'Who knows?'

' "Who knows?" ' repeated Charlie. 'He does. Susan does.'

'Susan was asleep, remember.'

'So she never knew he'd returned while she slept?'

'Still doesn't.'

'Christ, you lot are priceless,' spat Charlie, disgusted.

'Why does she need to know?' shrugged Slater.

Charlie made an exasperated sound. 'Because she *deserves* to. Byron Land might have killed Mark.'

'Nah, mate, not a chance.'

'Because he knew Mark was his?'

'Oh, yeah, he knew. And, according to her, he wanted to take them away. He had a whole future planned for them. Funny the way things turn out, isn't it? But no way Byron Land killed his son.'

'And Dad knew that?'

'No.'

'And you didn't tell him?'

'Couldn't, could I?'

'My dad might have died wondering if he'd helped cover up a murder.' Charlie felt giddy with hatred for Slater.

'Yeah, well, jumping to conclusions runs in your family, doesn't it? Now, you're going to have to excuse me. I've said everything I came to say.' He stood. 'Correct me if I'm wrong, but I'm guessing you won't be going to the police.'

'There's nothing to tell them, is there?'

'No, my friend, there isn't.' He thrust his hand into his pocket, pulled out a ten-pound note and dropped it on to the table. Charlie hadn't touched his coffee.

'You want to take my advice?' said Slater. 'Forget it. Forget the whole thing. Don't end up like your old man and your brother. It ain't worth it.'

# The Sorries

*I've got something to tell you, mate.*

Cheers, Leo, I got there in the end. What you wanted to tell me was how Dad took money to hide what he knew, and medicated himself to death because of the guilt. How the money he left wasn't a nest egg but blood money.

Oh, Dad. Why?

But Charlie knew why. He looked at Mary and knew why. Because dads do things to care for their children. Simple as that. But, Christ, there were so many messed-up people. A woman in a mini-skirt slept with her boss and decades later there were so, so many messed-up people.

Okay, okay, think – what next?

He needed to see Susan Slater.

'Sorry, baby,' said Charlie, as he drove, to Mary. 'I'm sorry for driving you around when I should be playing stimulating games with you. I'm sorry we're in the world's hottest car, which is like Death Valley with a Peugeot badge on it, only hotter. I'm sorry for being such a bad father.'

In response, she gurgled.

He guessed she'd understand, in time.


'Hi,' he said to the woman at reception in the council offices. 'Where do I have to go for the electoral roll?'

'Third floor,' she said, smiling down at Mary, who made a funny noise in return, like a gift.

'Thanks,' he said, picking up the car seat, already moving towards the lift.

After a wait at a window on the third floor, pressing the bell, baby seat dangling, craning round the window to see if anybody was going to bother bloody serving him, he requested the electoral roll, and moments after that he'd plonked Mary's car seat on a table and was sitting down, flicking through the register . . . Which was indexed by street.

'Excuse me,' he said, 'excuse me.' He managed to catch a council person as they passed the hatch. 'Do you have a copy of the electoral roll that's ordered by surname?'

'Sorry,' she said, looking at Mary on the table. 'Just by street.'

'But is there any way of looking it up by surname?'

'Telephone book?'

'But I need to . . . I need to find someone, so I have to check the Christian name and I need the house number. You don't have some way of accessing it here?' He gestured at a computer monitor that sat on the other side of the window.

'Not really, I'm afraid, not that's available to members of the public. Do you know whereabouts this person lives?'

'Erm, not really –' he remembered what Slater had told him – 'except that it's somewhere on the Eastern Estate.'

The council person reached through and took the register

from him. 'Well, that's in this ward,' she said, going to a middle section. 'Best you can do is go through it street by street.'

'But that could take . . .' He glanced at his watch, then back at her. She had the decency to look sympathetic.

He was about three-quarters of the way through the ward, had noted down two Susan Slaters, then came across a third.

Susan Slater. He noted it down. She lived on Freight Road. According to the electoral register, with a Selina Philips and a Paul Philips. Neither of the two previous Slaters had looked hopeful. One was clearly a married couple, the other a family with the Slater surname. This one fitted the profile.

He noted the Freight Street address on his damp pad, picked up the baby seat, thanked the receptionist and left.

# Susan and Byron

They met on Crosby Street. They had been meeting there occasionally. Not as much as he would have liked, but every now and then. At first they'd argued about the past, but in a roundabout way, without ever actually talking about it. Now they just spoke, finding comfort in each other, like two veterans from the same war. He tried to give her money. She refused. He tried to give her Charles Laughton and she'd refused him, too, until one night Byron had left the dog tethered and walked away, forcing her to take him.

'Hello,' he said now.

'Hello.'

Charles Laughton stared at Byron Land nervously, plainly hoping he wasn't about to be returned, but Byron Land wasn't looking at Charles Laughton. He was looking at Susan, who looked back at him.

He wore a polo shirt open at the neck, linen trousers, brown brogues. From the neck down he could have passed for the man he used to be. Attractive, well-dressed. The years had taken their toll on his face though: the stretched, besieged skin. He wore his orange-lens glasses, the ones he wore all the time, whatever the weather, inside or out, as if his eyes were afraid to see the world. He hadn't always worn them, she recalled, hadn't worn them in 1973.

Charles Laughton settled by her feet. She reached one hand down to scruff at his neck. If he was a cat, he would have purred. 'Thank you for coming,' she said at last.

Byron Land spread his hands, as though to say it was the least he could do.

She nodded. 'I wouldn't have asked you here if it wasn't something important. If there wasn't something I needed to ask you. A favour.'

'Anything.'

'Really?'

He took a step forward, emphasising. 'Anything it's in my power to do.'

'It's about Mark's grave.'

'Yes.'

'I know you're paying a man called Joe Parks to get the kids who did it.'

His face darkened. 'Don't tell me you disapprove?'

'I want you to stop it.'

'No.'

'Please. For me. For the friends we once were.'

'Tell me why.'

A car passed, blatting music. She waited until it had gone.

She smiled. 'You know, Byron, I've mourned Mark for more than thirty years. I tried not to – for so long. I tried to carry on. I had a little girl and I hoped she would replace Mark, but she didn't, and still I mourned him, until eventually I gave in. I decided that my role had been given to me. I had no choice but to mourn my son. It was my punishment, my duty.

357

That was ten years ago, and every week since then I've taken flowers to his grave and I've sat with him, and I've told him how sorry I am that he didn't live his life.

'When I saw what they'd done to his grave I felt like he'd died all over again, and I thought about the kids who'd done it, and I wanted them to feel some of my pain. I wanted them to know what it felt like to be desecrated.'

He was nodding. 'That's how I felt, exactly.'

'I wanted to *get* the people responsible.'

'Then . . .'

'Byron, if you really want to hurt the person responsible for desecrating Mark's grave, I'm the one you want.'

He raked fingertips down his cheek, leaving red lines which faded instantly. 'What do you mean?'

'The person who desecrated Mark's grave,' she took a deep breath, 'was Selina.'

They had spoken for a long time in the graveyard, Susan and Selina, sitting on the grass, with Mark at their backs. They had spoken for perhaps longer than they ever had.

Now Byron Land absorbed the information, his eyes behind the brown glasses screwed tight shut. 'Selina did it,' he stated flatly.

'Selina should have been my world,' said Susan. 'I hardly even knew she was in it. I hadn't only lost a son, Byron, I'd lost a daughter, too. Do you blame her? Her brother had destroyed her life, just by being dead.'

He nodded, understanding. 'You're asking me to call off Joe Parks?'

'Yes, please. Either he hurts me or he hurts no one. My daughter has suffered enough.'

'She and her friends are scum.'

She shook her head. 'They're kids who pay the price for their parents, Byron. You, of all people, should understand that. Mark would.'

Byron looked to his right, at the house. It had had a front garden in 1973, a small patch of grass, sapling in the middle. Other details he couldn't recall, but the grass and sapling he did. Now, of course, the front garden was gone. In its place was a tarmac drive. It was empty, the owners at work, presumably. 'What would you do if I refused?' he asked, looking back at Susan.

She smiled again. 'What could I do to you, Byron? All I can say is that if anything happened to Selina you'd never see me again. Not ever.'

He nodded slowly. 'There are two reasons that won't be necessary, Susan. First, because I'll speak to Joe Parks and nobody else will get hurt. You have my word on that.'

'And second?'

'Because this is the last time you'll see me.'

She gazed at him, then averted her eyes, shaking her head. 'No, Byron, no.'

'Yes, Susan. I can't handle it any more. I think the police will come soon.'

'The police?'

'You were asleep that day, Susan.'

Her head dropped. 'Yes.'

'So you didn't see.'

Now her head jerked up. 'Didn't see what?'

# Freight Street

Freight Street was lined on either side with uniform terraces, the kind that looked as though they'd been designed by somebody with only a ruler for company. Front doors opened on to derisory gardens, most of which were either overgrown or full of junk that the bin men had refused to collect, or both. This was where Susan Slater had ended up. Her ex-lover was one of the richest men in the Home Counties, her ex-husband a Rotary-pin-wearing pillar of the car-dealing community. But she'd ended up here.

Predictably there was nowhere to park. Charlie located the correct house, then found himself cruising to the end of the street before he found a space, squeezing the Peugeot between a rusty Metro and a green-covered motorbike, neither of which looked like they'd been moved since Thatcher resigned. He killed the engine and got out, un-folding the buggy and putting Mary into it, checking the sun visor, then deciding she needed the little brolly, too. He glanced at his watch. What time was she supposed to go down for her afternoon sleep? Would it matter if she fell asleep now? Again, how on earth did Bea remember all this stuff? He pushed the pushchair along the street to Susan Slater's house.

Joe Parks turned into Freight Street at the far end and parked the Toyota opposite a children's playground. Mums and dads played with their kids on one side, giving the big swings a wide berth. On the big swings a bunch of five kids had been sitting, hanging around, spitting, swearing and enjoying intimidating the mums and dads, who hurried extra fast to collect any curious toddler who wandered their way.

One of the youths looked up and saw the red Toyota. Joe Parks leaned forward, smiling at the group, which began to disband, the kids leaving the swings swaying in their wake, all five drifting off, snatching backward glances at Joe Parks, who watched them go, grinning.

Selina Philips wasn't among of them, but word had got round so he bet she'd either holed up at her mum's or was staying with a mate. Either way, she was his; didn't matter where she was. She was his. Bitch had vandalised her own half-brother's grave. He got out of the Toyota and slammed the door, leaning into the wing mirror and admiring his new diamond-cluster earring. It kind of made him look like David Beckham, he thought, when Becks had worn this sort of gear. He ought to keep an eye on what Beckham was wearing, he decided. That way he could always be ahead of the game. He straightened, began to walk down Freight Street, then heard his phone chirrup in his jeans.

It was him. Land.

'Yes, boss?' he said.

Byron Land told him the job was over. That he should forget about hurting the kids, and especially forget about hurting Selina Philips. Parks stopped on the pavement, frowning. Land went on to say that he would still get payment in full for the job (now Joe Parks smiled), and that if he wanted to drop by the house at some point today, he could collect his cash.

Which sweetened the pill for Joe Parks, who ended the call, gazed wistfully down the street at Selina's house and turned away.

Then turned back – something having caught his eye.

In the event, nobody answered the door. Charlie wasn't sure if the bell was working, so he knocked as well. When still nobody came, he felt his shoulders droop, either from relief or frustration, he couldn't decide. He pulled the pushchair back on its rear wheels and turned it, moving out to the pavement, about to return to the car.

He stopped.

About fifty yards away, between Charlie and his car, the guy with the high-visibility waistcoat stood with his feet apart and arms folded, as though providing pavement security. Through narrowed eyes he regarded Charlie, head tilted slightly to one side. He was smiling. The same smile Charlie had seen before, which held the promise of hurt. As Charlie watched, he unfolded his arms and held up one hand, in it a mobile phone. He appeared to press a button, doing it with a flourish, like a master villain with a detonator.

Charlie turned the pushchair, moving back down the street as his own mobile phone bleeped. He pulled it from his jeans, flicking it open as he walked.

One message. Sender unknown. It said, 'Saw you.'

He glanced behind him. The bloke in the high-visibility

waistcoat was following, keeping the same distance between them. He seemed to amble, as though he had all the time in the world. Charlie reached the junction with the main road, glancing behind him – bloke still there. He should go left, into town, he decided. More people. Guy wouldn't try anything there.

He tapped out a message as he walked, continually looking up to make sure he didn't accidentally ram Mary into a lamppost.

'Who are you?' it said. He pressed send. He'd reached the outskirts of town. There was a Chinese restaurant he and Bea had never visited, a shop selling office equipment, another specialising in seating for babies. He looked behind him and the guy was still there, now looking at his own phone.

Charlie's mobile bleeped. He was holding it on the handle of the pushchair, flicked it open with his thumb and keyed the message button.

'I'm Joe Parks. And you've been told to leave well alone,' it said.

'Just fuck off,' keyed Charlie back, pressing send, turning a corner on to the high street.

But was that such a great move? Not telling the high-visibility waistcoat guy – sorry, Joe Parks – to fuck off, but turning into the high street. There were more people here, sure, and he was pretty certain Joe Parks wouldn't want to try anything with shoppers standing by, but if Charlie had hoped to lose him, then how? He was out in the open.

*And even if you do lose him*, said a voice inside, *he knows where you live. He's been in your house. And if he's been in your house once, it's not exactly beyond the realms of possibility that he's going to do it again.*

'Sorry,' came the message back. 'Not poss.'

Charlie stopped, pretending to admire offers in the window of Thomas Cook. Looking to his left he waited for Joe Parks to appear round the corner.

And waited.

He looked to his right. No sign of him there, either.

And waited.

His phone went. He flipped it open and accessed the message. 'Behind you,' it said.

Fuck. He looked behind. On the other side of the road stood Joe Parks, who lifted a hand to wave as Charlie turned.

Charlie mouthed 'Piss off' at him. In response Joe Parks did a mock-hurt face, then, as if Charlie was a neighbour he'd spotted on the other side of the street, called, 'How's the little one, mate? She having a sleep in there, is she?'

'*Piss off,*' mouthed Charlie a second time, only this time with extra venom.

Again, Joe Parks did his hurt face, then grinned, enjoying himself.

Now Charlie began to wheel the pushchair along the high street, glancing at the other pavement as he did so. Past Superdrug, Waterstones, Iceland, Beauty and the Bump, Woolworths, a bike shop. Off to the Bone, Burger King, Help the Aged.

All the time Joe Parks shadowed him on the opposite pavement, his green waistcoat hanging open, bare-chested, lord of the street.

Charlie was thinking. Okay, so what were they going to do now? It wasn't like they could cruise up and down the high street indefinitely. But then he was vulnerable at home. They were all vulnerable at home.

I'm sorry, baby, he thought, sending the sorry to his wife and baby girl. I'm sorry I've brought all this on you.

He stopped. On the opposite pavement Joe Parks stopped too. Charlie flipped open his phone and pressed the green call button.

Across the road, Joe Parks raised his eyebrows and brought his phone to his ear.

'Yeah,' he said. His lips moved a fraction ahead of the word. It gave the conversation a weird, delayed feel, like it was happening via satellite link.

'What do you want?' asked Charlie. He turned the push-chair and began to walk back down the high street.

'I've got a job to do,' said Joe Parks. He, too, turned round; Charlie could see him keeping level with them.

'What job?' said Charlie.

'Protecting the interests of my employer.'

'Who's your employer?'

'That information, also, is classified, I'm afraid.'

'And does it protect his interests if I call the police?'

'And tell them what?' asked Joe Parks.

Charlie stopped. Joe Parks stopped, too.

'That I'm being followed,' said Charlie, staring across the road at Joe Parks. Cars passed. An old lady pulling an old-lady-trolley-on-wheels negotiated her way round him.

'Well, you are being followed,' said Joe Parks, cheerily. He reached into the back pocket of his jeans and held out something frilly that Charlie recognised. 'I saw your little girl drop this and I was hoping to return it.'

Charlie bent to look into the buggy. Mary was asleep, head on one side. Christ – that was the second sun-hat she'd managed to lose.

'Give me that back,' he spat into the phone.

'Happy to,' said Joe Parks.

Now Charlie began to walk again. 'Look, I know a policeman, a detective inspector. I can call him right now, and he's going to believe me. He's going to believe that you are threatening me and my family.'

'Believing you's one thing, mate. Being able to do something about it is another.'

'You've been in my house.'

'Not me,' said Joe Parks. 'Like I say, my mate Gavin needed a bit of help with his nose. I was with him all night, and nowhere near your computer, which could do with dusting, if you don't mind me saying.'

'What you're doing is threatening behaviour.'

'Oh, I'm not even started yet, mate. You should have done as you were told.'

Charlie pushed the buggy into Woolworths, through the electric door, which opened with a thick clunk. 'Look,' he hissed, 'whatever the police might say, you don't want me to call them, do you? I mean, you don't look like the kind of bloke who wants the police sniffing round him. Bet they sniff a bit harder when it comes to you, eh?'

'It's all right, mate. I know my rights. Anyway, guy that's paying me says you won't be going to the police.'

'He's wrong. I'd do anything to protect my family.'

'Funny. That's why he said you wouldn't go to the police.'

'Tell Byron Land he's wrong.'

'Why would I want to tell him that?'

Charlie stopped by the DVD section. 'That's who you're working for, isn't it?'

'Well, I do work for Byron Land, in a manner of speaking.

On grounds maintenance. But a man can have more than one employer.'

'You told me you were working for Byron Land.'

'When?'

'This morning.'

'*When?*'

'On the fucking email.'

'Oh. No. I think I said I was protecting his interests. Look, here's a good one.'

Charlie looked up. Joe Parks stood on the other side of the DVDs, holding a case for Charlie to see. *The Tweenies*.

'Your little girl might like this one,' said Joe Parks.

Charlie lowered his phone, leaning forward across the display. 'I don't know what game you're playing,' he whispered harshly, 'but it ends now.'

Joe Parks replaced the *Tweenies* case, took his time selecting another. *Postman Pat*. 'What about this one?' he said pleasantly. But his eyes were nasty slits.

Charlie snapped his phone shut and pushed it into his jeans. Ignoring *Postman Pat* he moved away from the DVDs, pushing the pushchair down to the children's clothes, the front wheel squeaking. He stopped, pretending to admire some Power Rangers pyjamas but waiting to see what Joe Parks would do next. Not such a good move, he mused, fewer people in this part of the shop. Now Joe Parks was moving away from the DVDs, visible over the top of the aisle, coming in Charlie's direction. He got to the end of the DVD aisle where there was a mounted poster display, the type with hinges that make a satisfying clacking sound as you look through.

Charlie watched him as he made a show of browsing.

Clack. A poster of Eminem. Next, a picture of an alien smoking a spliff with 'Take Me To Your Dealer' on it. A generic dollybird on a big motorbike. SlipKnot. Jordan. Then – clack, clack, clack – Joe Parks dragged a hand across the display, letting them fall against each another, turning to regard Charlie who stood with the bottom half of the Power Rangers PJs in his hand.

They looked at one another. Slowly Joe Parks knelt down, as if to tie a shoelace, but as he did so he held Charlie's gaze; held it as he pulled up his trouser leg to reveal the knife sheathed there. He winked.

Charlie caught his breath.

Joe Parks stood and began to walk more purposefully down the aisle.

Charlie turned the buggy, almost jogging with it to the end of the shop, towards the toy section. Joe Parks was coming up behind him, more quickly now. Charlie performed a U-turn, going round the end of the unit and back up again, looking behind to see if Parks had followed. He hadn't. Charlie stopped, trying to second-guess Parks. The other man had obviously stopped mid-aisle, either tracking back or expecting Charlie to try to out-bluff him.

Shit.

He glanced up. There was no way of looking over the top of the unit without climbing up and risking an avalanche of Noddy soft toys. He looked down. No gap between unit and floor. Think, Charlie. Think.

Okay. Parks wanted him at the quiet end of the shop. So there'd be no point in coming round the end of the aisle. He'd be waiting to head Charlie off at the top. He'd be listening for the squeak of the pushchair wheel, waiting for Charlie to make his move and banking on him heading for the front of the shop, the security of the people there.

'Try me!' it said on the Noddy box. An arrow pointed at Noddy's tummy. He took the box off the shelf.

Now he turned the buggy to his left, back in the direction from which he'd come, lifting the squeaky front wheel off the floor, going as quickly as he dared.

At the end he glanced to his right, terrified he might have got it wrong – that standing just round the corner was Joe Parks, the knife out of its sheath.

No one there. He darted left into the next aisle along and stopped.

Tupperware.

Charlie put the Noddy box on the floor, pressed Noddy's stomach, lifted the front of the buggy and began to run down the aisle.

'Hurray for Noddy!' came the music, gratifyingly loudly, from behind him. And now he had to bank on Joe Parks hearing it, darting to the end of the display and realising – too late for you, you *fucker* – that Charlie was no longer in the aisle.

As Charlie emerged from the top of the aisle he glanced to his left, half expecting to see Parks there, grinning at his own cleverness. But no. Thank God, no. Charlie was flying now, through the baby clothes, ignoring an 'Oops, careful,' from a woman almost bowled over. Only when he'd traversed the pick'n' mix did he dare look behind him, and there, arriving at the baby clothes, walking quickly past the oops-careful wo-man, was Joe Parks. Not happy.

Charlie allowed himself a moment of glee, a shiver of excitement. Then he was out of Woolworths and into the high street, not caring that he was running and that people were looking at him inquisitively, pulling out his mobile phone, which arrived with half his jeans pocket, sprinkling sweet wrappers and bits of fluff to the pavement, dialling nine.

Because it had gone too far. There was too much at stake. I'm sorry, Bea, and I'm sorry, Dad, but it's got to stop.

Nine.

His phone rang. It was Parks. He answered. 'What?'

'Clever boy,' said Joe Parks.

'I've just dialled the cops.'

'Because of a man trying to return your daughter's hat?'

'Because I've just seen that you're carrying a weapon. I trust you'll be as quick to show the police.'

He was outside Barclays now. He looked behind. There was the high-visibility waistcoat – easy to spot, at least – Parks's phone at his ear. He was on the street and hurrying, but Charlie had put a lot of distance between them now.

'Yeah, I'll show the police,' he was saying, 'but I work on the parks. I need a cutting tool, don't I?'

'Bollocks, it's a weapon,' Charlie said, 'and I'm calling the police.'

He pressed the phone's red button, holding the phone above his head so that Joe Parks would see, then dialling and very deliberately putting the phone back to his ear.

But it wasn't 999 he'd dialled. Above an empty shop front there was an estate agent's board, and it was this number he'd called.

'Good morning, Land Associates, how can I help?'

Snotty gum-chewing woman, probably.

'I need to speak to Mr Land, please,' gasped Charlie.

'I'm afraid Mr Land isn't in today. Can I help at all?'

'Where is he?'

'I really couldn't say. Can I help at all?'

He ended the call. Looking back, Joe Parks was the same distance behind, not hurrying, just following. Now Charlie was coming to the end of the high street. There were still shops but fewer people.

Charlie found another number and dialled again. This time Jane Land answered. 'Mr Watson,' she said cautiously.

'Where's your husband?' he barked.

'At home, as far as I know. Why?'

'Tell him to call off the bloke.'

'What *bloke*, Mr Watson?'

'The bloke who's threatening me and my baby. Tell Byron I'm not interested in him, or what he did in the past. *I just don't care.* I want to forget about the whole bloody lot of you and go back to being a not-very-successful wedding DJ. Okay? You got that?'

'Um, I don't think I have.'

'Just tell him,' Charlie snapped, and pressed the red button off. A look behind. Parks still there. They were coming past the station now. They were heading out of town.

Then, instead of going down the hill towards home, Charlie took a sudden left, was sweating and gasping as he thrust the pushchair up a footpath, the front wheels spinning madly on the uneven ground.

Christ, shaken-baby syndrome, he thought, but didn't slow down. And now the jolting disturbed Mary, who woke with a low yowl that swiftly became a scream.

Joe Parks would have seen him, would be quickening now, because Charlie had gone up the pathway and where better to do Joe Parks business than on a quiet, overgrown footpath?

Mary screamed. Charlie could hardly blame her. He didn't remember the path being so rough, but he'd never tried sprinting up it with a pushchair before. He could hear Joe Parks's footfalls behind him. And now, as he came over the brow of the incline, he could see the opening of the pathway, make out hedges beyond. Tall, well-maintained, screening hedges at that, because the footpath came out, he'd remembered, into Armitage Avenue.

No pavements. Just as he remembered it from the last time he'd visited, when he'd decided he was lowering the tone. Now he really was, pounding along with the buggy, spraying sweat, Joe Parks running behind him. Charlie heard his own running feet, felt his breathing in his ears, heard the buggy's squeaky wheel.

Mary crying. His own voice trying to soothe her.

He risked a glance behind. Joe Parks was jogging, gaining on them. He looked out of breath. Either he smoked too much or he'd misjudged the distance Charlie had put between them.

Ahead he saw the gate to the Land house, beyond that the gravel drive, the ornamental island, flowers in bloom. After that the house.

Something he remembered from the day of his visit to Jane Land was that the gate had a button on the inside; he'd pressed it himself to get out. He remembered thinking that someone could conceivably get their arm through the gate to push the access button.

He was about to find out whether or not it was possible.

Arriving at the gate he skidded to a halt, thrusting his arm through the iron bars in one movement, hand feeling for the switch.

Feeling for it.

Joe Parks gaining.

*Come on, come on.*

His fingers found the base of the unit. He stood on tiptoe, he strained, his fingers searching out the button and – finally – activating it.

Charlie swung through with the gate, pulling his arm back and grabbing the pushchair, shoving it through, turning and slamming the gate behind him.

Joe Parks reached it at that moment and, for a second, the gate was all that divided them and Parks grinned at Charlie, his arm already snaking through, fingertips searching out the access button.

Charlie didn't have breath to waste on abuse or reason. He spun the buggy and began to push, the gravel so deep that the wheels seemed to sink into it as if it was snow. With a grunt, he lifted the front wheels so that it ran on the fatter, rear ones.

From behind him he heard the gate go.

He heard the crunch of Joe Parks on the stones. Charlie pushed, almost bent double keeping the front wheels off the gravel, shaking his head as sweat poured into his eyes, blinding him, willing the pushchair on and to the front door. Then, as he reached the steps, a final effort as he lifted it, threw himself forward and hammered on the door.

He swivelled round, moving to the front of the pushchair so it was between him and the door. Joe Parks would have to get through him to reach it. Joe Parks would reach that pushchair over his dead body.

But Parks had stopped. He'd reached the ornamental island and remained there, wary. Charlie looked down at himself, his T-shirt wringing with sweat.

Nobody came to the door.

'Answer the door, answer the door,' he muttered.

Joe Parks took a tentative step forward. He, too, had noted the drought of people rushing to open the door. Mouth twisting into a smirk, he knelt, pulled up his trouser leg and unsnapped the knife from its sheath, bringing it out into the open. Sunlight glinted off the blade.

Charlie turned and hammered on the door again. Come on, come on. *Please come on!*

And still nobody came. Joe Parks moved forward, grinning now, teeth exposed.

There was a doorbell. Charlie hadn't seen it before, but there it was, and he pushed it, hearing the bell ring inside, loudly. At least it was working.

Joe Parks lifted the knife so Charlie could see the blade. He was just a few steps away. Mary was still crying.

*Come on, come on.*

There were footsteps from behind the door and Charlie turned as it opened. There stood Byron Land, his orange-lens glasses on, his silver hair, his drawn face with its look of permanent distress, eyes darting from Charlie to the baby, then to Joe Parks.

Charlie almost screamed, pointing at Joe Parks: '*Call him off!*'

# Wasted Land

For a moment or so, Byron Land stood on his doorstep. He swayed slightly, Charlie noticed. Christ, he's off his face, he thought. He's off his face and he's not going to offer sanctuary or call off his dog. He's going to let Joe Parks get on with the job, right here on his drive. Now.

'Call him off,' repeated Charlie, calmer now. 'This has gone far enough, Byron. Just. Call. Him. Off.'

Land looked at Charlie and his mouth struggled to work itself into a smile. 'Hello, Mr Watson.'

'Are you listening to me?' said Charlie, his voice breaking, a betrayal screech there.

Now Land stared beyond him and Charlie saw that Joe Parks had tucked the knife into the waistband of his jeans, just a tiny hint of handle at his waist. 'Parks,' called Land, 'what on earth is going on?'

'Just a misunderstanding, Mr Land,' said Joe Parks evenly.

Charlie was reaching down, unclipping the pushchair's restraints and picking up Mary, pulling her to him, smelling her smell, feeling her warmth. Almost immediately she seemed to calm, her head moving to take in Byron Land on his doorstep.

'What misunderstanding is that?' barked Charlie, over his shoulder. To Land he said, 'You know exactly what's going on.'

He jogged Mary gently as he spoke, her hair on his cheek. Smelling something besides her baby scent now, he realised she had a dirty nappy. Great.

'I'm afraid I don't,' said Land, sighing as though he neither knew nor cared.

'He's working for you.'

'He works for me, yes.'

'You've hired him to threaten me.'

Byron smiled a faint smile at Charlie. 'Why would I do that?'

'Because you didn't want me to find out about you and Susan and Mark. But now that I have, it doesn't matter. Really, you can all go back to living your fucked-up lives.'

Byron Land's voice was soft and dreamy. 'I intend to go on living my fucked-up life, thank you. Living the rest of my fucked-up life was exactly what I planned to do before you rang the doorbell. As for everything else, I really have no idea what you're talking about. I suggest you both take your argument somewhere else.'

For a second Charlie thought he might be hallucinating, but Byron Land really was stepping back. He really was about to shut the door. Charlie shot a look at Joe Parks, the other man's face registering surprise, too, but a pleasant surprise.

'What?' said Charlie. It was all he could manage. 'What are you doing?'

'I'm closing the door. Good day to you.'

'No, I don't think you understand.' His eyes went to Joe Parks again.

The door was closing.

'I know,' called Charlie through the gap, still jogging a now-silent Mary at his chest.

'Know what, Mr Watson?'

Charlie took a deep breath. 'That Mark wasn't your son.'

## Elsa Lanchester's Secret Life

He'd come across it poking around on the Internet a couple of nights ago. He'd keyed in 'Elsa Lanchester' and hit return. Moments later he'd been looking at biographical detail on her. She hadn't won that Academy Award for *Come to the Stable*. Figured. She'd been nominated for another, yet again a Best Supporting Actress Oscar, and yet again she hadn't won. This time it was *Witness for the Prosecution*, which co-starred her husband, Charles Laughton. She'd married Laughton in 1929 and they'd stayed together until his death in 1962. Which was all very sweet, and not many Hollywood marriages last that long, etc. Except.

After Laughton's death she had written a book, *Elsa Lanchester Herself*, an entertaining memoir in which she claimed that the reason she and Laughton had never had children was because Laughton was gay.

That was it. Charles Laughton was gay.

And he remembered one night at the cinema. They'd been at a midnight double bill of *Frankenstein* followed by *Bride of Frankenstein*. He'd sold it to Bea by telling her what a laugh it was so she'd brought along a couple of guys from

378

the band. 'You've got to dress up,' Charlie had said, and they had. The two guys had come as the monster, Bea as the Bride. Well, supposedly. She'd worn a white outfit, back-combed her hair, was wearing some extra-glossy lipstick and all right, she looked *nothing* like the Bride, but she still looked fabulous.

'God,' she'd said, glancing around, 'wish I'd made more effort now.'

'Yeah,' said Charlie, strangely proud of his clientele. 'Some of these guys pull out all the stops. She's bit of a gay icon, the Bride is. For Goth gays, I suppose. Like, if you find Doris Day and Judy Garland a bit Goody Two Shoes, there's the Bride of Frankenstein.'

Lanchester was a gay icon, and Charles Laughton was gay, and a decade after Bea had backcombed her hair and applied her glossy lipstick, Charlie played a hunch to save himself and their daughter.

'Mark wasn't your son,' he said again.

The door stopped closing.

'Please repeat,' said Land from inside.

'Mark wasn't your son. It's what Slater thinks but, then, Slater doesn't know you're gay, does he? But you are, so Mark's not yours – and you went back that day, didn't you? Did you kill him, Byron? Did you kill Mark?'

The door swung open again. Land's gaze went from Charlie to Joe Parks. He seemed to decide. 'I think you'd better come in,' he said. 'Both of you.'

'Not him,' said Charlie. 'He comes nowhere near my daughter.'

'Nothing will happen to her.' Land was beckoning Joe Parks in from the drive. 'You have my word on that. We really do need to sort this out, I'm afraid. His presence is necessary. Unpleasant,' he smiled thinly, 'but required, all the same.'

Charlie placed Mary in the buggy. She was quiet now, back in curiosity mode.

Joe Parks had joined them on the step. Suddenly Charlie felt as if he was back in the playground and had been caught getting beaten up by the school bully – felt the same surge of injustice. 'It was him,' he felt like saying. 'He started it.' But Byron Land was standing aside and opening the door wide for Charlie to push the buggy inside, Joe Parks at his heels.

'In here,' said Land, stepping to one side and ushering the strange convoy into his office, which was as Charlie remembered it, the Lanchester memorabilia along one wall, the desk and chair.

They waited obediently, like the domestic staff called together for an announcement, as Land pulled back his chair and sat down – then offered a rolled-up note to his nose, leaned towards his desk and snorted what Charlie could only assume was a line of cocaine.

Charlie looked at Joe Parks, who smiled back evilly and said, 'Good stuff, innit, boss?' At least now Charlie knew where Byron Land got his drugs.

Then Joe Parks's smile faded, his eyes widened and Charlie turned his head, following Parks's gaze to the desk where Byron, a man who now had cocaine stampeding in the direction of his bloodstream, sat holding a gun.

It was a pistol. He'd picked it out of a drawer, probably, and was holding it across the top of the desk, his hand shaking slightly. It pointed forward, at nobody in particular, Charlie noted, with faraway relief. But it pointed.

Charlie didn't know a lot about guns. His only experience

with them was second-hand, gleaned mainly from films and comics or the weaponry that action figures carried. This one looked like an automatic, though, the kind that used to be called a Browning: an old-looking gun, but a gun all the same. One that fired bullets. Pointing in his general direction and in the general direction of his baby daughter. Held by the trembling hand of a man who, if there was a line in his life, had clearly just stepped over it or, more relevantly, snorted it.

Again, Charlie glanced at Joe Parks. There, at least, was a gratifying sight. Finally his arrogance had drained away. He stood with his mouth hanging slightly open, as if paralysed by the dread-gas that seemed to have seeped into the room.

'Yes,' said Byron Land, 'I'm pointing a gun at you.'

'Byron,' started Charlie, trying to make his voice calm.

'Yes, Mr Watson,' said Land, as though Charlie was about to ask him a quesetion regarding the décor.

'Well,' said Charlie, stepping over his words as if they were mines, 'it's the gun.'

'Yes?'

'What are you doing with it?'

Land sniffed a coke-snort sniff and used his non-pistol hand to push his glasses up his nose. His sudden ascent to gunslinger status had done nothing for him. He still looked like a reduced person. Maybe even more so. Perhaps Charlie should have been reassured by that fact, but he wasn't. He thought only of Mary, sitting in her pushchair in front of him. Without craning over the top he couldn't tell if she'd fallen asleep or was at this very moment contemplating the gun.

'This isn't happening,' said Joe Parks, robotically, uselessly, at his side. And Joe Parks was bang-on. Because if you travelled the Met line into town, then maybe you might expect a drug lord in an opulent Mayfair penthouse to produce a gun. Fly British Airways, and perhaps a gangster might pull a gun on you in a Miami beachfront apartment. But not here. This was Bentham. Where they lived was knife-outside-the-boozer turf *at worst*. This was a kicking behind Southern Fried Chicken country. This was the Home Counties. People didn't pull guns on people here.

Vaguely, he imagined telling Bea. *See?* he'd say triumphantly, *I told you we should never have moved out of Hackney.*

'Byron, I don't know what you're doing,' said Charlie, as evenly as he could manage. 'All I know is, you don't have to do it.'

'Do what?'

'Please, Byron, put the gun away. I've got a baby here. She's ten weeks old, for God's sake.'

Land took a deep breath as though deciding something important. 'There are some things I need to know first.' He shifted the gun very deliberately in the direction of Joe Parks.

This could be my opportunity, thought Charlie, and began to move round to the front of the buggy, wanting to shield Mary.

'Stay where you are, please, Mr Watson,' commanded Land.

'Boss . . .' said Joe Parks.

'Shut up.'

'Please, just let me stand in front of her,' said Charlie.

'Stay where you are.'

'Boss . . .' whined Joe Parks.

'If it goes off, though, Byron.'

'You'd do anything for your daughter, wouldn't you, Mr Watson? Even stop a bullet if you could,' said Land.

'Yes. Of course,' agreed Charlie.

'Boss . . .' whined Parks, again.

'*Shut up!*'

His hand shook so much it thumped against the table top. From the wall Elsa Lanchester regarded them.

'Go ahead, then,' said Land, composing himself. 'Stand in front of the pushchair. No other moves, though, and do it slowly. You must understand that I'm not used to handling a gun. If I feel I'm under threat it might easily go off.'

'Right.' Charlie wasn't sure whether to be unnerved or reassured by this information. Rich guy on cocaine. First time with gun.

Very slowly he moved to the front of the pushchair, catching a whiff of Mary's nappy and glancing down as he did so. She was asleep. Thank God for that. Soon she'd want feeding, though. If Byron was on edge right now, he ought to see Mary when she got hungry.

But Land's attention was on Joe Parks, and now Charlie became aware of tension between the two. Either he hadn't seen it before or it had only just surfaced, but here it was, as Land said, 'Who's paying you?'

'Boss . . .'

The gun lifted. Joe Parks took a step back and raised his arms.

'I asked you a question,' said Land.

'You pay me, Mr Land,' answered Parks, voice honey-coated and desperate to please.

'I didn't pay you to attack Mr Watson, though, did I?'

Charlie's head whipped round so hard he almost cricked his neck. He stared at Joe Parks, who glanced nervously at him. *Not Land*, thought Charlie. Byron Land wasn't employing him.

'No, Mr Land,' said Joe Parks.

'I pay you to help fulfil our grounds-maintenance contract with the council, I pay you for drugs and recently I've also paid you to hurt the people who destroyed Mark's grave, isn't that right?'

'Yes, Mr Land.'

'But I didn't pay you to frighten Mr Watson. Somebody else has done that, haven't they?'

'Yes, Mr Land.'

'Who?'

'Listen, Mr Land . . .'

'Just say his name.'

'Look, this ain't funny any more.'

'It was never funny to begin with.'

'I ain't into someone holding a gun on me.'

'It's not supposed to be a new hobby.'

'Me and you are going to fall out, Mr Land, if you don't put the gun down.'

'Me and you were never friends to begin with.'

'If you don't put it down now, you can forget about the racket. You ain't having any more coke off me, never.'

'I can live with that.'

'Put the gun down.'

'Tell me the name.'

'Put the fucking gun down, mate.'

'Tell me the name.'

'*Put the fucking gun down!*' Joe Parks screeched, spraying spittle.

'Oh, forget it,' said Byron. 'I know who it is anyway.'

He lifted the gun, used his other hand to steady it, and shot Joe Parks in the face.

# A Thumping Headache

Mary was just ten weeks old when she witnessed her first fatal shooting. Had she been old enough to testify, she would have said that she was unable to see the bullet hit and the victim fall, on account of being strapped into a pushchair facing in the opposite direction, your honour. Nor did she see the accused fire the gun, as her father was standing directly in front of her at the time, so all she was able to see was Daddy's funny bottom. In fact, she wasn't even aware of the accused holding the weapon, as she herself was enjoying a an afternoon nap — a nap that Mummy would have been a bit cross about, as it meant she would have difficulty in sleeping later on. No, the only thing she was aware of was the almighty bang, which woke her up.

'No, Byron,' Charlie heard himself say.

They're right, time does slow down. Maybe it's so that you can savour every little detail.

'No, Byron,' he heard himself say, but in the space between him speaking and Byron pulling the trigger, he analysed his words and found he said them without much conviction. He would wonder later whether his terrible secret was that he had wanted Byron to shoot Joe Parks. Obviously he didn't want Byron to shoot him in front of his daughter, which was why he said, 'No, Byron.' Or he said it simply because it was the kind of thing you *should* say in such a situation – would have been rude not to.

But maybe a little bit of him cheered that finally – at last – a bad guy copped it. Only the innocent and good seemed to die in this story. Hurrah, the balance was redressed.

Because when Byron pulled the trigger, and there was the strange mixed-up chronology of sound – the wet noise of the bullet entering Joe Parks's face before the report of the gun – and Charlie turned to look at Joe Parks, he found his principal feeling was relief that Joe Parks was no longer his problem, plus curiosity. He had never seen a man shot before. This was to be his first. Of course he wanted to see.

The shot had more to do with luck than good marksman-ship. Despite Land using both hands he was clearly no Dead-eye Dick. It could just as easily have taken a chunk out of the wall as thumped into Joe Parks's face. Unluckily for Joe Parks, it missed the wall and found his face.

He staggered back as though taking a punch. The bullet had made a hole in one cheek. From it, blood poured. Not spurted, but poured. A bottle uncorked. Joe Parks put one hand to his cheek, bringing it away to look at the blood on his fingers. The expression on his face was of mild surprise. He swayed on his feet.

Mary was crying, Charlie realised. Still in slow motion he looked down at her, then back at Joe Parks, who was reaching for his waist, for the knife there, only he was reaching at the wrong side. And Byron Land was frowning, steadying the gun again.

'No, Byron,' repeated Charlie, leaning forward, placing his hands over his daughter's ears and holding them there as Byron fired a second time.

Which did take a chunk out of the wall.

And a third time, this last shot hitting Joe Parks in the throat.

Parks sank to his knees. Both hands went to his neck. Blood sheeted down his front.

'Christ,' said Charlie. He kept his hands over Mary's ears as Joe Parks gurgled, then pitched forward to the carpet. You'll never get that stain out, thought Charlie, distractedly.

One Joe Parks foot thumped away at the floor.

*Thump-thump-thump.*

There was another gurgle.

*Thump-thump-thump.*

Mary had stopped crying, her attention diverted by the sensation of her father's hands over her ears. She seemed almost to be enjoying it. Charlie allowed himself to believe that a man dying just feet away from her would not cause permanent psychological scarring.

He looked at Byron Land. The man still held the gun, but now it rested on the table, not pointing anywhere. It rested where he'd let his arm fall, as though all of a sudden the weight of the weapon was too much for him.

*Thump-thump-thump.*

'Byron,' said Charlie softly. He stooped, his hands still over Mary's ears. After gunshots, the second-to-last thing he wanted her to hear was Joe Parks's death rattle. 'Byron,' he repeated.

'Yes?' replied Land, in a sigh.

'You're not going to hurt us, are you?'

'No, Mr Watson. I give you my word.'

'Then can we put the gun away, do you think?'

'I'm afraid not. I'm going to be needing it when you've gone.'

Charlie understood. He knew that the noble, the ethical, the morally correct thing would be to try to persuade Byron Land not to kill himself, but he found, with a great wave of internal fatigue, that he didn't care. He'd have to wrestle with that later, he guessed.

'How long will that go on for, do you think?' he asked.

*Thump-thump-thump.*

'I don't know, I'm afraid. It must be something to do with the nerves. Beyond that I couldn't say. Not long, I don't think.'

There was a pause.

'You killed Mark, didn't you?' said Charlie.

'Ah, I do know the answer to that question. The answer's no, Mr Watson, I didn't kill Mark. You're right, I'm gay, and Mark wasn't my son. He was my brother.'

# 1973

Byron turned round, going back to Susan's house, tutting because he couldn't quite believe he'd forgotten his jacket but also secretly pleased, because he was about to see her again. Would she have spotted the jacket and be expecting him back, holding it up with a sardonic smile? Or would she be surprised? Pleasantly surprised?

He reached the house and began to move down the alley which led to the back door, to the garden.

He stopped. Another man was standing in the alley. Byron had come from bright sun into the relative dark, and it took a moment or so for his eyes to adjust.

When they had, he said simply, 'Dad?'

'Byron,' said Aubrey Land.

Byron had never seen his father anything but composed and in control, but now his expression betrayed him. 'What are you doing here?' he asked. 'What's wrong?'

'It's Mark,' said Aubrey, stepping forward in the alleyway. 'I think you'd better come with me, Byron.'

He had Byron's jacket folded over one arm.

'Mark? What about him?'

'There's been an accident.'

Suddenly Byron felt panicked, boxed in by the alley and his father, who stood blocking the light. *Accident? What accident? He'd only been in the garden moments before.* 'What on earth do you mean? Where's Susan?'

'Susan fell asleep.'

Byron looked at his father for a long time.

'Oh, Dad,' he said, 'what have you done?'

'I think you should come with me. Quickly, before the police arrive.'

Aubrey took another step forward, reaching out to Byron, taking him by the shoulder and trying to lead him out of the alley. Byron shook him off. 'But he's your *son*.'

'You're my son, Byron. It's you I have to protect.'

'I don't need protecting. What have you done to him?'

'Nothing's going to destroy our family, Byron, I've made sure of it. You'll understand one day, when you have a family of your own.'

'No!' Byron opened his mouth to shout, was just about to call for Susan, when Aubrey punched him.

He had been hit by his father before, of course, but never punched, and it was the surprise more than the pain that sent him staggering backwards, holding his mouth, suddenly aware of his teeth, a great *chonk* sound in his skull. Aubrey was shaking his hand.

'I'm sorry, son,' he said, 'I'm sorry. I know it doesn't feel like it now, but it's all been for you – everything.'

They left, walking along the road to the junction and on to Willow Street where Aubrey Land was parked. As they climbed into his car, Byron looked up and saw a figure in the window of a house.

# Another Shot

'That was your father,' said Byron now.

Of course, thought Charlie. When he'd turned up at Slater's garage that day, shouting that Land had killed Mark, he'd meant Aubrey, not Byron.

'So it was Aubrey who was having the affair?'

'No, not an affair. A one-time thing, as I understand it. Something that happened after hours one night. A moment of weakness, I suppose. Aubrey was my father. I have never really wanted to go into the details of any dalliances. I'm sure you understand.'

'But why? Why kill Mark?'

'Oh . . .' Land's head bent forward and he sniffed. At first Charlie thought it was a coke-sniff but then, as Land removed his glasses and squeezed the bridge of his nose, he realised the man was trying not to cry. 'Because . . .' he started, then stopped, took a deep breath and looked at the wall of Lanchester pictures, the mosaic there.

'I loved Susan, Mr Watson,' he said, after a long pause. 'I still do. With her it was never a sexual thing, not with me, and I really don't think with the majority of the straight men she came into contact with, funnily enough. You just wanted to be with her. I did, at least, all of the time. Others, I think, wanted to own her, cage her, keep her all to themselves. Her greasy husband certainly did.'

'You were above all that, though.'

'Mr Watson, I'll shortly be putting the barrel of this gun into my mouth and pulling the trigger. Please don't try to make me feel like some kind of fraud. No, I suppose I wasn't really above all that . . . I suppose I, too, wanted a kind of ownership of Susan. Which is why we're sitting here today, I imagine.'

'How so?'

'I wanted to go away with her. I wanted to get her away from her idiot husband, from my priapic father. I wanted to take Mark and was willing to raise him as my son. I made the mistake of telling my father. I – I—' Once again he squeezed his nose and Charlie saw tears glitter in his eyes. He looked up at Charlie, his face riven with remorse. 'I thought I'd be doing him a favour. I thought I was doing us all a favour. I was in my twenties still. I had this idea of arriving like some kind of big-hearted cavalry to solve everybody's problems. But, looking back, there were no problems to solve. None that I could help with, anyway. I had made assumptions. About Susan's happiness. About my father's willingness to accept culpability for his actions. They were errors of judgement that proved fatal. My father jumped to the conclusion that Susan was trying to take me away from him – to what life he imagined I'm not sure. He went to speak to her that day and . . . he saw a solution.'

'He drowned Mark?'

'Yes.'

There was a long pause.

'What about my dad?' said Charlie at last.

'I saw him in the window. He was a witness. We spoke to him. The garden, you see. From the window of your house on Willow Street you could see into the garden on Crosby Street.'

'Exactly what did he see, my father?'

'He saw my father in the garden. It was our good fortune that he didn't see my father hold Mark beneath the water. We were able to tell him that my father had walked in on a tragic accident. Much more I don't know. Timson made the arrangements. Whatever your dad saw, he was paid a lot of money to unsee it, so to speak.'

Charlie closed his eyes. 'And Susan never knew what Aubrey did?'

'Susan never knew, no – until today.'

Charlie started. 'You told her?'

'She deserved to know.'

Charlie nodded. 'Why did you tell her now?'

'A desire to put my affairs in order before . . .' He lifted the gun.

'But why this . . .' Charlie's turn to indicate the weapon . . . 'now?'

'Well, I've just killed a man, for a start, and I have no intention of serving any jail time for our friend Mr Parks here.'

'I still don't understand . . .'

'Listen, I'm going to kill myself because I've been involved in some terrible things, and because there is not a single moment since that day in 1973 when I have been happy, and because I have done nothing with my life other than fuck up other people's. Is that good enough for you? Now, I think

394

you'd better go, please. if you don't want your daughter to see me shoot myself.'

Charlie nodded and walked to the office door, pushing Mary in front of him, gingerly skirting Joe Parks's body.

He opened the door and pushed Mary into the hallway then turned, careful not to look at the corpse on the floor. He grasped the door handle. 'Why did you protect Aubrey?' he asked, half through the door.

Land laughed drily. 'He was my father. What else could I do?'

'Of course.' Charlie opened the door, looked at Land. 'I should try to talk you out of killing yourself, really, shouldn't I?'

'It would be the correct moral response to this situation, I believe.'

'Even from a man whose family you've helped to destroy?'

'I think, in that case, you're excused.'

'Right,' said Charlie. 'Well, good luck with the suicide, then. Hope it goes well.'

He was half-way down the drive when he heard the shot. Sighing, he pulled his phone from his pocket, and dialled 999.

# Sound and Vision

Charlie was shown into the top office of Land Associates, the cavernous room, its *Bride of Frankenstein* poster still taking pride of place. The main difference now was that where Byron Land had sat, Timson was behind the desk. Robert Timson: managing director.

He waved Charlie to the seat opposite, sitting as he did so, smoothing his tie, tanned and relaxed. 'I gather you've been helping the police with their enquiries,' he said. 'I'd like to thank you very much for that. The quicker we put all this behind us, the better. You've told them everything you know I take it?'

'Yes,' said Charlie.

'Good.'

'Well, *almost* everything I know.'

'Ah. What didn't you tell them?'

'Well,' smiled Charlie, 'where do I start? I didn't tell them that Aubrey Land had slept with Susan Slater. I didn't tell them that Mark was his child, or that Byron was gay and infatuated with Susan and planned to take her and Mark away, and that Aubrey killed Mark Slater, and that my father saw them both at the house that day, and that you bought our house and paid him to keep quiet about it.'

'Right. I see.' Timson looked watchful, resting his chin on his fists. 'I can understand why you wouldn't want to bring your father into this. Probably very wise.'

'Well, there's still time.'

'Really?'

'Oh, yes. There's still time. But I thought I should come to you first.'

Timson smiled knowingly. 'Really?'

'Yes. I was hoping you might be able to answer a couple of questions.'

'Is this a shakedown, Mr Watson?'

'Well, let's not jump the gun. Why don't we see if I'm right first?'

'About what?'

'About you and Jane Land sleeping together.'

Timson sat back, grinning. 'What makes you think we are?'

'Your aftershave in her car, for a start.'

Timson shrugged. 'Hardly concrete.'

'No, but at the very least you were working together, weren't you?'

'I don't follow you. What makes you say we were working together – and to do what?'

'To get the company.'

'Go on.'

'Something Byron and Joe Parks talked about before they died,' said Charlie. 'Byron didn't employ Joe Parks to try to scare me, did he? You did. And you did it so you could be sitting here today. You get the girl, you get the company.'

'Sounds good.' Timson laced his hands behind his head. He looked like a man enjoying a good joke.

'You wanted Byron out of the way, so you employed a detective. Or, rather, Jane Land employed a detective, the cover being that she thought her husband was cheating on her. But you both knew the trail would lead to Susan Slater, and that that trail would lead to the past. I'm guessing that, as Byron's trusty lieutenant, you kept him abreast of the latest developments, let him know how close that past was to catching up with him, to get him nervous. Am I right?'

Timson shrugged noncommittally. 'Go on.'

'Did it matter how he went over the edge? Either Leo or I could have gone to the police. How did you know he would kill himself?'

Now Timson leaned forward. His face became serious once again. 'Byron had attempted suicide before. It was pills that time. Jane, rather foolishly in retrospect, called the ambulance and he was saved. He'd left a note that, again rather foolishly, in retrospect, he intended me to deliver to Susan Slater on his behalf. A bit of a tear-jerking read, actually. About how he loved Susan, how he always had. How he forgave her for sleeping with his father. He went on to say that most of all he was sorry for deserting her. The pain of it was eating away at him, he said, but he had had a reason for doing so, and that reason was his darkest secret, the secret that was now killing him. He told her that Aubrey had drowned Mark. Only, unfortunately for almost everybody concerned, the dark secret *didn't* kill him. It just got him his stomach pumped. And he came out of hospital the same old Byron.

'The only difference was that I knew then how to get Byron out of the picture. As you say, to get the company, to get the

398

girl, and it was a question of arranging it. You know, when I saw your brother's advertisement, I swear I heard a choir. I saw it and I literally had a vision of what to do. Having vision was what it was all about in the end.'

Charlie did a pretend hand-clap. 'Looks like it all turned out peachy for you. You have every right to be proud of yourself.'

Another thin, on-off smile in response. 'Thank you.'

'Why the choir when you saw Leo's advert, though? Why Leo? And after that, why me?'

'Because the road that led to the past led also to your door.'

'So?'

'It meant you wouldn't go to the police.'

'I don't understand. Surely the plan relied on one of us going to the police at some point?'

Timson nodded thoughtfully. 'In a way, but the beauty of the idea was that it contained contingencies for both scenarios. The important thing from my point of view was that Byron believed that at some point you would call in the police – that the secrets of the past were going to be well and truly dredged up.'

'And if we had called the police?'

'Like you say, I half expected you to. In doing so, you would have brought Byron into the firing line, which was what I wanted. I expected the police to visit Byron and that probably Byron's role in the cover-up of a child's murder would be exposed. And after that I expected Byron to do exactly what he eventually did. Hiring you – as in you, and not somebody else – meant that it would go no further than that. That *our* role –' here he indicated himself and Charlie – 'in covering up a child's murder went undetected. Because, like me, you have a good reason to leave the past where it is. A lot of people did regrettable things in 1973, not least of them your father.'

Charlie looked away. 'So you always depended on one of us getting there in the end?'

'Absolutely.'

'Then Leo dying must have been . . .'

'It was inconvenient, yes. Until you came on the scene. Then it was a case of leading you in the right direction. That, and making sure Byron also knew where you were heading.'

'Leading me in the right direction? Then why were you trying to scare me off?'

'People are very rarely scared off. They simply realise what's at stake and pass the burden of it to someone better qualified to bear it. Joe Parks might have thought he'd been employed to scare you off. His real purpose was to make you realise what was at stake.'

'You said you thought I'd keep it quiet, about the murder and the money. Keep the past where it was. Maybe I would have done, if all things had been equal. You know, I applaud the thinking. But people have died because of your little company takeover. So I'm afraid things have moved on, and significantly, since you dreamed it all up. When I leave here, I'm going to the police.

'You could. But it won't stop me.'

'Apart from the fact that you'll be locked up.'

'I won't be.'

'In 1973 you covered up a murder.'

'Murder? What murder? The accident, you mean? No, I was simply asked by Mr Aubrey Land to help provide gifts to certain people to thank them for their discretion when it came

400

to not mentioning that his son had been having an affair with Susan Slater.'

'You've just admitted it.'

'Fortunately you're not the police. It won't stick.'

'What about Byron? He killed himself because of you.'

'Really? I thought he killed himself because he put a gun into his mouth and pulled the trigger. But I suppose I might be mistaken. We'll have to let the police decide that, won't we? Or let's not, because the police is pointless hassle that neither of us needs. I'll shrug my shoulders. You know you're not going to the police, but you know what I think? That it suits you for me to believe you might. And that's why you're here.'

Timson opened the top drawer of the desk and took out a chequebook. Not a small chequebook, but a large one, leatherbound. In it there were sheets and sheets of cheques. 'Do you know, I can't remember the last time I wrote a cheque. The last time the company wrote a cheque. Right, how much do you want?'

Charlie stared at him.

'I tell you what,' said Timson. 'Why don't we start you off with . . .' he began to write in the chequebook '. . . a hundred thousand pounds. How about that? A hundred grand, just for keeping it buttoned. Not bad for a day's work.' He finished writing the cheque, tore it from the book and held it out to Charlie. 'Take it, Mr Watson.'

Charlie regarded him.

'Take it,' offered Timson. 'At least look at it.'

Charlie leaned forward, about to take the cheque. Before he could, Timson snatched it back and tore it to pieces, which he let flutter to the desk. For a moment or so, the two men stared

401

at each other, a faint smile edging Timson's mouth. 'You don't seem too bothered,' he said at last.

Charlie shook his head. 'I'm not. I was going to do exactly the same thing.' He stood. 'And I was going to tell you where you could stuff it. Because now I'm going to the police.'

Timson still smiled. 'Suit yourself. As I've already pointed out, it's a futile gesture. Plus, of course . . .'

'What?'

'Well, you see this behind me?' Timson pointed upwards and back, leading Charlie's gaze to what looked like a coat of arms on the wall. 'You can't see it but there's a closed-circuit TV camera in there. No sound, unfortunately, just pictures. But, of course, those pictures will perfectly corroborate my story that you came here attempting to blackmail me, and are now only going to the police because I refused to co-operate.' He stood, too. 'I've got no sound, Mr Watson, but I've got vision.' Timson chuckled, looked around the office. 'Yes, you could say I got vision. Now, how about you get out of my office and we pretend this little meeting never happened, eh?'

Charlie went to the door, opened it and looked back at Timson. He stopped as if about to say something, then turned, let himself out.

He came through the downstairs office and went to the receptionist, who looked at him and chewed gum.

'Oh,' said Charlie. 'I forgot to give Mr Timson this.' From his pocket he brought a small, folded piece of paper, which he handed to the receptionist.

'What is it?' she asked.

'It's a receipt for the stationery shop in town. I bought a dictaphone there yesterday. Tiny little thing, fits in your

trouser pocket, picks up everything. Just give him the receipt –
he'll know what it's about. Oh, and can you tell him . . .'

'Yes?'

'Tell him he got vision. But I got sound.'

# The Kiss

Two weeks later, Charlie finally made the journey to see Chariot in north London. An evening visit.

She had Beyoncé on the stereo, ushered him in and waved him to the sofa, offering him a glass of wine. 'I'm glad you've come,' she said, holding out a glass, which he took. 'Those jazz CDs were beginning to look a bit neglected, to be frank.' She folded herself down next to him, bringing with her the smell of freshly cleaned clothes, a hint of perfume. 'I'm sure that my other CDs were massing the troops, ready to mount an attack.'

'Yeah.' He laughed. 'It's lucky I'm here.'

'Well, I'm certain my collection of Coldplay albums will feel thwarted that you've taken their prey but . . . I'm glad you're here.' She pulled her feet up on to the sofa, tucking them beneath her haunches. She rested one elbow on the back, put her head in her hand so that it was at an angle, and watched him.

'I'm sorry it's taken me so long,' he said into the pause. 'There have been things to, um, sort out. I've had to get my head together.'

'Right. What kind of things?'

'I don't know.' He took a sip of his wine. 'Well, I do, I'm just not sure if you're the person I should be telling.'

'Ooh, sounds interesting. Go on, do tell – tell me what it is you don't think you should be telling me.'

'That I envied Leo.' He looked across the back of the sofa at her.

She took a sip of wine and watched him over the rim of her glass. 'In what way,' she said, 'did you envy Leo?'

'In a lot of ways, really. I admired the way he'd stuck with his thing – the singing thing. I admired him for being his own person. Do you think you could ever have changed him?'

She smiled. 'Not a chance.'

Charlie laughed. 'That was the difference between us. Me, I just let myself get dragged into stuff. For the quiet life, I think. I cave in too easily, you know. I go along with things. I guess that makes me weak or too accommodating or something . . .'

'Or just "not selfish"?'

'Or just not selfish, yeah. Hopefully.'

'Because Leo was selfish. For all his charms . . .' She said it affectionately.

'He was selfish, sure. But he was his own person.'

'Oh, come on, now you sound like somebody off reality TV.'

Again he laughed. 'Maybe I do. But, you know, Leo and me, at some level our values were the same. We got them off our dad, so I suppose they must have been. I've wondered a lot lately about Leo – obviously. I wondered how he felt about himself when he died. I wondered if when he looked at himself he was the man he wanted to be.'

She was nodding. 'And by implication . . . You're not the person you wanted to be?'

He sighed. 'When I grew up, I wanted to leave Bentham, and where do I live now? I live in Bentham. I live there for all the right reasons – because it's a nice place, and it's a lovely town to raise kids in, and my wife likes it – but none of them has anything to do with me. Sometimes it feels as though I've become an observer in my own life. People tell me where to stand and I obediently go and stand there to watch proceedings. So, yeah, I envied Leo, because even though he lived in a shit-hole flat in a rough bit of London and he didn't have much money, nobody told him where to stand. He was Leo. He was being himself. And the other thing I envied about him . . .'

'Yes?'

'Was you.'

There was a silence. Her head on her hand, elbow on the back of the sofa. Jet black hair hanging in straight lines. 'Me?' she said at last.

'Yeah.' He looked straight ahead, holding his wine glass in both hands. 'The night I got pissed and stayed here, you told me he'd finished with you, and the thing was, I couldn't believe it.' He took a sip of the wine, a security sip. She did the same. 'I couldn't believe it, because – and I know how corny this sounds – I just couldn't believe that he, or anyone, really, would dump you.'

He turned his head to look at her. She smiled. 'I like this. Keep it up.'

'I was right, I think,' he said. 'I don't think Leo did dump you.'

'Really?' She shifted her legs. He tried to ignore it.

'I started looking into Leo's last case. Did he ever tell you about our dad?'

She nodded, yes.

'Well, Leo had found some stuff out. A lot of stuff. After he died his office was burgled. He'd wiped his computer, gone to work from home, but as far as I can make out he wasn't really working from home. He was hiding out because he was being threatened.'

'Really?'

'Yes. He wasn't dumping you, he was protecting you. By cutting himself off he was making sure that whoever was threatening him couldn't get to you.'

'Look,' she said, 'rewind. You've lost me.'

So he did. He rewound to the beginning, telling her everything. Almost everything. All the salient bits, anyway. Until their glasses were empty and she blinked hard, twice, and said, 'Charlie, I really don't know what to say.'

He laughed. 'I'm a bit freaked out by it all myself. One thing you think is certain is your past. Turns out mine was anything but.'

'Right.'

Again, a silence.

'Do you want a refill?' she asked.

'No, thank you. I'll take Leo's CDs and be going.' He stood.

'Right,' she said, and stood too. She walked to the other side of the room and brought him a tottering tower of CDs. He held them to his chest.

'Here,' she said, 'while your hands are full,' and she leaned forward, kissed his lips. The shock of it went through him. A bolt of desire. He tasted her. For a moment he felt dizzy.

Then he smiled. 'Thanks,' he said.

'My pleasure.' She smiled back.

And he turned to go.

'You know,' she said, as he was half-way out of the door, 'he envied *you*, Leo did.'

'Yeah,' he said, 'I did know that. It's funny, there's so much I wish I could tell him about how this ended up. But most of all I'd like to tell him that I was wrong to envy him, and he was right to envy me. I'm luckier than I know, that's my trouble.'

He said goodbye to Chariot, took the CDs down to the Peugeot and drove home. Back to Mary and Bea.